Billionaire Lumberjack's Bride

Gwyn McNamee

BILLIONAIRE LUMBERJACK'S BRIDE

To everyone who has lived with their scars and turned them into something beautiful.

BEFORE YOU READ

This book contains content that may be triggering for some readers.

If you would like to learn more about the content warnings for this book, please visit Gwyn's website: https://www. gwynmcnamee.com/lumberjacksinlove

Chapter One

SILAS

The first spring breeze of the year blows down Main Street, bringing with it the promise of warmer, longer days and hours spent out in the sun instead of cooped up inside the cabin.

A perfect day.

Everyone in Millsburg seems to be out, enjoying the shift in weather that could easily reverse itself this time of year. They bustle up and down the sidewalks, chatting with each other, ducking into the small shops that line the only real downtown area to say hello to friends or grab something quickly.

But no one dares approach me.

They know better.

All I get are darting glances and concerned looks from mothers ushering their children away from where I lean against the side of my truck outside Jensen's General Store.

It's always been this way. Even after over fifteen years of living on the mountain above them, I'm still a newcomer.

1

A stranger. Someone to watch with a wary eye and offer a wide berth.

And that's the way I like it.

If they have no desire to approach me, they won't ask questions or demand anything I can't give them. It's the only way I can keep living this way without somebody finding out who I am—if no one cares. And today, they're making it clear they still want nothing to do with the tattooed, bearded, long-haired madman from the mountain.

Good riddance.

Maintaining a conversation with anyone has become a chore after so long, and I have no intention of chit-chatting with any Millsburg locals while I'm down here with my wood deliveries. It's hard enough having to deal with Jensen —and I actually *like* the old man.

All I want is to get into town, get what I need for the next few weeks, and do my business. Then I can retreat to solitude and leave these headaches behind.

Like the one forming at my temples the longer I have to be here, surrounded by so many prying eyes.

What is taking him so long?

I glance over my shoulder toward the old building that's housed the general store for Millsburg for at least the last century and a half. Jensen shuffles around near the register, speaking with someone on the other side of the counter, his easy smile visible through the big windows at the front.

Huffing, I cross my arms over my chest and return to observing the people of this town who go through their days without the slightest idea of what goes on beyond their sheltered lives in this valley.

If only it were so easy for me to forget what is really out there...

A decade and a half alone hasn't helped with that at all.

The memories linger. The demons still attack. The same face flashes in my nightmares and haunts my days every time I close my eyes.

My knee starts bouncing incessantly the longer I wait. Down here, my anxiety sets in quick.

Too many people.

Too many sets of eyes on me.

Too much scrutiny.

Something cold and wet touches my neck, and I reach back and rub Whiskey's muzzle, my racing heart slowing almost immediately with his closeness. "Sorry, boy. We should be out of here soon."

God willing.

He gets just as anxious as I do when we have to be in town too long, and his nervous energy vibrates through his thick coat and into my hand. His observant gaze darts around in all directions, trying to keep track of everyone and everything, always searching for anyone or anything out of place, like I trained him to.

My constant companion. My protector. My best friend.

His body stiffens, and I follow his line of sight down the street to a sleek black sedan coming toward us.

Fuck.

Whiskey recognizes the same thing I do—that isn't a local.

People up here lead simpler lives. And *no one* would be driving a car like *that.*

I duck my head as much as possible, hiding behind a curtain of long hair while keeping my gaze on its approach. It moves slowly, as if the driver is scanning Main Street for something. Or someone. The languid approach gives me the opportunity to round the bed of my truck to the opposite side, where I can rest my forearms on the frame and get a decent view when the vehicle travels past us.

Elegant.

Expensive.

A *statement* ride.

Something from another life.

One I left behind me a long time ago—for good reason.

The darkly tinted windows protect whoever is inside from identification. A deliberate choice from a person who doesn't want to be seen. But the hair on the back of my neck rises as if someone is watching me.

You're being paranoid.

It might just be some rich fucker from Pittsburgh or Harrisburg looking to spend a weekend antiquing and soaking in the fresh air and "eclectic" culture of our small mountain town.

No one has found me yet.

There isn't any reason to think they have now.

The car reaches the end of Main Street and the single stop sign in all of Millsburg. Red brake lights flash. It pauses a moment, then turns right, going *up* the mountain.

Shit.

I suck in a shaky breath, and Whiskey trots across the bed of the truck and buries his face against my neck. But even his presence can't help quell the dread settling like a massive rock in the pit of my stomach.

"Sorry about the wait..."

Jerking at the voice behind me, I whirl toward Jensen, my heart thundering rapidly against my ribcage at being caught off guard. "No problem."

The first person I met when I arrived in Millsburg holds out an envelope. "Here you go."

I accept it and shove it into my back jeans pocket. "Thanks."

One of his white eyebrows rises. "You aren't going to count it?"

The old man's genuine shock almost makes my lips curve into a smile. I clap him on the shoulder and squeeze gently. "No. I trust you, Jensen. You've never done me wrong."

And if he hadn't helped me all those years ago, I never would have survived out here. I didn't know the first thing about living this way, but Jensen connected me with the right people to learn—trial-by-fire style.

For that, I'll be forever grateful to him.

A smile spreads across his weathered face, making the laugh lines deeper than usual. "Have a good day, Silas. I'll see you again in two weeks?"

Inclining my head toward him, I shove my hand through my hair and glance toward the empty intersection where the black sedan sat only minutes ago. "Yeah...say..." I peer back at him, trying to make this sound as casual as possible. "You haven't heard anything about someone visiting from out of town today, have you?"

If *anyone* has heard the gossip in Millsburg, it's Jensen. The people trickling in and out of his store tell him *everything*—which is precisely why he knows *nothing* about me beyond what he needed to when I arrived here, still a child in so many ways.

I was smart enough to keep my mouth shut then and now. I'm just the guy who brings him loads of firewood to sell a couple times a month, who has a German Shepherd named Whiskey, who loves the homemade dog treats his wife makes.

If he knew anything else, it could be catastrophic.

He rubs a hand along his gray-stubbled jaw, contemplating for a moment while he scans the street, searching for what might have brought on my question. "Can't say that I have. Why do you ask?"

"No reason."

Except I may be in deep shit.

That car turned up the mountain, and there isn't anything up there except a handful of cabins owned by people who don't want that kind of trouble—including me.

I give Jensen a parting wave and climb back into the truck. Whiskey crawls through the open cab rear window to take his seat next to me, still vigilant and watching everything outside, my anxiety putting him on high alert.

"It's probably nothing, boy."

He tilts his head suspiciously.

Yeah, I don't believe it, either.

My gut tightens, and by the time I reach the stop sign, my hands visibly shake on the wheel.

It isn't him.

It can't be.

There's no way he found me.

The same words I've repeated to myself over and over since I fled that life, those people, that world, and settled into this one ring in my head. In the past, it's been enough to settle my worries. Though, this time, I'm not so sure I believe them.

I turn right and start the slow climb up the mountain toward the cabin.

Knuckles white.

Jaw clenched.

Stomach in a knot.

Whiskey paces and shifts on the bench seat, sensing the unease and carrying it on his shoulders as much as I do.

Each mile we ascend up the old gravel road, my disquiet grows until I'm tapping my palm against the steering wheel so persistently that the noise starts to annoy even me.

As I approach each turnoff for the very few "neighbors" up here, I slow and glance down the unpaved paths leading into the woods, hoping to glimpse that sedan. But all of us have our cabins set well back, away from prying eyes, so if it were a visitor at one of their places, I wouldn't be able to see it.

It's a futile effort.

And deep down, I know that's not what the car is doing up here.

Whoever that is...they're here for me.

It was only a matter of time before someone found me, but it doesn't mean I'm going to go down without a fight. Years of anticipating this have prepared me for what I might have to do.

Each minute of the remaining hour up the narrow road leading to my property gives me more opportunity to consider my options.

There aren't many.

Only one that will end this for good.

I glance at the shotgun mounted behind me in the truck cab. Whiskey looks at it, too, like he's anticipating the same reckoning coming that I am.

The barely visible path tucked between two high hedges that leads back to my property comes into view, and I turn in. Thick, dark woods engulf the truck, and my entire body tenses.

Home.

My safe haven.

The only place I've ever truly felt protected from what lies below the mountain.

But today, it doesn't feel that way.

Whiskey stands at attention, focus forward through the windshield, waiting for whatever has me so rattled.

Good boy.

Even before I pull through the last of the trees and into the small clearing that houses my cabin, I know what I'll find—the black sedan parked in front of the porch.

Fuck.

Sometimes, I hate being right.

I stop the truck, throw it into park, and grab my shotgun. Whiskey issues a low growl, hackles up, as he stares at the car. He knows it shouldn't be here as well as I do, and he's ready to get rid of the intruder.

Me, too, boy. Me, too.

My hand tightens around the stock, and I throw open my door, racking it as I step out. Whiskey jumps down behind me, and the driver of the sedan slides out onto the dirt in thousand-dollar loafers and a suit that costs at least twenty times that.

Whiskey charges while I move forward, leveling the barrel at our "visitor's" chest. He sees me and the dog and staggers backward, his ass hitting the open door, hands raised in surrender.

Familiar, hard brown eyes meet mine, and my steps falter. Whiskey barks and snarls in front of him, but he won't attack unless I give the word. It sits on the tip of my tongue, yet I can't bring myself to issue the command or pull the trigger.

At least, not until I find out why he's here and how he found me.

Watching Whiskey carefully, the man I never thought I'd see again offers a tight smile as he examines me. I'm not the same boy he knew. Years of working alone up here have helped me pack on muscle, and the tattoos that cover almost every inch of my skin hide what he surely knows lies underneath. "Silas—"

"What the hell are you doing here?"

He glances down at Whiskey, still poised to lunge at him with a single breath of the command from me. "We need to talk."

"There's nothing to talk about..." I keep the gun on him, though it's really overkill at this point, with Whiskey ready to take him down. "How did you find me?"

And who else knows where I am?

Who else might be coming?

His shoulders tense, but he keeps his hands up. "We have a lot to discuss." He releases a shaky breath. "Your father is dead."

It takes a moment for his words to register.

Father is dead...

I should feel something.

Anger.

Anguish, perhaps at the loss of my last remaining parent.

But an overwhelming sense of relief washes over me, releasing some of the burden I've been carrying for years.

"Good riddance." I practically spit it at the messenger. "The world is better without Phillip Bolton in it." I motion to his car with the shotgun. "Now, get out of here, Ronald."

He shuffles forward, a move that Whiskey mirrors, bringing his jaws even closer to the attorney who has cleaned up all the messes for Father and Uncle Marty for decades. "I can't. We have to talk about—"

Two massive steps bring me to Whiskey's side, the barrel mere inches from Ronald's chest. This close, I can see the fear in his eyes—something I'm not sure I ever witnessed

9

during my eighteen years living with this man around almost every day. "There is *nothing* to discuss, Ronald. When I left, I told all of you that I wanted *nothing* to do with what goes on in that family anymore. I thought I made that *crystal* clear."

His head bobs nervously, his hard eyes darting from the gun to Whiskey. "You did, Silas. You most definitely did, but things have changed now that your dad is gone. Your uncle..."

He trails off and lifts his old brown gaze to meet mine again.

It's there—mixed with the fear.

The truth.

He *knows*.

He's *always* known.

He didn't do a damn thing to stop him then, when I needed a savior, when I begged for someone to help me. And now, he doesn't know how to.

————

LYLA

"I would just need a fifty-thousand-dollar retainer to begin—"

The attorney's words echo in my ears. Everything he said after that point is nothing but garbled *wah wah wah wah* like that old cartoon teacher. But that *amount*—I can't get that out of my head.

A week later, it rattles around, slamming against the inside of my skull. Taunting me. Toying with me. Incessantly reminding me exactly how far out of reach it really is

—how well and truly *fucked* I am—unless I do something *drastic*.

Something awful.

Something I never, in a billion years, thought I would ever find myself doing.

Something I may not be able to actually go through with...

"Ma'am, do you have questions?"

I tear my focus from the pamphlet in front of me and look to Carly, the beautiful blonde, with her dazzling white smile and porcelain face that's so tight and unwrinkled that she must have been shot up with a gallon of Botox.

She tilts her head, examining me. "I know it's a lot of information to digest, but I'm happy to answer *any* questions at all." One of her perfectly manicured hands presses against her voluptuous chest. "As someone who was once a mail-order bride myself, I can attest that this *works!*"

My eyes dip to the massive diamond on her left ring finger, then over the tennis bracelet at her wrist and matching earrings dangling from her ears. She certainly *looks* the part—though, I guess I don't really know what a mail-order bride is supposed to do or look like. Aside from what I've seen in movies, TV, and on social media, this is all new to me.

And terrifying.

I swallow thickly.

How can I ask this without sounding judgmental?

It may not be possible because I *am* judging her for doing this—the very thing *I'm* contemplating. No matter how hard I try, I can't see a mail-order bride as anything but a very expensive prostitute. "This is all...legal?"

It can't be, right?

Taking money from someone to marry them—that sounds awfully *un*lawful.

I glance around the offices of Wife Wanted Enterprises. While it *seems* legit, it also seems like prostitution, which might be legal in certain places, but it certainly isn't in Pennsylvania.

The woman purses her injected lips. "Lyla...can I call you Lyla?"

I nod. This bubbly blonde may be the only thing standing between me and the fifty-grand retainer I need to come up with. The least I can do is let her call me by my first name.

She smiles. "Good. Look, I see you're uncomfortable with being here, but since you *are* here, I'm going to assume you've found yourself in some sort of financial trouble because you do not seem like the type of girl who is here looking to make a true love match..."

True love match?

The bark of laughter floats out before I can stop it, and Carly flinches slightly in her chair at the sound.

I press a hand to my far-less-ample chest and shake my head. "I'm so sorry." Fighting another laugh, I try to regain my composure. "I didn't mean that to come out. I'm just... no...I am *not* looking for a true love match."

If I were, this is the *last* place I would ever be. Meeting a guy at a random bar or on a dating app would likely yield better results in the "true love" department than throwing my photo and profile into a literal bride catalog.

What kind of men buy *their wives?*

Desperate ones—that's who.

What does that make you *then, Lyla?*

Mom's voice now replaces the one of the attorney from last week, and her question makes me stiffen in my chair.

She has always been the angel on my shoulder, guiding me through the twists and turns life has thrown at me, steering me down the right path. But this feels like one *massive* detour down a dark, bumpy road filled with potholes big enough for me to disappear into forever.

She would hate this. All she ever wanted was for me to be happy and find love—something she said she never really experienced. My sperm donor certainly never gave it to her, and neither did any of the other men who came and went over the years.

Marrying someone for money...

Mom would climb out of her grave to wring my neck for this if she could—even knowing *why* I'm doing it.

Carly drums her nails on the desk, leaning forward slightly and drawing me out of my own head. "Sweetie, this is all perfectly legal. We provide a match-making service between a man who wants a wife and a woman who wants to be one. A financial transaction occurs between the parties to ensure commitment to the partnership, since often the women are moving across the country —or sometimes the world—to be with their new spouse. It's one hundred percent on the up and up legally *and* ethically."

What about morally?

My stomach sours, bile rising in my throat. I force it down and offer what I hope is a believable smile to the woman, who truly seems to mean well and believe in this business model. She seems open to answering anything, and if I am going to sell myself, I at least need to understand what I'm getting into fully.

"And what is...*expected* of the spouse..."

It's the only way I can think of to phrase it without coming right out and asking if I'm going to have to bone some ninety-year-old geriatric great-grandfather to get the money. There isn't any *appropriate* way *to* ask that question.

Carly gives me a tight smile. "That is to be negotiated between the relevant parties."

NEGOTIATED?

Sex is now something I *negotiate* with strangers...

What the hell am I doing even considering this?

The very thin line I've thus far been able to visualize between prostitution and *this* evaporates, and I climb from my chair onto shaky legs. "I'm sorry, I don't think I can do this..."

My purse tumbles from my lap to the tile, the contents spilling out across the smooth, polished surface—including my empty wallet.

It falls open to the photo I've always carried in it, and tears fill my eyes, stinging them and making it hard to see. I swipe them away and drop to my knees—something I likely will have to do if I am really doing this—and start gathering the scattered belongings.

Clicking heels round the desk, and Carly squats and helps me gather up everything, holding out my lipstick, cell phone, and a small bottle of hand sanitizer. "You seem agitated."

"You think?"

It comes out harsher than I intend, but I'm on the verge of a very real mental breakdown right now. I thought this was going to be the answer to my very expensive problem when no others presented themselves; instead, I feel *dirty* merely sitting here, discussing it so casually.

I push to my feet, shoving everything back into my purse. "I'm sorry. That was rude. You're right. I'm very agitated and..."

She raises a pale brow. "And uncomfortable with taking

money to marry someone you don't know and will likely have to sleep with?"

Well, I guess we're laying it all out there on the table now.

And I just deeply insulted this woman who told me *she* was a mail-order bride.

Before I can offer *another* apology, she holds up her hand to stop me. "It's all right, sweetheart. I've been doing this for ten years from this side of the desk. I know exactly what some people think of our arrangements, and I understand why they do." She sighs and motions for me to take my seat again. "Please sit. Let's talk this through."

As if that's going to help.

This mental block regarding what being a mail-order bride really requires doesn't want to break, but I slowly lower myself back into the chair with my purse clutched in my hands on my lap. Because I *need* that money. And I need it *fast*.

At this point, I don't have the benefit of being able to turn down opportunities based on my morals. Not if I want to protect the one thing I love in this world.

Carly retakes her seat and reclines, a smile playing on her red lips. "It isn't what people think—it isn't what *you* think. Not all the men are old or have some major flaws that make them physically unattractive. Many are just shy or live somewhere that they don't have the opportunity to meet eligible women. We do our best to set up couples who we believe might click naturally."

Nothing about this is natural.

The fact that this type of service exists in the twenty-first century blows my mind and shuts it down to the possibility of accepting it as the answer to my problem.

"I'm sorry, Carly. You're very sweet, and I appreciate

you taking the time with me today. But I'm not sure I can do this."

Her brows rise again. "Do you have any other options?"

Well, shit.

She drums her nails on the desk again. "I won't pry into your reasons for being here, but they have to be pretty good for you to have set foot into my office. Most of our brides are from foreign countries looking for marriage to someone in the States, and the ones who are from here tend to be..."—one of her shoulders rises and falls—"socially awkward. Women who might have a hard time going out and meeting a potential suitor the old-fashioned way. But you..."—she smiles brightly—"you don't seem shy at all. You've spoken your mind with me, the same way I am sure you would with any match when discussing final contract terms. You need the money, and that's okay. That's a completely valid reason to get hitched, and who knows, you may even end up falling in love with your husband like I did."

"You love your husband?"

Her laughter tinkles through the space. "Of course, I do, darling; otherwise, I would have ended this ages ago. As I said, our contracts are tailored to the couple, and when I signed *mine*, I ensured there was an out clause that wouldn't require repayment of his marriage gift as long as we remained married for five years."

Five years?

I'll be thirty-five.

That isn't *so* terrible. Still young enough that when all this is over, I can start a new life and maybe find *actual* love.

A tiny spark of hope ignites in my heart.

I can't believe I'm asking this.

"How long does it usually take to get...matched?"

Because I am running out of time.

Carly smiles, clearly pleased I'm still here and asking questions because it means I haven't *completely* ruled out going down this very uncertain path. "Well, our clients seeking wives will go through our gallery of potential matches and review their questionnaires to see if anyone sparks their interest. We arrange an in-person meeting, if possible; otherwise, a video chat between the parties, and if all goes smoothly, then we move on to the contract portion. The whole process typically takes anywhere from two to six months."

"Two to six months?"

That tiny flame of hope that I might have found a resolution to my very time-sensitive problem vanishes in an instant.

A frown turns down the corners of Carly's lips. "We do need to take care to ensure we're making complementary pairings and set you up to succeed."

Tears burn my eyes again, welling until the kind woman blurs in front of me. "I-I don't have that kind of time..."

And the sheer desperation in my voice makes me want to flip the desk separating us.

I'm not *that* girl. Never the damsel in distress. Not the one seeking someone to take care of her.

I take care of other people. I make things happen for myself with hard work and determination. But that has gotten me exactly *nowhere* in coming up with fifty fucking grand.

My best night at work wouldn't even get me one-tenth of that, and the more time that passes, the more urgent getting that money becomes.

Two to six months will *not* work.

Standing on the corner in fishnets and a miniskirt,

flashing potential johns suddenly seems like the more reasonable option.

"Of course..." Carly's voice momentarily stops my downward spiral into despair—"we can speed up the process, if both parties are interested in doing that."

I suck in a sharp breath, the sudden intake of oxygen and her words reigniting that tiny flame. "Really?"

She nods. "It wouldn't be the first time we've rushed the process a bit. Obviously, you grasp the potential consequences of that. We will thoroughly vet the potential suitors, but you won't have the lengthier process of getting to know each other before finalizing anything..."

The warning hangs in the silence between us.

There's a reason they have a rigorous process. They want these matches to succeed—not only for the people getting hitched, but also because it reflects negatively on Wife Wanted if their arrangements fail.

Arrangements...

I'm thinking of my *wedding* as an "arrangement" now.

All the dreams of big white weddings, full of happy tears, love, and forever promises I really mean, vanish in a haze of determination to do what needs to happen—not what I want.

What the hell am I doing?

What. You. Have. To. Do.

Squaring my shoulders, I wipe away the tears streaming down my cheeks. I'm going to have to learn to control my emotions if I'm really doing this. No man will want to marry me if all I do is cry over the situation.

I need to do things I will hate to get that money.

I need to become the perfect wife.

"Please find me a match quickly. As quickly as possible."

Chapter Two

SILAS

I slide the half-full cup of coffee toward Ronald, and he looks down at it and raises a bushy white eyebrow at me.

Scowling, I lean against the kitchen counter and cross my arms over my chest, well aware of the way he watches my biceps bulge against the tight T-shirt I wear. I'm not the skinny, terrified teen he remembers, and he's wary now. "You won't be here long enough to need a full one."

That makes his lips almost form into a grin. He raises the cup and tips it toward me in acknowledgment before he takes a sip. "Thank you. It was a long drive."

"It will be a long one home, too."

When I ran, I ran fast and far. Far enough away that I thought no one would ever find me. Yet the Bolton attack dog sits at the small two-person table I have against the front window, completely out of place. I never thought I'd see a man like him, who wears $20,000 Italian silk suits, relaxing on my worn handmade chairs, looking uncomfortable and nervous as fuck.

Ronald doesn't get nervous.

He's a rock that never cracks under pressure.

Scandal after scandal.

Bribe after bribe.

He took care of it all without blinking or questioning anything.

Which means it's just as bad for him to be here as it would be for Father or Uncle Marty to have climbed from that car.

I glance at my watch. "You have five minutes, and then I'm letting Whiskey have his way with you."

The dog stands guard at my side, intently watching Ronald, waiting for me to give the command.

Ronald holds up his hands and leans back slightly in his chair. "Then I'll make this quick. Now that your father has died, your uncle is in sole control of the company."

"They were always fifty-fifty partners, so that makes sense."

His gaze hardens. "It doesn't have to be that way, though."

I raise a brow at him this time. "Why not?"

He twists his lips and wraps his knuckles on the table, his entire demeanor shifting. "I know what he did to you, Silas." His tone drops. "I know what he did to a lot of people, and I don't want your uncle controlling a company your family spent two hundred years building. He'll have control of every dime. He will hold all the power and use it to do even worse than he already has without your father at least *trying* to keep him in check. The man should be in fucking prison, not making decisions that affect hundreds of workers' lives and well-being."

I snort and point an accusatory finger at him. "Yeah, and who helped keep him out of prison?"

Ronald takes another sip as he watches me, and while I can see the apology in his stare, it doesn't do any good now. "I didn't have a choice, Silas."

"Bullshit." Anger flares red-hot in my blood, scorching through me and threatening to ignite me from the inside out. I shove off the counter, advancing a step, Whiskey right along with me, baring his teeth at the focus of my ire. "You *always* have a choice. You just didn't make the right one because the wrong one was easier and got you more money and power."

He flinches but vigorously shakes his head. "It isn't like that, Silas. Your uncle..." He swallows slowly, his Adam's apple bobbing as he weighs his next words. "He *had* something on me, something that would've ended my career and my marriage."

Shit.

Not that it changes anything or wipes away Ronald's sins, but it does explain a lot of what he was willing to do for a man who is such a monster. "He was blackmailing you?"

He nods slowly.

"What about my father?"

A long, slow sigh slips from his lips, and he toys with the mug in front of him, not looking at me. "Your dad protected Martin. He tried to rein him in for a while but realized it was a vain effort and eventually went along with anything Martin wanted. Your dad may have been the older brother, if only by ten months, but Martin controlled him through manipulation of their relationship. I guess it's true what they say about Irish twins. They're as close as regular ones, even if they don't share the womb."

I always knew Father allowed Uncle Marty to get away

with heinous acts, but I never thought he might have tried to stop him. Because I never saw that. He never stood up for me or defended me against that madman; he only turned a blind eye and his back when I needed help.

"So, Father knew you were being blackmailed, and he knew everything Uncle Marty was doing, and he let it continue?"

Ronald nods, focus still ahead of him on the mug. "I'm sorry. Truly. The older I get, the more the guilt weighs on me."

"Is that why you came here? To try to unburden some of your guilt?" I release a sardonic laugh that holds zero humor. "Because that's not going to happen. If you're asking for my forgiveness, you can't have it."

What they let happen is unforgivable. It isn't something that can be forgotten, no matter how far away I ran or how deeply down I tried to bury those memories. The evidence of them still scars my body. I see and feel the reality of them every single day.

Just having this man in my home, what was my safe haven away from the past, already threatens to unleash the demons again. They dance around at the back of my mind, trying to break free, to wash me in a tidal wave of misery I can never escape.

"I'm not here for forgiveness, Silas. I would never expect you to forgive me for what I've done—or him or your father—but I do expect you to step up and help me save the company from him."

"I don't want the company." I spread out my hands. "This life is all I want. To be left alone. That's why I renounced my inheritance and left."

"*Verbally* renounced your inheritance."

I nod. "Yeah. What are you getting at?"

He offers a slight shrug and finally looks up at me. "Your father never changed any of the paperwork. He never removed you from his will or adjusted the trust after you left."

The thought that Father hadn't immediately run to Ronald after our blow-out fight and had him instantly remove me had never crossed my mind. It should have been the first thing he did.

"Uncle Marty didn't make him?"

Ronald shrugs again. "He had me tell Martin he had removed you."

He lied to Uncle Marty?

All the years of torture he put me through at the hands of his brother, all the times he defended him and stood up for the man who was hurting his son, I never thought he would openly defy him or do something that could literally cost him billions.

"So, what does that mean?"

Ronald locks gazes with me. "It means you just became a billionaire, fifty times over, and that's only the cash your father had in his bank accounts controlled by the will and investments he had you listed as the beneficiary on. If you take into account the funds and the business controlled by the trust..." He shrugs again. "Far more than that."

I scrub my hands over my face. "Fuck."

The business always did well. Even growing up, I understood the way we lived wasn't normal. And at eighteen, when I left, I knew what I was giving up and leaving behind. But I never imagined it would have ballooned into *this*.

"But there's a catch."

I drop my hands, burying my fingers on my right hand

into Whiskey's fur to brace myself for what's coming. "What catch?"

"The cash is yours, no matter what. But if you want to take any control in the company or the other assets controlled by the trust, your father put certain conditions on it."

"I already said I *don't want* control of the company."

He slams his hand down, the first sign of his anger leaking out from his always poised and controlled nature. "You want your uncle to have it?"

"No, of course not. But—"

"No buts. I'm done being his fixer. I'm done being their lackey. I want to take the man down, and you're the only person who can help me do it. You're the only one who hates him as much as I do."

Shaking my head, I snort. "I guarantee you, there are dozens and dozens of people who hate him as much as we do. All the other people he hurt..."

I don't have to extrapolate on that because Ronald was the one paying them off under the table, making sure Uncle Marty's proclivities never became public knowledge, ensuring there were never lawsuits or prison time.

"Listen to me, Silas. If you can meet the terms of the trust and take your fifty percent of the company, then, when we get him removed, you'll have full control. At that point, if you don't want it, sell it. I don't care. It's your family legacy, not mine, but we have to get him out first. It could be a temporary deal if you don't desire to be involved long-term. But it should be *your* decision to make. You're the last Bolton."

That had always been the plan...for me to take over when the Bolton brothers finally retired or passed away. Without an heir on Marty's side, it fell squarely on my shoulders to keep Bolton Steel in the family and secure its future. But that was a long time ago. And those plans ended the day I almost died. The day I ran.

"You make it sound easy."

It won't be.

Uncle Marty has far too much power. Too many people in his pocket. Too much money that can easily be passed under the table. And I've been living in this damn cabin for the last decade and a half. I never went to college, and I don't have the slightest fucking clue how to run a Fortune 100 company.

Ronald's jaw tightens. "It could be easier than you think. All those things I cleaned up for your father and your uncle—I have evidence. Recordings, videotapes, correspondence with the victims' families."

My ears perk up, and I still my hand on Whiskey's head. "You kept it all? I thought for sure Father would have you destroy everything."

"He thought I did."

Sly fucker...

I never thought Ronald had it in him to betray the men who were his best friends for half a century. But it isn't as simple as turning over the evidence. It will have a snowball effect.

Consequences.

"So, what? You're going to sacrifice yourself and come forward, go to the police, and explain everything that happened?"

He shakes his head. "No. Your uncle owns the police. I'm going to the FBI. A lot of his crimes involved transporting people across state lines for illegal activities. That makes them federal offenses. More prison time, much harsher."

Hope flutters in my chest after all these years that the people who destroyed me might finally get what's coming to them. "You really think you can take him down?"

"I do."

"And what about you? You'll go to prison, too, for all the things you've done."

He shrugs. "Potentially. If I can't negotiate a proffer agreement for my willingness to testify against him. I think they'll want the bigger fish, but if I have to pay for my sins behind bars, then so be it."

"You can do all this without me."

He twists his mug on the table, staring into it. "I can, but if I remove him and you have not legally inherited your fifty percent, then the company gets sold out from under you rather than you getting everything and being able to make a decision for yourself about what to do with it."

"That wouldn't be so bad, would it?"

Bolton Steel protected a monster for decades. Continues to. The only thing that mattered was profits. Turning a blind eye to a CEO who abused women and children wasn't even a question if it meant everyone walked away with more cash in their pockets.

Ronald's back stiffens. "What about the eight generations of your family who have worked there, who have pushed it to the top? Bolton Steel is the single biggest steel manufacturer in the United States, but only because your family worked fucking hard for it. You want all that to go away, or do you want to figure out a way to maintain it?"

For the last fifteen years, I've stayed up on this mountain, thinking I never wanted to go back, that I didn't give a flying fuck about what happened to Father or Uncle Marty or anyone else who let my torture continue all those years.

I thought I didn't want the money, and I still don't. But,

for some reason, the threat of Bolton Steel shutting down or getting bought and enveloped by another company, controlled by someone who isn't a Bolton, makes acid climb my throat.

For so long, the importance of that family legacy was drilled into me, and despite all the ways my own blood let me down, that company is the backbone of the community. People respect it. They respect the Bolton name. They rely on it for their salaries. If we sold or closed, it could destroy the lives of a lot of families—kids I grew up with who went to work for the Boltons, never knowing why I left.

Could I really live with that?

"Let's just say, for argument's sake only, that I agree to help you. What would I have to do?"

Ronald swallows thickly, averting his gaze slightly to some unknown spot on the table. "You would likely have to testify against your uncle in open court."

I flinch and squeeze my eyes closed. "And..."

There doesn't need to be an "and." The thought of publicly talking about what he did to me for my entire childhood is enough to make me want to scream, "No!" immediately.

"Well?" Ronald takes a sip of his coffee, and Whiskey rests his head against my thigh, offering me comfort against my growing unease. "The terms of the trust..."

"What are they?"

He hesitates a moment, almost like he's reconsidering asking me to do this. "You won't be able to take over your role as co-CEO of Bolton Steel unless you're married."

Married.

The word rings in my ears, and I shake my head to clear it. "Excuse me? I must have misheard you."

"You didn't." A muscle in his clenched jaw tics. "Your

27

father wanted to ensure that you were at a point in your life where you were stable before you took over." He holds up a hand when I start to interrupt him. "Obviously, he had anticipated you becoming a playboy like he and your uncle were. He didn't want you running around with various women and hookers and all the shit they got into. He wanted you to be an established family man so Bolton Steel would look good and have a more secure future. So, he put the provision in the trust. From the date of his death..."—he pauses for a second—"which, for what it's worth, was two days ago, you have exactly thirty days to get married."

"No." I shake my head, crossing my arms over my chest defiantly. "No fucking way."

My adamant rejection of the idea doesn't seem to deter him.

"And, in order to maintain your leadership role within the company, you must remain married, living together under the same roof, no separate lives. The moment you separate, you lose your stake in the company."

The sheer audacity of the absurd requirements makes me laugh. "This is some sort of fucking joke, right?"

He shakes his head. "Unfortunately...no. Your father made sure the trust was ironclad."

"So, what you're saying is I have twenty-eight days to find someone who will marry me, actually *get* married, then we need to *stay* married indefinitely."

Nodding, he finishes his coffee. "That pretty much sums it up."

I snort and shake my head. "Then you're out of luck. You're going to have to find another way."

"There isn't any other way. And, really, you don't even have twenty-eight days."

"What do you mean?"

He runs a hand back through his silver hair. "Your uncle called for an emergency board meeting in two weeks. If you aren't there, and this issue hasn't been taken care of already, I'm worried about what he'll do. The moves he'll make. He believes you were removed from the trust, and since no one has seen or heard from you in fifteen years, he would have a very strong argument that despite the old terms still being there, that you have renounced any claim, leaving him in full control as sole CEO. A court could rule in his favor if it got that far."

My stomach drops. "Especially one where he owns the judge."

Ronald smirks. "I wasn't going to say it, but yes."

"Well..."—I spread out my hands—"as you can see, my marriage prospects are pretty slim right now, so I think you're out of luck."

"Maybe not."

He reaches into his inside suit coat pocket and pulls out a pamphlet, holding it out to me. His eyes dart to Whiskey, as if he's afraid to get out of his seat to approach me.

I close the distance between us, tug it out of his hand, and unfold it. "What's this?"

"The answer to your problem. To *our* problem."

I read it, trying to make sense of the words above the photo of a smiling woman in a white dress. "Mail-order bride?"

What he's suggesting finally snaps together in my mind, and I whip my head up and meet his gaze. "This has to be a joke."

He shakes his head. "It's not. It's the answer."

———

LYLA

The farther this hired car drives me into the remote Pennsylvania wilderness, the more I shift in the plush leather seat, trying to get comfortable in the luxury vehicle that seems so out of place in this setting.

It's impossible.

Every single part of my body trembles, and it has been for so long that it physically hurts.

Muscles I didn't even know exist ache.

Joints scream in protest with each slight movement.

My stomach roils.

Sweat drips down my brow.

Two days of waiting, packing, and anticipating have all led up to this, and my body has reached a breaking point, trying to contain all the anxiety welling inside me.

We drive past dozens of small towns—the kind you see on postcards and in Hallmark holiday movies—then we keep driving farther and farther away from civilization as I know it.

The afternoon sun gets lower on the horizon, signaling the coming evening, and we still haven't reached our destination.

I clear my dry throat to get the attention of the man behind the wheel. "How much longer?"

The driver glances back at me and offers me a tight smile. "Another hour and a half or so, ma'am, I think."

I think?

That doesn't instill a lot of confidence, which I could certainly use right now. Because God knows I don't have any in the choice I made.

You're really doing this?

I suck in a deep breath and let it out slowly, then roll

down my window to get some fresh air. Instantly, the smell of pine and musty, decaying wood from all the foliage around us hits me. So different from the smell of the city.

Rather than being refreshing, it makes me gag slightly. But it really isn't about the nature enveloping us and invading my lungs; it's more the thought of what I'm about to do...

That I've been trying *not* to think about this entire ride.

You're driving to meet your husband.

I shudder, and my phone call with Carly two days ago runs through my head again.

"Good news, Lyla! I really didn't think we'd be able to find you a match so quickly, but I have someone for you."

The realization that this mystery man needed a wife so fast quickly overshadowed my spark of excitement. Suspicion replaced it. *"But it's only been two days."*

"I know, but he's in quite the rush."

"Why?"

It was an obvious question, but her answer didn't help my concern. *"I can't reveal that information to you, unfortunately."*

"What can you tell me about him?"

Her hesitation sent a chill through me then, as it does now. A signal of her shared unease over the situation. *"Well, this is a bit of an unusual case because he's asked for confidentiality and for me not to reveal certain information that he would like to give you himself when he meets you."*

"Has anyone ever done that before?"

"No, which is why I'm telling you that you don't have to accept this. I will let you know that I do trust this individual and understand the reasons for the secrecy. I don't have any concerns for your safety, if that worries you."

"Of course, I'm worried about it. Going to live with a

stranger, marry him, and you can't tell me anything about him."

"If you get there and you're uncomfortable, if it doesn't feel right, anything like that, you can always leave. You don't have to go through with signing the contract."

"They'll have it?"

"Yes, he has asked that the final contract be signed in his presence. He wanted to meet you first in person, as I said."

"You can't even tell me where he lives or his age, what he does for a living, anything?"

"I'm sorry, Lyla. I can't, so I would totally understand if you say no. But you seemed a little desperate the other day, so I had to give you the opportunity before I went on to any other potential matches."

"I'll do it."

The words came out of my mouth so fast that I can't believe I said them.

"You will?"

"Yes. I assume he knows about the gift."

"You can discuss all that with him in person, but it won't be a problem."

That's the only thing that keeps me from throwing open this door and jumping out of the moving car, knowing that $50,000 is going to be mine, hopefully by the end of the day. All I have to do is sign on a dotted line and say "I do" to a complete stranger, then play wife for God knows how long.

I release a heavy breath and roll up my window.

You can do this, Lyla.

A sign for Millsburg appears along the side of the road, almost covered by bushes encroaching from either side, and my back stiffens. Another mile or two goes by, and the town finally comes into view—if you can even call it that.

Two dozen or so tiny shops line each side of the main street. People meander along the sidewalk, but each and every one stops to stare at the Lincoln Town Car as it passes. We make it to a stop sign on the other side of town, and the driver puts on his turn signal.

My hand tightens around my purse strap. "Where are we going? I thought you said Millsburg."

He glances at me again. "Millsburg is the closest town, ma'am."

"And how much farther is it?"

We make the turn. "Another hour."

"The closest town is an hour away?"

He nods.

Who the hell would live an hour outside of here?

Who the fuck is this guy?

I scan out the windows all around us. Nothing but towering mountains and a stunning vista filled with impenetrable trees for 360 degrees around us.

We start up a narrow gravel road that winds along the side of the mountain, a giant drop-off to our right that makes me clutch the handle on the door, as if it could actually be of any help if we slide on these tiny rocks and go careening off the side.

It gets more rugged, more bumpy, less of an actual road the higher we climb. I grit my teeth, holding my breath in anticipation. The last few weeks have been nothing short of soul-crushing, but if this works, it would be a step in the right direction.

You'll make it work.

After what feels like an eternity, the driver finally slows and turns into a narrow opening protected by bushes.

"This is it?"

He nods. "I confirmed how to get here before we left."

Holy shit. What have I gotten myself into?

The towering fir, maple, and birch trees create a dark canopy above us, making our drive increasingly ominous. My driver flips on the headlights to illuminate the unpaved path that looks more like the game trails I've seen in movies and on television than an actual *road* to somewhere a human being might live.

I lean forward to watch out the windshield. Almost ten agonizing minutes later, the trees open up to a small clearing where a black sedan sits in front of a tiny A-frame cabin with a porch attached to the front.

This can't be right.

Carly said he wouldn't have any problem paying the gift.

This can't be right.

I shake my head. "No. No, no, no, no, no, no. I need to call Carly."

The driver parks and turns back to me, giving me an apologetic look. "Ma'am, there's no phone service up here."

Shit.

I pull out my cell phone—zero bars and that damn "no network" warning sits where my coverage indicator should be.

Fuck.

The nerves I've been trying to tamp down on the drive up here have turned into full-blown panic, tightening my chest, making it impossible to bring air into my lungs. "Turn around. Let's go."

He raises his brows. "You sure you want to do that, ma'am?"

"Yes..." I shake my head. "No."

Do I?

This is likely my only hope of getting the retainer

money. But this isn't at all what I expected. Not what Carly suggested it would be.

I can find another way.

I always do.

"Yes, I do. Go."

He shifts the car back into drive as the front door to the cabin opens, and a silver-haired man in an immaculate suit steps out.

I freeze.

Not exactly who I thought I'd see coming out of a place like this.

While certainly not what I would consider handsome, he holds an air about him that says he holds the wisdom of the years that his hair color and the lines on his face suggest he's lived.

God, he must be old enough to be my father.

Another shudder rolls through me at that thought.

Beggars can't be choosers, Lyla.

The older man offers a tight smile and a little wave from the front porch and makes his way down the few steps in shining black shoes that seem completely ridiculous in this remote place.

He approaches the vehicle—not the driver's side, but mine. Stopping outside my door, he motions for me to roll down the window. With a shaking hand, I press the button and it descends.

His lips curl into that same tight smile. "Lyla, I presume?"

I nod slowly. "Y-y-yes."

"Please come in so we can discuss the contract."

I bristle.

Well, that's a little formal coming from a man who's

going to say, "I do" and undoubtedly try to stick his dick in me.

But another voice pops into my head, one constantly there to remind me why I'm doing this.

At least hear him out.

That won't cause any harm. Just sit down with him and discuss this rationally, like two consenting adults. I can always say no and leave.

I glance over at the driver, who has been watching the conversation quietly from the front seat while trying to appear disinterested. "You'll wait for me?"

He offers a sharp nod. "I have been told to remain here until you confirm that you'd like to stay."

The air in my lungs rushes out in one relieved breath.

My driver gives me another look. "It'll be fine, ma'am. I've done a lot of these."

I bark out a laugh that's full of all the tension I've bottled up inside me. "You've driven a lot of women to the remote wilderness to cabins in the middle of fucking nowhere to sign a contract to marry somebody they've never met?"

He finally cracks a grin. "Okay, not *this* exactly."

"Ronald..."

I turn back toward the silver-haired man. "What?"

"My name is Ronald Page." He extends his hand through the window. "I know this must be uncomfortable for you, and you're surely nervous. I realized I never introduced myself."

As if that somehow makes any of this better?

I slide my hand into his and shake it, expecting a revulsion at having to touch the man interested in buying me. But I feel nothing really, except that same churning in my stomach that's been going on for hours.

"Please, Lyla, come in. It looks like it might start raining soon."

Give him a chance...

I nod, release my palm from his, and roll up the window. He opens the door for me and offers his hand to assist me out, a true gentleman.

Stepping from the elegant car with my purse slung over my shoulder, I scan the woods and cabin suspiciously. "Is this where you live?"

He doesn't answer, just climbs the stairs and opens the front door, motioning me forward. I take one last look at my only means of escape idling in the clearing, then step in.

The smell of fresh burning wood hits me immediately, and I scan to my left and find the floor-to-ceiling fireplace with river rock running up it. A fire blazes inside it, sending flames leaping up the chimney and warming the inside of the small space. Other than a stack of books sitting to one side of a plush leather reading chair that faces it, there isn't much else in the open room aside from a bed against the far wall and a dresser opposite it.

The door clicks closed behind me, and I flinch.

Ronald steps up and motions to the right to a small kitchen and a two-person table. "Let's sit and chat, shall we?"

"Oh, okay." I step on shaky legs over to it and slowly lower myself down onto a chair that rocks slightly on uneven legs.

He approaches. "Would you like something to drink? Water? Coffee?"

"No. I'm all right."

Ronald doesn't seem completely convinced, but he takes his seat across from me, then opens a folder sitting on the table and turns it around to face me. "Here's the contract. It's the standard one the company uses that I've made a few adjustments to, based on personal necessity."

Personal necessity? Who the hell talks that way?

"I insist you take the time to read it."

I reach out and flip through the pages. "There are like thirty pages here."

He grins. "I know, but you should never sign something you haven't thoroughly reviewed. I understand Carly gave you one of their sample contracts, but as I said, I've made some changes. They're all tabbed on the side for you. Please"—he holds out his hand—"read it. Make sure you're comfortable with the terms, and then, we can discuss specifics."

Talk about transactional.

This must be what a hooker feels like when they're trying to negotiate with a client.

I clear my throat, then begin reading page one. The first five or six contain the same standard language I saw in the version Carly gave me, until I hit his first tab change.

Length of contract term—indefinite.

"What does this mean?"

Ronald glances to see where I am in the paperwork. "It means there is no end to the contract unless both parties agree in writing."

"What? You mean this is permanent?"

His silver eyebrows rise. "Isn't that what marriage is meant to be?"

Touché.

But it isn't what Carly described to me. "Carly said we could have an out clause."

He purses his lips. "That isn't an option unless both parties agree."

Parties...he's talking about himself in the third person.

Jesus.

That will get annoying.

Especially if this is supposed to last *forever*.

That clause *alone* should be enough to make me walk out of here and climb into that waiting car, but something makes me keep reading—maybe the desperate voice in the back of my mind that keeps telling me there is no other way.

I keep reading through more standard clauses until I get to the gift section. "I think you have a typo here."

He leans over to see what I'm looking at. "What do you mean?"

"This has a few extra zeros. The agreed-upon amount was supposed to be $50,000."

Ronald gives me another tight grin and crosses his arms. "That isn't a mistake."

"But"—I read the number again, then back up at him —"this says a guaranteed $5 million."

He nods. "$50,000 of that will be sent to you immediately. We can have a bank transfer done in a matter of hours."

We?

"The remainder will be paid on the schedule provided on the next page."

I flip to the next page.

Half a million dollars a year for the next ten years as long as we remain married and living together. After that, one million a year for each year wed.

I try to process the words in my head. "I don't..." I blink and survey the small cabin. "Where are you getting all this money?"

Shit, that made me sound like some gold-digging bitch.

"I mean, I'm sorry. It's none of my business. I just wasn't expecting that."

He smirks. "Lyla, if you go through with this, you'll never have to worry about money again. I can promise you that. But I need you to read through all the provisions."

I gulp and keep reading, but the other changes are minor. Wording choices mostly. Which means the only thing holding me back from doing this is the *indefinite* clause.

Which might not really mean forever.

He said if both parties agree.

Surely, if we don't get along or something negative happens between us, he would be agreeable to part ways amicably and end the contract.

Right?

It doesn't have to be forever...

Does it?

My throat suddenly goes dry.

Damn, I wish I had that water he offered.

Almost as if he can read my mind, he rises from his chair, steps into the kitchen, pulls a bottle of water from a small fridge, and brings it over to me. "You might need this."

Oh, God. What's coming up in here?

I flip a few more pages and get to his next addition.

Bride will be bound by a confidentiality agreement, preventing her from discussing any of these terms with anyone at any time.

"So...I can't tell *anyone* what I'm doing or discuss it with anyone, even ten years from now?"

Ronald shakes his head. "Unfortunately, it would be a requirement in this case. To anyone asking outside of these four walls, you fell in love the old-fashioned way and are forever happily married."

I stare at the man I'm going to have to marry, who I'm going to have to have sex with, if I want this money. If there were any other way, I would walk out of here, get into that car, and drive back down the mountain.

But at this point, there isn't.

And the clock is ticking.

Time is running out.

Sacrificing my future, my happiness, is nothing compared to why I'm doing this. Owing your life to someone else means sacrificing it when necessary.

I inhale deeply and keep reading until I finish the contract. Under the clause for "intimate relations," a simple "*TBD* between parties" fills the space, which I guess means it's open for negotiation. I guess that's better than it saying I have to fuck him on our wedding night...

Two blank lines for signatures occupy the final page, with a spot for Ronald and me to print our names under.

You're literally signing away your life...

It all seems so surreal, but so does everything that's happened over the last few weeks. Like I'm living in some movie, watching someone else's life unfold before me.

This is someone else asking the question. "Do you have a pen?"

The old man who will become my husband reaches into his breast pocket and pulls one from it. His steady hand holds out the pen to me, and I reach for it with my shaky one.

God, don't let him see how nervous I am.

That would automatically put me on uneven footing with him, and I don't want to start whatever this is with Ronald thinking I'm a weak woman who breaks down under the slightest signs of stress.

I force a smile. "I think we can make this work between us. You seem—"

His white brows fly up, eyes wide. "Oh!" He holds up

his hands to stop me. "Oh, God. I'm sorry. You have it all wrong." He points to his chest. "I'm not the one you're marrying."

"What?"

"Sorry if I gave you that impression..."

I shake my head to try to clear the confusion now overwhelming me. "But, if I'm not marrying you, who *am* I marrying?"

A floorboard creaks to my left, and I whip my focus in that direction, just in time to see a massive, muscled, bearded, tattooed mountain man step out from one of the few doors along the wall in the tiny cabin.

His hard gray eyes meet mine—devoid of anything but the simmering heat of anger. "Me."

Chapter Three

LYLA

All the air rushes from my lungs. My body trembles so hard that the rickety chair's uneven legs rattle against the worn wood floor. Blood rushes in my ears as the man who looks like he stepped straight out of a police line-up for one-percenter motorcycle club members approaches me with heavy-booted steps. Long sandy-blond hair falls past his shoulders, and he rubs a hand over his bearded face, the only place on his body seemingly not covered by intricate tattoos.

Icy-blue eyes stay locked on me, and the closer he moves, the clearer the fire burning across their surface becomes.

I don't dare look away, even though the longer he holds my gaze, the tighter my chest becomes. "Who are *you?*"

He finally darts his attention to Ronald, who offers a non-committal shrug and motions to the contract still in front of me.

"If you're really going through with this, you're going to have to tell her, eventually."

The man who claims to be my future husband finally stops a few feet from the table and stares down at me like he's looking at something he's never seen before and isn't quite sure what to do with me or what to say. "My name is Silas Bolton, and he"—he points to Ronald—"is the attorney for my family's company."

Silas Bolton.

The name rattles around in my head for a moment.

Family company.

It takes another few seconds before it finally clicks.

Holy shit.

"Bolton, as in *Bolton Steel?*"

He nods slowly. "Now you understand the need for discretion."

"I..."

Shit.

For perhaps the first time in my life, I'm actually speechless, and not just because the man I'm supposed to marry has changed from the clean-cut, much older, yet seemingly kind and gentle one sitting across from me to the sinister-looking, massive mountain man now towering over me with an unfriendly sneer on his lips.

All the money makes sense now.

But none of the rest of this does.

I hold up a hand. "Wait a minute. Why do you need to *buy* a wife?"

There's no point in beating around the bush because that's exactly what's happening. He is, for all intents and purposes, buying me, and I'm letting him. But it doesn't make sense for a man literally worth billions to *need* to do it or so quickly that he made this arrangement with Wife Wanted in a matter of days.

His jaw tightens, and a muscle there tics under his thick beard. He glares at Ronald, who rests his forearms on the small table, making it wobble in protest.

"We aren't asking you why you need the money." Ronald raises a brow. "Do you want to share that with us?"

Good point.

I shake my head no. There isn't any reason to drag *that* part of my life into whatever *this* will be. Once the money is secure in the hands of Attorney Fields, I can let him take the wheel, and all I'll have left to do is pray.

Ronald smirks. "That's what I thought. Whatever is said and done here today, whether you end up signing this or not, is protected by the NDA you already signed when you met with Carly."

The NDA, right...

Silas stares at me, the inferno building in his gaze. When I believed I had to marry Ronald, the thought of it being indefinite wasn't all that terrifying. He's old enough that it wouldn't last forever. A few decades at most. And all I needed to end it was his agreement—something that might not be so hard to get, given how agreeable he seemed.

But Silas is about my age, which means this could very well be a lifetime thing with this grumpy, irritated, angry, handsome, and scary-as-hell man who makes my entire body vibrate just by standing near me.

That *indefinite* clause is there for a reason, something that's important to Silas Bolton—which means I'm *fucked*— literally and figuratively if I sign this contract.

Ronald offers a tight smile. "Do you still want to go through with this, Lyla? Because we don't have a lot of time."

Neither do I.

I guess that's the one thing offering me solace in all this...Silas seems about as happy to be doing this as I am. Maybe that means it won't be as bad as all the possibilities I've built up in my head getting up here.

Looking between Silas and Ronald, then down to the contract, I try not to focus on the what-ifs and instead the "I musts" that I *know* are true.

"$50,000. Today."

Ronald gives a sharp nod, and I peek at Silas again out of the corner of my eye. He stands with his arms crossed over his barrel chest, tattoos covering every inch of the exposed skin on his arms and neck.

I wonder where else they are...

My cheeks heat at the thought, and I quickly return my attention to the piece of paper that will change my life.

This is not at all what I'd expect the heir to a multi-billion-dollar fortune to look like, and I don't know enough about him or his family to ask any more questions. Like why we're meeting up here like this and why everything has to remain so hush-hush. Or why the hell a man like Silas needs to *buy* a wife.

Not that they'd answer them, anyway.

Does it really matter if it's him or Ronald?

I was prepared to agree to marry this old man, but now, butterflies dance in my stomach at the thought of it being Silas. And they aren't the ones I felt thinking I would spend the indefinite future with Ronald.

These are different, feeding off the intensity of the man standing next to me. They loop and flutter rapidly, spinning and rolling inside me, unnerving me more than anything has in a very long time.

Apparently, it does matter who I'm getting hitched to.

But I don't have any time to consider what that means or the complications it could bring. It's irrelevant if I'm afraid of Silas or if the way my body reacts to his proximity is something else. I don't have the luxury of being choosy with my betrothed.

"I still want to go through with it."

Instead of relaxing, Silas visibly tenses at my statement, his scowl peeking out from under his beard. He shifts in his boots, his unease matching mine, and looks away, out the front window toward the woods opposite the cabin.

Ronald claps his hands. "Good. You two will be married tomorrow in a civil ceremony. You understand that?"

I gulp, swallowing past the lump in my throat. "Tomorrow?"

"Time is of the essence."

It is for me, too.

But *tomorrow*...

I open my mouth to ask what all of this is about, but I quickly snap it closed because it's none of my business. They aren't grilling me about why I'm in a rush to marry a stranger for money, so I shouldn't be questioning why a billionaire needs a fake wife, either.

"Okay..." I let myself trail off, unsure what to say to any of this. "I guess."

Silas' back stiffens, and he averts his gaze, staring back at the door he just came through. "I want to make sure you understand that this is a business arrangement. You need money, and I need a wife on paper." He returns his steely, cold eyes to mine. "That's all it will ever be." He issues a long sigh, running a hand through his thick hair. "Before you sign, there's one more thing..."

Oh, God.

Please don't tell me there's another agreement, something else I have to do...

Silas walks back to the door he originally came through and opens it wide. A massive German shepherd darts out toward the table, barking and snarling at Ronald, stopping immediately in front of the man but clearly still a threat despite not ripping him apart.

My future husband follows the dog over to us, a smirk on his lips as he watches the dog terrorize the man who's supposedly helping him.

What kind of sadistic asshole is he?

Silas stops his approach and snaps his fingers. "Whiskey, off."

The dog immediately sits and stops barking. His soft brown eyes move to me, but none of the aggression he showed toward Ronald gets directed my way. He merely assesses me the way animals do, like they can see straight through you, to the depths of your soul.

"This is my dog, Whiskey. He's the best judge of character I know."

He whistles sharply, and the dog returns to sit at his side, still eyeing me. Silas drops to one knee next to him and wraps his arm around Whiskey's neck, whispering something to him.

The dog approaches me cautiously.

I immediately tense, ready for the welcome Ronald received, but instead of charging at me with full-force aggression, Whiskey trots forward, tail wagging, and sits at my feet, then rests his big head on my lap.

The humor in Silas' face fades as he watches the dog nuzzle against me. "Holy shit."

"What?" I run my hand through the dog's fur. "What's wrong?"

His scowl returns as he pushes to his feet. "Whiskey hates everyone. I'm the only one who can get close to him."

I grin as I rub my finger along his muzzle to the tip of his cold, wet nose. "He's a good boy."

"Or a *traitor*."

The way he says the word tells me it means something different to him than it does to me. He trusts this dog to watch out for him, to read and see people for who and what they are. And apparently, he thinks Whiskey misjudged me.

I can't help but smirk at him. "So, did I pass your test?"

Part of me thinks he released Whiskey, believing the dog would scare me away and he wouldn't have to go through with this sham marriage.

Silas' agitation returns. He points to the contract. "I want you to understand something. Just because I'm a Bolton doesn't mean you're going to live that lifestyle. This"—he motions around the cabin—"is my only home and the only one I ever want. I've never taken a penny of my father's money, but I'm doing it now to pay you.

"You will get the sums owed to you in the contract when the terms are met, and you're free to do what you want with it when that time comes, but you won't be leaving here for some mansion in Pittsburgh. This place—me and Whiskey—this will be your life."

My back stiffens at the anger in his voice. Whatever happened between him and his father, it has clearly wounded the man standing in front of me deeply enough to truly make him hate the Boltons. And me, apparently, based on the ire in his harsh warning. "Do you even *want* to get married?"

Maybe it's a stupid question to ask, given the circumstances. Every single moment since he entered this conversation has screamed his disdain for the situation.

He reaches up and runs his fingers through his long, dirty-blond hair. "No, *never*." His gaze cuts to Ronald. "But sometimes, we have to do things we don't want to in order to protect those who need it."

Who the hell is he protecting by marrying me?

I don't understand any of what's happening, but that seems to be intentional on both Silas and Ronald's part. I'm not *supposed* to know. I'm just supposed to say, "I do," accept the money, and move into this claustrophobic cabin with this burly, tattooed, reclusive grump of a man and hope all goes well because I'm stuck with it the rest of my life.

Whiskey licks my palm, almost as if he can sense the anxiety ramping up in every cell in my body. I return to petting him, his soft fur sliding through my fingers, helping ease a little of my discomfort. But even him snuggling against me contently as Silas scowls at his apparent attraction to me can't make any of this okay.

You can leave.

The car is waiting...

For a split second, I start to stand. I actually *consider* walking out of here, driving back to the city, and trying to figure out another way to come up with fifty grand. But I drop back into the chair before I can get up an inch... because there isn't anything else—short of *actually* prostituting myself.

And God knows I'm not skilled enough in the bedroom to make any decent money at that, even if I *could* bring myself to try.

Ronald's gaze darts between Silas and me before he holds out his hands. "Are we doing this thing or not? Because if not, I need to call Carly and discuss other options as fast as possible."

I hold up my free hand, tightening my other into Whiskey's fur. "No, we're doing this."

The tattooed man in front of me may be physically intimidating. He may have a shit attitude, and living in this cabin isn't exactly top of my dream home list, but one thing he does have is money, and it's the only thing I need right now.

A lot of people marry someone they don't love. Arranged marriages still happen every day in other countries. Surely, Silas and I can come to an understanding, learn a way to co-exist here so we can both get what we need.

I grab the pen from where I dropped it on the table and immediately scrawl my name on the contract. Ronald looks at Silas expectantly. He ambles toward the table and snatches the pen out of my hand. His scent—a heavy mix of pine, wool, and fresh mountain air—fills my lungs as he scribbles his name almost unintelligibly on the line for his signature.

Ronald claps his hands together sharply once. "I'll just notarize this and go take care of the certificate."

I raise a brow at the man I had readied myself to marry before Silas walked out of that door and apparently stole my sanity, along with my breath. "We're really doing this tomorrow?"

Silas releases a heavy sigh beside me, full of frustration and pain and something I can't quite place. "We're really doing this tomorrow."

———

SILAS

Though, I don't have a clue why.

Even after having a few days to think about it while Ronald worked out the arrangements with Carly, I'm still not one hundred percent confident I'm doing the right thing —for me or for this girl who has no idea what she's getting herself into.

The world would be a better place without the Boltons in it, if Bolton Steel were to go under or get sold to some other company that would absorb it or completely dismantle it.

It would end the vehicle that allowed Uncle Marty to be the vile, disgusting piece of shit he is. Without Bolton Steel—the money and power it created—he never would have gotten away with any of it. The company has blood on its hands, and I would be the one running it—something I never wanted once I left.

But I can't shake that nagging feeling that I'd be letting down all those generations of Boltons who fought so hard to build it into what it is, that I'd be making a huge mistake I'd regret later by letting Uncle Marty "win" and continue hurting people until the day he finally keels over like Father.

The fact that he *will* continue if I don't step in and remove him keeps me moving forward with this horrifically stupid plan Ronald concocted, despite the reservations my future wife clearly shares.

She seems so sweet and innocent—exactly the type of woman Uncle Marty likes. One he can *break*. But in the end, I'm the one who will break her.

This place isn't meant for people like Lyla. *I'm* not fit to be around someone so pristine. I'll taint her with the permanent dirt that clings to me—literally and figuratively. Then the mountain will eat her alive.

But what other choice do I have?

If I continue to keep my head buried in the sand, trying to pretend what Uncle Marty did to me hasn't continued the entire time I've been gone, the guilt will destroy me.

Ronald rises from the table with the contract. "I'll see you two tomorrow at the courthouse at nine. Have fun getting to know each other."

Fuck.

Scrubbing my hand over my face, I avoid looking at the woman I'm going to spend—potentially—the rest of my life with.

I don't have any intention of getting to know Lyla. What I just said was true. This is a business arrangement, nothing more. It doesn't matter that my breath caught in my chest when I walked out of the bathroom where I'd been listening to their conversation. It doesn't matter that the moment I saw her and my eyes met her evergreen ones, I stumbled a step and remembered what it was like to be that teenage boy I was when I left home, the one who still reacted to beautiful women and *wanted*.

None of that matters.

It can't.

I haven't touched a woman in fifteen years and with good reason. Just because we say "I do" doesn't mean I have *to do* anything with this woman other than live in the same house and pretend we like each other long enough to get rid of Uncle Marty once and for all and secure the future of Bolton Steel the best I can.

Then, I can set her—and myself—free.

Lyla's eyes widen as she watches Ronald walk to the door. "You're leaving?"

He pauses with his hand on the doorknob, brows raised. "Yes." He sweeps out a hand. "There isn't a whole lot of room for me to spend the night, is there?"

She winces, and I can almost *feel* her anxiety building. Maybe the reality of her situation is finally sinking in. The sooner, the better.

Her gaze darts around the small cabin, from the queen-sized bed against the far wall to the chair and fireplace, as Ronald steps out. "Is there another bedroom?"

I shake my head. "Nope, this is it, except for a bathroom."

"Do you have..."—she looks around again, almost frantically—"electricity, running water?"

Fuck.

Not bothering to answer her annoying question, I stalk out after Ronald. Part of me wishes he *would* stay, or at the very least, take Lyla with him back to town and get her a room at the B&B so I don't have to deal with her in my space tonight—but that would only be delaying the inevitable.

I need to get used to Lyla being around.

Her citrusy scent.

Her soft footsteps.

Her assessing gaze always raking over me, judging me.

But not at this second.

My heavy boots thunder down the few steps from the porch to the clearing where the parked cars wait. Ronald starts his and pulls away to do a turn and head back down the mountain, and I walk over to the idling sedan Lyla arrived in and motion for the driver to pop the trunk. He does, and I grab two small suitcases most people would bring for a week-long trip—not to somewhere they are planning to stay permanently.

By the time I close the lid, Lyla stands in the open door of the cabin, eyes shimmering with unshed tears, arms wrapped protectively around herself again. She's on the verge of completely breaking down, and though I can't blame her, given the circumstances, it's the last thing I need right now.

There are more important problems to worry about than trying to figure out a way to reassure her. I can't even reassure myself that this is the right action to take, so there's no way I can do it for a complete stranger. Not when my *bride* looks at me like her life is ending the moment we say, "I do."

It just might be.

She certainly won't find a good one up here with me.

All she's getting is a broken man who can't be repaired and doesn't want her to try—something I need her to understand.

I stalk up the steps and stop in front of her, holding up the two suitcases. "This is all your stuff?"

She swipes away the tears and nods. "Yes."

"Good...because I don't have room for any other shit in this cabin."

It comes out more like a growl than words, and she stiffens as I move to brush past her. My shoulder bumps hers, and a spark shoots through my arm and straight to my groin.

Ignoring the strange electric current rolling through me, I stalk over to the bed. She follows me in and closes the door behind her. Out of the corner of my eye, I catch her wrapping her arms around herself again. Without Ronald acting as a buffer between us, the tension immediately starts to grow in the one place that has always been my refuge, where the only people I have to deal with are the ones who haunt me in my head.

I drop her bags next to the bed. "You can sleep here. I'll take the chair."

Her gaze darts to my worn leather armchair and footstool in front of the fireplace. "You can't sleep there. It'll destroy your back."

Snorting again, I make my way to the kitchen, trying to ignore the warmth her concern brings to my chest. It's been so long since anyone gave a shit about me that I have forgotten what it feels like until this moment. "Years of being up here and lumberjacking have already done that."

"You're a lumberjack?"

I pull out a tumbler and snag the bottle of whiskey that I've barely touched in the last few months from the cabinet.

If there's ever a day to drink it, it's today.

I pour myself two fingers and down it. Then I rest my hands flat against the counter and let my head drop low, closing my eyes, relishing the burn of the fiery alcohol in my gut. Better *that* than actually enjoying the way Lyla's worry about me makes me feel. "I had to make money somehow."

And that's all she's ever going to get out of me.

Ever.

I have no desire to rehash my past with her or discuss what happened in the Bolton mansion, what I was forced to endure. Those memories, that pain, they need to remain buried deep in the darkest recesses of my mind.

If I ever let them claw their way out of the grave where I secured that part of me, I'll never be able to function. The truth will tear me apart, and I'm barely hanging on by a thread as it is.

One quick tug on it will be enough to make me completely disintegrate.

I sense her moving toward me, and Whiskey sits behind me, pressing his body against the back of my leg, putting himself between us protectively though he seems to like her.

The sound of Lyla's footsteps stops a few feet away—though I can't tell if it's because of Whiskey or if my *get-the-fuck away* vibe is preventing her from advancing. "What do we do now?"

Her question is quiet, spoken to someone she clearly doesn't trust.

And why should she?

Fuck if I know what we're supposed to do now.

All of this was just dumped on me. The weight of putting away a man as horrible as Martin Bolton crushes my shoulders. So damn heavy. I'm not sure I can be the one to carry it. The thought of setting foot back in that building, of having to look into his eyes again, is enough to start my body trembling.

I pour myself another drink and down it before I turn back to face her. Whiskey shifts to lean his head against my thigh but keeps his focus on our new roommate.

Lyla still stands with her arms wrapped around herself, her thick brunette hair spilling down around her shoulders. Her soft green eyes rimmed with red from her tears seek an answer I don't have. One I'll *never* have because I'm as confused as she is.

She looks so small, so terrified. Lost and desperate. This woman doesn't belong here, doesn't belong with me.

It isn't safe.

Not for her.

Not for anyone.

The only way this works is to put as much distance between us as possible while maintaining the necessary façade for as long as needed. Once Uncle Marty is gone for good, Lyla can get back to her *real* life.

But until then, what do *we do next?*

Definitely *not* just stare at the beautiful woman in front of me. Yet, I find it impossible to look away. Her vulnerability draws me in, makes me want to offer her comfort I can't possibly supply another human being anymore.

Instead of giving in to that desire, I shrug because I only have one answer to give. "I guess we figure out a way to live together for the rest of our lives."

Though I leave out the "without hating each other," she still knows what I mean. Neither one of us really wants this. Whatever she needs $50,000 for must be important, as important as taking down Uncle Marty and protecting Bolton Steel has apparently become to me because I'm willing to do this despite a thousand reasons not to.

Neither of us is looking for more, which should make all of this that much easier.

And it would be, if she stopped staring at me with those sad eyes.

It's fucking worse than when Whiskey gives them to me. Any longer stuck looking at her, and I'll be liable to say or do something that will make her run after that car that just pulled away without her.

That can't happen.

We need her for this to work.

Which means I need to get the *fuck* away from Lyla Sinclair.

I push off the counter and storm past her toward the door, Whiskey hot on my heels.

Lyla tries to follow me but stops short when I whirl back to face. Her wide eyes watch me, her deep fear coming to the surface. "Where are you going?"

I open the door. "None of your business." I step out but pause halfway on the porch. Eyes locked on the forest outside, I inhale a deep breath of fresh mountain air before saying what I have to. "I want to make something very clear. You will be my wife on paper and in name only. I will continue to live my life exactly as I have been here—alone. If we're really doing this tomorrow, you better figure out what you're going to do up here because you are about to have a lot of fucking free time on your hands."

For years, I've had no one to answer to, no one questioning what I do or why. It's the only way I've managed to survive what happened to me. And I can't let this woman unravel that.

I jog down the steps, some of the tension instantly melting from my body being out here. The cabin always felt right for me—the right size, the perfect space, my own little sanctuary in the mountains. But now, it's filled with her light, citrusy scent, and her voice already rings in my ears.

And she's going to be here for the indefinite future.

Fucking hell.

Whiskey trots after me, tongue lolling out of the side of his mouth, bright eyes watching me.

"You like her, don't you? You *are* a fucking traitor."

He bounds ahead to grab a stick, then runs it back to me as I approach the edge of the clearing where the woods start to thicken. I take the stick from him and toss it. He bolts after it, scoops it up, and returns it to me quickly.

I kneel and take his face between my palms. "You better not get any ideas with her."

He tilts his head sideways like he's trying to process what I said to him.

"We can't like her, Whiskey. We just can't. But we need to figure out a way to keep her content because if what

Ronald said is true, this marriage has to last at least until Uncle Marty is taken care of, potentially forever if we can't get the terms of the trust amended."

Forever.

Tomorrow, I'm going to stand in front of the justice of the peace and say "I do" to a woman I just met, one who was shaking, terrified, and full of tears the entire time.

I drop my head back and stare up at the last light of day creating a brilliant orangey-pink sky.

It's too clear and bright. Too beautiful. Utterly wrong for the moment. It should be dark and foreboding, full of storm clouds signaling the approaching tempest. It's almost as if God is trying to force the sunshine onto me and into my life at the worst possible time.

I just can't let it blind me.

Chapter Four

LYLA

When little girls dream about their weddings, it certainly isn't standing in a justice of the peace's office at a tiny courthouse in Millsburg, Pennsylvania, with only the clerk of courts and your fiancé's attorney as your witnesses.

But it's been a long time since I was one who dreamed about it, anyway.

Things got too complicated. By the time I was eighteen, all I could concentrate on was surviving day to day.

I always thought I'd have time later, time to figure out life, time to figure out love, time to figure out any of it, but now, all that's left to do is say "I do" to a man I don't even know and pray he isn't some sort of psycho.

The few hours I've spent with him haven't done anything to appease my worry over that. I've barely seen him since he ran from me yesterday. If Whiskey hadn't climbed up onto the bed with me, I might not have known Silas had returned at all, but his muttered curse calling

Whiskey a "traitor" again filled the silent cabin before the leather of his chair creaked as he settled into it for the night.

Apparently, he was serious about sleeping there and letting me have the bed—not that I slept at all.

How could I, imagining what today would bring?

Nothing could *truly* prepare me—or anyone, really—for something like this.

I take one last peek in the mirror in the women's bathroom at the courthouse and release a heavy breath. The white sundress I changed into when I got here after the hour-long, awkward, silent drive down here in Silas' truck is the closest thing I had to a wedding gown.

Given the circumstances of these nuptials, I probably could have worn my jeans and sweatshirt I had on this morning, but though I didn't expect the big white wedding as part of this arrangement, something just felt wrong about that.

It cheapened it.

And no matter the reason for the vows, they do *mean* something.

I tug at the thin strap on my exposed shoulder, making sure it stays up instead of slipping down like it always wants to, then flatten my hand down the front of the dress to remove the last few wrinkles being stuffed in my suitcase and bag on the drive down here left.

This is likely the only time I'm ever going to be able to wear this dress. If I had known I'd be living in a remote cabin rather than an actual house somewhere, I might have chosen my clothes differently. But I came into this fake marriage totally blind, and now, I've been blindsided by Silas Bolton.

His stoic silence.

His moody huffs and heated, angry looks.

His huge presence in that tiny one-room cabin.

It's worth it. It's worth it. It's worth it.

I keep telling myself that as I throw my bag that holds my other clothes and makeup bag over my shoulder, tug open the bathroom door, and walk down the short marble hallway toward the clerk's office, where everyone's waiting for me.

Where my future husband *waits for me.*

That word will take some getting used to.

To go from painfully single to hitched for life to a stranger in a handful of days feels like being tossed into a tornado and not knowing where it will dump me when it finally ends its violent, tumultuous path.

I swallow past the rock lodged in my throat, tightening my grip on the bag to have something to ground me, and I step into the office. Whiskey lifts his head from where he rests on the floor at Silas' feet, giving that inquisitive head tilt. Ronald and Silas turn toward me, and both their eyes widen like they're seeing me for the first time.

A grin spreads across Ronald's face, deepening the crow's feet at the corners of his eyes. "Lyla, my dear, you look lovely." He holds out a hand for me, and I step forward and accept it. He brings it up to his lips and brushes them across my fingertips. "A beautiful bride."

Bride...

Jesus, I really am *doing this.*

My stomach clenches, and not for the first time, I consider racing out of the courthouse and running as fast as I can down Main Street until I find someone willing to drive me the fuck back to civilization.

I try to avoid looking at Silas, but it's impossible not to with the heat radiating from his gaze drawing me in like a moth to a flame. His eyes devour me—eating me up from the top of my head, where I've let my hair down out of the bun I tied it in this morning, stopping to examine my face that has makeup on for the first time since we met. It dips over my exposed shoulders and cleavage, across the lacy, flowing dress, to my bare legs and feet in the sandals I slipped on in the bathroom to replace the basic white tennis shoes I wore yesterday and this morning.

Every inch of my skin burns under his assessment.

During our drive down, he didn't glance at me once, but now, he can't seem to look away.

I glance down at myself, trying to see what he does. But all *I* see is the dress I've worn to summer parties for years, my pasty-white skin that desperately needs some time in the sun, and an old pair of sandals that show off an old indulgence—the pedicure I got before my whole life went to shit weeks ago, that's already starting to chip.

Nothing to look at, really.

Nothing special.

And I guess that's good because something tells me I won't be seeing a lot of people or needing to dress up for anything any time in the near future. The way Silas lives will be a dramatic change—so remote, so intentionally isolated, almost like he's hiding.

From what?

Given what little he said yesterday, I can surmise he doesn't have contact with his family, but whatever drove him up here is far more than a basic familial squabble. And I'm about to have a *long* damn time to find out.

If I can ever crack his rocky exterior.

I am wholly unprepared for any of this—to be a wife, to be a partner to someone who doesn't want it, to live like that —but it'll be worth it in the end if Attorney Fields can do what he says he can.

Ronald tugs at my bag. "Let me set this down on the bench for you during the ceremony."

I let him take it, and his palm presses at my lower back, ushering me toward a side room where the justice of the peace waits. We move past Silas on our way. He doesn't say a word, just continues to stare at me with an intensity that somehow sends goosebumps skittering across my skin.

Why is he still looking at me like that?

Do I look that terrible?

I thought the little bit of makeup I put on helped hide the puffy eyes from crying last night, but apparently not. It doesn't matter what he thinks, anyway—since this is all a sham.

He doesn't have to like me. He just needs that marriage certificate, and I just need his cash. If I don't start thinking of it as a business arrangement, I'm going to drive myself nuts, wondering what he thinks of me.

Seal the deal and get it over with.

Ronald leans in and motions for Silas to come over.

He clears his throat and approaches, Whiskey at his side. "What?"

His attorney gives him a reproachful glare. "Can you two *please* pretend you *want* to do this? I need to take some photos of the ceremony."

Silas stiffens, his jaw tensing, but he gives a curt nod.

I force a smile. "Yep, no problem."

That's what I'm being paid for, right?

Though, I always was a shitty actor and a horrible liar. I wear my heart on my sleeve far too much to conceal my emotions, especially when they're running as wild as they are today—as wild as the man I'm about to marry.

He couldn't even be bothered to dress nicely for the wedding. Dark jeans, tan work boots, and a long-sleeve light-blue Henley that barely contains his bulging muscles and shows hints of the tattoos covering his arms and chest. They swirl up out of the neck of the garment, all the way up behind his ears and to where his beard starts under his chin.

Someone clears their throat. "Are we ready to proceed?"

I jerk my head away from staring at Silas and force another smile at the justice of the peace who waits not so patiently to get the ceremony rolling.

Ronald claps his hands. "Yes, absolutely."

Our officiant nods and motions for Silas and me to come forward. "Excellent. We're gathered today to bring together Silas Bolton and Lyla Sinclair as they begin their new life together, founded in love and respect. Promises made today are an everlasting, lifelong commitment..."

Each word is a stab straight into my heart.

"Your future will be filled with new adventures, laughter, and challenges, but through your love and unfailing support of one another, you will meet these inevitable bumps in the road together and see each other through them. Silas, do you take Lyla to be your wife?"

Silas cuts his gaze over to me, seemingly unaffected by the vows the way I am. He only hesitates a second before his lips part and those two small, important words slip out. "I do."

Two more stabs.

The pain makes my legs wobble.

"Lyla, do you take Silas as your husband?"

The clicking of a camera and Ronald moving around the edges of my vision to get different angles of the ceremony draw my focus away from the question long enough for me to forget it was asked.

"Lyla?"

My name finally draws me back to the moment, and I

shift and force a half-smile.

It's now or never.

"I do."

The officiant looks to Silas. "Do you have rings?"

Rings?

I never even thought of that. There are so many things I haven't had the time to consider or wonder about.

Ronald holds up a hand. "Hold on. I have them."

Of course, he has them.

The man seems endlessly prepared for any potential hiccups in this process—unlike the two of *us*. Silas seems just as surprised at the mention of the rings as I am, watching his attorney suspiciously as he fumbles in his inside coat pocket and comes out with a blue velvet box.

He flips it open and turns it toward us.

A massive solitaire diamond sits in an intricate setting made for a queen, and below it, a simple gold band intended for Silas.

Silas' breath hitches. "Is that..."

Ronald gives him a sharp nod and holds it out for him. Silas reaches for it with a shaking hand and slips the elegant ring from it. He turns back toward me, lips pressed together firmly, averting his gaze, and takes my hand in his tattooed one.

Electricity sizzles through the connection—the power of all the built-up tension between us.

He slips the ring onto my finger, looking to the justice of the peace, refusing to meet my gaze while he says his hollow vows.

"Repeat after me: I give you this ring as a symbol of my love and devotion as we join our lives together today, tomorrow, and for as long as our love shall last."

Silas pauses a moment, his gaze cutting down to the ring

on my very important finger. His hand under mine trembles. "I give you this ring as a symbol of my love and devotion as we join our lives together today, tomorrow, and for as long as our love shall last."

More slices at my already-flayed heart burn in my chest.

Ronald steps forward and holds the velvet box toward me, urging me to take the band intended for my fiancé. I take it and turn his hand, my fingers brushing over the thick, calluses on it as I slide the ring down over the ink on his finger and say the words we both know neither of us means.

"I give you this ring as a symbol of my love and devotion as we join our lives together today, tomorrow, and for as long as our love shall last."

"And by the power vested in me by the state of Pennsylvania, I now pronounce you husband and wife. You may kiss the bride."

Shit.

We haven't discussed any of...*that* yet.

It wasn't really something I wanted to bring up in front of Ronald. While this is all contractual, discussing potential intimacy with anyone else as a witness would have surely pushed me over the edge.

My shaking legs weaken more, threatening to give out from under me. Silas keeps his eyes locked on mine but doesn't move to take the man's suggestion.

The justice of the peace doesn't know what to do, glancing between the two of us and chuckling awkwardly. "All right then, I'll just finalize the paperwork."

"One for the photos, please!" Ronald's command echoes in my ears.

Silas takes a minuscule step forward until I can feel his body heat radiating off him and the scent of pine and sandalwood envelop me. "For the photos..."

His large, rough palm slides over my cheek, and a shiver rolls through me as he tilts my head up toward him and slowly lowers his mouth to mine.

————

SILAS

The moment my lips hit hers, electricity flows through my blood, lighting me from the inside out and making my cock stir to life for the first time in years. Her mouth moves against mine, slow and unsure, and my hand involuntarily tightens against her cheek, urging her chin up higher, giving me a better angle.

Against my better judgment, I give in to what my body wants and deepen the kiss, dragging my tongue along the seam of her lips, requesting entry, wanting to know what she tastes like. Needing it. Craving it more than I have anything in recent memory.

But Whiskey shifts against my leg, causing reality to slam into me like an out-of-control semi-truck.

What the hell are you doing?

I've made a tremendous mistake.

I could barely breathe with her in the cabin and my truck. If I had tried to talk to her last night or on the drive this morning, that scent that clings to her would have invaded my lungs again, the same way it did when I got close to her yesterday to sign the damn contract.

And now I've gone and kissed the damn woman.

Inhaled her taste—mint, passion, and the kind of sunshiny happiness *other* people get to experience.

But not me.

Before I can let this go any further, I jerk away from her,

tugging my hand free from her smooth cheek and stepping back, almost knocking Whiskey over with my abrupt movement. Her eyelids flutter open, and the green staring back at me has darkened in a way that makes my heart stop momentarily.

Tiny breaths slip from between her perfect pink lips, and her chest heaves in the tiny white dress that barely contains the swell of her breasts.

Fucking hell.

What have I done?

Ronald barks out a laugh and slaps me on the back. "Congratulations."

I tear my gaze from her to glance at him. "What?"

He squeezes my shoulder. "You're officially a married man now."

I can't even acknowledge the words. Rather than being something to celebrate, each syllable sends ice shards through my veins, instantly snuffing out the conflagration the kiss sent surging through me only moments ago.

It's a frigid reminder of what we've done and of what's coming.

And he's the one who got me into this mess.

If Ronald hadn't shown up to tell me about Father's death, I'd still be blissfully unaware, living my life on the mountain, not giving a fuck about what happened to any of the Boltons. The past would have stayed buried where it belongs. But instead, I have allowed myself to be thrust back into the life I fought so hard to leave behind forever.

Now, I face an uncertain future—and I've dragged this woman into it without her knowledge.

Things are about to get very messy, and as my legal wife, Lyla's going to have to suffer some of the blows that are sure to come.

Martin Bolton doesn't play fair. He doesn't even play the same game anyone else does. His is evil. Depraved. Sinister. So twisted that once you get caught in it, there's only one way out...

I thought I had escaped, but I've been drawn back in by guilt and some deep-seated need to ensure he doesn't hurt anyone else. And it could end up hurting the woman standing in front of me. The one who just made me *feel* something other than pain for the first time in my entire life.

There's very little I can do to protect her from what's coming, but I can protect her from *me*.

Lyla twists the material of her lacy white dress between her hands, nervously glancing up at me every few seconds with her bottom lip between her teeth.

Fuck.

This is so damn fucked up.

I turn to fully face Ronald, stepping closer while Whiskey moves to Lyla, apparently more concerned with her right now than me. "So, what's the next move?"

He inclines his head to indicate we should leave and have this discussion elsewhere as Jon Franks, the Millsburg justice of the peace, returns with the signed paperwork.

Jon offers a tight smile, undoubtedly uncomfortable with the awkward ceremony we had. Especially since he and I have never shared a word before in all the time I've lived here. "Here you go, your finalized marriage certificate."

I reach out and take it, trying to hide the fact that my heart still beats a rapid tattoo from that single kiss. "Thanks."

"Good luck, you two." He says it with a wary look, almost like he knows exactly what's happening—the fakeness of this wedding.

But that's impossible. Until this ceremony, no one in Millsburg knew my last name. Even now that he does know it, there's no way he suspects I am one of *those* Boltons or why I'm doing this—our entire plan depends on that.

If the truth gets out and back to Uncle Marty before Ronald and I can get everything in place, it will doom our attempts and draw him from his cave of depravity to place a target on my back—and Lyla's.

Ronald opens his arm and wraps it around Lyla's shoulder. "Come on, dear."

He ushers her toward the door, and she pauses to grab her bag from the bench. Her hand tightens around it until her knuckles whiten.

I know how you feel.

Everything about this is wrong—the person, the timing, why we're doing it.

Marriage was never on my radar for too many reasons to count, and now this poor girl is locked into it with me.

Fuck you, Father, for putting this stupid requirement in the trust.

Though I can understand why he did it. He and Uncle Marty were notorious womanizers who tore through anyone who had somewhere to stick their dicks. That kind of life-style would eventually tarnish the company beyond repair.

If Father was really trying to protect the future of Bolton Steel, he needed me to have a different life, a real family with a solid base to stand on as CEO. He probably didn't formally disown me because he held on to some hope that when I left there, I found just that and would reconsider my distance from him and the company, eventually. But that *never* would have happened if Ronald hadn't shown up with this wild plan...and brought this unsuspecting woman up to the mountain.

I glance over at a silent Lyla as we make our way down the front steps and out of the courthouse. Her silence eats away at me the same way it did last night and this morning on our drive to town.

Why are you doing this, Lyla?

She's far too beautiful and intelligent to be selling herself like this, but whatever brought her to this place in her life, it's enough to make her as desperate as me.

I try to stop staring at her while we walk, but Whiskey rushes ahead toward her, trying to rub his head on her hand. It forces me to keep an eye on her.

Yeah, that's why you're doing it...

The eyes of everyone out on the street follow me, suspicion hardening their gazes. It isn't like me to be back in town so soon after my last trip, and they sure as hell have never seen me with anyone like Ronald, or Lyla, for that matter.

My stomach churns, thinking about the gossip that's no doubt already spreading through the entire population of our tiny mountain oasis. It won't be that for long.

Ronald pauses beside his car parked on the street in front of the courthouse. "I'm heading back to Pittsburgh to start on some of the things we discussed, Silas."

I narrow my eyes on him. "What am I supposed to do?"

He has to leave. I knew it was coming. But I am not prepared to be left alone with Lyla...my *wife*...yet.

"Prepare yourself for a battle at the board meeting."

"How the fuck do I do that?"

He gives me a stern look. "You were always a strong-willed kid, Silas. Don't let anything that happened to you change that. You're going to have to face him, and you're going to have to lay down some pretty horrific accusations if you want any chance for the board to turn against him and support you."

I can feel Lyla watching me, her inquisitive gaze locked on me as she listens to a conversation she can't possibly understand.

Ronald grabs the paper Jon just gave me. "I'm going to have these photos and the marriage certificate ready as evidence to support your claim for the trust. But it's still going to be a battle, and it's only round one. The morning of the board meeting, I'm going to deliver the envelope to the FBI."

I release a heavy breath and rub my beard. "You really think any of this is going to work?"

He peeks at Lyla and turns back to me. "It has to if we have any hope of stopping him."

"That's the *only* reason I'm doing any of this."

"You're doing the right thing, kid. I'll see you at the board meeting?"

The last thing I want to do is drive five hours into the city to step foot in that room with those people again, but I suppose I've made my bed and now I have to lie in it.

I glance at Lyla, who still looks so lost, shifting restlessly in her sandals, scanning the surrounding street. "Should I bring her with me?"

The corner of Ronald's lips turns up. "She is your wife, isn't she?"

"She is, but it doesn't mean I want her privy to any of the family's deepest, darkest secrets. Any of *mine*. If I have to stay married to this woman, potentially indefinitely, she's going to have to learn that some things are private and better left that way. If she needs to be there, she can wait in one of the offices during the board meeting."

Ronald holds up his hands. "Whatever you're most

comfortable with." He climbs into the car. "Hey, and Silas..."

"What?"

He opens his glove box and holds out a prepaid cell phone still in the package. "Take this. I need to be able to get in touch with you without driving up here."

I shake my head. "There's a reason I don't have one. Even if they worked on the mountain, which they don't, I don't want anyone to find me again."

Lyla's mouth hangs open. "You mean there's no phone? What if there's an emergency or—"

Turning toward her, I level her with a hard glare. "Or you want to leave?"

She swallows thickly and takes a little half-step back from me.

Good.

It would be best for both of us if she's afraid of me. Keeping her distance.

"If you want to leave, then...you *walk* into town."

She gulps, undoubtedly imagining the *long* climb up the mountain she made yesterday and the steep way down this morning.

Ronald points to the phone. "Come into town and call me as often as is feasible so we can touch base. I'll see you in a week and a half. If anything happens to me in the meantime, if you can't get in touch...assume the worst."

The worst.

He mutters the last part under his breath, but the way Lyla stiffens, she must have heard him.

He peels away from the curb and down Main Street toward the two-lane highway that will eventually take him back to the city. And now, I'm left alone again with my wife.

My wife.

I shake my head and rub at my temples, where a headache is starting to form. Too much has changed too fast —and it's only going to spiral further out of control as we approach the date of the board meeting. "What a clusterfuck."

"Just what every girl wants to hear on her wedding day."

Fuck.

I flinch and reluctantly open my eyes, though the last thing I want to see is the hurt. It's been so long since I had to think about anyone but myself that it never crossed my mind that what I said might actually *hurt* her.

It's there in her evergreen eyes—this may be a business arrangement, but it's still the only wedding day she's likely to ever get if we succeed and I decide I want to keep control of Bolton Steel in the end.

And I just said it was a clusterfuck.

Real fucking smooth, Silas.

I release a heavy sigh, a thousand different things I probably *should* say refusing to come out while looking at this beautiful woman who has been brought into a quagmire. "Look, I'm sorry, Lyla, but..."

She holds up a hand to stop me, her body tense, ready for a fight. "No, it's okay. Don't apologize. This is a contractual agreement, right?"

I give a sharp nod. "Right."

The word feels like acid coming from my lips after having them pressed to hers today, but it's the painful truth we're both going to have to live with.

We signed a deal—a *business* arrangement. It can never be more than that, no matter how long we may be stuck together. We stick to the requirements in the contract. That should be easy enough.

Keep reminding yourself of that.

Chapter Five

LYLA

The higher we climb up the bumpy mountain road leading to my new home, the heavier the reality of my situation settles on me. Every muscle in my body tenses. Each little dip we take over uneven gravel sends my ramrod straight spine slamming against the seat of Silas' truck hard enough to make my teeth clank together. My fingers tighten around the handle on the door until my knuckles whiten and ache.

A vise starts to tighten around my chest, squeezing the air from my lungs each mile we ascend—and it isn't going to get any better.

Coming down the mountain earlier this morning to get *married* in dead silence was awkward and uncomfortable—especially after a night of Silas avoiding me and offering nothing more than a grunt if I asked a simple question.

But this...this is something else altogether.

A new kind of torture I didn't know existed.

One of my own making.

My eyes drift to the massive diamond on my finger—the single thing I've seen since I got to this Godforsaken place that in any way suggests the man I'm now married to is worth billions—aside from those numbers in the contract I've been promised for many years of wedded "bliss." But apparently, coming from all that money and high-class stock doesn't mean he has any manners.

How can he ride with me for an entire hour after just getting married and not say a single fucking word?

He seems completely content to drive with his eyes locked on the road, Whiskey between us, the dog alternating between sitting up to watch our progress and resting his head on my lap and staring up at me with soft, sad eyes.

Like his owner, his bark seems worse than his bite, and if dogs weren't such good judges of character, I might be even more worried about what will happen when we get back to that cabin.

He's your husband, Lyla. You're going to have to do your wifely duties.

The man didn't kiss me like someone who is going to let that *"TBD"* clause go...

I really signed those damn papers without discussing *that* part of our relationship first. There's desperation, and then there's *that* level of desperation.

My stomach flips hard enough for me to slap my hand over my mouth to keep myself from losing its contents—the bitter black coffee Silas made this morning as the only breakfast offered on our big day.

I squeeze my eyes closed, drop my hand, and suck in a little sharp breath, trying to regain control of the panic threatening to send me spiraling.

"Are you okay?"

Silas's first words in over an hour since we left Millsburg and our "I dos" behind us make me flinch—loud and gravelly in the tight space, like he's barely reining in something he really wants to say and feigns concern instead.

I open my eyes and glance over at him. Our gazes meet for one moment—long enough for me to see he *is* genuinely asking before he darts his attention back to the road as we approach the turn-in for his place.

The fact that he seems like he might actually give a shit *should* make me feel better, but the man could just as well be wondering if I'm going to be "up" for consummating the marriage when we get back to the cabin.

Swallowing back my unease and the bile threatening to make its way out, I nod. "Yeah, the bumpy road is just messing with my stomach."

Seems plausible.

A good explanation.

Better than telling him I'm freaking the fuck out about having to have sex with my new husband.

Silas doesn't appear to be the kind of guy who will take it easy on me—ever. He's already proven how demanding he is, how he expects me to walk on eggshells around him in *his* space and not ask questions about why he's doing any of this, to simply *accept* this is my life now and roll with it.

Which means a roll in the proverbial hay I am so not ready for.

I tighten my grip on Whiskey's fur as Silas takes the turn into the woods that leads back to his property.

He snorts, as if my discomfort is somehow funny. "You get used to it."

"I guess I'll have to get used to a lot of things."

Like his grumpy, shit attitude toward everything, especially me.

Still, it comes out a little harsher than I intend, and he

doesn't miss the bite in my voice. His hands tighten on the wheel, the ink that covers them drawing my attention. The man hasn't been in a room with me long enough for me to examine any of the swirling tattoos that cover every exposed inch of his skin. I take the opportunity to zero in on a brightly colored parrot on his right hand—so out of place on a man who seems to only see things in black and white.

And I'm not helping anything with the way I just snapped at him.

I bite my bottom lip, and for a split second, I almost apologize. The only thing that stops me is the confidence that I won't be able to get through it without bursting into tears.

For so many reasons.

Before the last month, I prided myself on always being strong, of facing anything life threw at me with a smile and positive attitude. But the last few weeks have battered and bruised me beyond what I ever thought I could survive—and it is *far* from over.

It's just beginning.

And the only reason I'm here is because I got myself into this situation. I *knew* sex was going to have to be on the table for anyone to give me fifty grand.

I shouldn't take it out on Silas, especially when it seems as though he has his own very complicated reasons for this, far beyond anything Carly could have anticipated when she was explaining the typical mail-order bride arrangement to me.

But I did what had to be done, and now, I have to live with all the consequences—even the gruff, tattooed, angry one sitting on the other side of this massive dog who now acts as the only buffer between us.

Thank God for Whiskey...

We return to our uncomfortable silence, and Whiskey sits up as we finally approach the small clearing in front of the cabin. Silas pulls the truck around the side of the house, and I finally see more of the property.

A barn sits back in the trees, surrounded by fenced-in livestock pens that hold a cow, goats, chickens, and what looks like a horse in the far field.

He has a whole farm up here—probably so he doesn't have to go into town.

How long will I be stuck up here without any other human interaction except this *man?*

Silas turns off the truck, opens his door, and climbs out with a huff, Whiskey jumping down after him. My husband dips his head to peer back in at me, his long, sandy hair hanging around his face, giving him an almost angelic appearance if it weren't for the tattoos covering every inch of exposed skin. "You coming?"

I tighten my grip on the door, using it to ground myself so I don't say or do anything to make this situation worse.

What's going to happen when we set foot in that cabin? What is he going to expect from his wife?

Acid crawls up my throat, and I fight to swallow it back. "I-I..."

His brow furrows, those icy-blue eyes of his growing colder. Any potential goodwill I may have built up with him disappeared the moment I snapped at him.

"You *what*?"

I can't even look at him when I say this. *If* I can get it out at all. I squeeze my eyes closed and muster up every ounce of strength I have left, clutching my wedding dress in my hand. "I'm just wondering what it is you *expect*...now that we're officially hitched."

The chill emanating from his glare raises goosebumps

on my entire body without me having to peek his way, but I force my lids open and meet his gaze.

He doesn't say a word, merely stares me down with icy daggers.

I hold up my hand with the ring on it, as if that's enough explanation for what I'm asking.

TBD...

We really left that to be determined.

His jaw tightens under his beard, so much so that I'm surprised I can't hear his teeth crack, and his shoulders tense under his Henley, the thick muscles rippling as he grips the truck frame hard enough to crush it.

He lets out a long, heavy sigh and averts his gaze to something in the distance rather than on me. "I need to make something very clear, Lyla. Maybe I should have yesterday because it might've changed your decision..."

I hold my breath, waiting for whatever *requirements* he's going to lay down.

What will TBD mean for our future?

"I have no intention of being a husband to you. You'll get the money that's been guaranteed in the contract, and I won't ask anything of you." He finally glances over, his typically cool eyes unreadable, carrying almost an apology in them. "I'll never lay a hand on you in anger or any other way. We'll live as roommates. Nothing more. If you came here looking for a husband in anything more than name, you came to the wrong place."

He slams the door shut, rocking the entire truck and making me jerk in my seat. Instead of relief flooding me with his assurance that I won't have to do my "wifely duties," the anger and disdain in his words tighten my chest, and the sting of impending tears threatens.

Blinking them away rapidly, I can barely make him out

through the windshield as he stalks off toward the barn with Whiskey at his side.

He doesn't look back.

Do I really want him to?

Maybe after he cools down—*if* he ever does.

The man vacillates between frigid and fiery so fast that I can't keep track of what might set him off.

We can't continue on like this, can't have this much tension and anger building and compounding until one of us says or does something they can't take back.

Neither one of us wanted this, but it doesn't mean we have to be miserable for the rest of our lives together.

Does it?

I grab my bag from the floor of the truck, open my door, and step out. Soft dirt immediately covers my feet in the sandals, and I wince.

Useless up here.

So is half of what I brought with me—the slinky black cocktail dress, the matching bra and panty sets—just in case my future husband was someone I might actually want to use them with—the cute tank tops and shorts that now seem ridiculous to even *think* about wearing.

I scan my surroundings, getting my first *really* good view of my new home.

Towering trees.

Thick, dense underbrush.

Not another living soul around.

This is about as remote as it can get. If I'm going to survive here, I'm going to have to figure out how life works and how that man ticks, but something tells me it'll be the hardest thing I ever do in my entire life.

———

SILAS

The sun disappears behind the treetops, and as the light fades, the temperature begins to drop, instantly chilling the sweat covering my skin. Early spring in the Allegheny Mountains means dramatic shifts in temperature that seem as erratic as my moods around Lyla.

I glance at the cabin from where I stand next to the woodpile, axe in hand. Maybe it was a dick move to walk away from her earlier, to leave my wife—*Christ, I can't believe I have to say that word*—alone in an unfamiliar place while I came out here to do chores and avoid having to see her and what I've done to her.

She signed up to be a mail-order bride, but she didn't sign on for *this*, for *me*, for my fucked-up situation that we haven't even seen the worst of yet. Lyla thought she was getting a husband, a life partner. Someone who would take care of her and ensure her needs were met. Instead, she got me—a damaged, moody, gruff, scarred, broken man who can barely look at her without being overwhelmed by the demons of my past and threats to my future.

And what a fucking sad excuse for a man I am...

Releasing a heavy sigh, I drop my axe into the stump I use to split logs. There's still a lot to do tomorrow to prepare my next delivery for Jensen's store, but my shoulders and back ache from pushing myself too hard all day, and my stomach rumbles, reminding me I haven't eaten.

I couldn't, not when I woke with a crick in my neck from sleeping in the chair to find Lyla asleep in my bed— that traitor, Whiskey, snuggled up against her like he's *her* best friend and not my constant companion.

Something twisted in my chest. Something I don't want to examine or acknowledge, no matter how badly it wants me to. No matter how intensely it has clawed at me since the moment I laid eyes on her sitting at the table with that damned contract, looking so innocent and desperate.

I took advantage of her when she was in a shitty place.

She needed money, and I needed a wife. It should have been a simple proposition. But it's far from it. It will never be simple with the Boltons involved.

And things have already gone to shit...on day fucking one.

This morning, with her satiny dark hair fanned out around her head on my pillow like a fucking halo, she looked so peaceful. For those brief few minutes when I stood and watched her—the easy rise and fall of her chest, the soft part of her perfect pink lips, the way she clung to Whiskey—I knew I would shatter that peace the moment we said, "I do."

Which is precisely what happened.

Now, I can't seem to say anything to her that doesn't come out clipped and harsh and full of animosity that really isn't directed at her at all. I should continue to give her space because Christ knows I won't be able to form the words to apologize, but I can't continue to avoid her.

At least, not today—our *wedding* day.

Her earlier question about what I expected of her makes me cringe again as I head back toward the cabin. Whiskey trots alongside me, tongue lolling out, seemingly oblivious to what we're likely to walk into—another argument with the woman I need if I want any chance of taking down the monster who lurks in my nightmares.

I pause outside the door, kick off my boots, and suck in a deep breath to prepare myself for what might come flying at me the moment I walk inside.

A rich, mouthwatering scent hits me, and my stomach

rumbles again. Whiskey lifts his head and sniffs, and I turn the handle. He bolts against the worn wood, nudging it open and rushing in front of me toward the best thing I've ever smelled in this cabin.

"Oh, hey, boy!" Lyla's tinkling laughter comes from my right—the small kitchen I use solely to satisfy the most basic caloric needs to maintain the sheer amount of physical work I need to accomplish daily alone up here.

I close the door behind me and follow Whiskey in there, toward whatever's making the house smell so fucking good and the woman who has rattled me more than I care to admit.

Lyla squats in front of the stove, petting Whiskey, letting him lick her face.

Fucking traitor...

That damn dog hates everyone, but the moment she sets foot into the cabin, he's her best friend and I've become an afterthought. Though it isn't his affection for her that makes the green monster rear its ugly head—it's the way she's looking at him.

Pure, unadulterated joy.

This woman doesn't look for trouble. She doesn't enjoy angst and arguments. Her brilliant smile directed at a damn dog says everything I knew the moment I saw her and just didn't want to admit it.

She's too good to be stuck on this mountain with the likes of me.

Lyla looks up and jumps to her feet, wiping her hands on the front of her Steelers T-shirt. "Oh, hi." She scans the kitchen and motions to the pans in front of her. "I hope you don't mind"—she shrugs slightly—"I was getting hungry, so—"

I hold up a hand to stop her needless apology. "It's fine."

More than fine. I shove my fingers through my hair, suddenly very aware of how sweaty and filthy I am after working all day. "I should have told you to help yourself to anything in here." Releasing a heavy sigh, I squeeze my eyes closed. "Fuck, I have been a real dick. I'm sorry."

And that feels wholly inadequate for the situation.

I open my eyes to find her staring up at me, a soft crease in her brow.

"What are you apologizing for?"

Such an innocent question, but the long list of answers to that would take days to get through.

I snort and move past her to the fridge, tugging it open so I can grab a beer. The brief blast of cool air helps give me a moment of reprieve from the strange heat that seems to tighten my skin every time I'm around her, but I can't stand in the open door forever. Or go hide in the bathroom and clean up so I'm at least *somewhat* presentable.

Snagging a beer, I pop off the cap on the opener attached to the wall, then down half of my favorite brew— Locked and Loaded from Lockwood Brewing.

The hoppy liquid glides down my throat easily, refreshing and definitely what I needed after today. I finally turn back toward her and incline my bottle. "You want one?"

She shakes her head. "I don't drink."

I raise a brow. "Okay...is there—"

It isn't any of my business if there's a reason she doesn't drink.

Or is it?

She's your wife, idiot. These are the things you should know.

Maybe if she were really my wife, if this were some sort of genuine relationship, I would be asking, trying to find out everything about the woman I'm now attached to for the foreseeable future.

But it isn't real, is it?

I need to build a bridge while maintaining my distance —a feat that becomes increasingly more difficult the longer Lyla stays in my world.

She quickly turns back to the stove and stirs whatever's on there, but I can't tell whether it actually needs it or she wants to avoid where the conversation was going.

I rest my hip against the counter and stare at the wall. The longer the silence stretches between us, the more I shift uncomfortably, trying to figure out *anything* I might be able to say. "It's weird."

Her gaze darts over to me. "What is?"

Shit. Dumb way to start this, Silas.

But now that I've gone and stuck my foot in my big mouth, there isn't any reason not to keep going and just say what's on my mind with Lyla cooking dinner at my stove. "Having someone else here."

She stiffens slightly before she returns to stirring, keeping her focus anywhere but on me. "I'm sorry this is happening."

Her unexpected and ambiguous apology makes me push off the counter to retort, but she holds up a hand this time, stopping me from opening my mouth and saying something else stupid.

A tiny sigh falls from her lips, and she blows some of her loose hair from her forehead. "Look, you don't have to pretend this is something you want. Yesterday, you made it very clear you're doing this for some reason *other* than you actually *wanting* a wife. And you confirmed that today, which is fine because I don't actually *want* a husband."

The massive weight that's been sitting squarely on my

chest since I stormed away from the truck this morning lifts, and I release a huge breath.

Thank fucking God.

Because the man upstairs knows I couldn't give her that even if I did want to.

She returns to stirring whatever is on the stove. "I just needed the money. It's as simple as that."

Something tells me it isn't, but this isn't the time to press her—when it feels like we may actually be making some headway toward a wobbly, rickety bridge between us.

"And now that you have it?"

She pauses and glances over at me, uncertainty in her green eyes. "I made a call from the courthouse this morning and got the money where it needed to go."

I nod slowly and take another sip of my beer. "And what did you tell the person on the other end of the line?"

"Nothing about you, if that's what you're worried about. I understand what the NDA means. I won't tell anyone who you are, where we are, or that we did this."

Won't tell anyone.

For some reason, the thought of *no one* knowing where she is or why raises my hackles as much as Ronald did Whiskey's. The dog sits next to her in front of the stove, leaning against her thigh, staring up at her adoringly while I debate whether I should even ask.

"What about your job? What about your family? Won't there be people wondering where you went, worried?"

She squeezes her eyes closed, her pain palpable and radiating from her in a way I recognize all too well. "No one is looking for me. You don't have to worry about that, either..."

Her assurance should be enough to release the knot

from my stomach, but the way she speaks about no one looking for her makes this entire situation worse.

I left the world behind intentionally, fled here to protect myself. Since the moment I arrived, I've relished my solitude. Needed it to survive what had been done to me. But Lyla craves human interaction and affection.

She *wants* someone to miss her, to be looking for her. She may say she didn't want a husband, but she wanted *something* other than that fifty thousand dollars when she came up this mountain.

Something I can't possibly ever give her.

She pulls the pan from the stove and turns off the heat, then forces a smile that doesn't reach her eyes as she turns toward me. "Dinner's ready."

I glance down into the pan. "What did you make?"

One of her slender shoulders rises and falls. "A stir-fry, of sorts. I found rice in your pantry and what I *think* is pork and some vegetables in your fridge. I didn't have what I needed to make anything even remotely resembling a proper sauce, but"—she shrugs again—"it will have to do."

The way she tries to downplay what she's created from whatever random crap she's found in here doesn't sit right with me. "It looks a thousand times better than anything I've ever made for myself, and it smells delicious."

She moves over to the table and sets the pan on a pot holder, then grips the back of the chair for a minute, staring down before she looks over at me. "I know neither of us wants this, but since it has to happen, I'm going to have to figure out how to live here, and you're going to have to figure out how to live with me, as roommates."

The word makes me flinch. "Yeah, roommates."

"I can cook. I can clean." She motions absently toward the side of the property where I keep the livestock. "I can learn to help you with the animals and whatever else you need done."

I snort as I make my way over to the table and pull out the chair opposite her to take a seat. "You don't know the first thing about taking care of animals on a homestead."

"No, but I know about taking care of other human beings."

Her words come sharp and with a bite to them that makes me pause with my beer bottle halfway to my mouth. It's the first real crack she's shown in her armor. There's something in what she said, a hint about why she's here, but she doesn't offer anything more. And I don't dare press her and risk damaging this fragile truce.

Lyla returns to the stove, grabs a pot of rice, and brings it over to the table. Setting it down, she takes her seat, Whiskey settling under her feet. "So, we're on the same page?"

I down the rest of my beer and set the empty on the table, peeling at the label. It isn't much—more of an uneven, rolling log we're both trying to walk across without falling into the raging rapids of uncertainty threatening to sweep us away, but it's as much of a bridge as we're going to get right now.

"We are."

Roommates.

Absolutely.

Positively.

Nothing more.

Chapter Six

LYLA

Apparently, despite us coming to what I thought was a relatively friendly agreement about our predicament last night over an awkwardly silent dinner, Silas would still rather spend his time with the animals than with me.

I stare at the empty chair where he slept last night, trying not to remember what he looked like with the fire flickering in front of him, illuminating his strong, angular features. The way, even in his sleep, his brow furrowed and he flinched like something was chasing him, something he didn't want to catch him.

He's running; I'm trying to hold on.

The irony of the situation isn't lost on me—that *his* money—that he never wanted to touch—might be keeping me from losing the only thing I really give a shit about in this entire world.

As comfortable as Silas' warm bed is this morning, I owe it to him to try to help in any way I can around here. No doubt it's a lot of work for him to run this homestead alone. If I'm going to be here, I can't sleep my days away, only getting out of bed to cook and do what little cleaning the small space requires.

It's been so long since I haven't had a job that *not* doing anything feels wrong. And helping him can only make things easier.

Theoretically.

I throw back the covers and pull on a pair of jeans and a T-shirt that I dig out of one of my small suitcases—likely the only type of clothes I'm really going to need up here.

And we're going to have to talk about that...

My thorough examination of the cabin yesterday after he ditched me revealed only the single small dresser that holds his basic clothing—consisting mostly of a hell of a lot of flannel and jeans—and no closet to actually hang anything in.

Not that I would need something fancy up here, anyway.

I stare at the lacy white sundress I wore yesterday, where it's draped over the end of the bed and release a heavy sigh. The next time we go into town, I'll see if there's a thrift store or somewhere else I can get rid of the stuff I won't need and grab more jeans and workwear, since that's apparently what my life is going to be like.

Not that it's necessarily a bad thing.

Working hard never scared me before, and I'm not above getting my hands dirty to be useful to my new *roommate*.

I pull my hair back into a ponytail and step out into the warm spring morning. Unlike on the ride up here, the pervasive piney, woodsy scent of the air doesn't immediately make my stomach revolt. Birds chirp and soar through the blue sky. Leaves rustle in the light breeze. An energy permeates everything—the world coming back to life after being in a winter slumber.

Something tells me it isn't pleasant up here once the temps drop and snowflakes start flying, and being cooped up in this cabin with *that* man for months on end won't be, either.

Despite the tiny fissure in his hard exterior last night, the wall is still there. It might always be. Towering between us. Preventing him from telling me why he's so closed off and volatile.

It's only been two days—two very stressful and confusing ones—but somehow, it feels like Silas will go out of his way to keep me locked out forever.

That's going to make for a very lonely marriage for both of us.

That sense of dread that won't stop lingering in my head at the thought of this potentially being forever tries to push its way to the forefront again, but I will it back down.

Just keep reminding yourself of why you're doing this.
Love.

I step out onto the porch, closing the door behind me as I inhale another lungful of the fresh mountain air.

A quick scan of the small clearing makes it obvious why Silas loves it up here. Though wilderness certainly has never been my thing, it would be impossible not to see the stunning beauty of the endless towering trees and understand the benefits of the unpolluted air.

But there's no sign of Silas or Whiskey.

Without having explored the property yet, I have no idea where to search for the enigmatic man, but the barn seems like a safe bet.

I round the corner of the log cabin and get my first sight of Silas Bolton in his element.

He stands with his back to me, shirt off, axe raised high overhead before he swings it down, slamming it into a piece of timber propped up on a large stump off to the left side of the barn.

I stumble mid-step.

Holy hell...

The morning sunlight blazes down on him, creating a sheen of sweat across his tattooed, thickly muscled back and shoulders. Each step closer I take allows me to appreciate him even more—his Adonis-like physique and the raw power his body contains.

That man could snap me like a twig.

I get within a few yards, unable to tear my eyes from him as he works his way through log after log, splitting them easily, the axe almost an extension of his own body. The ink moves across his skin, the scene of two pirate ships battling coming to life across his broad shoulders.

He changes his attack slightly, the sunshine hitting his back at a different angle, and my breath catches. I freeze, coming to a halt as I examine what lies beneath all the ink.

Scars.

Woven into the tattoos.

Everywhere on the vast expanse of visible skin—the shiny, tight texture visible with each movement he makes.

Whatever was done to him left literal reminders.

He places another piece of wood on the stump and raises the axe again, swinging it down with a force that makes me jump back a step. My foot snaps on a twig. Whiskey's head turns from where he lies inside the door of the barn, and his eyes zero in on me. He leaps to his feet and charges my way.

Silas quickly whirls around to face me, giving me a view of his chiseled chest and abs, every inch covered with similar dark ink and a myriad of scars.

Is that why he has so many tattoos, to conceal them?

That thought makes my stomach roil as Whiskey reaches me.

He rubs his head against my thigh, and I squat and bury my fingers in his fur, scratching at his neck. "Hey, boy, good morning."

Silas scowls and turns away to set up another log and drive his axe into it without acknowledging me. This man has no intention of letting me distract him from his work.

I push to my feet and slowly approach him, despite all the vibes rolling off him that I should move in the opposite direction. If this thing has to work—and it seems like it does, for both of us—then I can't let him keep icing me out.

Stopping a few feet from him, I watch him split a few more logs before he finally pauses, resting the axe head on the ground and leaning against the handle. Sweat trickles down his thick neck, over his massive pecs, across a tattoo of a ghostly pirate captain, past the word *"Ruthless"* covering his perfect abs, and then disappears down into the waist-band of his torn jeans.

I swallow against my suddenly parched throat, trying not to stare at his bulge and the way the sunlight makes his tattoos seem almost alive. "Ummm...good morning."

Christ, you sound like an idiot, Lyla.

He glances up at the sun. "Almost afternoon..."

I scowl at the judgment in his tone. "I have no idea what time it is. My phone can't connect to the network up here."

The corner of his lip twitches. "You should get yourself a *real* watch, one with hands"—he points up—"or learn to tell by the sun. You don't want to get stuck out here when it goes down."

"Why is that?"

He smirks—the first true humor I've seen from the man. "A lot of things live in those woods that would enjoy tearing you apart in the dark, and even if you survived their teeth and claws, the temperature drops wicked fast this time of year, enough that hypothermia can set in before you realize it."

His warning removes any warm and fuzzy feelings I was having about the day. "Oh." Instinctively, I wrap my arms around myself and rub at them, though I'm not cold in a T-shirt on this bright spring day. "I thought maybe you could show me what I could do to help."

He raises a brow. "Really?"

I nod and motion toward the cabin. "Like I said last night, I can't just sit in there, doing nothing the rest of my life. Can I?"

His lips twist down into a scowl. "No, you can't."

Though, I doubt any other Bolton wives have ever had to feed animals and muck out stalls.

He slams the axe into the stump, wedging the head in halfway. "Come with me."

Without waiting to see if I am following, he gives me his back and heads toward the barn. I chase after him, hustling to keep up with his long, sure strides, almost tripping several times on the uneven ground.

Whiskey stays at his side, prancing along happily, completely oblivious to the scars his owner bears that I can't seem to look away from. He tried to hide them in the tattoos —that much is glaringly obvious now—but the way the skin puckers and the strange sheen when the sun hits them makes them impossible to miss.

The intricate sea battle across his shoulders looks so real that it seems like if I reached out and touched it, I would feel the spray of the water and the blast of the cannons from each galleon.

"Your tattoos are beautiful."

I don't know what possessed me to say it, but it makes him stop mid-stride and peer back at me over his shoulder. He doesn't say anything, just stares at me for a beat too long to be comfortable. I brace myself for his anger, for *any* response, really, but after a moment, he simply continues into the barn as if I hadn't spoken.

Should I be relieved or annoyed?

It seems with Silas Bolton, I never know *how* to feel.

When he first stepped into the room the other day and said I would have to marry *him*, a new kind of fear overtook me. Of the huge, angry man I would have to figure out how to live with. But over the last few days, I've come to realize he's just as trapped as I am.

Whatever secrets he holds close to his scarred, muscular chest, he doesn't want me to know them. And I have no intention of revealing mine, either.

But I'd be lying to myself if I said there wasn't some sort of attraction.

That flutter in my stomach when he first approached me at that table in his cabin. The way my body came to life when his lips pressed to mine yesterday at the ceremony. The unexpected tiniest hint of disappointment that hit me when he said he had no intention of ever touching me or being a husband to me in anything but name only...

It should have been a relief because I never wanted any of that. Yet, the idea of living my entire life without that kind of intimacy again makes my heart ache in a way I never could have anticipated.

But Silas doesn't want that.

He doesn't want me.

This is a business arrangement. Pure and simple. Whatever fleeting attraction I might have toward the confounding man has to stay buried, along with the reason I'm up here.

I have to stop staring at him like I've never seen a half-naked man before and concentrate on the task at hand—mainly lending one.

He walks through the open double barn doors and through the long building to another set that leads into one of the animal paddocks. "On the right is the goat pen, the left is Mae, my cow, and Lasher, my horse. The chicken coop is tucked into the far corner, where they're protected from predators. If you want to be in charge of getting the eggs in the morning, that would be great."

"We have fresh eggs?"

He nods. "They lay a lot. Sometimes, I'll bring some to the closest neighbors or into town if I have too many. But with you up here, that might not be an issue anymore. Can you handle feeding the goats, Mae, and Lasher and look after the animal pens, keeping them clean?"

Mucking out shit—that's what he means...

The closest I've ever been to farm animals was at a petting zoo when I was a child. And now, I have to care for them.

I force a smile. "I can learn, if you show me."

He makes his way over to the goat pen and stops with his hand on the gate. "Make sure this gate is latched at all times. Billy and Bobby like to run and cause trouble. Mildred and Peabody are older and slow, but the twins, you have to keep your eye on them."

"Billy?" I raised a brow at him. "Billy goat?"

His lips curl into a half-grin barely visible beneath his

beard, which now seems a lot like another way for him to hide. "So, I wasn't that creative..."

Another crack in that armor.

A tiny one.

Each time the man shows any emotion but anger, I'll have to consider it a win.

He opens the gate and slips inside the pen, allowing me to follow him, and I pull the gate closed, making sure it latches behind me.

Silas meanders to a small shed in the corner. "All their feed is in here. They get fed twice a day. Every morning before nine. If you wait this long to serve them breakfast, they'll be angry."

"So, you're telling me I need to become a morning person?"

He chuckles lightly, the sound foreign from a man who seems to spend his days fighting anything that might make him more human. "Living like this requires you to be a morning person."

"I've always been more of a night owl."

By necessity.

But things change, and I have to adapt.

Silas motions to the trees. "We have those here, too. You'll hear them come winter mating season."

Mating season...

The mere mention of it is enough to bring heat to my cheeks that has nothing to do with the warm spring sun beating down on us. Silas seems to sense the shift in the mood and averts his gaze to the two small goats approaching us.

I take a step back, allowing them to run around him excitedly while I try not to get nipped. "It might take me some time to figure everything out."

Without looking at me, Silas waves out a hand absently. "All we have is time."

————

SILAS

Lyla's gaze heats my skin all afternoon, far more than the high sun does, even at this elevation. It rakes over me any chance she gets, searing through me like an out-of-control forest fire. A conflagration of judgment and pity threatening to consume me and leave me a pile of ashes.

Each assessment brings the original pain again.

Reliving each strike that left me this hollow shell.

She can't look away.

Lyla sees them, despite all the efforts I went through to hide the scars. That woman sees *too much*. From the first moment I laid eyes on her, it was like she stripped me bare, and the more time I spend around her, the more convinced I become that she can see right through everything I've done to bury my past.

She's close enough today that she can memorize every single reminder on my skin and is no doubt running through scenarios in her head, trying to figure out how I got them. But I have no intention of reliving that trauma to satisfy her curiosity.

It's bad enough I'm going to have to do it in front of the board.

I won't with that woman there. If it means forcing her out of the room before I reveal Uncle Marty's sinister deeds to the people who hold the fate of Bolton Steel in their hands, so be it.

We may have to figure out a way to live together, but it

doesn't mean Lyla has to become my confidante. There won't be any pillow talk, opening up old wounds. Because she isn't *really* my wife. Not in any way that matters.

But she *is* a hard worker.

She may not be used to living like this, yet she hasn't complained about cleaning out the stalls or loading the wood I've been splitting to the shed for storage or to my truck for my next delivery.

Lyla will need that drive to survive up here.

She'll need that to survive me.

I raise the axe over my head and take another swing. The log splits perfectly, and I toss both chunks onto the pile for her. She returns from the shed, rubbing a hand across her brow, wiping away the sweat, and I pause my work to watch her for a moment.

She raises a brow, her already pink cheeks darkening slightly under my assessment. "What? Why are you staring at me like that?"

Because it's been a long fucking time since I've seen such a beautiful woman.

Even sweaty, with her dark hair trying to break free from the cute ponytail she has it in, Lyla still shines in a way that would make any man lose his control.

Any man but me.

I don't have the ability to explore what it might be like to have a woman here for any other reason than the current one—to secure the trust and put myself in a position to control Bolton Steel. And even if I could, the last thing she needs is to battle the demons that will always chase me.

Shaking my head to clear away those thoughts, I let my gaze drift to her lips. "Nothing. I just didn't expect you to do all this without complaint."

She scowls at me, crossing her arms over her chest. "Do you know what I did for a living before I moved up here?"

Fuck.

I don't.

I didn't ask.

It was all such a whirlwind. As soon as I agreed to Ronald's mail-order bride scheme, he drove back into town to make the call to Carly. It became clear we wouldn't have a lot of options since we needed it to happen fast.

All we had were the basics on Lyla—enough to run a cursory background check for any criminal history or anything else that might leap out. But she came up squeaky clean. And I never bothered to try to get any other information about her—from Carly *or* from my wife.

Real fucking nice, Silas.

I rub the back of my sweaty neck and shake my head. "No. I don't know."

She huffs and blows a strand of loose hair off her forehead. "I was a waitress and a bartender. I've been on my feet for long shifts, carrying heavy trays, cleaning tables and equipment, dealing with asshole patrons and co-workers who sometimes have shitty attitudes. All this"—she waves a hand around the barn area and at me—"might be new to me, but hard work isn't."

I flinch at her completely warranted reproach. A shitty attitude seems like an understatement for how I've treated her since she set foot here. "I'm sorry. I shouldn't have assumed..."

Just because the women I knew before I came up here would rather sit on their asses and be catered to hand and foot doesn't mean all women are like that. It's becoming abundantly clear that I vastly underestimated Lyla Sinclair.

She weighs my apology for a moment, then dismisses it

with a wave of a hand. "Don't worry about it. Really. I'm sure we've both made a lot of assumptions that aren't true."

What the fuck does that mean?

I don't get to ask because she grabs a few more logs and walks away without another glance at me. Whiskey watches her go from his spot in the rapidly fading light next to the barn, and I glance at the sun starting to set.

The temperature will start dropping soon, and there's no reason I can't finish this myself so she can get cleaned up and relax after a day that will likely leave her sore.

She reappears, arching her back and rolling her neck, clearly feeling the exertion of the day as much as I am.

Guilt at making her do my work twists my gut, despite her insistence that she can handle it. That chivalry ingrained in me growing up won't disappear, even after so much time on the mountain.

I motion to what's left of the woodpile. "We're almost done here. I can finish up. I need to restock the house from the cured wood in the shed and throw this stuff in there to dry. It shouldn't take more than another hour."

Her brows rise, and she looks prepared to argue with me before her eyes dart toward the barn. "So, I should feed the goats a second time before I head in?"

Smart girl.

She was paying attention.

I fight a grin. "If you don't want them screaming all night because they're hungry."

A smile plays at the corner of her lips, and she shakes her head. "We can't have that, now can we?"

I shouldn't enjoy watching her walk away so much. Or rather, I shouldn't enjoy watching the way her jeans mold to her ass with each deliberate step she takes. I should be happy she's leaving me alone—that I won't have to feel her eyes on me while I finish this load and restock the house. Instead, I lean against my axe, gaze locked on her until she disappears around the side of the barn toward the goat pen.

"Fucking hell, Whiskey..."

He looks up at me from his spot in the grass, clearly asking permission to go with her.

"Stay here, buddy."

None of the goats are particularly fond of him, and the last thing Lyla needs is them getting unruly because he's riling them up tonight.

I'm riled up enough for everyone as it is.

The extra hour and a half of work I do moving, stacking, and rearranging the fresh and already-curing wood in the shed doesn't do much to relax the tension being around her all day has built up in me. And by the time I'm done, night has fully descended, the stark drop in temperature sending a chill across my exposed skin.

My stomach growls, imagining what Lyla might come up with for dinner. "What do you think she cooked for us tonight, bud?"

Last night's meal was...superb.

She tried to brush it off as nothing, but she somehow managed to create real food from the scraps of random things I had left in the kitchen. Maybe having her as a "roommate" won't be so terrible after all.

I trudge up to the cabin and open the door, but no mouthwatering scent hits me tonight. Stepping in, I scan the small space and kitchen, but the stove is off—no pots or pans out. No sign of Lyla.

"Lyla?"

Whiskey rushes past me and around the cabin, searching for her in the bathroom, and comes back, his brow furrowing over his dark eyes.

"Where is she, buddy?"

I step back outside and call her name into the night. "LYLA?"

It echoes through the clearing with no response, then gets swallowed by the surrounding trees and darkness.

Shit.

Dread wraps around my chest as I descend the porch steps and jog over to the barn. I throw open the doors, but there isn't any sign of her inside.

"Lyla?" My voice startles Lasher in his stall. I walk over and rub his flank to settle him. "Have you seen her?"

He snorts and shakes his head, almost like he can actually understand what I'm asking. But he likely senses my growing anxiety at her disappearance.

I slide open the back doors that lead to the pens and pasture, Whiskey following closely at my side. "Where is she, boy?"

He tilts his head, staring at the goat pen, and I follow his gaze to find three where there should be four.

"Oh, hell..."

Scanning the dark forest along the back fence of their pen, I can almost picture what happened. Billy must have gotten out when Lyla came to feed them...and that damn stubborn woman went after him without calling me for help.

"Fuck."

I race into the barn and grab a flashlight from my workbench, then hustle back to the forest edge. "Let's find her, Whiskey."

He bounds in front of me, leading the way through the thick brush. The flashlight beam illuminates the rugged non-path into the woods she must have taken, given the snapped twigs near my feet.

"LYLA!"

My voice seems to get swallowed up by the towering pines and firs, but I keep calling for her, trudging over fallen trees and dead leaves, trying to track her path through any small evidence she may have inadvertently left.

Tangled limbs try to grab at my booted feet and hold me back, but I break free and push on, sweeping the narrow light beam in front of me.

"LYLA!" The panic rises in my voice each time I call out for her and the farther Whiskey and I move away from the safety of the cabin. "Can you hear me?"

Knowing Billy, he'll head toward the river, where his favorite flowers grow along the bank. And they could be miles into the forest if he got away from her when she first disappeared to feed them. That determined little shit likely led her away so quickly that she didn't realize how far she had gone until it was too late.

My chest tightens more the deeper I get into the forest. Every breath I take puffs out in front of me, the icy air biting at my exposed skin since I never bothered putting my shirt back on. Even my jeans and constantly moving can't protect me from the bitter chill.

She isn't dressed for this in that T-shirt...

At these temperatures, hypothermia can set in fast, despite how warm it was during the day. With no moon tonight, it's almost pitch black out here. She won't be able to see where she's going, and this forest goes on for hundreds of miles all around us—with steep ravines, creeks, a rushing river, and any number of living things and other dangers ready to take her down.

Fuck! Fuck! Fuck!

"LYLA!" I push deeper into the woods, following what I hope was her path, trusting Whiskey to help. "LYLA!"

I scream her name over and over again, until my voice goes hoarse and my throat is raw. Whiskey races ahead, zigzagging in front of me, darting to the sides into areas too dense for me to reach, hopefully catching her scent. But he isn't trained to locate people, and I can tell by how frantic he is that he hasn't found her yet. And he knows something is wrong, just like I do.

Dread starts to coil around my spine.

Lyla's barely been with me for a few days, and I've already managed to get her lost in the fucking woods.

What the hell was I thinking bringing a woman up here who knows absolutely nothing about this lifestyle, about how to stay safe?

She probably thought she was doing the right thing going after Billy, that she'd easily catch him and she wouldn't have to admit to me that she let him out of the pen. And then he led her deeper into the woods until she had no idea where she was.

It happens a lot to people out here, but it shouldn't be happening to my wife.

"LYLA!!!"

A branch scratches along my arm, but I barely feel the pain. Running solely on adrenaline now, I surge onward, casting the light everywhere I can in hopes she'll see it if she can't hear me.

Whiskey barks somewhere unseen ahead and rushes back to me, bouncing on his paws excitedly. He charges forward, then spins in place and looks back to make sure I'm following him.

"Did you find her, boy?"

He rushes toward me, circles, then takes off with a determination I haven't ever seen in him before.

He found her.

109

Hope starts to bloom in my chest as I race through the dark, clambering over fallen trees, through sharp branches, and across uneven ground. "Lyla?"

Whiskey leaps over a giant log, and I swing my leg across it and come down on the other side, almost on top of Lyla.

Fuck.

She lies huddled up against the log, her eyes closed, arms wrapped around herself, shaking violently.

"Shit. Lyla?" I drop to my knees and pull her up by the shoulders. Her head lolls to the side and her eyes flutter, but she doesn't open them all the way. "Lyla, can you hear me?"

Her lips part, her breaths visible in the frigid air. "I'm s-s-sorry..."

Fucking hell...

I scoop her up into my arms, and the ice-cold of her cheek against my already-cool skin tightens that coil of dread around me. If I don't get her warmed up fast, I'm going to lose her.

Chapter Seven

SILAS

"Lyla, stay with me." The panic I'm trying to tamp down threatens to bubble out with each word. She's barely conscious, but I can't let Lyla hear it in my voice. I swallow it back, fighting the pitch-black night toward my only hope of saving her in time. "We're almost there..."

Her trembling body held tightly against mine, each stumbling step I take through the woods back toward the cabin, reminds me of how long she's been out here in the freezing temperatures.

Too long.

And the light, cold drizzle that's started to fall has already dropped my body temp noticeably.

The forest seems endless and hostile—branches reaching out to try to hold me back inside it, brambles and bushes blocking the most direct path to safety.

But I finally make it to the tree line.

My cabin comes into view—along with it, an intense sense of relief. But we are far from out of the woods yet.

Whiskey bounds ahead, darting between me and the door as I advance toward it. He knows how serious this is. How deadly it could be. The dog is smarter than anyone gives him credit for.

Look how attached he is to her already...

I climb to the porch and manage to turn the knob behind Lyla's back and nudge open the door with my knee while balancing her in my arms. Her eyelids continue to flutter, but she doesn't fully open them, and she stopped responding to me before I got the cabin in sight.

Whiskey rushes inside, turning back to watch us, his brows raised, head tilted, while he watches everything unfold.

I kick the door closed behind me and freeze, staring at the empty fireplace.

Fuck.

We spent the entire day outside, and I never stoked the fire. My gaze darts to where the stack of dry firewood should be beside the hearth, knowing full well what I'll find.

Empty.

Because I was *supposed* to bring in more when I stopped working today since I've been burning through it faster with her here, keeping it warmer than usual so she's comfortable.

But it isn't warm now.

The deep chill permeating the inside of the cabin matches the one settling over my heart despite having come in out of the rain. I can't warm her up when I'm freezing from being outside for hours searching for her, and there's no way to light a fire. If I take the time to run outside, grab wood, and get one going, it could be too late.

There's only one other option to help get her core temp back up—and it isn't great.

Please fucking work...

I beeline straight for the bathroom. Whiskey trails after, nervously pacing near the door as I kneel next to the steel trough that acts as my tub. I gently set Lyla down on the bath mat, propping her against the counter. The moment I move my hand away, she starts to tip sideways.

"Shit."

Supporting her head with my left hand, I reach over and crank on the hot water with my right, then add a half turn of the cold handle, too, since putting her into water that's too hot too fast could fucking kill her.

Irregular heartbeat. Damage to her near-frozen skin. All of it is a real risk.

Dry and warm is best.

But in a pinch, wet and warm is going to have to do.

Please, God, let this work...

If there were any time I wish I believed in someone upstairs, it would be now. When I'm desperate and praying for something I don't deserve. I've failed so many people, and looking at Lyla's pale skin and slightly blue lips, the very real evidence of my most recent failure is impossible to miss.

"Lyla, come on." My voice cracks, and I clear my throat. "Wake up."

She issues a little groan, which at least means she's conscious, and tilts slightly into my hand. I brush my thumb across her pasty cheek and bring my right hand to the other side, tilting her face up toward mine.

"Lyla"—I shake her gently—"I need you to wake up."

A strangled sound slips from her lips, like she so badly wants to ignore my command and let sleep claim her again.

She tries to wrap her arms around herself, but she's shaking so badly she can't control her limbs, and her arms fall back to her sides.

"We have to get you warm."

She nods a tiny bit, no doubt all she's capable of in her current condition, and I glance over at the tub starting to fill —but not fast enough for my liking. The tankless water heater I splurged on was a necessity for me up here after a long, hard day of work on the homestead. It could also be what saves her life. If I had to heat water on the stove like many who live up here do, it could be too late.

And I need to get her out of these cold, wet clothes in the meantime.

"Shit."

Stripping her while she's barely conscious makes my cold skin crawl, but I reach down with one hand and grab the hem of her shirt. Slowly, I work it off her, maneuvering her limp arms through the sleeves with very little assistance from her.

I pull it off over her head, and her eyes flutter open and meet mine.

Unfocused. Confused. Terrified.

Me too, Lyla.

I brush my fingers across her abdomen, above her pants, reluctant to do what needs to be done. "We need to get you undressed and warmed up."

She bobs her head again and fumbles with the button and zipper on her jeans with fingers that won't seem to work. I reach down and do it for her, and she wraps her arms around my neck to steady herself.

Instantly, I freeze, my entire body stiffening at the contact. Though, it isn't only her ice-cold skin pressed to mine that sends goosebumps over me. My instinct to pull away wars against the knowledge that I *have* to do this. My old demons threaten to interfere with the current necessity, but I have to push them away if I want her to survive.

Just breathe, Silas.

Repeating that in my head, I shift the material down over her ass, and she uses me for leverage to lift herself from the floor so I can maneuver them down her thighs to her calves, where the shoes she's still wearing stop my progress.

I manage to peel them off and toss them onto the floor, then tug her pants off, letting the soaked material splat against the wood floor.

Don't look.

It's hard not to as I scoop her up in her bra and panties and swing her over the metal edge of the tub. She clings to my neck, refusing to let go, using what little strength she has left to ensure I can't set her in the tub.

"You need to let go, Lyla."

She presses herself closer to me, undoubtedly seeking what little body heat I have and not realizing what I'm trying to do.

There isn't any time to argue with this woman.

"Fuck."

I step over the metal side, sinking down into the tepid water with my boots and jeans still on. Even the minor difference in the temperature instantly heats my bare skin—exactly what she needs to get hers up—but we need to do this *very* slowly and carefully, or I'll end up doing more damage than actually helping.

She presses her face against my neck, arms still linked around me, chest to mine, and her body curled on my lap as the water rises around us. Violent tremors still wrack her body, and I hold her firm, rubbing my hand along her chilly arms and back, trying to get the blood circulating through her again.

Water laps close to the edge of the tub, and I use my booted foot to nudge the hot and cold water off before it overflows. I hold her close for what feels like an eternity. Sheer terror that I might do this wrong or too fast and kill her keeps me from moving except to continue gliding my hands along her body, hoping the friction will somehow help.

Only the steady rise and fall of her chest against mine assures me I haven't fucked it up too badly yet—but there's plenty of time for that.

I let a few more minutes pass, until she relaxes slightly and the tremors seem to come less frequently. Tightening my grip on her, I bend forward, taking her with me to unplug the drain and let out some of the water.

She moans a protest at being lifted, but I press my lips to her temple.

"Shhh. It's all right. It's going to get warmer."

I crank the hot water back on, letting it mix with what's left in the tub, then slowly lower us back down into it.

Lyla releases a little sigh as it engulfs her again, and the gradually increasing temperature starts to help her skin feel less chilly against my own.

The tiniest bit of relief starts to fill my chest as the water inches toward the edge of the tub, threatening to spill over onto the pine floors. I kick the hot water handle off and sink as low as I can, getting Lyla fully submerged, only her face against my neck above the waterline.

Her light breath flutters against my beard, and she shifts restlessly against me, inadvertently grinding down on my crotch. I grit my jaw, tightening my hold on her so I can adjust her slightly and nuzzling my face into her thick, damp hair.

The image of her huddled against the log, her normally pink lips almost blue, skin a deathly pallor, flickers through my head, and I squeeze my eyes closed against the panic I've barely managed to dispel as it threatens to return.

I almost lost her...

"What were you thinking, Lyla?"

In the quiet stillness of the bathroom, my words sound as hollow as I felt when I saw her like that. Knowing it was my fault—that someone else got hurt because of another massive failure on my part.

Lyla shakes her head slightly, like she doesn't know the answer, but she may not have even registered the question. She presses more firmly to me, her grip around my neck almost frantic, like she can't get close enough, and she releases a little sigh of contentment usually reserved for that moment right before you drift off.

"Don't fall asleep." I pull my head back slightly and tilt her chin up so I can see her face. The color has started returning to her cheeks and lips, which I hope means she's out of the woods, but I'm no fucking doctor. "Lyla, open your eyes."

Despite the fact that she's finally warming up, falling asleep right now would be a bad idea—I might not know anything about how to interact with another human being, especially a woman like Lyla, but I know *that* much.

Her eyes flutter open.

This time, they're a little more focused.

She's a little more *there*.

This close, the little flecks of gold sprinkled through the evergreen seem to shine, and I can't tear my eyes from hers, lost in the subtle beauty I would never allow myself to recognize before.

"Stay awake, okay?"

She nods and buries her face back against me, seemingly unbothered by the fact that she's nearly naked on top of me and my harsh beard is rubbing against her.

But I'm *far* from unbothered.

My entire body vibrates with barely restrained frustration.

With her...

With the situation...

Mostly with myself...

It never should have happened—none of it. And even though she's safe in my arms at the moment, hundreds of horrific things that could have hurt her out there haunt the parts of my mind usually reserved for other horrors.

A bear.

A coyote.

Hell, a fucking wolf could have been brought in by Billy's scent and killed her instead.

I shudder at the thought, and she shifts against me, her ass grinding my crotch in a way that makes me immediately freeze again.

Millions of men would clamber over each other to have an almost-nude Lyla in their arms, moving against them like this, but I'm not most men. I'd give anything to go back to that day she sat in the kitchen and signed that contract and do it differently, warn her how fucked up I am and how twisted this entire situation would become.

Do anything to stop *this* from ever happening in the first place. To save her from this pain and what is coming once we have to face what waits back in the city.

"I-I-I g-g-got lost." Her words are so soft I can barely

hear them over the sound of my own psyche crying out at me that I'm fucking everything up. "I-I—"

"Shhh, I know."

Lyla shouldn't be wasting her energy trying to explain herself to me.

"Billy g-g-got out when I went in to f-f-feed them." She fights back a sob, her body shaking again. "I th-th-thought I could c-c-catch him inside the woods before he got too f-f-far away."

I squeeze her tighter, rubbing my palm along her spine. "I know."

"It g-g-got so dark." She shivers and clings to me more frantically. "I c-c-couldn't see the cabin or even the lights from it."

The panic building in her voice at reliving the night makes my chest tighten, and I bury my face in the top of her head, the light citrus scent of her shampoo and the rain and crisp night air filling my lungs.

I let my eyes drift closed.

This shouldn't be comfortable, curled up in my jeans and boots in this old metal trough tub with this woman I barely know in my arms. A woman who unnerves me every time her eyes cut my way. But somehow, it is. And that's more terrifying than the thought of anything that could have happened to her out in those woods.

"These woods are easy to get lost in. You should have come and got me."

She sniffles, and even with her head angled down, I can tell she's fighting back tears. "I know, but you were busy, and I didn't want"—she sucks in a breath and releases it slowly—"I didn't want you to think I couldn't do it. I couldn't find Billy...he's still out there...I fucked up."

Aw, hell.

119

This is my fault.

I'm a total jackass for making her feel that way—that she couldn't come to me to ask for help.

She's afraid of me.

I've *made* her afraid of me.

That's what I wanted.

That's what I *should* want...

I run my hand along her arm draped around my neck, trying to offer a soothing touch when I don't even remember what one feels like. "Don't worry about Billy. He'll hunker down somewhere for the night, and I'll find him tomorrow." I release a heavy sigh. "And don't apologize anymore. I know this is all new for you. Having you here is new for me, too."

New and fucking terrifying.

People have always been the problem.

Caring about anyone only ever led to pain.

I'm supposed to be alone here—forever.

I'm not supposed to like this, like *her.*

"I've always done all this on my own, Lyla. It's the way I like it. Looking out for someone else..."—I sigh—"it just really isn't in my nature. I should have protected you, made sure you were all right..."

Lyla lifts her head and looks up at me, her eyes brighter now, more alert. "You didn't do anything wrong. And I don't think that's true, that it isn't in your nature to look out for someone else." Her fingers brush along my beard, the light touch sending a little shiver through me. "I don't understand what's going on with your family, why you're doing any of this, but I know you *wouldn't* be if you weren't trying to protect someone else."

Her words carve at my chest the same way the painful implements that left my scars did.

This woman has only been here a few days, and she already sees too much, understands too many things I never wanted her to, and I don't know how to respond to her right now without completely unraveling.

"You think far too much of me, Lyla, and give me credit I don't deserve." The day I left flashes through my head—what a fucking coward I was. How easily I ran and never looked back. "I've hidden here for fifteen years, hidden from my past and my responsibilities and the people I should have protected." I look away from her, unable to stare into her innocent face while I say the words I know are true. "I'm a coward."

She raises her right hand out of the water and presses it against my cheek, my beard likely rough against her palm. "You're far from a coward, Silas. You saved my life."

———

LYLA

In more than one way.

He didn't just find me when I was lost in the menacing, dark forest; he rescued me from the nightmare I was living before we signed that contract—one which I never could have escaped without him.

Hearing him discount himself, downplay what he's done and what it meant to me hurts as much as the cold did out there.

I almost come clean and tell him everything—the reason I was willing to marry a complete stranger and live up here like this, why that money is so important to me, but the real fear in his eyes stops me.

The usual icy-blue filled with animosity has melted away, replaced by alarm I've never seen from Silas before.

What's he so afraid of?

That I might have died, and whatever reason he has for this sham would become more trouble for him...

That I might file for an annulment after my near-death experience and get the hell off this mountain permanently, leaving him hanging in whatever quagmire he has with the Boltons...

That I might actually break through the seemingly impenetrable wall he hides behind...

All seem like real possibilities.

And after staring into icy eyes for so long, the warm pools now looking back at me seem deep enough to drown in if I let myself.

He brushes his thumb across my cheek, the move sweet and almost reverent. A heavy sadness settles over him, darkening his gaze and making his jaw harden. "I didn't save you, Lyla. I doomed you."

Doomed me?

I struggle against the fog still enveloping my brain from the cold, attempting to wrap my head around his words.

Because they don't make sense.

None.

This man gave me fifty thousand dollars without asking what it was for. He took me into his home, brought me into his extremely private world, opened himself up to scrutiny from a complete stranger. And he just spent what must have been *hours* searching through a damn pitch-black forest in the cold rain to find me when I got lost because I did something *stupid*.

But he says he *doomed* me.

If anything, it's the other way around.

I never imagined my personal drama had the potential to negatively affect whoever I matched with, but the moment I learned who Silas Bolton was, I knew the truth could hurt him.

His family isn't the type to invite scandal into their lives. And that's exactly what it would bring if it got out. Which is why I bite back what sits on the tip of my tongue, what I *want* to say to help him understand what he's done for me.

Silas squeezes his eyes closed, as if he can't bear to look at me, and when he reopens them, there's a resolve there that I haven't seen before during any of our conversations. "I pulled you into something you should never have been involved in, Lyla. It wasn't fair of me to do that without telling you what was in store for you. And now you're stuck with me, maybe forever."

Is that how he sees this?

Like he's stuck *with me?*

A moment of silence hangs between us, the tension building the longer neither of us says anything.

I guess I shouldn't be so surprised. He never wanted any of this, doesn't like me invading his space and his life. And now, I've lost his goat and almost got myself killed.

I'm a liability.

My attempt to do anything useful around here backfired worse than my first car used to. Everything went to shit so fast it has left my head spinning. Or maybe that's the after-effects of nearly dying and currently having my almost-nude body pressed against Silas' under the hot water.

Hard muscle under me and all around me.

Strong, secure arms, holding me tight, keeping me safe.

Exactly what a husband *should* do.

It would be impossible not to think about what he told me yesterday—that he has no intention of ever touching me, no intention of being a real husband or partner.

The very things I was so afraid of when I agreed to the mail-order bride idea and came up here have suddenly been replaced with the unexpected fear that I might have to live as a roommate with this moody, confusing, powerful, and frustrating mountain man the rest of my life without ever experiencing a man's touch again.

Without experiencing *this* again.

His warm, hard body pressed to mine.

Complete focus on me and ensuring I'm all right.

I lightly trail my fingertips over the tattoos on his neck and upper chest. The dark, swirling display follows the theme of most of his ink—vicious, violent images of pirates and sea battles. Of death and destruction. The same dark sadness that seems to permeate the man wearing them like armor. "You're not as big and scary as you think you are, Silas."

He flinches at my words and pulls his hand away from my face, shutting down again instantly, putting that wall firmly back before I can pick away at any chips I may have made it in. "Are you warming up?"

The violent shaking stopped a while ago, and pressed up against him in the still-warm water, I could almost forget the trauma I just endured if I weren't still randomly shivering every few minutes and breaking out in goosebumps remembering the bone-chilling cold.

"Yeah...I feel a little better..."

He stares at the open door where Whiskey sits watching us, rather than looking at me. "We should get you in bed."

Those words could have such a different connotation, but after all the warnings he's given me, I know not to take them that way. Silas has drawn a very firm line, and I don't have any intention of crossing it and making things more uncomfortable between us.

I nod my agreement. "Okay."

He returns his gaze to me. "Can you sit up by yourself?"

With my hand planted against his inked, firm chest, I try to push off to sit up in the tub, but a massive wave of dizziness engulfs my head immediately, making me waver.

His strong hand slides around me and holds me upright, and he watches me, waiting for me to catch my balance and ensure I'm okay. He slowly pulls his legs from around me and stands in the tub, hand still keeping me steady.

Water pours from his soaked jeans, and I follow it down to see his boots submerged under him. "Your boots are soaked."

He glances at them and offers a half-shrug that makes the scene on his chest move like the real ocean. "I have others." His lips press together in a firm line as he stares at me, his body tensing more the longer we lock gazes. "I'm going to have to take these off so I don't traipse water through the entire cabin."

It takes a second for me to understand what he's saying and why.

Silas Bolton is about to strip in front of me, and I'm not sure either of us can handle that right now.

I grab onto the water nozzle and place my other hand on the edge of the metal trough tub to keep myself upright, then squeeze my eyes closed, giving him the privacy he needs to get out of his wet clothes and hopefully also shed any lingering awkwardness tonight may have caused.

The water sloshes around me as he kicks off his boots. The air thickens around us with the sound of the button on his jeans popping and the zipper going down.

I hold my breath.

A big splash hits me, and my eyes snap open.

To Silas Bolton in all his glory.

The tattoos and scars cover him *everywhere.* Not just his chest and back and arms, but swirling over his rock-hard abs and down his thighs and...

I suck in a sharp breath and squeeze my eyes closed again.

Shit.

There's no way he didn't notice that.

The water sloshes as he climbs from the tub, followed quickly by a rustle of fabric. "You can open your eyes...*again.*"

Busted.

Reluctantly, I open them to find Silas standing on the bathmat with a towel wrapped around his waist, barely covering anything and precariously secured with a single tuck at his side. "Are you okay for a minute while I go get dry clothes?"

I nod because I can't seem to form words, staring at my husband and the myriad of scars that cover him under the ink. It would be easy to blame my inability to look away on my brain still slowly coming back online as my body fights to regain some normalcy, but that would be a lie.

Silas Bolton is hauntingly beautiful.

It would be impossible for *anyone* to look away.

He turns and stalks from the bathroom, and I sink back into the water as low as I can on top of his pants and boots still lying on the bottom. Whiskey trots over, resting his head on the side of the tub, examining me closely.

"Jesus, I really fucked things up tonight, didn't I, boy?"

His ears perk up, and he tilts his head and shuffles forward to lick my face.

At least someone isn't mad at me.

Though Silas has every right to be. Not only did I lose Billy, but I also almost got myself killed, ruined his clothes and boots, and made him grumpier in the process.

My only consolation is that it can't get any worse...

Silas returns quickly, dressed in a tight white T-shirt and dark-gray sweatpants, using the towel that had been wrapped around his waist to dry his long hair as he examines me in the water. His light-blue eyes drift from my face down over my chest, abdomen, and legs, making me *very* aware that I'm only in my bra and underwear.

He swallows slowly, his Adam's apple moving under the ink. "Let's get you out of there."

As great as the hot water felt, it's already starting to cool, and without Silas' body heat added to the mix, the chill has started to return, making me shiver again.

He approaches the tub slowly, almost like he's afraid of what will happen if he gets too close. I keep my eyes locked on him, trying to see through the wall he keeps building higher and higher around himself to keep me out.

Silas is so used to living that way that the thought of having to open up to me terrifies him worse than whatever drove him up the mountain in the first place.

I saw that definitively tonight.

Our chance to break through it—to *potentially* have a single second where we're completely open and raw with each other.

But he shut down so fast I barely had an opportunity to glimpse it.

His legs brush the side of the tub, and he nudges Whiskey with his thigh until the dog finally trots away to wait outside the bathroom door.

Silas stares at me for a moment too long—long enough

that I instinctually move my arms protectively over my body like he shouldn't be seeing it. His jaw hardens again, his teeth clenched as tight as his fists at his sides before he reaches down and slides his hands under my arms to help pull me back up into a sitting position.

It takes a moment for the spinning in my head to clear, and Silas seems to understand that, giving me a few seconds before he tugs gently, trying to get me to my feet.

My entire body trembles immediately when the much cooler air hits me outside the warm water. "Jesus, am I ever going to be warm again?"

"It'll pass."

His words come gruff and gritted out, like it physically pains him to say them and see me like this. But that would mean he *cared*, and he's already told me he doesn't. Not like that.

My teeth start chattering as he wraps a dry towel around me and lifts me easily from the tub, setting me onto my feet on the bathmat. I wobble immediately, but one strong arm wraps around my waist while the other rubs against my wet skin—hard.

I begin to protest that it hurts, but he gives me a stern glare that instantly silences me.

"It'll help get the blood flowing."

It feels more like a punishment—some sort of torture designed to make me fully break when I'm barely holding it together right now.

He squats and does the same with my legs, beginning down at my ankles and working his way up until his face is directly in front of my soaked white panties that can't hide anything.

Jesus.

Heat spreads through my cheeks, and I clench my

thighs together and grip the edge of the counter to keep myself from passing out from sheer embarrassment.

He quickly climbs to his feet, darting his gaze toward the door. "I'll get you dry clothes. Are they in your suitcase?"

I nod. "The pink one."

His lips twitch almost imperceptibly before he stalks back out into the cabin and returns a minute later with a bra, underwear, sweatpants, and a long-sleeved T-shirt. "These should keep you warm. Can you get undressed by yourself?"

"Seems you've already done most of the work."

He flinches.

Shit.

Nice mouth, Lyla.

Not the time for those jokes...

"Sorry, I didn't mean it like that." I wince, squeezing my eyes closed. The last thing I should be doing is trying to push the boundaries with Silas right now. "Thank you, really. I think I'm all right."

I release the edge of the counter and let the towel slip off me. Immediately, my legs start to shake so badly that I almost collapse. I reach back for the hold that kept me upright, but Silas' strong arm wraps around me, and he tugs me against him and holds me tight.

"I don't think you're fine, Lyla. I'm going to help you."

It isn't a question.

It's a statement of what he's going to do, whether I like it or not.

The man who said he had no intention of ever touching me is doing an awful lot of it tonight, but I'm too weak to argue or try to stop him, even if I wanted to.

I give him a little nod of understanding and approval,

and his fingers at my back shift up to the hook of my wet bra. He unhooks it and takes a half-step back, keeping his hand at my waist so I don't collapse.

He turns his head to the side to look away, and I let the bra slide from my arms. Then I reach to the counter for the dry one and tug it on as quickly as I can. "Okay."

His fingers move to the hem of my soaked underwear, and I lash out and wrap my hand around his wrist, stopping him before this gets more awkward.

"I'll do it."

I don't think I could handle his callused, rough, yet somehow gentle touch there right now—or ever.

He sucks in a sharp breath, turning his head away as I release his wrist. His hand slides from me, and I shimmy the old underwear off and the new, dry ones on.

My head spins again, the effort it took to do such simple things wiping me of any energy my body has left. I grip the counter behind me again, my legs wobbling under me.

And Silas is right there again, offering me his strength, wrapping his arms around my waist, and taking my weight. "I got you."

Darkness starts to creep into the edges of my vision, just like it did as the sun set outside and I realized I was lost and freezing in the damn woods. I was terrified then. Alone. Cold. Hopeless.

But this time, Silas' strong hold and warmth assures me everything will be all right.

Even if it isn't true.

Chapter Eight

LYLA

I wake to an unmovable wall of warmth behind me, strong arms wrapped around my waist, and a heat block of fluffy fur in front of me. Whiskey's cold nose brushes against my chin, and I turn my head away from it slightly, only to have rough whiskers scratching at my cheek.

Bright light streams in through the windows, indicating it's already late morning, if not early afternoon, and I blink against it, trying to regain my bearings when it still feels like everything is spinning out of control.

I shift slightly to peek at Silas. Eyes closed. Lips parted slightly. Rhythmic rise and fall of his chest against my back.

Relaxed.

Comfortable.

Not at all the Silas I know or expected to find.

Fuck. What happened last night?

Billy darted out of the gate...

I chased him to the edge of the woods, then into them.

Then it got very dark.

I got very lost.

And fuck, was it damn cold.

A shiver rolls through me at the memory, and Silas' arms tighten around my waist, drawing me against him more. I freeze and glance at his face again, but his eyes are still closed, breathing still regular.

I release a relieved breath and try to relax into the warmth of the bed.

More memories of last night return.

The bathtub...

Silas stripping in front of me.

Shit.

Me peeking.

Heat floods my cheeks and other places.

Thank God he's asleep...

The last thing I remember was being embarrassingly naked before the man currently snuggled up behind me and getting very light-headed again. I don't even know how I got into bed, but I can guess.

Just like he carried me out of those woods, climbing over fallen logs and through all sorts of bushes and other things that made me lose my way, Silas lifted me and brought me to this warm bed and crawled in beside me, ensuring I was surrounded by his body heat and Whiskey's.

He took care of me.

More than anyone else in my life ever has.

Even though he didn't have to.

Even though it clearly scared him.

That memory remains crystal clear—of him telling me he has *doomed me.*

It certainly doesn't feel that way, lying here in his arms, his warm breath fluttering across my cheek. In fact, I sink deeper into him, pushing myself closer, needing it and him more than I want to admit to myself.

"Are you still cold?" Silas' low, gravelly voice in my ear makes me flinch. "Lyla?"

Shit. Answer the man.

"No, no...I'm okay."

His eyes flutter open and meet mine only inches away. And up this close, it's so easy to see all the complexities of the man, the varying shades of blue that match the different moods he seems to have.

Icy and cold and hostile one moment.

Soft and warm and inviting another.

Like going from the arctic to the Caribbean in a split second.

And right now, they're so calm and peaceful. None of the tumultuous waves or brewing tempests threatening to erupt on the horizon.

It lulls me in, makes me roll closer to him.

Even though I shouldn't.

Even though it's dangerous.

My thighs press against his crotch—and his *entire* body stiffens. I trail my fingers over his chest, sending a shudder rolling through his massive frame.

"What happened last night after the bath, Silas?"

I regret asking it instantly because it sounds like an accusation instead of a genuine question designed to learn what he had done for me.

His arms slide out from around me, and he shifts back. I wince as he throws back the covers and climbs from the bed, then tosses them back on me.

"You think I would've"—he tightens his jaw, hands fisted at his sides—"when you were like *that*."

He stalks away from the bed, and I push myself up into

a seated position, my sleep-clouded brain trying to process how badly I just fucked up. Whiskey lifts his head to see where Silas is going.

His owner pauses at the edge of the kitchen, hands on his hips, facing away from me, his shoulders tense. "I told you I would never touch you like that."

"I know. I'm sorry. I just—"

He glances over his shoulder, that icy look back in his eyes. "You just what? Thought I would take advantage of you when you were almost dead?" His hand goes back through his hair, and he tugs on it. "Is that what you really think of me?"

"No. *God* no! I—"

Silas whirls to face me, his jaw set hard. Every muscle in his body tenses for the fight we're apparently going to have—all because I couldn't keep my damn mouth shut and simply enjoy a fucking moment with him. "You *what?*"

"That's not what I *meant.*"

His nostrils flare, a red-hot fury building in him, threatening to erupt right before my eyes. "Then what the hell did you mean?"

"I just..." I run my hands back through my disheveled hair and glance toward the bathroom, then motion to the bed where he slept beside me. "You found me. You took care of me. We...almost kissed in the tub..."

And I have no memory of you putting me to bed or holding me all night like you must have.

I want those memories.

I want to *know* what that was like.

He stiffens again and follows my gaze toward the closed bathroom door, then lets it drift to the bed. The man who spent the night caring for me seems to be reliving every moment—and despising it, given the curl of his lip. "It was a mistake." He grits out the words. "It won't happen again."

That same inexplicable pain that hit my chest the first time he announced he would never touch me or be a husband to me hits me again. Ten times harder this time because now I've seen glimpses of who Silas really is—under all the ink and rage and self-loathing.

Silas was broken by something. Shattered. And he carries the guilt of it like a badge of honor. He will never see how good he is, how much good he can do, while he's blinded by his own pain.

But I can't force him. Attempting to push things with him will only make him retreat further.

If that's even possible.

He sighs and turns away from me, disappearing into the kitchen.

I lean back against the carved wood headboard and listen to the stillness of the cabin. Something rattles and bangs in the kitchen, and I bury my fingers into Whiskey's fur. He shifts to drop his head onto my lap, looking up at me with raised brows like he's trying to figure it all out, too.

Wish I knew, boy.

Truly.

The more time that passes without a word from Silas, the more I shift restlessly in his bed. Like waiting for a ticking bomb to go off.

A high-pitched whistle makes me jump, and Whiskey lifts his head, watching the kitchen until Silas reappears with a mug in his hand.

He holds it out to me, the bright-blue parrot on his right hand staring at me. "Drink this."

I reach up and take it from him carefully, averting my

gaze from his. The bitter coffee smell makes me gag slightly, but I need to drink it. "Thank you."

"You should stay inside today. Your body needs to recover." He rubs his hand down his bearded jaw, staring out the window toward the side of the property with the barn and animals. "Maybe it was a stupid idea for me to allow you to help..."

"No!" I shift to try to get up, but the coffee almost spills, and I resettle before I make an even bigger ass of myself. "I want to help. Jesus, Silas..." I fight back the tears stinging my eyes—the overwhelming frustration finally starting to boil over. "This place is my home, too, now. Right?"

He gives a reluctant nod.

I swing out my free hand. "What am I supposed to do in here? The only skills I have are that I can stay on my feet for a long time and I don't give up easily."

His gaze softens for a moment. "You're tenacious. I'll give you that."

The genuine compliment gives me the slightest hint of hope that he'll get over his anger at me. "I'm not going to let one stupid night and bad decision stop me from helping you around here. I just need to be more careful."

"You do." He grits his jaw, and he shakes his head, releasing a heavy sigh. "You fucking terrified me last night."

I freeze with the mug halfway to my mouth and glance up at him, but he's looking away out the window at something else or nothing at all.

What was he so afraid of?

I shouldn't ask.

I *know* I shouldn't.

But I can't stop myself from digging for the truth, even when it might hurt.

"Were you afraid you'd lose your bargaining chip with

whatever's going on in your family?"

His head whirls around back to face me, and his jaw tenses again under his heavy beard.

I've clearly hit a nerve with my question, and it might be my only chance of really getting the truth about what's happening with him.

"Are you ever going to tell me what's going on? Why you needed this marriage in the first place?"

His hands fist at his sides. "You should stay out of things that don't have anything to do with you, Lyla."

The reproach should be enough to stop me, but the push and pull, back and forth, hot and cold with him over the last few days, has forced me to the edge. And almost dying and waking in his arms apparently pushed me over it.

I can't keep going on like this, not understanding why he's like this or why he's doing something that clearly hurts him so much.

"But it *does*, doesn't it, Silas? Ronald said I'm going to have to go with you to some board meeting. What's this all about?"

"Don't worry about it until you need to."

I sit up straighter, trying to show him how annoyed I am with him shutting down. "And when's that going to be?"

"When I tell you."

He stalks to the dresser, tugs open a drawer, grabs something, and disappears into the bathroom, slamming the door behind him. The sound reverberates through the cabin, making me flinch and almost spill the coffee I have zero desire to drink.

Instead, I wrap my hands tighter around the warm mug and wait for the inevitable hurricane that will come out when he's done changing.

The bathroom opens again, and Silas storms out in a

pair of jeans and a button-down plaid shirt. "Come on, Whiskey."

The dog reluctantly climbs from my lap and jumps off the bed.

Silas stomps toward the door, tugs on a pair of boots sitting next to it, and yanks it open. He steps out onto the porch, then pauses and turns back toward me. "There are things I'm never going to discuss with you. Things you shouldn't ask about. I'm not delving into your personal life, and I expect you to give me the same courtesy. I'll tell you what you need to know when you need to know it."

The door slams like a final exclamation point on his words.

Shit.

Every time we take a step forward, it's three steps back. This time feels more like a mile.

Because something happened last night, something *beyond* me getting lost and Silas rescuing me. Through the frigid, inky blackness of almost dying, there was a spark. The tiniest hint of something that could become a flame. It flashed hot for a moment, only to be snuffed out by the man who doesn't want to feel the warmth because he's so terrified of getting burned.

And he is going to do anything and everything in his power to douse it every chance he gets.

———

SILAS

Wind blows my hair back, whipping around me, taunting me with its warmth today after contributing to almost killing Lyla last night. Combined with the high sun, the beauty of the day is only clouded by the dark mood over-whelming me that hasn't dissipated since I climbed onto Lasher.

Riding usually helps.

The freedom pushing him to his limits and putting what haunts me behind brings should be hitting me now.

Should be but isn't.

I urge him into a gallop, and the horse does as he's asked, just like he always will, charging ahead while Whiskey races beside us, trying to keep up with our pace.

We move along the river that meanders down the mountain, taking the familiar path quickly, as if we're being chased by some unseen pursuer instead of looking for signs of Billy.

This is exactly what I needed: to put as much distance between me and that woman as humanly possible.

If I didn't, things would have only gone to shit worse than they already have. Somehow, I went from falling asleep in bed with Lyla safe in my arms to arguing with her and making her fucking cry in the span of only hours.

Another epic failure on my part.

I hurt Lyla.

I tried to save her, and I ended up *hurting* her.

A better man never would have let that happen. A better man never would have let *any* of this happen. He would have *ensured* Uncle Marty couldn't keep hurting people. He would have come forward years ago and exposed him so others wouldn't suffer.

Instead, I ran, and I hid; now, it's all coming back to bite me.

And her.

It's only a matter of time before he finds out about Lyla, and once he does, it will put a target on *her* back. And no amount of running on this horse is going to escape that reality.

I warned her that I doomed her, but she has no idea how badly. She couldn't possibly understand when I can't tell her, when I can't seem to form the words to explain what was done to me and what I'm going to have to do soon.

Keeping her in the dark is the only way to protect her right now.

The painful truth will come soon enough.

But riding along the river, I can pretend I've left all that behind and lose myself in looking for Billy and casting the line.

Theoretically.

I catch sight of a familiar flash of white, and I pull on the reins and slow Lasher to a trot.

Billy...

The little prick is exactly where I thought he'd be—grazing along the shoreline where his favorite dogwoods grow, near my fishing spot.

He lifts his head at my approach, bleating softly before returning to munching away like he didn't cause that catastrophe last night with his shithead behavior.

I slide from the saddle and tie Lasher loosely to our usual tree. Whiskey runs ahead toward Billy, spooking the goat and sending him racing a few yards farther down the bank.

"Whiskey, stop."

He slows and turns back toward me, waiting for me to catch up, and I rub his head. "Stay here."

I approach Billy slowly, and he's too busy searching for another snack to notice me get close enough to slip a rope on him. He lets me lead him back to Lasher, and I secure him to another limb and release a relieved breath.

Lyla will feel better knowing he's okay, but finding him doesn't undo anything that happened last night. I can't take back those moments with Lyla, the ones that came out of nowhere and have made everything far too complicated now.

She's too sweet. Too vulnerable. Too caring. Too open in a way that only makes me want to shut down more.

All I can do is try to forget last night. What it felt like to have her in my arms. To have her body pressed to mine. To see the trust and longing in her eyes.

Even if it may be a fruitless effort.

I grab my fishing rod and bait from the saddlebag and make my way toward my favorite spot on the river. Whiskey nips at my heels, excited that he might get a piece of fresh fish if I do well today.

"I'll see what I can do, boy."

It's far too late in the day to expect much. The pre-dawn magic hour has long passed, but I wasn't about to leave Lyla in that bed—for a lot of reasons. Most that scare the ever-loving shit out of me and sent me running out here.

That woman is *dangerous*.

She pushes me in directions I didn't know existed and twists me in ways I couldn't have imagined in my wildest dreams. Lyla is everything I shouldn't have, yet the longer she's here, the more I don't want her to leave. And that's a big fucking problem when this is all supposed to be fake.

When it *has* to stay that way.

For both our sakes.

I set my gear on the massive flat rock that hangs out over the river and lower myself onto it, casting my first line to the center of the rapids, where the biggest pool collects the largest fish.

Birds swoop overhead, swirling in the warm breeze

before darting into a nearby tree. The smells of spring permeate the air—fresh flowers, trees in bud, the long, marshy grasses along the shoreline sprouting up all around us.

It's moments like this that made me fall in love with this place. The pure, simple, unadulterated beauty of it all. Nothing compares. Except maybe the brunette back in my cabin...

"What are we going to do about Lyla, Whiskey?"

He lies down next to me, ears perked. Part of me wishes he understood what I was saying, so he could give me some fucking advice about what to do. Because it feels like I'm a stick caught in the middle of this river, getting carried in the rushing water, smashed against jagged rocks, pushed miles and miles a day, tumbling and spinning with no end in sight.

Out of control.

She was right about what happened in that tub last night—things got wildly out of control. We got far too close to doing something that would be wrong. Something we would have regretted in the harsh light of morning.

She's your wife...

That voice at the back of my head keeps reminding me of that fact, and it won't shut the fuck up. It taunts me, trying to stick me in an even worse place than I've already found myself. Somewhere there's a possibility of something more than the life I've been living up here alone.

I need to lock it away, at least for today, so I can try to find some peace and quiet out here before I have to return and face *her* at the cabin. Maybe the fresh air and solitude I've always relished will help me get some clarity.

Wishful thinking.

Something tugs at my line, and I reel it in, the small-mouth bass wiggling at the end as I drag it up on top of the rock. I pull out my knife and quickly end its suffering, then immediately give it to Whiskey.

"You can have this, boy. I've lost my appetite."

The only thing my body craves now is the woman I can never have. The one who wears Grandmother's ring and is sitting back in my home, thinking I'm a huge jackass for the way I've been acting and treating her.

I recast my line and try to focus on the surrounding sounds, of the bubbling water, the birds chirping and flying overhead, the rustling of leaves. A twig snaps off to my left, and Whiskey's head jerks up before he launches himself off the rock in that direction.

"Hey, Silas."

I turn toward the man approaching along the riverbank.

Fuck. Just what I don't need today.

I force a tight smile and give Travis a quick wave. "Hey, Trav."

The older man ambles toward me with his fishing gear, Whiskey watching him intently and following alongside him on his approach—though he knows him well enough not to bark and charge at him like he would so many other people.

My closest neighbor up here on the mountain stops next to the giant rock and stares at my line. "Catch anything today?"

I nod slowly. "Bass. Whiskey's breakfast."

He chuckles, his lined face wrinkling more, and sets his gear on the rock as he climbs up and settles next to me. "Lucky dog. You know I'm usually out here earlier, but the missus had a honey-do list a mile long for me today."

I snort. "Is that what I'm in for?"

Fuck, I hope not.

The days of letting someone else control my life ended long ago, and I don't plan on going back to that way of living.

"So..." He casts his line, peering at me from the corner of his eye. "I heard a rumor in town."

I stiffen and glance over at him. "Yeah, what's that?"

He stares off into the water, watching the lines bob. "That you got hitched to some pretty young lady at the courthouse the other day."

Fucking hell.

Nothing ever stays a secret in a small town. We only had two other people who saw anything, aside from Ronald. But two is enough to start the rumor mill.

Hell, even one is.

"That is an interesting rumor."

He looks over at me. "So, it isn't true?"

There isn't any point denying it. The entirety of Millsburg probably knows by now, anyway.

I release a heavy sigh. "It is."

His white brows rise. "You're married?"

Bobbing my head slowly, I suck in a sharp breath. "Uh-huh."

He adjusts his line and chuckles lightly. "I've never really seen you as the marrying type."

I snort. "Me, either."

"Who's the little lady? I haven't seen you around with anyone..."

That's because no one sees me around at all. Other than heading into town once or perhaps twice a month for supplies and to make deliveries, I avoid human contact at all costs.

"No one you would know. She's not from around here."

He clicks his tongue. "I see. She's doing well living up at your place?"

Considering how bougie Travis' homestead is compared to mine, his question is valid. He even paid to be on the grid with electricity and water rather than relying on solar and a well, like I do. Because he's so much farther down the mountain, he could afford to do that. I guess I technically can, too, if I touched my inheritance, but God knows I don't want to.

Just taking out the $50,000 to make the payment to Lyla felt like admitting defeat and making a deal with the devil.

"What's her name?"

Fuck. Can't the guy take a hint that I don't want to be talking about this?

"Lyla."

"Pretty name."

"She's a beautiful woman, too."

The observation slips from my tongue easily despite not wanting to discuss her or the current situation with him. But it's hauntingly true.

Lyla is beautiful—inside and out.

She's the type of woman who deserves to be given the world, not a shitty cabin in the fucking woods.

Travis returns his focus to the river, a long silence drawing out between us like it usually does when we run into each other. Over the years, he's learned not to press me when it comes to conversation, and I usually greatly appreciate the wide berth he gives me.

But something feels off today.

Like there is something unspoken between us that should be said.

A reason he showed up in the *same* place at the *same*

odd time to come fishing.

Maybe to offer the kind of advice only a man who has been married as long as he has can provide.

"Can I ask you a question, Travis?"

"Of course." He looks over. "What do you need, son?"

Son?

Even after fifteen years of hearing him use it, the word stiffens my spine. It was always used as a weapon before—a reminder of who and what I was to the Boltons.

Someone without power.

Without a voice.

But the warmth in the way Travis always says it has prevented me from asking him to stop using that term over the years.

"You've been married what? Thirty, forty years?"

He issues a low, deep chuckle. "Almost fifty. We met when we were eighteen, married within two weeks."

I whip my head toward him. "You got married two weeks after you met her?"

A slow grin spreads across his face, thinking about his wife, the genuine love he has for her radiating from him. "I knew she was the one from the moment I laid eyes on her. The only reason we waited two weeks was because she was seventeen, and we had to wait for her birthday before we could get legally married."

"Jesus..." *Two weeks...* "And it's lasted this long?"

Travis gives me a knowing smile. "I doubt there's much that could tear us apart now, short of me keeling over after the hike up here to fish."

I give him a once-over since it's been a few weeks since we last saw each other. "You seem to be in pretty good shape."

He pats his growing belly. "The wife says I need to lose

a few pounds, but man, she is a great cook. It makes it hard."

"Yeah, Lyla's a pretty decent cook, too."

The longer she stays, the more I am going to get to enjoy the benefits of her skills in the kitchen.

"Then you're a very lucky man. Beauty, a good cook, and now, you have someone to help you on the homestead and a warm bed to crawl into every night."

That's the last thing I want to think about: crawling into bed with Lyla.

Last night was hard enough, and waking up with my cock very interested in the woman tucked into my arms was a new form of torture.

I can't do that again.

I can't do this with her.

I'm going to have to draw a line in the sand.

One I will never cross.

Still, the question lingers in the back of my head until I finally have to ask it. "You said you knew the moment you saw her, but...how?"

Travis releases a long sigh. "That's harder to explain, son. I just...felt it. One look at her and I knew I would never want another woman again until the day I die."

He makes it sound so simple.

He wanted her.

He made it happen.

They've shared an incredible life for fifty years...

But that's the difference between Travis and me—he saw her and held on tight; I saw Lyla and wanted to disappear.

This will never be a happily ever after, and I need to make sure Lyla understands that, that we maintain a business-only relationship until I can free her from the contract and send her back to her normal life.

Chapter Nine

LYLA

The moment Silas pulls the truck over to the curb in front of the general store and throws it into park, I toss open my door and leap out.

He leans over Whiskey to see me. "Where the hell are you going?"

I stop before I slam the door in his face and scan up and down Main Street in Millsburg, searching for any means of escape. After four days with the man barely saying a fucking word to me, I just need to get away from him, from the tension, from the anger and hate-filled looks, even if it's only for the hour or so he says we'll be in town to make his delivery and pick up a few things we need for the cabin.

Not only will it give me a break from Silas, but I can make the calls that might quell some of the anxiety that being stuck up the mountain without any means of communication with the outside world has built up inside me.

I point at a sign with a loaf of bread hanging above a

small shop a few feet to my left. "That looks like a bakery. I'm going in there."

They likely have sugary desserts and other things I haven't had a taste of since I got here...and hopefully, they have coffee, too. Real coffee. Not that sludge Silas makes at the cabin that turns my stomach and makes me fantasize about a Starbucks drive-thru on the mountain.

Silas scowls and glances at the clock on the dash. "Meet back here at the truck in an hour."

Not nearly enough time.

But I am not about to start another argument with him right now.

Things have been uncomfortable enough since that night. His eyes always on me, following me, despite him not uttering a word to me and pretending I don't exist.

The man has made the silent treatment an Olympic-level achievement.

"Fine."

I slam the door, and Whiskey stares at me through the window with sad eyes, begging me to bring him along. Pointing at him, I shake my head. "Don't give me that look. You know you can't come with me."

Silas hates me enough without me stealing his best friend, who seems to be so much more than a dog to him.

God knows the last thing I need is that man more wound up and grumpier.

I stalk away, down the perfectly manicured sidewalk, smiling at the strangers who stare at me with wide eyes— who hopefully didn't witness my little exchange with Silas.

In small towns like this, it's impossible to keep a secret. No doubt our wedding has already become a source of gossip. We don't need to give them more to talk about—like how our marriage is already on the rocks.

It would only draw more attention to us, which neither of us needs.

I don't know how the hell Silas managed to prevent everyone from finding out who he is, but something tells me that won't last long, not with a marriage certificate on file with his full name on it.

And mine.

My stomach churns, imagining what might happen if anyone does a deep dive. It could make things worse with Silas, and I'm not sure I'd survive that.

In the meantime, all I can do is manage one day at a time until the mysterious board meeting. That will be a lot easier with some of the supplies I put on the list for Silas... and some *real* coffee.

I make it to the bakery, and the wide windows in the front display all sorts of cookies and cakes, along with fresh baguettes and bread. My stomach rumbles, and my mouth waters.

This is exactly what I needed.

It's been bare-bones cooking up at the cabin since I got here, making use of what I can find in his fridge. But Silas lives like a bachelor. Aside from meat that he apparently either goes out and kills himself or buys in town and the vegetables he grows in the small greenhouse, the man doesn't have much in the way of making anything extravagant or special, like the massive cupcake with the pink frosting that's calling my name.

I tug open the door, and a bell above it jingles.

A blonde with bright-green eyes looks up at me from a book on her lap, perched on a stool behind the small register. "Oh, hi. Welcome in!"

Her unexpected perkiness takes me aback for a moment. "Um, hi, and thank you."

I've spent so much time with nothing but an icy, stoic "roommate" that the genuine warmth in the reception seems like coming home. I make my way toward her with what I hope is a genuine smile because I've forgotten what they feel like these days.

"I could really use one of those cupcakes with the pink frosting in your window."

She grins. "No problem. Do you want a cup of coffee or hot cocoa to go with that?"

"Coffee would be great."

Hopefully, it's better than the bitter junk Silas has.

She slides off a stool behind the counter and disappears into the back through a swinging door. A few minutes later, she returns with a steaming mug and a cupcake on a plate. "Here you go."

"How much is it?"

I reach into my purse for my wallet, but she shakes her head, grinning almost conspiratorially.

"I'll tell you what. It's on the house...as long as you tell me everything about Silas."

It takes me a moment to process her words. "What?"

She laughs and motions toward the street with the plate. "You're the talk of the town. Are you really his *wife*?"

The word is still so foreign that it sounds wrong to my ears.

I chew on the inside of my cheek and consider my options. Since this is a permanent situation, and I'll likely be coming into town with him again and again, there's no use in lying. But I have to be careful about what I say.

"Yes."

It's public information. I'm not revealing anything protected by the NDA confirming we got married.

She opens her eyes wider, her pink-glossed mouth falling open. "Woooooooooooow."

Her reaction makes me bristle. "Why *wow*?"

Does she know something about Silas I don't?

Her tinkle of laughter fills the small bakery, easing a bit of the discomfort, and she motions toward one of the small bistro tables. "Let's sit."

Oh, Lord.

I probably shouldn't be sitting down with this woman who seems to want all the gossip, but I could really use a friend right now—even somebody who's only talking to me because they're trying to get information I shouldn't be revealing.

"Look, I was born and raised in this town." She takes a seat across from me, resting her elbows on the table and her chin in her hands. "And when Silas showed up about fifteen years ago, I was ten, *almost* eleven." She corrects that point like it is important. "And every girl in town has had a crush on him since that day."

I sputter on my hot coffee—which is actually delicious and drinkable. "Excuse me?"

She grins. "He didn't always look like that—like he's trying to scare people off."

As his *wife*, I should probably be insulted on his behalf at her description, but it's one hundred percent true. Silas pushes everyone away and does anything he can to remain as lonely and reclusive as possible.

She reclines in the chair and sighs, getting a wistful look in her eyes. "I love the whole tattooed, bearded, long-haired, I'm-going-to-chop-you-up-with-my-axe look he has going on, but when he arrived, he was as clean-cut as they come."

"Really?"

It shouldn't surprise me, given his family background. I

doubt the Boltons are a family who appreciates tattoos and the scruffy-outdoorsman appearance at their elegant dining room tables.

But imagining Silas any other way proves difficult.

She nods. "His blond hair was cut perfectly, face shaven. He was just a baby back then, couldn't have been more than eighteen or nineteen."

I've already gotten more information from her in two minutes than I have from my own husband in the week I've been with him. I peel the wrapper off the bottom of the cupcake and take a massive bite, chewing as I consider the information she's provided. "So, he's been here for fifteen years, huh?"

Her blond head bobs. "Yep. And as far as I know, you're the only woman he's even ever talked to."

I swallow my bite and laugh. "That can't be true."

"No, no." She nods. "It is. He showed up on the bus one day, looking lost, stayed in the apartment above the general store for a few weeks, then bought Jensen's brother's property and disappeared onto the mountain. I think he worked with Travis and Jensen a bit on some things, but other than that, he doesn't interact with anyone. He only comes down here to make his wood deliveries to the store and grab supplies. But I'm telling you, he avoids conversation with anyone, *especially* women. Like he's afraid of *them*. Which is funny since most people won't make eye contact with Silas because they're so afraid of *him*."

"Afraid of him?"

I think back to my first impression of the man when he stepped out of that bathroom and announced he was my fiancé.

Yeah, I can see that.

He's big and mean-looking—intentionally so—but I've learned in the last week that there's far more to Silas than what meets the eye. The mountain might offer him refuge from the rest of the world, but it can't give Silas anywhere to hide from his own demons that seem to eat him alive from the inside out.

Most days, it seems he lets them win.

Yet, underneath all the ink and attitude lies a man with a good heart. I caught a glimpse of it the other night. He showed me what he tries so damn hard to conceal. Someone who cares too much, so much that he thought secluding himself and pushing everyone away would be the only escape from the pain and guilt he lives with.

I may not understand what drove him up this mountain or what happened with the Boltons, but I am getting to know Silas. Enough that I can say one thing with confidence. "He wouldn't hurt a fly."

She leans in, elbows on the table, face nestled in her palms again. "Really? So, he's a total sweetheart teddy bear under that gruff exterior?"

I laugh and shake my head. "I wouldn't say he's a sweetheart or a teddy bear. But..."

"But what?"

"But I think he's a good person, underneath it all."

One of her blond brows rises. "You *think*? You *married* the guy. Don't you *know*?"

Oh, shit.

I've said too much.

I shove the cupcake into my mouth to occupy myself and try to cover my mistake while she watches me suspiciously. As soon as I swallow, I take a drink of the coffee, hoping to buy myself more time.

My new friend watches me suspiciously, green eyes

narrowed. "How come no one ever saw you around here before the wedding?"

I offer a nonchalant shrug that I hope she buys and then swallow another sip of coffee. "We're both private people."

She nods as she drums her fingers on the tabletop. "Uh-huh."

"Look..."

Crap, I don't know her name...

She perks up and smiles. "Carrie Ann."

"Look, Carrie Ann. I really appreciate the delicious cupcake and cup of coffee. You don't know where I can purchase any of these coffee beans, do you?"

She leaps from the table and rushes into the back, returning with a bag of grounds. "Here."

"You're giving it to me?"

Her blond head bobs enthusiastically. "You can't get it at the store here. I have it shipped in because the coffee they sell here tastes like ass."

I bark out a laugh. "Yeah, it does."

"If you like it and you want to get it on the regular, I can start ordering a few extra bags. Just let me know how much you need a month."

"Really?"

She smiles, almost giddy, bouncing on her feet. "Girl, this has been the biggest excitement to hit Millsburg in fifteen years—since that man first showed up. I've learned so much from you."

Shit.

Exactly what I hadn't intended.

I take the final bite of the cupcake and hold up my mug. "Can I get the rest of the coffee to go?"

Carrie Ann climbs to her feet. "Of course."

As she disappears into the back to grab a to-go cup, I

release a relieved sigh. If she isn't here, I can't inadvertently tell her things I should be keeping to myself.

I may have accidentally revealed too much about Silas, but Carrie Ann has given me a few things to think about, too. Whatever happened to him to make him leave his family and come up here at only eighteen, it must have been something horrible. Coupled with the memory of the scars covering his body, that knowledge makes the delicious cupcake in my stomach roil violently.

Carrie Ann returns and pours my coffee into a travel cup, clamping on the lid and handing it to me. "Here you go."

I rise from the table and take it from her. "Thanks so much. I suppose I'll see you next time I'm in town."

"Stop by anytime." She offers a wide smile. "I own the place and always love to chat."

In another life, my life before coming up here, that would have been something I would have avoided. But living like this has made my soul desperate for a friendly face, someone who doesn't fight me at every turn or seem to hate having me around.

Carrie Ann may have ulterior motives for offering me friendship, but beggars can't be choosers.

I smile at her as I make my way to the door. "Thanks again. I'll see you soon!"

Relatively speaking.

I'm still in the dark about what this board meeting is about or what—if anything—it might do to our schedule in terms of returning to Millsburg.

But suddenly, the thought of being away from here for too long feels strange to me.

It isn't home—far from it.

Yet that little cabin on the mountain has grown on me.

Even Billy, who caused so much trouble and continues to try to escape every time I feed the animals, has started to weasel his way into my heart.

I hustle out of the bakery before Carrie Ann can ask me any other questions and suck in a deep breath of the fresh mountain air outside.

Almost immediately, the hairs on the back of my neck rise. I scan the street and find Silas kitty-corner across the street, watching me with his arms crossed over his muscled chest, Whiskey at his side.

He's getting antsy being here. I can see the unease in his eyes. The way he's standing, like he's preparing himself, always on the defensive. He wants to get back to the cabin as soon as possible.

But I'm not ready to leave yet.

I turn and walk in the opposite direction, not caring what's at the other end of Main Street. It doesn't matter. All I need is privacy, somewhere I can make a call without the threat of Silas overhearing me or interrupting.

A few shops down from the bakery, I find a bench in front of a bookstore and take a seat.

I pull out my phone, which still only has one bar of service down here, and call Attorney Fields with my heart in my throat.

Each ring through the line ramps up my nerves until I'm practically vibrating by the time someone answers. "Attorney Matthew Fields' office."

"Hi. Is he in? This is Lyla Sinclair calling."

Or is it Lyla Bolton?

The idea of changing my last name never crossed my mind, but if people are supposed to believe this is real, that's something I'm probably going to have to do—sooner rather than later.

"Oh, yes, he is. Just a moment."

His assistant puts me on hold, and I take a sip of my coffee and watch people buzz along Main Street. I can see the appeal of Millsburg, why Silas might have chosen this place to settle. The chill, laid-back atmosphere draws you in, and with the forest surrounding it, it's also the perfect place to disappear.

But it seems it wasn't enough to keep Silas' past from catching up to him.

I just hope mine doesn't do the same.

The line jostles, and someone clears their throat. "Lyla, my dear, it's Attorney Fields. I'm so glad you called."

Hearing his voice after so many days of no news releases the vise from around my chest slightly, but it still presses down with the weight of what I've put into his hands. "Hi, I wanted to check in while I had phone service to see if there's been any progress..."

Attorney Fields releases a long sigh. "Well, I've gotten the ball rolling. But as I told you during our initial meeting, things like this take time. It could be a few months before anything happens."

I squeeze my eyes closed.

A few months.

It seems like such a long time, when so many weeks have already passed. But in the grand scheme of things, compared to a lifetime and what could happen if he fails, it isn't.

I have to be patient and trust he knows what he's doing. "All right. Should I plan on calling you whenever I have phone service?"

"Sure. I'll let my assistant know she can update you if I'm not available, so if we miss each other, you can still find out what has been happening."

"I'd appreciate that."

Just like the first time I met him, the confidence he truly cares and is going to do his best settles over me. None of the other attorneys I discussed the situation with gave me any hope. They all said it was an impossible ask. But Matt Fields said he would *fight*, and that's what I need right now.

A fighter.

It was worth it, Lyla.

All this.

The heartache. The contract. The wedding. A potential lifetime with Silas giving me whiplash.

All worth it if Fields does his job well.

"And Lyla?"

I fight back the sting of tears. "Yeah, I'm still here."

"He's in good hands. I want to reassure you of that. I'll do everything I can."

And I believe him.

I don't know why. Attorneys are notorious for telling people what they want to hear. But when he says it, I believe this may all work out.

Somehow.

I end the call and swallow the emotion threatening to choke me. The last thing I need to do sitting on a bench on Main Street in Millsburg is break down into hysterics.

It would only add to the gossip already swirling around town about me and Silas.

I have to keep my cool here and back up the mountain with him.

Anything that happened between us the other night has to be forgotten, as if it were a bad dream instead of the harsh reality of my new life.

———

SILAS

Lyla steps out of Jensen's with two plastic bags hanging from her hand and approaches me at the truck, her eyes slightly red as if she's been crying.

After watching her sit on the bench and make phone calls for half an hour, then walk this way and duck into Jensen's without a word of acknowledgment or glance my way, my entire body is so tense, it feels like I might snap in half. But now that I can see she's upset, my chest tightens with concern instead of the annoyance I've been harboring all morning.

She finally reaches me, stopping a few feet away, and Whiskey walks over to her, rubbing his head against her thigh, waiting for her to scratch him.

Traitor.

The longer she's around, the more attached to her he seems to get—which means I'm losing my best friend *and* my sanity to this woman. She shifts her bags into one hand and scratches the top of his head, murmuring something to him without looking at me.

"You ready to go?"

Her head snaps up, and she narrows her gaze on me. "Yes...are *you*?"

I push off the truck, crossing my arms over my chest. "I've been ready for half an hour."

She offers me a saccharin-sweet smile that doesn't reach her eyes, which I probably deserve after my snide remark. "Well, I'm glad I gave you some time alone then, to think."

To think?

Lyla brushes past me, her shoulder bumping into mine deliberately, sending a little zing of electricity through me, along with renewed annoyance. She opens the passenger side and climbs in without another glance my way.

I bound around to the other side and yank open my door. Whiskey jumps in first, and I slide into my seat, slam my door, start up the truck, and suck in a sharp breath to keep my blood from boiling. "What the fuck is that supposed to mean? Time to think?"

She sets down her bags at her feet without looking at me and offers a shrug. "About how you've been behaving."

I gape at her. "About how *I've* been behaving?"

Her green eyes finally cut my way, filled with a seriousness and resolve that wasn't there when we drove down the mountain. "Yes."

"What about *you?*"

I throw the truck into drive and pull away from the curb a little too fast, the tires squealing slightly. It draws the attention of several people on the street who cast dirty looks our way. But it isn't anything I'm not used to around here.

Now, it's Lyla's turn to gape at me. "And what exactly have *I* been doing to you other than cooking for you and cleaning the cabin and helping with your chores and the animals? Tell me what has been so awful."

She has a fair point there, but none of that is what I am talking about.

For days, she's given me the cold shoulder, barely acknowledged I'm alive and acted like *I* somehow did something horrible to her when she was the one who damn-near died and almost killed me in the process. And the first chance she got, she started making calls.

Calls that were serious enough that she came back puffy-eyed and angry.

"Who were you on you on the phone with?"

A thousand possibilities ran through my mind during

that half hour—from a secret boyfriend to a gossip magazine to the worst option of them all...

Carly to tell her she wants *out*.

Lyla turns toward me in her seat and urges Whiskey to lie down so she can see me better. "*Excuse* me?"

"Who were you on the phone with?"

We reach the stop sign, and I turn to look at her, raising a brow as I wait for her potentially catastrophic answer.

She scowls and crosses her arms over her chest, looking out the window at the road leading up the mountain to my place. "None of your damn business."

I throw on my blinker and make the turn. "Oh, I think it is my business now that we're married."

Lyla scoffs, releasing a sardonic laugh. "Oh, we're going to play *that* game?" Her head bobs. "Okay, so why don't you tell me why you moved here at eighteen and have been hiding out on the mountain like a fucking recluse when you could be living in a mansion anywhere in the world? Hell, probably on your own private island? Tell me why you had to *pay* someone to marry you."

Fucking hell.

A low growl slips from deep in my chest, and she flinches but continues to glare at me, heat in her eyes. Any fear she may have had of me early on has quickly been replaced by a fiery defiance that heats something low in my belly.

I return my focus to the road. "I see you've been talking to someone local."

She shrugs again. "So, what if I was?"

"You signed an NDA."

An important one.

If Uncle Marty or anyone else in the company gets word of our marriage, it would ruin the plan Ronald and I devised. One word out of Lyla's mouth to the wrong person could end it all before I ever have a chance to *try* to save Bolton Steel.

"I didn't tell them anything that isn't public record."

I tighten my grip on the wheel. "What happened with my family is none of your business. Why I'm here is none of your business. It has *nothing* to do with you and me."

Her jaw drops. "It has *everything* to do with you and me."

"How do you figure?"

She turns to face me fully, resting against the door. "Because it sure as hell would explain why you act like this."

I bark out a laugh and shake my head. "Act like what?"

"Like I'm the fucking *enemy*."

The words come out so full of anguish that it actually feels like I'm being cut again. She might as well be driving a knife into my heart and twisting it. I flinch and inhale deeply, continuing to stare at the road ahead, unable to look at her, knowing she believes I think of her like that.

The gravel path winding up the side of the mountain seems to go on forever today. Each bump and dip jarring the tense silence between us that only worsens the higher we climb.

By the time we reach the halfway point, Lyla is vibrating with anger—her small body trembling where she still sits defiantly with her arms over her chest, jaw locked, eyes never leaving me as if she can bore a hole straight through me by glaring hard enough.

Whiskey leans against her, offering her comfort the way he usually does to me. Which I guess means *I'm* the asshole...

"Look, Lyla, I'm sorry if you feel that way, like I think you're the enemy. I don't. I just…"

Living alone for so long with no one else to talk to except Whiskey has made me even less of a conversationalist than I was before I moved onto the mountain. I can't ever seem to find the right words when I'm around her, and everything I *do* say seems to only upset her or piss her off.

She stares at me, waiting for me to finish my statement. "You just what?"

"I just can't trust anyone anymore, even you."

Trusting someone who should have had my best interests at heart is what made me this way. It is what twisted me so badly inside and out that I no longer know how to live a normal life.

Lyla sinks back in her seat a little bit, her eyes starting to shimmer with tears. "Then you shouldn't have married a total stranger and brought them into your life."

"I didn't have a fucking choice…" I mutter it under my breath and instantly regret it as she flinches.

Smooth, Silas.

"Stop the fucking truck."

I whip my head back toward the road to make sure I'm not about to hit something like a deer or a goddam bear. But it's clear. "What?"

She clenches her teeth. "Stop. The. Goddamn. Truck."

I slam on the brakes and turn to face her. "Why?"

Her hand darts to the door so quickly that I don't have time to register it. She snatches her bags from the floorboard and leaps out onto the narrow gravel road with the steep drop-off only a few feet to her right.

"What the fuck are you doing?"

She whirls back to face me, a tear trickling down her cheek. "I'm walking back to town."

"Are you insane? That'll take you hours."

Given how high we are up the mountain already, potentially longer. Thirty miles on this road on foot is nothing I'd ever want to attempt, especially in the afternoon when the sun is going to start going down.

Lyla shakes her head. "I don't care. I'm used to being on my feet for eight to ten-hour shifts. It'll be a nice, brisk walk."

She slams the door so hard that it makes the truck shake, and Whiskey leaps into the seat she vacated and presses his face against the glass to watch her walk away.

"Fucking hell."

I throw the truck into park, toss open my door, and climb out after her. She's only managed to make it a few yards, and I jog to catch up with her, then grab her bicep to jerk her back toward me.

"Lyla, stop."

She whirls to face me, the tears streaming down her face now after she's apparently abandoned her attempt to keep them at bay. "Why should I?"

"Because I asked you to."

"And what? You're my husband, so I'm supposed to do whatever you say?"

Hell.

I probably deserve that.

I try to take a deep breath to calm my thundering heart, but staring down into the tear-soaked eyes of this woman makes it impossible. Somehow, in the last several days, in all the time we've spent together, she's worked her way under my skin, scarred as it may be, and managed to reach a part of me I never wanted to admit was there.

The part that secretly needed companionship, that craved some sort of connection, the part that enjoyed waking up next to her in bed the other morning, the part that was fucking terrified I was going to lose her the night before.

"Please, Lyla. I don't know how to do this."

Her brows fly up. "How to do what? Be a fucking human being?"

I snort at her incredibly pointed remark. No one has ever been so bold with me. When I was still a child, living under Father's roof, no one dared challenge the prince, and now, people in Millsburg are too afraid of the tattooed man from the mountain to ever say anything like that to my face.

"It's been a long fucking time since I've had to interact with anyone, Lyla, since I've had to live with anyone, since I've had..."

Biting back the words that will only cause trouble, I wrack my brain for any other way to get out of this, for another way to make her stay.

But God knows, Lyla isn't one to let this go.

She's too worked up, finally unleashing all the pent-up emotion she's been holding in since she got here, and there isn't any way to return it now that it's floating out here between us.

"Since you've had what, Silas?"

I can't believe I'm going to admit this to her.

It would be easier to turn around, storm back to the truck, drive away, and never look back, letting Lyla walk back to town and find her way out of Millsburg and far away from me.

It would be better for her if I did.

Ronald's plan would fall apart. I would lose the company. Uncle Marty would win...

But it would save Lyla from all the anguish and pain I'm

going to cause her by not only keeping her here with me but by revealing this truth.

I stare down into her vibrant emerald gaze, wishing like hell that I could lie to her and knowing I won't. "Since I've had any sort of feelings for someone other than disdain or anger."

An agonizing few seconds tick by without her reacting, and I avert my gaze before Lyla releases a laugh that doesn't hold any actual humor.

"Oh, you definitely have those for me. I see it every time you look at me."

I shift my gaze back to meet hers. "That's what you think? That I hate you?"

The tears flow freely now, leaving little red lines across her pale cheeks. "You have barely talked to me in four days other than to bark orders at me when I'm doing something wrong at the homestead. Every time you look at me, I *see* it."

"You see what?"

"The anger in your eyes."

I release her arm and shove my hands back through my hair, tugging at it until the sharp bite of pain matches the one in my chest. "Hell, Lyla, I'm not angry at you. I'm angry at myself."

Her soft brow furrows. "Why?"

Too many fucking reasons to count.

I turn away from her to walk to the edge of the drop-off to stare out at the vast expanse of wilderness spread out below us on the mountainside, Millsburg barely visible in the distance, over thirty miles away, but still not far enough for my liking most days.

This was what I wanted. What I needed. A place where I could disappear and cut myself off from ever feeling pain again. But there is no hiding anymore. No amount of ink or hostility is going to keep the real world from infiltrating my life now.

It's too fucking late to pretend it hasn't already.

Finally, I face her again, knowing what looking at her soft face and tears is going to do to me. "I'm angry at myself for caring and wanting something I can't and shouldn't have."

Her lip trembles as she watches me slowly advance. "You don't mean that."

"I do." I stalk toward her slowly, giving her every chance to tell me to stop or to back away, but she doesn't move until my chest brushes against hers. I tilt her chin up to look at me, making her tears roll back along her temples. "The last week since you got here has been fucking torture for me because I fought so fucking hard for so fucking long not to want anything or anyone in my life, and you were forced into it against my will. I want to hate you. I want to look at you and see nothing but that world I tried to leave behind and resent you as much as I've resented all those people. It would make things so much easier. But..."

"But what?" She asks the question so softly I barely hear it, but it's an invitation to say the words she knows are coming as much as I do.

She wants to hear them.

She *needs* to.

As much as I need to say them.

"But I can't."

No matter how hard I try, I can *never* hate Lyla.

I can never resent her.

I can never blame her for becoming tangled in this same stupid scheme I have gotten myself involved with.

I can never intentionally hurt her, even if it makes it easier for me.

God, it would be so much easier to hate this woman.

But my heart thunders against my ribcage with something other than hate—a need, a desperation to taste her again the way I did the day of our wedding.

Before I can talk myself out of it, I lower my head and crash my lips against hers, wrapping my arm around her waist and dragging her up against me more firmly, so she can feel my cock hardening against her, the way my body craves as badly as my soul does.

I've already said far more than I should, and I sure as hell shouldn't be doing this. But I can't stand to see this woman cry, can't bear for her to think that she's done anything wrong or that she's the problem.

I'm the fucking problem.

I always have been.

I'm not strong enough.

I wasn't strong enough to end what was happening back then, and I'm not strong enough in this moment, either.

Chapter Ten

SILAS

My lips move against hers greedily after wanting to do it for so damn long, and initially, Lyla freezes, like she can't believe I've actually kissed her. But just like the other day at our sham wedding, after a moment of shock, she melts into me, her mouth as eager as my own.

The world disappears as I come back to life again, as I allow myself to forget all the reasons this is a horrible idea and simply feel the way she gives herself over to me. The way I give myself to her. How easy and natural it is.

How right.

Lyla drops her bags so she can loop her arms around my neck, and the sound of glass shattering finally breaks through the fog enveloping my brain and brings me back to my senses.

"Fuck."

I jerk back from her and focus on the bag on the gravel, where a red liquid oozes out across the uneven stones. The scent of tomatoes and basil hits me, replacing her light, citrusy one that had filled my lungs, and I drag my eyes up to meet Lyla's wide, unfocused ones.

She stares at me, soft, pink, swollen lips parted slightly with her heavy breaths, not bothering to peek down to see what broke.

My head still spins, and I waver slightly as I squat and glance in the bag, pulling out the few things that are salvageable and putting them into the other one. "I hope you weren't personally attached to this jar of pasta sauce."

Lyla doesn't respond, just continues to watch me with wide eyes filled with a tempest of conflicting emotions. I push to my feet and use my boot to kick the glass off the road so no one ends up with a flat tire if they come up here, especially me.

When I turn back, Lyla still hasn't moved. She stands dumbstruck in the middle of the mountain road, her hands hanging limply at her sides.

Jesus Christ...

What the hell have I done?

I scrub a hand over my beard. "Get back in the truck, Lyla."

She shakes her head like she's trying to clear it, her eyes snapping back into focus on me. "What?"

I approach her slowly, trying to rein in my body before I have to climb into that enclosed space with her again. "Get. Back. In. The. Truck."

It comes out low, almost like a snarl, and I can suddenly understand how she might think I've been angry with her. Anyone being talked to like that would assume the same. But like every single day since she arrived on my doorstep, it's my own failure that's pissing me the fuck off.

Why'd you kiss her again, you fucking idiot?

172

Why did you say any of that?

Clearly, living up here alone for so long has made me lose my mind.

No, this woman has.

I've become what everyone here has always thought me to be—the crazy, dangerous recluse. Lyla almost died on my watch, and I've pissed her off again enough to make her want to *walk* back to town. Which is almost as dangerous as trying to chase a damn goat into the woods after dark.

And then I went and *kissed* her to try to make her stay when all it really did was complicate things more.

She still stands immobile. Her gaze darts past me down the road toward town before moving back to the truck—like she's weighing her options.

I point a finger at her, tightening my grip on the bag in the other hand. "Don't even think about it."

Her mouth opens like she's about to argue with me, but I stalk over to her, drop my shoulder, and flip her up over it to carry her toward the truck.

"Hey, what the hell are you doing?"

She pounds at my back and tries to twist out of my hold, but I wrap my arm around her ass, holding her tightly to my shoulder.

"I'm making sure you don't do something stupid, like try to walk back to town."

"You can't do this." She flails her legs and tries to smack my back hard enough that it would hurt, but there's very little that could faze me at this point in my life. "Let me go—"

"You are not going back to town, Lyla. Stop pretending you are."

"Who the hell are you to make that decision for me?"

I get back to the truck, open the passenger door, and let

173

her slide down to her feet. With my arm still wrapped around her, holding her body tightly against my own, she stares up at me, her eyes heated with anger.

"Your *husband*."

She almost flinches at the word, like it's something that shouldn't be said, by me or anyone else. And maybe it shouldn't be.

It seems to have become a weapon, something we throw around to make a point as opposed to being something sacred as it is intended to those who give a shit about the sanctity of marriage.

We both understand what this is, and it doesn't matter that I've developed a soft spot for Lyla because it can never be anything else. *I* can't be anything else. I don't know how to be.

My eyes dip to her lips, and I release her before I do something stupid again and open her door, then nudge her back.

She mutters something unintelligible—but definitely not complimentary—under her breath and climbs in, snatching the remaining bag from my hand. "I really wanted that sauce for dinner tonight."

I scowl at her and slam her door, then make my way around the front of the truck and climb in. Whiskey continues to sit there, his eyes darting between the two of us, like he's trying to figure out what the fuck just happened. But of course, the traitor lays his head on her lap, and she immediately starts petting him.

"Your daddy is an arrogant, brutish, grumpy asshole, you know that?"

I snort as I shift the truck into drive and head back up the mountain.

She isn't wrong.

174

In fact, Lyla seems to have me pretty well figured out in only a matter of a week. Her hand threads through Whiskey's fur, rubbing along his neck the way he likes it. "He likes to throw around his weight and muscle, doesn't he?"

The road dips, making the entire truck bounce violently. I cast another quick glance at her and scowl. "That's not what I'm doing."

"Oh, really?" Her dark brows wing up. "You just threw me over your shoulder, hot shot. What do you call that?"

"I call that, ensuring you don't get stuck in the dark trying to make it down the mountain and freeze to death again."

That shuts her up.

She sits back in her seat and crosses her arms over her chest defiantly, staring out at the woods and the mountain landscape as we climb higher and higher, closer to my property.

By the time we reach the turn-in, the tension between us is so thick that Whiskey has his ears up, waiting for something to happen, for one of us to snap.

And we're both pretty fucking close.

I pull around the side of the cabin and throw the truck into park, then open my door. Before I can climb out, Whiskey jumps over me and races out into the open field— either to go to the bathroom or because he can't stand being stuck between Lyla and me.

Lucky dog, making a quick escape.

My turn to do the same.

I start to slide out of my seat, but Lyla grabs me, her nails digging into the ink on my forearm. She looks at me with an intensity that makes me freeze, any thoughts of

175

escaping washed away by the need to hear whatever it is that's so important for her to say.

A little sigh falls from her lips, and she shakes her head. "You can't do that to me ever again, or I'll leave."

I should let her threat go, climb out of this truck, and go cool down somewhere far away from the woman who gets me so heated, but all the feelings that have been pent up since I found her almost frozen to death in the woods have been bubbling just under the surface. Our confrontation on the road cracked a fissure across the hard exterior that allows me to keep everyone away, but it's too late now to seal it over again.

If she's going to give me ultimatums, then I have one for her, too. Something that has been threatening to unravel me completely for days.

I incline my head toward her, getting right up in her face, as close as I can be, without kissing her again. "You can't do what you did the other night to me *ever* again. I can't..."—I shake my head, trying to figure out how to explain this in a way that isn't going to give her the wrong impression—"I can't go through that again, almost losing you like that."

And it *isn't* just because I need her by my side for the board meeting.

Her eyes soften slightly before she leans in and presses her lips to mine, stealing anything else I might have said with the way my mind goes completely blank every time she touches me.

It isn't like the other two kisses we've shared.

This one is almost sweet.

Slow.

Like she doesn't want to scare me away.

Her lips glide along mine in a silent plea, and despite

knowing how bad this will end, a low groan of appreciation rumbles in my chest. I reach out and drag her across the bench seat toward me, as close as our bodies can come in the confines of the truck.

Every fiber of my being awakens at her touch, her kiss, her scent seeping into my lungs. She reaches up and buries her fingers in my beard, scraping her nails along my jaw in a way that makes my hard cock jump against my jeans.

From the very first time Ronald mentioned it, I knew it was a horrible idea to bring someone up here, doing this mail-order bride thing as a desperate attempt to get ahead of Uncle Marty, but I *always* thought I was in control.

I thought I could handle it, handle *anyone* who showed up here after all the things I've suffered.

But I was in no way prepared for Lyla.

I'm not sure anyone ever could be.

I pull away from her reluctantly, and she follows me, keeping her lips linked with mine before I finally capture her face between my palms and hold her away. "What the hell are you doing, Lyla?"

She *has* to know what this will lead to, the dangerous path neither of us will be able to get off once we take this step. She *must* understand what she's doing and what she's asking for.

Her green gaze locks with mine, searching for the truth that I'm not even sure I grasp at this point. "I'm showing you I'm not the enemy."

Sweet mother of God.

This woman has already completely shattered everything I thought I knew about this world and what I wanted out of it in only a handful of days.

Her sweetness.

Her drive.

Her almost naïve innocence.

I don't know what the hell she did to need $50,000 so fast, what she could possibly have gotten herself into that would've cost her that much and forced her into this life.

But this isn't her, living up here like this, being with a guy like me.

Brushing my thumb across her cheek, I shake my head. "I know you're not the enemy, but this can't happen."

If I let it, it will only hurt her even more.

Lyla lifts her right leg and slides across my lap, settling her thighs on either side of my hips, her ass pinned against the steering wheel.

Fuck.

She feathers her lips over mine again, adjusting her position until I can feel the heat radiating from her core pressed against my hard cock, through my pants and the thin leggings she wears.

"Bloody hell, Lyla."

Her name comes out strangled—half plea and half curse.

She drags her head back, locking eyes with me again, feathering her fingers through my hair. "Tell me again you don't want this, you don't want me, that we're just *room-mates,* and I'll leave it at that, never bring up the subject again..."

Devilish woman.

I've given myself away with my words on the road back here.

She knows I can't look her in the eye and say that because it would be a lie, one of the great many I've told in my life, and also the one that could have the biggest conse-quences.

LYLA

It's there, swimming in the icy-blue waters of his eyes, the fear of letting himself give in, of letting himself care, of letting himself be anything other than the reclusive, self-sufficient man he's made himself into. Allowing this to happen, admitting what he has today, ripped him open wide to me and showed me everything I suspected about him that he tried so hard to hide.

He *does* care.

Silas may have set out to live up here alone, away from any human interaction, to allow whatever demons chase him to do so endlessly on the mountain.

But he has been lonely.

He still feels and wants, even when he thinks he shouldn't.

He needs this as much as I do.

I didn't want to admit my attraction to the man I married for money, but it was there all the same. And after his confession on the road, there was no way we were ever going back to pretending to only be roommates.

It would be impossible.

To ignore this spark, this heat crackling between us, would mean turning away from something you might feel once in your life, if you're lucky. And after everything that's happened to lead me to this mountain, this man, this moment, I don't want to let it go.

Only it isn't up to me.

I just placed the ball in his court.

And if he's not ready or truly doesn't want this, I will walk away.

I wait for him to pull out from my touch, to push me off him like he so easily could, to tell me he can't and go back to pretending he hates me and everything I represent...

I wait for him to do exactly what he did that night and the next morning—look for any reason to run away. But it doesn't come.

Instead, he threads his calloused hands in my hair and drags my mouth down to his in a fevered desperation I wasn't aware he was capable of.

The hesitation, the worry, the uncertainty all seem to melt away with the intensity of his kiss. I roll my hips and grind down on his cock, eliciting a deep groan from his massive chest.

"Fuck, Lyla." He tears his mouth from mine. "It's been a really fucking long time..."

I kiss him again, gliding my tongue along the seam of his lips. "Me, too."

Not that I want to get into any of *that* right now, but hopefully, he knows me well enough by now to understand I am not the type of person to jump into bed with anyone —though I guess I did sleep in *his* bed the first night we met.

"Recline your seat."

His brow furrows. "What?"

I nudge his shoulder. "Recline your seat."

Silas' hand slips free from my hair and down to the left, and his seat falls back, allowing me to move more freely between him and the steering wheel. Hooded blue eyes watch me as I undo his jeans and slide my hand in, wrapping my palm around his hard length.

He hisses at the contact, dropping his head back and closing his eyes tightly. If what Carrie Ann said this morning is true, this is probably the first time any woman has touched him in fifteen years—the first time any woman has touched him in his entire *true* adult life.

His body twitches with each slow stroke, and I gently brush my thumb across the head, spreading a bead of pre-cum in a slick glide of skin on skin. Another rumbled groan reverberates in his chest, and I lean in, catching it in my mouth as I release my grip on him so I can shove my pants to my thighs.

In the tight confines of the truck, it isn't sexy or easy to do, but something tells me if we took the time to get into the house, he'd find a reason to stop this.

Any excuse.

He would deny himself what we both want because of some deep-seated fear of hurting me or opening himself up to getting hurt. But for the moment, whatever made him this way, whatever holds him back, he seems to have pushed it aside. And I don't dare risk losing it.

His fingers tighten on my exposed hips, his eyes zeroing in between my thighs. The normally pale blue darkens, the storm raging inside him that he always tries to keep contained about to be unleashed.

I shift my position, dragging my slick core along the length of his cock.

His hips buck, fingers digging in almost painfully to my skin. "Fucking hell..."

He drops his head back again, eyes closed tight, muscles in his inked neck straining as he struggles for control.

I reach between us and grip him, aligning the head at my ready entrance, but I don't sink down yet. I can't. "Silas, look at me."

Why is it so important that he does?

Maybe because I need him to understand, need to convince him that all the fighting since I got here has been a buildup to this. That this was inevitable. That I felt that same spark with him the first time we met.

I may not have known *what* it was. I may have mistaken it for fear, but it was there all the same. Simmering under the surface. Arcing between us every time we were together. Threatening to combust if he didn't keep dousing it every chance he got.

His eyes open and meet mine, and I slowly start sinking down on him. His lips part, and a strangled groan slips from them as his body goes rigid under me.

I take him inch by inch, on a long, slow glide, allowing his thick length to stretch me wide and fill me completely. My breath catches, and I squeeze around him, drawing him deeper.

His grip on my hips tightens, like he's using them to ground himself into the moment somehow. My body trembles, and I finally take him all the way to the hilt, grinding my clit against his pelvis to get the friction I need in exactly the right spot.

"God, Lyla..."

I capture his gasp with another kiss and clench around him again, then slowly lift myself up so I can sink down and begin a languid rhythm that will hopefully bring us both the release we crave.

He grits his jaw, watching me shift back and move on him, his entire body so tense it looks like he's about to snap. The heat building inside me threatens to do the same— combust into something that will light both of us aflame.

I increase my pace slightly, bracing my hands on his rock-hard chest, and he shifts his hands up the back of my shirt and along my spine. Goosebumps break out over my skin at the rough calluses dragging along my skin, and he tugs me down fully against him, taking my mouth again in a searing kiss that finally starts to hint at the connection we have.

Because he doesn't just kiss me.

He eats me alive.

He devours all the reservations I had about being here, all the concerns about what the future with him will be like, all the worries about the things I don't know and what they might mean.

He makes it all go away in an instant.

Then he rolls his hips and thrusts up, meeting me every time I come down, burying himself even deeper. I gasp, pulling away from his mouth, and he follows me, capturing the sound like he doesn't want to miss anything.

Every advance and retreat.

Every roll and arch of my hips.

Every move I make is designed to bring him something he hasn't had in so long—release.

Of the guilt he carries over whatever happened.

Of his confusion and frustration over our situation.

Of the demons that chased him up here so many years ago.

Of the pain he seems to relish living with.

He needs to release it all.

And I do, too.

I need to forgive myself for what happened, keep moving forward without the things that try to pull me back taking too much control. I need to forgive myself for agreeing to marry Silas for money, for doing what *had* to be done.

Silas closes his eyes and shakes his head, like he's fighting what his body wants. His grip on me tightens again as he moves back to my hips to help me set a faster rhythm. "Lyla, I can't. I'm going to—"

I grind my clit against his pelvis, getting the perfect friction to ignite an inferno building between my legs. "It's okay, Silas."

Close.

So close.

I keep pushing myself up and thrusting back down, harder and harder, his hips rising to meet mine each time in the most delicious way, until I finally start to see stars on the edges of my vision.

We keep moving together. In the most awkward place possible, we're finally making a breakthrough in this "fake" relationship, one that stopped feeling fake at some point without either of us realizing it. And it's going to change everything between us.

"Fuck!"

He tips his head back, the muscles in his neck straining, as my orgasm finally hits me, a blinding white light filling my vision.

I squeeze my eyes closed and keep going, my rhythm faltering slightly, only his help lifting me at my hips, keeping me going. Then his cock hardens impossibly more inside me before he comes on a roar that fills the truck and echoes out his open door across the clearing in front of his cabin.

He collapses back again, and I fall on top of him, burying my face against his neck and scratchy beard. That woodsy, piney, masculine scent I've come to associate with Silas fills every labored breath I take, but I savor it, relishing the way his chest rises and falls under mine.

I don't know what any of this means for the two of us, but it seems like a step in the right direction, which means we're probably going to take a five-mile leap back.

Chapter Eleven

SILAS

The sun hasn't come up yet as I drive down the mountain, but I still recognize the spot where we stopped and I kissed Lyla yesterday.

My entire body stiffens.

Everywhere.

Memories of her moving over me, taking me into her hot, tight body and decimating any ability for me to think come flooding back. For those few brief moments when we were locked together like that, it was easy to forget why it was such a bad idea.

But the moment clarity returned, so did the realization that I'd made a horrible mistake.

I knew, if I ever let myself give into that woman, it would destroy any willpower I had, and that's exactly what happened. Lyla shattered me completely with her kiss and her touch, the way she never looked at me with pity, despite being able to see all my scars and knowing how completely fucked in the head I am.

She gave herself to me fully, opened herself up to all the pain and trauma I carry and will bring to her life.

And I can't do this to her.

Not after *that*.

I can't continue to put her in this position and force her to face what's coming for me in this showdown with Uncle Marty. It will only hurt her—expose her to my darkest secrets and the most vile human being I've ever met. Which is exactly why, as soon as we both came down from our high yesterday and she rolled off me, I fled as fast as I could.

Like the coward I am, I ran.

Again.

Needing the space, the distance.

Some damn quiet in my head when she won't stop racing through it so I could try to hatch a plan, figure some way *out* of this mess.

The only reason I needed this marriage was to secure my position with the trust, but maybe there's a way to defeat Uncle Marty without it. I never wanted the company or the money, anyway, just him gone and someone who actually has a heart and some morals and isn't a deviant piece of shit at the helm.

There has to be another way.

I spent the entire night in the barn, going over every possibility, and by morning, my resolve to end this was even stronger.

It's what allowed me to leave before sunrise without seeing Lyla or telling her where I was going. She would have tried to stop me, would have argued and pushed and insisted that I am only doing this because I don't know how to let someone in.

But it isn't about that.

It's about protecting her from what's out there—who's out there.

And there's only one way to do it.

I pull over on the side of the road near Millsburg's single stop sign, between the intersection and the beginning of Main Street, where hopefully no one will notice me this early but I can get some damn phone reception.

I pull out the burner phone Ronald gave me the day of the wedding and dial him, resting my head against the headrest and closing my eyes. But all that does is bring visions of Lyla straddling me in here yesterday. Couple that with the scent that still permeates the air in here and my cock is going to stay hard all fucking day.

Fuck.

It's the last thing I need occupying my brain right now, and I adjust my semi away from under my zipper and wait while the line rings.

After the eighth ring, when I'm about to give up for now, Ronald picks up. "Silas, what's wrong?"

Literally everything.

I spent the night planning what I was going to say to him, preparing for this moment, but now that it's here, all the eloquent words I thought I should say disappear.

All that's left is the one truth that won't go away, no matter how long I agonize over it.

"I can't do this to Lyla..."

Something rustles on the other end of the line, like he's trying to move to a different room, and a door closes with a loud click. "What do you mean, you can't do this to her?"

The way her eyes darkened from emerald to evergreen while she rode my cock yesterday flashes through my head, making it throb in my jeans. My body has a very different idea of what I'd like to be doing with Lyla right now instead of being down here making this call, but with the meeting in only a few days, there isn't any time to be distracted by some primal need to take that woman ten ways from Sunday.

I squeeze my eyes closed. "I can't expose her to what's going to happen at that board meeting with Uncle Marty. You know what he's capable of...what he might do. And I just can't do that to her."

Ronald is silent for a moment, considering what I said. "Holy shit, you *like* her, don't you?"

I drop my forehead against the steering wheel, wishing I could say no, wishing I could go back to yesterday and throw her back into that truck without ever saying a word, without giving in so selfishly and ensuring Lyla is going to end up hurt.

"She's sweet and innocent, and she doesn't deserve any of this. Uncle Marty could really hurt her, in so many ways, and you know it."

"Not if what I'm planning works. I have everything prepared to take to the FBI before the board meeting. You come in, expose him, claim your rightful place, and by the time he's done ranting and objecting, the Feds should be on the premises to arrest him—before he can do any damage."

"Should be."

Those words stick in my head because others have tried to bring him down...and failed or were paid to disappear. Nothing is assured in this—except that he poses a very real danger to anyone connected to me. Mainly Lyla.

I lift my head from the wheel, staring down Main Street at Jensen's, the bakery Lyla disappeared into yesterday, and the bench where she sat and made the phone calls that started our argument.

Everything looks so peaceful and quiet at this time of the morning. It could lull someone into a false sense of security, but I learned long ago to expect the worst because things aren't always what they seem.

Which is why that nagging feeling that something is going to go wrong won't go away.

"But even if he's taken into custody, he has connections. He has the kind of power that could hurt me and Lyla, even from a distance, even from behind bars, and you know he could do it *easily*."

A tidal wave of memories washes over me.

Each bite of pain brand new.

Stinging my skin.

Tearing me open.

Breaking me.

The thought of anything happening to her because of me makes my chest tighten until I can barely breathe. I suck in a sharp breath, pushing away the nightmares that live rent-free in my head and trying to focus on what needs to happen.

"I have to let her go, Ronald." The words burn like acid on my tongue. "Annul the marriage—"

"You can't do that, Silas."

"I can. I'd be giving up something I never wanted in the first place, something I probably would turn over to someone else in a couple of years once everything settles, anyway. We can still take down Uncle Marty without me complying with the trust, can't we?"

Ronald sucks in a deep breath and releases it slowly. "I don't think you have a very strong position if you're not going to step up as CEO. If you come in and throw around these accusations against your uncle and then disappear again, there won't be a Bolton at the helm for the first time in almost two hundred years. That could throw everything into turmoil. Force a sale...I thought it meant something to you, your family legacy. I've worked hard to ensure that it stayed in place for years after you left, so you could come back and take over—"

"Including covering up my father and uncle's crimes."

"You know why I did that."

I offer him an indignant laugh. "I know why you *say* you did that."

"I'm making amends now."

His defensiveness comes with the territory. Ronald has been fixing problems for the Boltons since before I was born, and he's used to having to defend others—not himself. Now that the target will also be on him when he brings all the information forward, he's going to end up in a very uncomfortable position—likely publicly.

I don't give a fuck what happens to Ronald or me, but I stare at the seat where Lyla sat only yesterday, so full of piss and vinegar, so angry at me.

Rightfully so...

Whiskey lifts his nose and looks up at me, tilting his head. Leaving her alone up there without Whiskey this morning felt wrong, but she couldn't be a witness to this phone call.

She's going to be pissed when I get back and tell her what I've done, what I plan to do. But protecting her from what's coming is far too important to worry about her hating me for it.

Ronald clears his throat awkwardly. "I didn't want to have to tell you this, Silas..."

Acid churns in my stomach. "Tell me what?"

His voice drops low, like he's concerned someone might

be listening to his end of the conversation. "Your uncle might suspect something."

Icy dread floods my veins, and my entire body goes rigid. "What do you mean, he might suspect something?"

"He's been acting shiftier than usual since I came back from Millsburg."

"What's he doing?"

"A lot of closed-door meetings with people. A lot of phone calls to board members that they won't discuss with me. It's almost like he's preparing an offensive, but he shouldn't know there's anyone coming in for the attack."

I slam my fist against the steering wheel, making Whiskey jump. "Fuck, I need Lyla out of this, even more then."

Ronald sighs. "There's no way we could get an annulment between now and the board meeting, anyway."

"Fine. Then we'll do it after. But there's no way I'm bringing her into that room with me. If Uncle Marty never meets her and doesn't know who she is, I have a chance at keeping her safe. If your friends at the FBI do what they're supposed to and take him into custody and ensure he stays there, then maybe she can get out of this unscathed."

At least, any more than she already has been by me...

Silence lingers on the line between us for a moment before Ronald releases another sigh. "The contract you signed with her said *both* parties have to agree to end the marriage—"

"I don't think that'll be a problem from her end. I know how to piss her off enough not to want to be here. She came close to leaving yesterday already."

He chuckles, the sound so out of place in such a serious conversation. "Somehow, that doesn't surprise me. We'll discuss it more after the board meeting. I need you to really think about if that's what you want to do, if you want to give up the company and your family legacy."

"I'm not going to change my mind."

All that means nothing if it requires me to put Lyla in the middle of the crossfire between me and the other last remaining Bolton.

I end the call as a familiar blue pickup truck approaches the intersection and stops next to me. Brent looks over at me and raises a brow, then rolls down his window.

Shit.

Forcing a half-smile, I roll mine down, too.

"Silas, what are you doing back down here? Forget something yesterday?"

Apparently my sanity.

Because as soon as I started up that mountain with her, I completely lost my ability to resist the pull that woman has.

"Yeah. A jar of pasta sauce got broken on the way up. Just coming down to grab another one."

His already wrinkled brow furrows. "You drove all the way down here for a single jar of pasta sauce?"

It does sound pretty fucking ridiculous when he says it like that—a two-hour round trip for one item isn't something I would normally do. But by now, no doubt everyone in town knows about the wedding.

I offer Brent a shrug. "I have a new wife to keep happy."

He barks out a laugh and nods, tipping the brim of his old baseball cap at me. "Happy wife, happy life. Congratulations, by the way."

"Thanks."

Brent gives me a wave and rolls up his window before continuing in the opposite direction, and I throw the truck into drive and proceed down Main Street toward Jensen's general store.

I hadn't actually planned to get her another jar of sauce, but now that I am here, it wouldn't hurt to bring her a peace offering of sorts before I drop the bomb that is sure to set her off.

———

LYLA

I stare at the note resting on the pillow beside me.

I had to run back into town for something.

Releasing a frustrated groan, I reach out and grab it, crumpling it up in my hand and tossing it toward the already dying fire.

Running back to town, my ass.

He just *ran*.

The same way he has any time I get remotely close to breaking through the walls he tries to keep up in order to continue to deceive himself into believing this is all fake.

And yesterday was the ultimate slap in the face.

I can't say a man has ever *literally* run away after having sex with me before, but that's precisely what Silas did. He stared at me as I climbed off him, then redid his pants and slid out of the truck without another word, walking out into the field after Whiskey like nothing happened.

Like we hadn't just done the *one* thing that should change everything between us.

How the hell can he do that?

He shuts down and leaves me to try to decipher his cryptic actions like I'm a goddamn treasure hunter with a map but missing the fucking key.

My frustration prevents me from lying in his bed any longer, surrounded by the scent of the man who is as volatile as he is tender, as petulant as he is generous, as loving as he is closed off...

I throw back the covers, climb from the mattress, and stomp into the kitchen, despite no one being here to see my temper tantrum. At least I'll have good coffee this morning, thanks to my stop at the bakery yesterday.

Carrie Ann did me a tremendous solid. Shitty coffee today would only sour my mood more. I tear open the package and throw a few spoonfuls into the French press, then start water boiling on the stove.

Leaning against the edge of the counter, my foot bounces rapidly. I cross my arms over my chest and glare at the door I walked through less than two weeks ago and got myself into this mess.

That man is so emotionally shut down that there may never be any truly getting through to him. I might be wasting my time and effort. But if it's going to be like *this*, we can't go on potentially *forever*.

If he doesn't want any sort of relationship with me besides roommates, then we're going to have to figure out a different living situation—at least until I can get him to agree to end the marriage.

I got the fifty grand I needed out of it.

What if you need more money? What if the attorney comes back and says he needs more?

The five million I'll get if I stay in this marriage for five more years would take care of a lot. It would set me up for life. I don't need anything extravagant, enough to take care of the basics—because if the attorney does his job, I'll need to be thinking about more than just me.

I've tried not to dwell on what's happening so many miles away, the things out of my control and in the hands of people with far higher pay grades than I'll ever have. I've done my best to think about the here and now, the things I *can* control.

But Silas Bolton is *definitely* not one of them.

I huff out an annoyed breath and check on the water. Now that it's finally boiling, I pour it into the French press and send up a silent prayer for meeting Carrie Ann yesterday. The rest of the day may have gone to shit after some of the best sex of my life, but at least I got some decent joe out of it. Simply knowing I'm about to get a caffeine kick from it lightens my mood a bit.

It seems up here, the simple things are what I'm going to have to cling to in order to survive.

I press down the plunger on the old-fashioned brewer and let it sit while I grab a mug and sugar. The aroma starts to fill the kitchen, and I pour myself a cup, taking a long, deep inhale of the fragrant steam.

Man, I could really go for another cupcake from the bakery.

But I have to take what I can get up here.

Which means attitude from Silas, unconditional love from Whiskey, and this cup of coffee I can sit and enjoy while I contemplate the inner workings of that man's head.

I settle into his big chair in front of the dwindling fire and take a sip as I stare into the low flames. Even with the heat still radiating from it, I shiver and snuggle down deeper into the old leather.

It feels so empty without him here, knowing he isn't on the property hiding from me somewhere like he did last night. I've gotten used to his presence, as cold and unwelcoming as it can be sometimes, but I can't do this anymore.

I won't dance around the man who seems to want to run from happiness.

When I first decided to do the mail-order bride thing, I thought it would be a death sentence when it came to actually finding someone I *wanted* to spend my life with, but somehow, over the tumultuous days I've spent with Silas, I had started to believe it could actually happen for us if he gave it a chance...

I take another sip of my coffee and start to set my cup on the small table next to the chair, but the sound of wheels on the gravel outside makes me freeze.

He's back already?

My stomach flip-flops—unsure whether I actually *want* to see Silas and have the inevitable confrontation with him or whether I want to enjoy the quiet for a few more minutes before everything implodes.

You can't avoid it any longer.

I push out of the chair and make my way over to the door, tugging it open before he can run off and hide from me again. But it isn't his big truck pulling in front of the cabin. A black SUV comes to a stop near the bottom of the porch steps, its darkly tinted windows hiding the occupants.

Who the hell is this?

The rear passenger door opens, and I glimpse silver hair.

Ronald's back? With a driver this time.

Only, the man who steps out in expensive Italian loafers and a perfectly tailored suit isn't Ronald. Familiar blue eyes assess me, the same ones I stared into while I was riding Silas yesterday.

This man must be a Bolton.

He buttons his suit coat and offers me a smile that sends a shiver down my spine. I take a half-step back so I'm fully inside the cabin, should I need to slam the door closed in his face.

Something about the man screams *run*, and I'm prepared to do just that in a fucking heartbeat.

"Hello." His smooth voice holds a hint of icy chill that tells me everything he says is carefully chosen and well-practiced. "Good morning."

"Uh, hi."

He approaches the porch but stops at the bottom of the stairs. "I'm looking for my nephew, Silas."

Nephew?

I glance behind me into the cabin, even though I'm not going to find who he's looking for. "He is not here at the moment, but he should be back soon."

A slow grin spreads across the man's face as he takes a few steps up to reach the porch, now only a handful of feet from me. "Then I guess that gives us time to get to know each other." He extends a hand, flashing cufflinks with an engraved *B* on them. "Marty Bolton, and you are?"

One of his silver brows rises slowly. He's asking, but something tells me he already knows. It's the way he looks at me, picking me apart. Almost like a boxer entering the ring and sizing up his opponent to determine the best way to demolish him with the fewest blows.

I transfer my coffee to my left hand and accept his in my right. "Lyla."

Another shudder overtakes me at the contact of his smooth palm against my own, and he leans in quickly, pressing a kiss to each of my cheeks before I can pull away.

What the fuck?

He pulls back and glances down into my cup of coffee

as he releases my hand. "I see you have a cup of fresh coffee. May I trouble you for one?"

So casual, so smooth, the way he invites himself into the cabin without *actually* doing it.

What I wouldn't give to have Whiskey here right now...

I never realized how safe the dog and Silas made me feel here on the homestead until they were both gone.

My unexpected visitor holds up his hands and offers an apologetic half-smile that doesn't touch the frigid chill in his gaze. "Only if it isn't too much of a bother."

I glance behind him at the SUV, where a man sits in the driver's seat, looking down at something and not paying us any attention.

Marty waves his hand backward. "Oh, my driver will be fine. You said Silas should be back shortly, correct? We'll just wait for him and have a chat."

I sure as hell hope he will be.

Whatever happened between Silas and his family, something tells me he won't be happy to see his uncle here when he returns. But this may be my chance to find out what caused the rift and sent Silas up the mountain. I might figure out why this fake marriage was so important to him and Ronald.

I step out of the way to allow Marty to enter, and his shrewd gaze darts around the cabin, from the unmade bed to the low fire, the leather chair in front of it, then over to the small kitchen. Less than thirty seconds to see the entire place.

"Quaint. Not exactly how I expected my nephew to be living."

The clear judgment in his observations makes me stiffen with the need to defend the way Silas lives. My fingers tighten around my mug while I try to remove the annoyance from my voice. "He loves it here. Living off the grid and on his own terms."

He nods slowly as he follows me into the kitchen. I set my coffee on the counter and pour another cup from the French press for him.

"Sugar?"

"Black."

He slowly lowers himself into one of the chairs at the small table that rattles unevenly underneath him. His eyes dart down to the legs and hand-hewn floors, and he smirks, like he finds it funny that his nephew would walk on anything other than imported Italian marble.

I hand him the mug, and he accepts it, his fingers brushing against mine in a way that sends another chill through me. Lowering myself into my seat opposite him, I grab my coffee and bring it to my lips.

"So, Lyla"—he grins—"tell me what you're doing up here with my nephew."

I almost choke on my coffee, but I manage to swallow it down before I answer him. "I don't think that's really any of your business."

He recoils slightly, like he isn't used to people not answering his questions, then chuckles. "I guess you're right. It isn't. But it's been a while since I've seen my nephew. So, I'm obviously quite interested in what's been going on in his life. A beautiful woman like you, and he's keeping her a secret, living up here like this?" He raises a shoulder and lets it fall casually, though the way he's sitting tells me this is anything but a casual visit. He takes a sip of his coffee, keeping his eyes on me. "You have my mother's ring on a very important finger."

Fuck.

I quickly pull my left hand from the mug and put it under the table on my thigh, but it's far too late to hide it.

Marty smirks. "You're married?"

Answering him feels wrong, like admitting it will be throwing Silas to the fucking wolves, but I can't very well deny it when he's already seen the multi-carat evidence.

"Yes..."

He checks a very expensive-looking watch on his wrist and glances up at me. "And I assume Silas has told you that he renounced his inheritance and doesn't have a fucking dime to his name anymore."

That certainly isn't what the contract I signed suggests, but there is clearly far more going on with the Boltons than Silas or Ronald ever let me know.

I take a sip of my coffee as I try to assess the man sitting across from me.

He's up to something.

Maybe he came to rattle me, or more than likely, he came to rattle Silas. Either way, I'm not going to let it happen. I may not be thrilled with the way Silas has been acting, but I am not about to let this old man walk in here and intimidate me or threaten the only person who has shown me any true kindness and affection in a very long time.

I rest my elbows on the table, squaring my shoulders and doing my best to appear unfazed by his clear intimidation tactics. "Look, Mr. Bolton, I don't know what you expected to find here. If you want to talk with Silas, I suggest you start making your way back down the mountain. You'll cross paths with him, eventually. There's only one way up and one way down."

A sinister grin spreads slowly across his lips, the kind that screams *you're in trouble* to anyone with any common sense. "Oh, I'm well aware of how remote and trapped you are up here, sweetheart. Well aware."

His words wrap around my spine like a sinister hand ready to snap it.

It's a threat, a very real one.

And I'm up here alone with no way to protect myself.

Chapter Twelve

LYLA

I tighten my grip on the coffee mug. Unless I'm going to risk trying to get to the knives in the drawer on the far side of the kitchen, this is the closest thing I have to a weapon if I need one.

And something tells me I might.

The menacing glint in Uncle Marty's eyes shines brightly at me, the man taking great pleasure in making me squirm. He waits and watches, searching for any signs that he's gotten under my skin with his comment.

I won't give him that satisfaction.

Calmly taking a sip of my coffee to test how hot it still is, I watch him over the rim of the mug. He takes a drink of his as well, never breaking eye contact with me. We both know whoever ends the stare-down will be the loser and have given the other a victory neither of us can afford to lose.

Not looking away, I push up from the table, nudging my chair back with my thighs. "While I've enjoyed our chat, Mr. Bolton, I think it's time for you to leave."

Feigning surprise at my request for him to exit, he glances down into his mug. "But I haven't finished my coffee yet."

"Oh"—I give him a sweet smile the man is surely intelligent enough to grasp isn't real—"we're definitely done here."

He pushes to his feet, the corners of his mouth lifting. "My nephew must like you."

The words make me stumble slightly on my way around the table.

I shouldn't ask, but the question comes out before I can bite it back. "Why do you say that?"

A low chuckle slips from his lips, and he takes one large drink from his coffee before answering, setting the mug on the table and turning toward me. "Because you do something he never could—you fight back." He takes a step closer until I can smell his cloyingly strong aftershave. "That's how I prefer it. I could have some real fun with you."

Any question of *who* and *what* Marty is evaporates in an instant, replaced by the cold, sheer certainty of knowing exactly how Silas got the scars.

This man standing in front of me is a monster. The kind that will haunt your awake hours and nightmares every day of your life once you've been touched by his sinister hands. Given the opportunity, he wouldn't think twice about hurting me the same way he did Silas.

I quickly dart around him to the front door, tugging it open and stepping into the jamb so I can run out onto the property, maybe to the barn where I can find a weapon better than this mug of now-lukewarm coffee if this asshole tries anything. "*Go.*"

He slowly saunters toward me, unbuttoning his jacket like he's getting ready to do something athletic and needs it loose. His gaze travels up and down me as he steps out onto the porch, intentionally brushing his shoulder against me on his way. "I don't think I'm quite ready to leave yet..."

"Get off my property."

The distance between us disappears so fast that I don't have any time to react. His hand knocks the mug from mine, and the porcelain shatters against the wood porch. Strong fingers close around my wrist so tightly that pain slices through my forearm. He twists it up behind my back, pressing his body to mine and pinning me against the solid doorjamb. "You don't know who you're fucking with, sweetheart. But I'll tell you right now, you're going to regret it."

I believe him.

His moves are too fluid, too well-practiced.

He's done this before.

Many times.

He's *comfortable* doing this to people.

Which does not bode well for me being able to get the upper hand.

His grip on my wrist behind my back increases, and he uses his hold and body to try to force me back into the cabin.

Don't let him get you back inside.

At least out here, there's a chance to get away, somewhere to run. Hope that I can escape this madman. If he gets me inside, this doesn't end well for me.

Vivid images of another man's hands on me assault my brain.

Another harsh touch.

Another threat.

The day my entire life went to shit.

Those memories threaten to overwhelm me, to make me shut down when faced with another piece of shit wanting to take something that doesn't belong to him, but the familiar sound of Silas' truck coming down the narrow path through the trees fills my heart with a glimmer of hope.

His uncle intensifies his grip, wrenching my arm harder. Pain shoots through my shoulder and wrist, and I bite my lip to keep from crying out and giving him the satisfaction of hearing me in agony.

Instead of shoving me inside, he yanks me out onto the porch fully, putting me between him and what is sure to be a very pissed-off Silas.

Gravel flies as Silas pulls to a stop behind the SUV and throws open his door. He grabs the shotgun from the rack behind his head in the cab as he steps out. Whiskey leaps from the truck and barrels toward us, barking and snarling, only stopping because Marty uses me as a human shield.

Silas levels the gun at us. "Take your fucking hands off my *wife*."

A deep chuckle sounds from directly behind my ear, Marty's warm breath fluttering my loose hair as he tugs me closer to him. "Or what? You're going to shoot me? Sick your dog on me? You wouldn't dare risk hurting her, would you? Because you need her, you and Ronald."

The mention of the family attorney makes Silas stiffen, but his gun doesn't waver. Nor does his gaze that's locked with my own. Of the dozens of emotions I've seen welling in the pale blue, the one he looks at me with now is new—a mix of panic, resolve, and something I don't think anyone has ever shown me before.

"Come now, Silas. Did you think I wouldn't find out what you two were up to?" Marty releases a mirthless laugh, jostling me painfully. "Ronald thought he was so smart renting a car to come up here instead of using one of the company vehicles, but he didn't think to do it under someone else's name." He shakes his head, tsking in my ear. "It took me a bit to locate the right rental company and car. But once I did, it was simple enough to track the GPS and figure out where he'd gone. I knew he was up to something. Ronald never was very good at keeping secrets, but I hadn't anticipated it being *you*, Silas."

The way his name rolls off the older man's tongue makes bile rise in my throat—filled with so many unspoken atrocities that made Silas into the man he is today.

Scarred. Broken. But not weak.

Never that.

Silas advances until he's standing next to Whiskey, only a few feet from us. The dog's low growl fills the air as he bares his teeth and snaps at Marty. But Silas's uncle is right about one thing—Whiskey isn't doing anything and neither is Silas. Not when I'm standing between them and their target.

He wrenches my wrist behind my back against, so hard it feels like a bone might snap—a reminder to Silas that he's in control. I try to cry out, but my gasp of pain gets stuck in my throat.

"Whatever you and Ronald think it is you're going to accomplish, you will fail. And I'll make you pay for even attempting it. This is the only warning you're going to get."

Silas snarls at his uncle, his finger slipping closer to the trigger. "Let her go and get the fuck off my property."

Marty shifts behind me, keeping me close while inching toward the steps that will take him down to his waiting SUV. "Somebody grew a backbone in the last fifteen years. You're not the same little, sniveling, crying boy, begging me to stop, are you?"

The harsh words darken Silas' gaze, but he doesn't buckle under their weight. His wide shoulders remain hard, jaw clenched, grip on the gun tight. "No, I'm not that little boy anymore."

Marty sneers in my ear. "But you're still a fucking pussy, like you always were. I never understood why your father didn't just take care of you when you were a child and put you out of your fucking misery then." He urges me forward, each step moving me toward the steps. "Now, you're going to let me leave, and I'm never going to see or hear from you again. I'll make sure Ronald gets the message when I get back to town, too."

Silas swallows thickly, knowing full well what the threat means to Ronald. But there isn't anything he can do about it, not from up here. Not when I'm stuck between him and a madman.

He motions with the gun for Marty to head toward the SUV. Marty keeps me in front of him as long as he can, then shoves me to the side, knocking me to the porch as he leaps down the steps.

Marty reaches for the door of the SUV, but Whiskey lunges at him and latches on to his arm, sinking razor-sharp teeth into the flesh. The man who undoubtedly would have done unspeakable things to me if Silas hadn't returned howls and tries to kick Whiskey off, but he stays latched on, hanging from the man's wrist with powerful and determined jaws.

Silas walks over to them calmly and places the barrel of the gun against his uncle's chest. "I could end you with one pull of this fucking trigger. The only reason I'm not doing it is because I don't want to go to prison. That would be a win for you. You've taken too much of my life, and I'm not going to let you take any more of it."

He pulls the gun back and grabs Whiskey's collar. "Whiskey—release."

Instantly, the dog lets Marty go and takes a step back to stand next to Silas.

Marty grabs his wounded arm, scowling at both of them while blood drips to the dirt. "You'll pay for this, Silas. Watch your back."

He manages to tug open the door and climb in. His driver pulls forward and does a Y-turn, then barrels down the gravel drive as Silas rushes toward me on the porch.

"Lyla!"

The anguish in the way he says my name matches my own, and he sets the gun on the pine boards and pulls me into his arms.

"Are you all right?"

I mean to say, "I'm okay."

But that would be a lie.

And the only thing that comes out of my throat when I try to say anything else is a strangled sob.

He grabs my injured arm gently and examines the bright-red marks already starting to darken into bruises. "I'm so sorry, Lyla. I never thought he'd find me, but I knew this was a possibility, that you could end up hurt. It's all my fault."

———

SILAS

The guilt of knowing I am the reason Lyla's hurt threatens to crush me. It sits squarely on my shoulders and chest, making it impossible to breathe or see anything but the damage that *monster* did to her.

But somehow, I push through the agony wracking my

body and scoop her up, carrying her into the cabin on unsteady feet.

Whiskey follows us in, and I kick the door closed behind us, then move her over to the bed and lay her down on it.

Was it only this morning I left her sleeping soundly here?

I should have climbed in with her, apologized for running from her yesterday, come clean about *everything* so she would be prepared for this, so she wouldn't have been blindsided by him showing up and attacking her.

I should have.

I should have.

I should have.

Yet...I ran.

Again and again and again, I've *run* from this woman, from what she brings me, the glimpses of happiness and what really living can feel like. I've *run* and hurt her, again and again and again.

And now, she's paying the price for my weakness, like everyone else who has been victimized by Uncle Marty has since I left so long ago.

Lyla stares up at me, tears soaking her green eyes, and I brush the hair back from her face, wanting so badly to take away her pain and erase everything that just happened from her memory.

"I'm so sorry..."

"It's not your fault." She shakes her head, her lower lip trembling as she cradles her wounded arm against her chest. "You couldn't have known he would—"

I shove off the bed to my feet, pushing my hands back through my hair. "But that's just it, I *did*." I scrub my palms over my face, unable to look at her and the damage he did without wanting to destroy something. "What he did to you is nothing compared to what he's capable of."

Her breath hitches, and I know she's putting the pieces together. "It was him, wasn't it? All the scars?"

I suck in a shaky breath, battling with the memories I've tried so hard to forget, to leave behind me when I came up here. It was inevitable that she would ask. The talented artist I found who has spent years trying to hide them hasn't been able to fully conceal what was done to me. And now that she's met Martin Bolton, now that she's felt the sting of his violence, I can't keep the truth from her anymore.

Not even if I wanted to.

And the truly terrifying thing is that I don't want to hide it from her anymore.

I want her to know, to understand why I can't ever be what or who she wants and needs me to be.

Slowly, I pull my hands away from my face and lower myself to the bed beside her. She lets me pull her bruised arm onto my lap, and I feather the tips of my fingers across the marred skin, feeling the same anger I've carried for so long welling inside me again.

"My uncle's a monster. And my father, he wasn't much better."

"He knew?"

I nod, remembering the looks he would give me that would silence me in an instant. "He never brought it up, never acknowledged it openly, but the one time I tried to say anything, he made it very clear to me that he didn't want to know what happened when I was alone with my uncle."

The smells and sounds and agony come racing back, threatening to drown me in the anxiety that keeps me up here on this mountain instead of living a normal life below it.

My heart thuds wildly against my chest, my breaths coming in hard, heavy pants as the past meets the present. Lyla slips her hand over mine, squeezing it gently, giving me an anchor, something to keep me grounded and help me remember where I am while I relive the horrors of my childhood.

I swallow against my dry throat, closing my eyes and picturing the house that was my home my entire life before coming up here. "We all lived together in the family mansion that's been the Bolton home since the early 1800s."

"What about your mom?"

It's such an obvious and innocent question but such a complicated answer.

I shift my position so I can prop myself against the head-board beside her, her hand draped on my lap, the bruises darkening every minute we sit here. "My father made sure she wasn't a problem."

Lyla looks at me, her brow furrowed, and the tears momentarily stop in favor of listening to the story she's wanted to hear since the moment she saw my old wounds. "What do you mean?"

"She had issues with drugs, self-medicated for her depression. After she had me, it got worse, but my uncle and my father kept her well stocked in anything she ever wanted." I give a half-shrug because I'm not entirely sure what happened—but I can make an educated guess. "I have brief memories of her from when I was very little. Then they just stop. My father and Marty told me she OD'd when I was four, but for all I know, it was staged that way to get rid of her."

"Jesus..." Lyla shifts to turn toward me, using her free hand to brush hair back from my temple. "Silas, I'm—"

I turn into her touch, locking my gaze with hers. "Please don't. Please don't say you're sorry. I don't want to hear those words come from your mouth, from anyone's. Losing my mom didn't change anything. If she had been there, it still would've happened. She couldn't have stopped them."

The emotions threatening to choke me fill my chest, but I fight them back, needing to get all this out now, or I know I never will again.

I owe it to Lyla to tell it *all*.

"My father and my uncle had too much power over the staff, everyone in the company, hell, even the police. No one was ever going to stand up to them. My uncle's sadistic tendencies, they got him into a lot of situations that would have looked very bad for the family and Bolton Steel. He needed an outlet, someone they could control more than the random women they paid to silence or made sure went away some other way."

Lyla turns her wounded arm and laces her fingers together with mine, and I stare down at her pale skin marred by a Bolton's hand against my inked skin that can't hide the evidence of what was done.

We're so different, from completely opposite worlds, yet I've dragged her into this quagmire we may not escape from.

She brushes her thumb across mine gently. "What did he do to you, Silas?"

My entire body trembles as memory after memory slams into me. I can feel every hit, every strike, every implement he ever used on me as if it were happening now instead of all those years ago.

No matter how much time has passed, the memories never go away.

They never dissipate.

If anything, they only grow stronger, more incessant,

banging around in my head to get my attention, to make me feel and see and experience them again.

"It would be easier to ask what he didn't do."

She flinches, but she doesn't pull away. "And you never told anyone?"

I shake my head. "Not after my father warned me the first time, but as I got older, I knew I had to get out..."

"That's why you came up here."

I nod. "I started saving all the money people gave me for birthday presents, Christmas, special occasions like that. I took items from the house that I could sell easily at pawn shops or on the street—watches, jewelry, things I thought they wouldn't miss. I knew I'd need cash they couldn't trace, and I didn't want to have to take anything out of bank accounts that they might notice and be able to use to find wherever I managed to settle down."

"Pretty smart for a teenager."

"No." I shake my head, clinging to her hand. "Smart would've been stopping it in the first place, going to the police until I found someone they didn't have on their payroll." I clench my eyes closed against a vision of a young woman, covered in bruises and welts and cuts being led from the house by one of the many servants paid to keep their eyes and mouths shut. "I wasn't the only person they hurt, especially Uncle Marty. There were women..." I swallow through the lump in my throat. "And I wasn't strong enough to do anything about it then. I just ran."

Lyla shifts up until she's kneeling next to me and takes my jaw in her palms, turning my head until I'm facing her, my eyes still closed. "Look at me, Silas."

Reluctantly, I open my eyes and meet hers. Resolve shimmers where her tears once did.

"A child can't be expected to bear that burden, Silas. You saved yourself. That's all you could do."

Her words seem so sure, her voice and gaze unwavering as she says them, but despite all this time agonizing over whether that's true or not, I can't believe them.

"Is it, Lyla? *Is* it all I could have done? Because it doesn't feel like it. It feels like I ran and left him to create more years of victims."

A single tear falls down her cheek. "Don't do that." She rests her forehead against mine, and that brief connection is enough to send warmth spreading through my chilled body. "I can't listen to you blame yourself."

I pull my head back. "How can I not? I have all this." I wave my hand around the cabin. "I had enough money to buy this cabin on this land that Jensen's brother couldn't maintain himself anymore on the mountain no one wanted, to hide out here, to cover my scars, to try to forget that life altogether, while everyone else continued to suffer because of the Boltons. What does that make me other than a fucking coward?"

"No. Not that." She shakes her head. "You *had* to leave."

Her eyes drift down my face to my neck, and she reaches up and trails her fingers over the thin scar that runs under my chin at my throat. "What made this?"

I squeeze my eyes closed at her soft touch and the goosebumps that spread across my skin with it.

Of course she would see it.

Through the beard, and the ink, and everything else I've done to give myself new skin, Lyla found the one thing that tells the worst of the story.

I don't want to tell her. I want to keep it buried. But

we've come this far that holding anything back wouldn't be fair to her.

"That's why I left, finally, what convinced me I had to. I was three weeks from leaving to go to Harvard. I was getting out, starting college hundreds of miles from my father and uncle." I swallow thickly, and she slowly brushes her fingers across the scar again. "Uncle Marty, he cornered me, said that just because I was leaving that house didn't mean that anything was changing, that he was still in control, and that if I ever said a fucking word to anyone about anything that had happened, he would kill me."

The pure rage in his voice when he made that threat still resonates in my ears. At barely eighteen, after years of him abusing me every way he could think of and getting away with it, it wasn't out of the realm of possibility that he could end my life and get away with it, either.

"I tried to stand up to him. I thought leaving was going to give me some leverage over him. I told him if he ever laid a hand on me again, I'd go straight to the police. But he grabbed a lamp and ripped the cord off it so fast I didn't have time to try to defend myself. He had it wrapped around my neck and was choking me before I could take another breath."

Lyla's grip on me tightens.

"I only managed to get away because my father came in the room and stopped him."

"What did your father say?"

I snort and shake my head at the absurdity of my father's words. "He told him that he couldn't kill the only heir, and right then and there, I understood why my father had never intervened, had always let him get away with everything." I lock gazes with her. "Because it was so important for him that the company stayed with the Boltons. If anything happened to him, he needed Marty to take over, and after him, I was the only one left. So, I renounced it. Once I managed to be able to speak again, I told him I didn't want any of his fucking money and I didn't want to be a Bolton anymore."

"And they let you leave?"

It's the obvious question, and when I consider what I went through to get away, a sardonic laugh slips from my lips.

"Fuck no. They knew they fucked up, that I wasn't going to accept what had been happening anymore. They tried to keep me there, with guards at my door. And that night, I left with almost nothing. Climbed down the trellis outside my window and walked to the bus station. I had no idea where I was headed. Just away."

She runs her fingers through my beard, the corners of her mouth turning up into an almost smile. "To this mountain."

I nod, remembering how terrified I was getting off that bus, walking into Jensen's, asking for somewhere to stay. "I grew up out here. Learning how to live like this through trial and error and the generosity of a few good souls like Travis and his wife down the mountain and Jensen in town. They taught me how to swing an axe and so much more. And I prayed no one would ever find me..."

"But someone did..."

I nod. "Ronald. Likely through property records. I registered this land under my mother's maiden name—not exactly the most brilliant plan to hide my identity."

Lyla shifts onto my lap, resting her head against my chest, curling into me like it's the most natural place for her to be. "What does he want you to do?"

"Take down my uncle. Get him removed from Bolton Steel and hopefully arrested for everything he's done."

She tilts her head to look up at me. "How do I fit in?"

Fuck if I know...

When Ronald suggested this cockamamie mail-order bride plan, it was supposed to be a simple business arrangement with a woman who needed some cash. It was never supposed to involve feelings. And it sure as hell wasn't supposed to be a woman who deserves far better than this cabin on this remote mountain occupied by a broken asshole like me.

"We had a plan, but it didn't involve Uncle Marty ever finding out where we were or threatening you. Now, it's too dangerous to go through with it..."

Chapter Thirteen

SILAS

I throw another log onto the fire and watch the flames catch it and climb higher, but the blast of warmth can't help against the icy chill that's settled over the dark night.

What happened today changes everything.

If I hadn't come home when I did...

Panic wells inside me, and I grasp the mantle and tighten my fingers around it, letting my head drop low and eyes drift closed.

I know what Marty would've done to her, how he would've hurt her even worse than he already did.

If I had stayed in town only a few minutes longer...

My gut twists, and I try to shake those possibilities out of my mind before I drive myself insane.

He's ready for us now.

Completely prepared.

He may not have known the trust was still valid, but

once he saw that ring on her finger, he had to at least suspect what we were planning.

I'll be walking into a trap set by a man who gets off on making people suffer—especially me.

The tangled web he's woven over the years threatens to strangle me, and I step away from the fire, shoving my hair back from my face.

Lyla shifts restlessly in a tense sleep, her brow furrowing and eyes darting behind her closed lids.

Of course, she's having nightmares.

How could she not after what just happened, after what I told her?

Now she knows—and it isn't safe for her here or anywhere anymore.

I'll release her from the contract tomorrow. Tell her I'll give her anything she wants. Ten million dollars if that's what it takes for her to leave and go somewhere safe where he can't find her, where he can't threaten her, where he can never *touch* her again, and then, I'll deal with the board the best I can without her.

Even without complying with the trust, they still have the power to elect *anyone* as CEO. It doesn't solve the issue of Uncle Marty actually owning Bolton Steel outright, but it would keep a Bolton in control through a sale. I could, at the very least, ensure the employees are taken care of and that our legacy isn't tainted by what Father and Marty allowed to take place.

Lyla cries out and jerks upright in the bed, panting heavily. Her eyes frantically dart around the cabin until they find me, and I make my way back and climb up beside her.

"It's all right. It was just a dream." A tear streams down

her face as I tug her against me and press a kiss to the top of her head. "I got you."

At least for now.

For a little while, I can try to protect her.

"Try" being the operative word.

She buries her face against my chest and clings to me like I'm the only thing in the world keeping her grounded when really, that's what she's somehow done for me since she arrived.

All I want to do is take away her pain and fear. Lift it onto my shoulders because I'm the one who should carry it.

"You can't let him win." Her words are soft but determined. She looks up at me with her tear-soaked eyes. "We are *not* going to let him win."

Even after what he did to her, she still wants to fight.

"I told you it isn't safe for us to try to go through with the original plan now."

She shakes her head. "I don't care. We're going."

Her resolve makes me appreciate who she is even more. This isn't her fight, isn't her battle, but she's willing to step in and stand at my side, despite the potential consequences.

I lower myself onto my elbow and stretch out beside her, brushing her hair off her temple. "You don't have to do that, Lyla. You're better off going somewhere safe where he can't find you until all of this is cleared up, until he's not a threat anymore."

She reaches up and palms the side of my face. "I'm not leaving you to fight that man on your own, Silas. You didn't give up on me when I was lost in the woods, and I'm not going to give up on you. He may think he's ready for us, but he has no idea who you are now."

"I think I gave him a pretty good idea when I pointed that gun at him."

Her lips twitch. "Maybe. But you're strong enough to go in and do what you need to do. So am I."

Was it really only yesterday she was threatening to leave?

Now, she's not going to allow me send her away, even if it is what's best for her.

"Christ, Lyla. I don't deserve you. Not even close."

A tear trickles across her temple, and I drop my head and kiss it away. The salty taste against my lips brings horrific memories with it of all the tears I shed that never stopped that madman from doing whatever he wanted.

She leans into me, wrapping her arm around the back of my neck and dragging my mouth to hers. The kiss is slow and sweet, unhurried and needy.

It stirs my body to life again when, only moments ago, all I could feel was panic.

My cock presses against her thigh, and she rolls closer to me, crushing her chest to mine.

I try to pull away and stop this before it goes too far, but she clutches me even tighter.

After what she just went through, the last thing I should do is touch her like this, but her hands go to the waistband of my sweatpants, and she shoves at them.

"Lyla..."

Her eyes flutter open and meet mine. "Don't say no because you think you're protecting me, Silas. I need you. I need this."

Fuck.

Like I could ever deny her anything after she said that to me. After she promised to stand at my side, even though I don't deserve it and it's going to expose her to the kind of ruthless evil that shouldn't exist in this world.

I kiss her deeply again, drawing her against me fully as

her hand finally finds my hard cock. The soft, sensual brush of her palm along my sensitive skin makes sparks shoot through me. I groan into her mouth, shifting to grant her better access, and she throws her leg across my hip, dragging my lower body against her despite the barrier still existing between us.

Her frantic need spurs something primal inside me. The desire to give her everything, to make her feel like she's flying away from all the trouble I've created for her.

But I don't have a fucking clue what I'm doing when it comes to women, when it comes to *this*.

It doesn't mean I won't fucking try, though.

I retreat from her and shift to my knees as she rolls onto her back again, watching me expectantly.

In all the years I've lived up here in seclusion, all the nights I spent alone in this bed with my demons, I never dreamed I'd have a stunning, intelligent, frustrating, determined, infuriating woman like Lyla spread out before me, offering herself to me with so much trust and patience and affection in her gaze.

I'll never believe I deserve any of it, but I won't make her beg.

I reach for her shorts and slowly drag them down her legs, exposing her black thong. My eyes zero in on it—so lacy and delicate. Just like the woman wearing it

Beautiful.

Silky.

Soft.

Far too lovely for the likes of me to have my rough, callused hands against her unblemished skin.

I hesitate for a moment, looking at her, that same voice in my brain that always told me to run from anyone who might hurt me, screaming at me to get off this bed before I expose myself.

Lyla lifts her hand and lays it over mine, directing it to the lacy material, dragging me out of my own head and back into the present.

Here.

Now.

I pull on the thin waistband and slide it down her legs, tossing it off the edge of the bed and fully exposing her to me. "Christ, Lyla."

She reaches for the hem of her shirt and tugs it up and off, letting the material fall onto the bedspread beside her. Her breasts peek out from a sports bra she pulls off just as quickly, freeing them and stealing my breath.

My hand shakes as I skim it along her inner thigh, and her body quivers under my touch, goosebumps pebbling on her skin. She opens her legs wider to show me her arousal already glistening at the apex.

She does want this.

Needs it.

Needs me.

No matter how unprepared I might be, how confident I am that I'll probably fuck this up, I have to at least try to give it to her.

I glide my finger through her slick core and over her clit. Her body jerks, her hands clenching the comforter under her.

"Silas." My name comes out like a plea. "Please..."

"I'll take care of you, Lyla."

It's a promise I mean.

I'll do whatever it takes to keep her safe, to make sure she's happy at this moment. As much as I can, I'll try to be the type of man a woman like her deserves tonight, even if it's far beyond my reach.

Shifting back, I drop onto my stomach and press my face between her legs, gliding my tongue through her arousal. Her hips buck as the most delicious thing I've ever tasted floods my mouth. I issue a low groan of approval, and her hands shift from the mattress to my hair, tugging on it sharply.

Fuck.

That shouldn't feel so damn good, but it makes my hard cock ache.

I thrust my tongue into her, savoring her, then slide up across her clit, making her entire body tremble under me violently. Her fingers tighten in my hair, twining around the strands. I have no idea if I'm doing this right, if it's what she wants, or how she likes it. But she shifts her hip slightly, urging me to keep going, and I won't stop until she comes.

One way or another, I'm going to make her forget everything that happened—at least for a few minutes.

I glide my tongue over her, lapping up every drop of her arousal until she's panting and clawing at my scalp.

"Silas..."

Her plea claws at my chest, knowing she needs something I'm not giving her.

"Please, tell me what to do."

She pants and bows her hips up toward me. "Your hand, just—"

It's all she has to say for me to slip two fingers inside her easily. Her head drops back, her mouth opening with a low moan, and I curl them and drag them along the wall of her pussy.

"God, yes. Like that."

Her words come out strangled as she tugs my hair,

holding me in place, and bucks her hips against my face. I lap at her clit while I move my fingers inside her, plunging in and out, trying to draw everything she has out of her.

I shift to sucking on that tight little nub, and her hips bow up so hard that I practically suffocate on the woman's cunt, but as long as she's happy, I could die like this.

She rolls her hips, undulating under me with every flick of my tongue until her pussy tightens around my digits, clamping on them the same way it did my cock the other day. The walls ripple along them as she spasms under me, her mouth falling open on a silent gasp.

I keep going, trying to drag it out and make it last for her, until she finally collapses against the bed and pushes at my head. "Stop. It's too much..."

It is too much.

All of it.

All of her.

Too much for a man as broken as I am to ever keep.

I pull myself back and take her in post-orgasm.

Lips parted. Breaths coming in short, heavy bursts. Pink cheeks. Eyes hooded, watching me, assessing what I'm going to do next.

My cock throbs, my entire body trembling, screaming to get inside her, but I have no intention of giving it what it wants.

———

LYLA

I can see it in his eyes, his desire to pull away, to shut me out again despite what he just did to me.

My heart beats wildly. My blood still rushes in my ears,

and my body tingles from the incredible orgasm he brought me.

Silas may not have a lot of experience with women, but what he lacks in experience, he sure as hell makes up for with his determination to figure it the fuck out.

It's like he knew exactly how to touch me, where to, the right pressure and motion that would set me off. And now, staring into his blazing blue eyes, his hard cock straining against the front of his sweatpants, my pussy clenches, my clits throbs.

I've never needed anyone as much as I do him in this moment, which is somehow equally terrifying and comforting at the same time.

I grab his hand and tug him down onto me before he can pull away or shut down. His solid chest presses to me, his heart beating the same rapid tattoo mine does, and I loop my arms around his neck, burying my hands in his hair. "Don't run away from me again."

Something flashes in his gaze—guilt at being caught. "I wasn't going to."

"Yes, you were." I draw him even closer until our lips are practically touching and his rough beard rubs against my skin. "What are you so afraid of, Silas?"

He palms my cheek, searching my eyes briefly before he answers. "I thought that would be obvious... For so many years, all I knew was fear living in that house. Fear of the people who were supposed to take care of me and love me unconditionally. But now a new kind of terror has replaced it—that I'm going to hurt you, that you're going to wind up hurt in the end."

My heart aches for the sweet, caring man Silas is underneath the rugged exterior. He's fought for so long merely to survive up here, battling against his memories, and now he's about to face an even greater battle and doesn't want me dragged into it. "I'm a big girl, Silas. I can take anything life throws at me—even you."

I shift slightly to press my hips up against his erection, and his eyes drift closed as he lowers his forehead against mine, breathing heavily.

His body tenses, and he shakes his head. "I don't have any idea what I'm doing, Lyla."

He doesn't just mean in bed with me.

Silas is lost in so many ways, but I refuse to let him stay that way. Not when he deserves so much more.

I press a light kiss to his lips. "You're doing just fine."

He chuckles, his chest vibrating against my own. "I feel like a fumbling idiot."

"Definitely not that."

I reach down for the waistband of his sweatpants and snap it against him. He shifts back to shove them down his thighs, freeing his cock. Towering over me, his inked skin on full display, I feather my fingers over the word "*Ruthless*" across his abs.

"Why *Ruthless*?"

His lips curl slightly. "Because that's what Boltons are, and I knew I would have to become that to survive."

"And the pirates?"

"My favorite book growing up was *Treasure Island*."

"You wanted to be Jim Hawkins?"

He nods slowly. "I wanted to be anyone but me..."

The sadness in his words tugs at my heart, and I yank him back down to press my lips to his hungrily—to show him he is exactly who he's meant to be.

He hesitates before returning the kiss and kicking his pants free. His hard cock pinned between us jerks against me, and I adjust my hips to allow his length to slide between my legs, coating it in my release.

Silas groans and lifts his head to drop kisses across my collarbone, up my neck, over my cheek, and finally back to my mouth. Goosebumps travel behind each press of his lips, my body anticipating what's coming. "You need to tell me what you want, what you need if I'm doing something wrong."

I grin against his mouth. "Believe me, I'll tell you."

He issues a little growl of satisfaction and shifts his hips, reaching between us to position his cock at my slick entrance. I lift my hips, giving him a better angle, and he slips the head inside me.

My eyes close as he slowly pushes forward, sinking in. "God, Silas."

His hair falls over his shoulders, and I score my nails down his back, over jagged, rough scars he never wanted me to see.

A low groan rumbles through him, and with a final thrust of his hips, he buries himself fully inside me. "Fucking hell, woman. You feel so incredible."

I squeeze around him, making his body spasm, and he pushes himself up to look down at me as he draws his hips back and eases into me again slowly.

The light from the fireplace coming from the side illuminates his honed physique, so perfectly constructed, like it's hewn out of marble, created by some ancient artist to stand the test of time. But underneath all that and the stunning artwork covering his skin lies the scars. I can still see what made him who he is—a beautiful, broken man I'm somehow now trying to put back together.

If it's even possible...

He starts a slow rhythm of long, deep strokes that are

sure to build my orgasm. It's sweet, almost reverent, the way his hands brush across my exposed skin like he's memorizing every inch of me, as if he'll never see it again.

I reach up and lay my hand over his heart, the rapid thudding proof that he's just as worked up as I am, barely restraining his desire to take things harder and faster.

Knowing what he's pent up all these years, the conflict he's had within himself over his actions and what happened to him, makes tears well in my eyes again.

He needs to let it go, needs to let himself go, needs to forgive himself before we set foot in that boardroom and expose his family's darkest secrets.

"Harder." The word hangs between us, and his thrusts falter slightly as he contemplates my request. "I won't break, Silas. Harder."

He issues a low growl, then drops back down onto me to press his lips to mine again. As his hips increase their pace, our bodies slam against each other, his cock bottoming out deep inside me in the place no one else has ever reached.

My clit throbs, his pelvis grinding against it with each downward drive, and I roll mine to meet his faster and faster as our desperation reaches that frantic point.

He kisses me like he's trying to suck my soul straight from my body, and I'm more than willing to let him take it. I match his fervent movements, and when he drags his head back, the look in his eyes makes me grasp his face in my palms and hold him there before he can glance away.

"We'll figure it out."

Why did I tell him that when I don't even know what I'm talking about?

The board meeting, his uncle, us...

All the above?

I just know he needs the reassurance, the promise that

I'm not going anywhere. He needs someone to be in his corner, to fight with him, to remind him of how strong he is.

He squeezes his eyes closed and leans into my touch, his hips pumping wildly now as the low heat builds between my legs again.

"Fuck." I let my eyes close and feel every inch of him filling me, completing me in ways I never knew a man could.

His thrusts become erratic.

He's close.

He's holding back.

I clench around him on each retreat and open my eyes to watch him go primal.

His neck strained...

Head tossed back...

Long hair flowing down over his shoulders...

He looks so beautiful, his tattoos moving as if they were alive as his muscles ripple and strain with his restraint. My orgasm finally hits me, a sharp burst of heat and electricity sizzling through my body.

I gasp and cling to him, my hips meeting his erratic rhythm. He plunges into me again and again, gritting his teeth until he grows impossibly harder inside me and comes.

Knowing he's found his release drags mine on as he keeps pumping into me even after he's done, until he collapses on top of me, burying his face against my neck, his long, blond hair spilling out across my chest. I brush it back, running my fingers through the silky locks as our hearts thunder against each other.

His hot, warm breaths over my skin make goosebumps pebble over it, and I hold him against me, not caring that the man weighs twice as much as I do, making it hard for me to take a deep breath with his entire body aligning with mine because he needs this, the connection.

He needs me.

I clench around his still-hard cock buried in me, and he quivers. He rolls to the side, taking me with him, then pushes my hair out of my face. I open my eyes and find him staring at me as if I'm something he's never seen before.

"You know, I don't deserve you, Lyla."

An ache forms in the center of my chest, hearing those words out of his mouth. I hate that he thinks he doesn't deserve to be happy. "Yes, you do. You deserve the world, Silas. And once we're done with all this, you can have it."

Something lies deep in his gaze, an uncertainty I don't want to see there, before he drops a kiss on my forehead. "The board meeting is in two days."

"I know."

"We should head into the city tomorrow and get ready."

I bite my lip and nod.

The fear and doubt in his words and the thought of him having to return there is like a bucket of ice water being dumped over my sweat-slicked body. I shiver and press against him more closely, and he wraps his arm around my back, keeping me pinned to him.

"We can do this, Silas. *You* can. I promise."

I never thought I would survive what happened that sent my world crashing down, but I somehow did—and it brought me to him. Through something horrific, I was given this man who cares more than he will ever admit, who wants nothing more than to protect me.

Even after the terrifying interaction with his uncle, I know I would never go back. I would never change my decision to come up here now that I've finally gotten through to Silas.

But there's a tempest brewing on the horizon—dark, sinister, billowing clouds that threaten to unleash a torrent on us.

I hope we're strong enough to survive because I've already promised him we are. And I never break my promises.

Chapter Fourteen

LYLA

I pace the length of the floor-to-ceiling windows that create one entire wall of our hotel suite, casting quick glances toward the closed bedroom door while I wait for my phone call to connect. If Silas comes out and overhears any of this, it will create a whole heap of questions and stress he doesn't need right now.

It was uncomfortable enough for him when we checked in and the manager realized who he was and upgraded us to the penthouse, against Silas' protests that we just wanted the room we had booked this morning.

He doesn't want to be recognized. He doesn't want the attention. And he's about to be thrust into the spotlight again.

I'd be nervous, too.

Someone finally picks up the call, and I watch the door even more carefully to ensure he's still safely out of earshot. "Attorney Fields's office."

"Hi, this is Lyla Sinclair calling."

"Oh, Lyla." His assistant jostles her phone. "Good timing. He just walked in from court. Let me connect you with him."

"Great, thank you."

I chew on my nail as I return on the same path while trying to keep an eye on the bedroom. Normally, I'm not a pacer, but I haven't been able to sit still since we got into town. Silas' anxiety matches my own, not only because of what we face at the board meeting but also because I need an update and need to get it without Silas overhearing anything.

"Lyla, so glad you called." Attorney Fields' familiar voice floats through the line. "I only have a minute before I have to jump onto a conference call, but I do have a little bit of an update for you."

My steps falter, and I stand still for the first time today. "You do?"

"Yes. I spoke to a few people, did a little digging since we last spoke, and I think there's a potential for a quick motion on a few important issues."

I hold my breath for a moment, his words bringing a flicker of hope. "Really?"

"Yes."

"But you said it could take months."

Papers rustle in the background, and I can picture his large desk covered in various files like it was when I met with him in person before coming up here. "I'm not saying it won't, but there are things I can file, tactics we can try that can move things quicker."

"Oh, thank God." A little bit of tension releases from my chest. "That's amazing news."

"I'm still waiting on some paperwork I need to make a

final call on that, but I'll file right away if everything lines up."

The possibility that something *can* be done almost overwhelms the fear I've been harboring for this board meeting, but I can only deal with one situation at a time.

"Do you need anything from me?"

"Not at this time, but..."

The *but* makes me freeze. "But what?"

"But we'll likely need to hire an expert to submit supplemental affidavits to my motion and to testify at any motion hearing."

Dollar signs flash before my eyes the same way they did when Attorney Fields first told me his retainer fee. No one tells you how much it costs when you need a good lawyer—probably for good reason. The numbers alone are enough to put you into an early grave, or at the very least, the poorhouse. Where I, unfortunately, already was.

"Can that come out of the retainer I've already paid you?"

"Unfortunately, as we discussed when we met in person, there's always the potential for additional expenses. The expert's fee is one of them that would need to be paid separately."

Shit. Shit. Shit.

I squeeze my eyes closed and try to suck in a deep breath before I start panicking. The less than $500 I have in my bank account after paying Attorney Fields is unlikely to get me anywhere with the kind of legal expert he's talking about, which means I'm right back to where I started before I signed my contract with Silas. "Okay. Do whatever you have to do, and I'll figure something out to get you any fees."

"All right." His voice softens slightly. "Just keep having faith, Lyla."

"I will."

I end the call, knowing I just told him a lie.

It's hard to have faith when everything seems to be spinning out of control, not only with Silas but now with Attorney Fields needing additional funds I certainly don't have and can't get.

I can't ask Silas for more money.

The terms of the contract were very clear—I don't get anything else for another year, and even if he were willing to give it to me, this *isn't* the time to bring it up to him.

Not when he's about to have a showdown with his uncle.

My gaze drifts down to the very obvious bruises on my forearm from Marty's harsh grip.

It simultaneously feels like weeks ago and only hours ago.

The memory of my fear still as real now as it was then.

I slip my phone into my back jeans pocket and resume my pacing, glancing at the door every few moments for any signs of Silas. It's been well over an hour since he disappeared into the bedroom, saying he needed some time alone. Given how anxious he was the entire drive, I can't help but worry about what he's doing in there and if he's all right.

The man has lived alone for a very long time and isn't used to having someone with him every waking moment. I've been trying to give him his personal space, but I also know how deep Silas can get in his own head. With the board meeting tomorrow, I can't risk him getting lost in there.

I make my way over to the door and knock on it lightly. "Silas, are you all right?" I press my ear against the door, listening for any signs of what he might be doing, but only silence greets me. "Silas, I'm coming in."

My hand shakes on the knob, and I turn it slowly, nudging open the door and stepping into the elegant hotel bedroom. The massive king-sized bed occupies the middle of the large space, and Whiskey lifts his head from where he lies in the middle of it, tail wagging when he sees me. My small suitcase rests on the floor next to it, and the duffel bag Silas threw his clothes in sits beside it.

But there's no sign of him.

"Silas?" His name echoes through the room, and I head for the bed to pet Whiskey. "Where's your dad?"

He tilts his head and looks toward the closed door to the ensuite bathroom.

I walk over to it and knock lightly. "Silas?"

He doesn't answer, but I twist the knob and start to push open the door.

"Don't come in."

Shit.

I stop my advance, with the door only cracked. "Sorry. You didn't respond. I was worried..."

"I'll be out in a minute."

He can't hide the slight panic and hesitation in his voice.

I may not have known Silas for very long, but in the few weeks we've spent together, I've learned to read him better. And right now, he's teetering on a very narrow ledge. It would only take a slight push for him to fall onto the wrong side and send him running home instead of toward what we both know he needs to do.

Sinking down into the chair in the corner of the room, I stare out the window at Pittsburgh laid out before me. I knew how hard this was going to be, coming back to the city where so many horrible things happened to him, but it's only the tip of the iceberg. Tomorrow, he's going to have to set foot in Bolton Steel for the first time since he fled his family.

It's no wonder he needs some space and time alone.

Still, my knee bounces up and down as I wait for him, trying to figure out what he's doing in there that he didn't want me to see.

Whiskey jumps off the bed and comes over, leaning against my leg and resting his head on my lap. I thread my fingers through his fur, rubbing at the spot he loves right behind his left ear.

"What's he doing in there, big guy?"

Knots form in my stomach the longer he stays in the bathroom, but finally, the door opens all the way, and he steps out.

My breath catches. "Silas?"

The man standing in front of me has somehow transformed from the rugged, rough mountain man I first met into something else entirely.

His long, sandy-blond hair that usually falls past his shoulders is now pulled back in a tight bun at the base of his head...

An immaculate black suit covering him instead of his usual jeans or work pants and T-shirt...

A crisp white dress shirt and dark silk tie help conceal his tattoos that would normally be on display, only the slightest hint of ink visible above the collar and on the knuckles and backs of his hands.

I must be gaping at him because the part of his cheeks not covered by his beard redden, and he averts his gaze out the window, tugging at the tie awkwardly. "I look fucking ridiculous, don't I?"

It takes me a moment to regain my ability to think, and I climb to my feet and shake my head, approaching him slowly with Whiskey trailing after me. "No, you look fucking incredible."

The corners of his lips twitch, but he still gives me an incredulous look. "No, I don't."

I walk around him, examining the way the dress pants hang off his tight ass perfectly and the suit coat accentuates his narrow waist and broad shoulders. "Where the hell did you get a suit?"

He releases a sigh. "When we stopped to get gas and you went to the bathroom, I called ahead to the hotel concierge and asked if they could have one waiting in the room in my size. If I am going into that board meeting tomorrow, if I'm really going to do this, I need to look the part, or the board's going to laugh me out of there."

The thought of anyone having the balls to laugh at Silas makes me grin. I may be over his intimidating look, but in this suit, it's impossible not to feel the power the man possesses. Even Whiskey stares up at him with his head cocked sideways, as if he's seeing someone he's never met before and isn't sure how to react to him.

I step in front of Silas and press my hands against the crisp white shirt. "It wouldn't matter if you walked in there in ripped jeans and a fucking flannel, Silas. What you have to say is important enough that what you're wearing doesn't matter."

He raises a brow. "So, I should ditch the suit?"

Laughing, I take a step back and examine him again. "No, I think you should definitely keep the suit."

This time, he returns my grin.

"Really, you look good—kind of what I would've expected the Bolton heir to look like, if you were going for that, minus *this*." I grab his hand and drag my thumb across the tattoos on his knuckles and the top of his hands. "We'll just think of it as added flair."

He releases a heavy sigh and pulls his hand out of mine. "The Bolton Steel board doesn't like flair, and they aren't going to appreciate *this* either." He motions to his long hair, tied back for the first time since we've met. "At all."

"Fuck them." I poke my finger into the center of his chest. "You're here for a reason, a good one. And don't ever forget that you *are* a Bolton. Don't let *them* forget that."

Silas moves over to the window and stares out at the city below us from the top floor of the hotel. "I don't like being back here, Lyla. The closer we got, the more I wanted to turn around and go back to the mountain."

I step up behind him and press my face into his back, wrapping my arms around his waist and squeezing him tightly, wishing I could take some of his pain. "I know, but I knew you wouldn't."

He turns his head to the side to look back at me out of the corner of his eye. "How?"

"Because you're one of the strongest people I've ever met in my life. You're strong enough to do this."

SILAS

I wish I could believe her.

I wish I felt like what she said was remotely true.

But standing here in a suit for the first time in fifteen years, I don't feel strong.

I feel weak, exposed.

Even though every scar and almost every tattoo is

covered, I still feel naked. Like I'm going to walk into that board meeting and every single person in that room is going to see straight through me, is going to pity me when they hear what was done, is going to think that I have no business stepping up in Bolton Steel.

There's every chance this is going to backfire because I'm not strong enough to make it happen. Because I fucked up by running all those years ago when I should have stayed and fought for what I knew was right, even if it would have been a losing battle.

Fuck...

I scrub my hands over my beard and squeeze my eyes closed, wishing I was back on the mountain with Lyla and Whiskey, sitting in front of a fire and forgetting the world outside our tiny piece of it.

Lyla tightens her arms around my waist, hugging me until I finally get out of my own head. Whiskey finally trots over and presses against my leg. I dig my hand into his fur and rest the other over Lyla's, threading our fingers together, Grandmother's ring pressing into my palm.

"I don't know what I'm going to say to them, Lyla."

"You're going to tell them the truth." She squeezes me again, almost like she's trying to give me some of her strength through the motion. "You're going to tell them what you told me."

Acid churns in my stomach at the thought of having to repeat any of that, of having to go into details I couldn't with her. "He'll deny everything..."

"Of course, he will, but that's why we have Ronald."

"I'd feel a lot better if I could actually get a hold of him."

The dozens of calls we've made since we regained phone service after leaving the mountain have gone unanswered. Each time his voicemail picked up, I got more and more nervous. Uncle Marty's threat that he was going to issue the same warning to Ronald as he did me the other day repeats in my head on an endless loop.

I squeeze her hand under mine. "I'd be lying if I said it doesn't worry me that we can't get in touch with him."

"Do you think..." Lyla pauses for a moment, almost like she doesn't want to say what's on the tip of her tongue. "Do you think Marty did something to him?"

My spine stiffens at her question, even though it's the one that's been running through my mind, too. A dozen different scenarios have all popped into my head—some worse than others.

"Possibly. It wouldn't be out of the realm of what he's capable of, or Ronald might have gone to the FBI and gotten taken into custody immediately, either because they're going to charge him or to protect him from Marty."

Lyla nods against my back. "Let's hope it's one of those, right?"

"Yeah..."

Hope.

It's always brought me nothing but disappointment in the past, but since Lyla's arrival in my life, I've started to think it might not be something to fear anymore.

During my entire time on the mountain, the only memories that ever chased me were the bad ones, the ones that had me screaming out in the night and waking up in a cold sweat, the ones that had me sobbing at times and praying for them to go away. But now that I'm here, even though things have changed, seeing the familiar buildings, the park where I used to play lacrosse, my high school, the library, and all the other places I spent time when I wasn't home, not all the memories are bad.

Laughter with friends—who had no idea what was

really happening in my life. Holding hands and kissing and having sex with the few girls I got close to, even while staying mostly clothed because I couldn't undress and have them see my wounds and scars. Escaping that house for a while to play the games kids should, instead of the sinister ones under that roof.

I learned how to hide things while living an outwardly normal life, but now it's time to reveal what was going on behind closed doors. The thought of looking into the eyes of the men and women who have worked with Father and Uncle Marty for so long and telling them everything makes this tie feel more like a noose.

It chokes me, threatens to take my breath and my ability to speak my truth. I reach up and tug at it again, undoing the knot I tied so easily, even after all this time.

Muscle memory is such a strange thing—I wore so many ties and so many suits like this to so many functions in my eighteen years in that house that it all came flooding back to me as soon as my hands touched the silk.

Lyla slips around me, keeping her arms locked around my waist, and stares up, those gold flecks in her eyes shimmering with the same affection that was there last night.

She reaches up and runs her fingers through my beard. "I'm glad you didn't shave this in your attempt to look more clean-cut."

I smirk at her. "Why? You like the beard?"

A grin plays on her lips, and she nods. "I do very much."

"Duly noted."

"And I really do like the suit." She pulls her head back slightly to examine the coat. "They got you sized pretty well."

I nod and roll my shoulders—the fabric is tight and uncomfortable compared to what I normally work in.

"Close enough that it'll work. I should go take this off so it still looks good in the morning."

"You want some help?"

The promise in her question makes my cock stir to life between us. "I would say yes, but I feel like this suit would end up in a pile on the floor and be very wrinkled tomorrow."

She fights a grin and presses her hand over my heart. "You're probably right."

Her gaze darts to the window, and she pulls her bottom lip between her teeth, like she's biting something back.

I tug her back up against me fully. "What is it?"

Lyla returns her attention to me. "I was just wondering if there's anywhere you want to go tonight, a favorite restaurant from when you were a kid, anything you want to see? Should we drive past Bolton Steel or the mansion?"

My spine stiffens again, and the mood instantly shifts. I release a heavy sigh, which makes Whiskey push against me tighter at my side. "You know I own that house now?"

Her brows fly up. "You do?"

I nod. "The trust left the house to me, so Uncle Marty is technically a squatter."

The green in her eyes sharpens. "So, kick him out."

As if it would ever be that easy with him.

Staring down at her, it's impossible not to see her determination and want to believe we will succeed. "Tomorrow."

"As part of the meeting, you make sure it's clear that he's not allowed in that house anymore. I mean, hopefully, the bastard gets taken into custody, right?"

I nod again. "That's the plan."

"So, as soon as that meeting's over, we go to the mansion and we clean out all of his stuff, have a fucking bonfire with it. We eliminate *any* evidence he was ever there. Either he will be in jail, or he'll have to watch all his possessions *burn*."

I contemplate her suggestion.

With everything else going on, I hadn't even thought about going by the house. That place holds the worst memories. It isn't home and hasn't been for a very long time, if it ever really was.

Home is that mountain.

It's those woods.

It's that cabin.

It's the bed I share with Lyla and sometimes Whiskey.

"I'll pay someone to clean it out when the time comes. I don't think I can ever set foot in there again."

She gives me a sympathetic look. "I can understand why you wouldn't want to. I'm sorry I suggested it."

For two centuries, that house held our family. It was the place everyone came for holidays and parties, where Bolton Steel was built into the most successful steel company in the world. But it was also Father's and Uncle Marty's playhouse, where they got away with anything they wanted, where they used and abused people.

"Don't apologize." I press a kiss on her forehead. "I don't want the house. I want nothing to do with it, but I will relish seeing Uncle Marty's face when I take it from him."

I drop my head and bury my face in her hair, clinging to her tightly. That citrusy shampoo scent that always clings to her wafts over me, and I inhale it deeply. "Your hair smells so good."

She laughs against my chest. "Um, thanks?"

I pull back and tilt her chin up. "Really, I love that smell."

She stiffens slightly, and I realize I've said a very important word in kind of a strange context.

All the air sucks out of the room, and she searches my face as if she's waiting for me to say something else, something more.

But I can't.

I don't know if I would recognize love when I never saw it myself. Saying it to her wouldn't mean anything when I don't understand it or know if I'm even capable of it.

All I know is that I wouldn't be here if it wasn't for Lyla. I would've stayed on the mountain, kept hiding, kept trying to forget this life that always haunted me. It's *her* strength that allowed me to get this far and will get me into that board meeting tomorrow.

I capture her face in my hands, tilting her head up. "Thank you."

Her soft brow furrows. "For what?"

"For coming with me."

"Isn't that what I'm supposed to do, be by your side in sickness and health, good times and bad, all that jazz?"

The playful, light way she references our vows makes my heart clench.

What was supposed to be fake has turned real so quickly, but there's still so much I don't know about Lyla Sinclair—like why she needed that money in the first place.

But I don't ask her, no matter how badly I want to know.

I still have my secrets, the worst of what he did to me, that I'll never tell a soul, and I can let her have that one.

Chapter Fifteen

SILAS

Bolton Steel hasn't changed in fifteen years.

The same building towers over me, and the familiar suffocating sense of dread settles on my chest before I've even walked in the door.

As a child, this place was Father's and Uncle Marty's, so I avoided it whenever possible. Each time I was dragged here with them, I spent as much time as possible exploring the hallways and back offices, as far away from them as I could get for as long as possible. This building represented the men I feared, but now, I don't have a choice because Lyla's right. If I don't do this now, Uncle Marty wins, and he will continue to hurt people, putting the company in jeopardy.

Something the Boltons have struggled for and built up for centuries could be gone in an instant with that man at the helm. He would destroy our family name and legacy and continue his reign of terror, and I can't let that happen.

I can't let any of this continue. I have to do what I should have done back then.

End it.

Once and for all.

Lyla loops her arm through mine and squeezes. I shift uncomfortably in the suit, tugging at the neck of the shirt, tight against my throat, for the millionth time since I put it on at the hotel this morning.

"Stop fidgeting when we're in there. Okay?"

I glance down at her. "You make that sound easy."

She gives me a smile that I can tell she isn't feeling because she's just as nervous as I am this morning. The usual confidence in her gaze wavers, but she still stands by my side, shoulders back and head held high, unwilling to let what we're about to do faze her. "I'll be right there with you."

Only a few short weeks ago, it was the last thing I would have wanted, for Lyla to be by my side in there, for her to hear what I'm going to tell the board, but now, I can't imagine going in there without her.

How the fuck did that happen?

Thinking back to when she arrived, I can't deny there was something about her that instantly made what lies at my very core twist. A feeling that she was going to change everything. That my life would be different once we signed that contract. But I never could have dreamed she would be the one to find a way to break through the walls I built around myself and somehow reach a part of me I didn't think lived anymore.

Now, everyone will see what she has—the scars, the trauma, what Marty did, and what Father allowed to happen. And I'm going to have to figure out a way to live with people knowing my darkest secrets and the thing I regret most in my life—running when I should have stayed and *fought*.

I reach into my coat pocket and glance at my phone. "Still no word from Ronald."

"So, do we wait or go in without him?"

Scanning the lot, I don't find any sign of him or his promised support from the FBI.

This would be the perfect time to panic, to turn, climb back into the truck, and retreat to the mountain. To bury my head in the sand once again and leave the people in this building to deal with the ramifications of Uncle Marty's actions.

But I could never look Lyla in the eyes again if I did that.

I release a heavy breath. "We can't wait. We have to go in. The meeting's supposed to start now."

She tugs my arm gently and takes a step toward the doors. "Come on, then."

I roll out my neck and shoulders and slide my hand into hers to walk toward the main entrance of Bolton Steel. The uncomfortable dress shoes pinch my feet and feel foreign after so long in nothing but work boots.

Play the role, Silas.

All of it will be worth it in the end, if this works.

If...

The sliding glass doors open, and I step into the immaculate reception area. Though they've renovated a little over the years, including new Italian marble floors and updated décor, it still looks pretty much the same. So much so that I half expect Victoria, the old receptionist who was always stationed at the information desk down here, to be sitting behind it like she always was when I was a child.

But a young blonde lifts her head as we walk in.

Her eyes immediately zero in on me and drop from my head all the way down to my feet, then come back up. Even though I donned this monkey suit, I'm still out of place here.

Her gaze darts to Whiskey at my side, then to Lyla. And though Lyla is absolutely stunning in her black dress, the woman barely contains a sneer looking at her. "Can I help you?"

I force myself to give her a half-smile. "Yes. I need to confirm where the board meeting's being held this morning." There are any number of conference rooms they could be using, and if Uncle Marty suspects I may show up, he might go out of the way to hide their meeting space from me. "Up on ten?"

The woman's brow furrows. "Yes. How did you know that?"

Anyone walking in off the street wouldn't, since rarely *anyone* who isn't a Bolton executive makes it up to ten, but this woman clearly has no idea who I am.

"Because I own the company."

Her eyes widen, and she reaches for a phone in front of her. "Sorry, I don't know who you are, but you can't go up there. It's a restricted floor—"

"Not for me, it isn't. My name is Silas Bolton. You likely knew my father and my Uncle Marty."

All the color drains from the woman's face, and she dials a number quickly, but I tug on Lyla's hand and drag her toward the elevators before the receptionist can try to stop us.

We're not standing around, waiting for her to warn Uncle Marty or whoever else she might be calling who will try to intervene. Two huge security guards round the corner and block our way to the elevator bank.

Whiskey releases a low growl, sensing the threat immediately, and I hold a hand in front of him to tell him not to move.

The older man eyes me, his gaze dropping to Whiskey briefly before returning to meet mine. Familiar dark eyes narrow. "Silas?"

It takes me a few seconds to remember him, but Barry has been the head of security at this building since I was born. If anyone was going to recognize me despite how much I've changed, it's him. "Hello, Barry. We're going up to ten now."

His jaw hardens, and for a moment, I think we're going to have a serious issue. The man was always loyal to Father and Uncle Marty. A "lifer" who has been with Bolton Steel since his early twenties. They've relied on him forever to prevent unwanted people from getting anywhere in the building, but he steps to the side, motioning toward an open elevator. "I hope you know what you're getting yourself into, kid."

It's the only warning we're going to get, and it's clear Barry knows precisely what Uncle Marty is capable of. He's likely cleaned up more than one mess for him here within these very walls over the decades he's been here.

I incline my head toward him and step into the elevator with Whiskey at one side and Lyla on the other, wrapping my arm around her to keep her close.

She loops hers around my waist and squeezes as she presses the button for ten and the doors slide closed. "Don't forget to breathe."

I'm trying, but my chest is so tight I can barely suck in any air.

Even the smell of the elevator makes me want to run—the "fresh" scent they pipe in here triggers memories I don't want to relive.

I shake my head to try to clear them and breathe through my mouth to stop myself from inhaling any more of the smell. "I never thought I'd be back here."

Lyla rubs my arm. "I know. Just remind yourself you're doing the right thing and that he can't hurt you anymore."

Her words are meant to be reassuring, but we both know they're not true.

Not by a long shot.

Marty has any number of ways to hurt me—to hurt *us*—and we still don't know what the hell happened with Ronald or if anyone's even going to show up to have my back today.

The elevator dings at the tenth floor far too quickly, and the doors slide open to the executive offices where Father and Uncle Marty ran the company my entire life—their ivory tower. They could do no wrong here, their staff willing to do anything and cover up anything to get their payoffs and secure their jobs.

It's the kind of power no man should have—especially one like Marty.

Another receptionist—this one a redhead—sits directly in front of us, and we step out slowly, each of us scanning the elegant space for threats. The redhead's eyes dart to Whiskey briefly as she pulls her phone away from her ear and returns it to the cradle.

"Mr. Bolton..." She stands and walks around her desk, extending her hand to me. "It's nice to finally meet you."

I narrow my eyes on her.

What's with the welcome party?

As soon as they called up from downstairs, Uncle Marty should have tried to put this place into lockdown to prevent me from interfering with the meeting.

Something about this isn't right.

Whiskey senses it, too, his ears perked and his eyes assessing every inch of the space.

I pull my arm from around Lyla to shake the woman's hand, despite the unease crawling up my spine. "Nice to meet you, too. This is Lyla."

They shake hands, but Lyla doesn't say a word. The woman doesn't ask *who* Lyla is, either, almost like she already knows.

She extends her arm, her manicured nails flashing red. "Everyone's already waiting."

Waiting.

It seems Uncle Marty knew we'd be coming despite the threats he issued the other day. That makes this ten times more dangerous. He's already a move, if not two, ahead, and he isn't the kind of man to let you catch up so the game is fair.

Lyla and I follow the receptionist down the hallway, hand in hand, with Whiskey's nails clicking on the tile. The glass-enclosed conference room comes into view, and eight sets of eyes all turn to watch us approach.

The receptionist pulls open the door and ushers us into absolute silence. Uncle Marty sits at the head of the table where Father used to sit, reclining slightly in his chair, arms steepled in front of his lips, though even he can't conceal the smirk that lies under it.

Shit.

Something's very *wrong.*

The other seven board members watch me as I approach the opposite end of the table where Marty used to sit. I pull out the chair and lower myself into it slowly while Lyla takes one in the corner of the room, back away from the table. Whiskey settles next to me, his lips curled back in a low snarl as he keeps his gaze locked on Marty.

Marty lowers his hands, and I catch a peek of a bandage wrapped around his forearm where Whiskey bit him. He leans forward slightly, a sinister grin on his lips. "Silas, how nice of you to join us."

The tension is so thick in the air that you could cut it with a fucking spoon. Each board member darts their gaze between him and me, but no one dares say a word.

They're waiting to witness the showdown, and they aren't about to stick out their necks until they see how things pan out.

Marty raises his good hand. "Should we start the meeting? Since everyone's here?"

I shake my head. "Everyone's not here. We're waiting on Ronald."

Every single board member shifts restlessly, avoiding eye contact with me.

Fuck.

Marty tilts his head slightly. "I'm sorry, Silas. Ronald won't be joining us today. We received the devastating news that he passed away yesterday evening. Heart attack. He went quickly." He *tsks* and shakes his head as that sense of dread that started early threatens to strangle me. "To lose both your father and him in such a short period of time...tragic."

He's trying to get me to back down.

To quit.

To run.

I swallow thickly, the tight tie making it more difficult than normal, then raise a challenging brow at him. "Quite. Let's start the meeting. There is a lot to discuss."

And I have been left hung out to dry.

I don't know if Ronald ever went to the FBI or anyone else with the information he had, nor do I know where he kept it. So, I can't go look for the evidence I'm going to need to support any accusations I make today, even if I manage to hold off any decision from the board.

The only thing I have is my word, and I am going up against a man with more power than God and board members who are loyal to him and Father.

I knew this was going to be a battle; I just didn't realize it was going to be D-Day.

———

LYLA

Watching Silas stare down the piece of shit who brutalized him for so many years and tried to intimidate him to keep him from claiming what's rightfully his while I have to sit off to the side and stay out of it takes every ounce of self-control I have in me.

The man truly is a monster.

He *enjoyed* telling us Ronald was dead.

I saw the gleam of satisfaction in his eyes.

He truly relished watching us as we learned our plan had gone completely to shit and was waiting for us to crumble under the realization that no help was coming.

Now they glare at each other from opposing ends of the long conference room table while the silent board members wait for the fireworks. Whiskey waits, too—for a command from Silas. One word and that dog will launch himself across that table and latch onto Marty's throat like he so badly wants to. And I'd pay to see it.

If I had any money.

But I can't worry about my continued financial woes when Silas has been left hanging without any of the evidence Ronald was supposed to provide or the backup of law enforcement he had promised.

We don't even know if he ever *made* it to the FBI in the first place, but given the smug grin Marty wears, my guess is he made sure nothing incriminating ever saw the light of day. Then he ensured Ronald wouldn't be a problem again. The only reason Silas and I are still alive is probably because he didn't have time to send anyone after us since our little confrontation on the mountain.

Too fucking bad. I would have liked to see him try to come for us again.

It takes a lot for me to hate someone, but I truly *loathe* the silver-haired man sitting in that chair like he's ruling from his fucking throne.

The "king" spreads out his hands over the table. "By all means, Silas, tell the board what brought you down from on high to today's meeting. Typically, we wouldn't allow non-board members in the room, but since it seemed you were intent on attending, we thought we'd make an exception."

From my angle, I can only see half of Silas' face, but I catch the tight smile he offers his uncle. "You know as well as I do that I *am* a board member, and in fact, I am *more* than a board member. I am now half-owner of Bolton Steel, as is laid out in my father's trust documents, which have remained unaltered since my childhood."

The board members shift restlessly in their seats, refusing to meet his gaze, shuffling through papers and folders in front of them rather than have to acknowledge the statement he just made and what it means for everyone in the room.

Marty issues a low chuckle. "There must be some confusion, Silas. I very vividly remember you renouncing your inheritance right before you disappeared, so even *if* what you say is true about the trust, you no longer have any claim to anything in it."

I tighten my grip on the armrests of my chair, waiting for Silas to respond.

He calmly sits back in his chair, resting a hand on Whiskey's head and stroking his fur. "Well, interestingly enough, Ronald assured me that legally speaking, a *verbal* renunciation isn't sufficient. It needs to be in writing." He gives his uncle a cold grin. "Apparently, things said in anger by teenagers aren't binding in court."

Marty's jaw tightens, and a muscle there tics. He clenches a fist on the table.

Yes! Score one point for the good guys.

But the victory is short-lived.

Marty looks to one of the other men at the table and motions for something. The man opens a folder and hands him a single sheet of paper. "What you *said* might not be, but this letter you wrote before you left town is..."

All the air gets sucked out of the room with the statement, and Silas' gaze cuts to me—his blue eyes holding the same confusion rushing through me now.

What letter?

If there had been a letter, Silas would have told me. We would have prepared for this scenario. Ronald would have discussed ways around it—if any—when he prepared the plan with Silas.

Marty motions for Silas to come to take it, and Silas slowly pushes his chair back and rises, making his way down the long table with sure, steady steps I certainly couldn't take right now with the way my knees are shaking.

Whiskey watches his every move but remains in his place beside the vacated chair, ready to move if he needs to in order to protect his master.

When Silas reaches the other end of the table, his uncle holds it out for him, and Silas snatches it from his hand and immediately reads it.

His eyes narrow, his mouth pressing into a thin line, knuckles whitening the more he reads. "I didn't write this." He holds it up so everyone in the room can see it and points to the short, three-sentence text and signature. "This is a forgery."

A sneer twists Marty's lips. "Not according to the court. I filed a copy with them yesterday, in reference to the trust, in case there was any question as to whether or not you would inherit under it."

The anger that's been building since the moment that man stepped foot onto the mountain boils in my blood until I can't stay silent anymore. "You lying bastard!"

Everyone's eyes dart over to me, and Marty offers a sinister smile.

"Lyla, my dear. So nice of you to join us today."

Silas immediately closes the distance between him and his uncle and grabs his shirt, lifting the smaller man straight from his chair easily. "You don't fucking talk to my wife. You don't *look* at her. And you sure as *hell* never *touch* her again."

Whiskey gets to his feet, his snarl ripping through the room, matching that of his master.

Marty holds up his hands in surrender, but that same little grin plays on his lips that tells me that he has something else up his sleeve besides the bandage. "Such violence, Silas. Is this really the way you handle yourself? It isn't a very good look for a Bolton." His eyes roam over his nephew. "Though, apparently, your appearance hasn't been a concern for you for a very long time..."

Silas releases him and retreats, his hands fisted at his

sides. He backs away from his uncle toward me until he's standing next to me and can tug me up against him. Whiskey shifts over to us and sits directly in front, creating a protective barrier against the man who clearly has an agenda today.

"I didn't come here to threaten you, Uncle Marty." Silas' voice comes steady and calm despite what just happened. "I came to tell the board the truth about you and to take what's rightfully mine."

The low chuckle that falls from Marty's lips fills my veins with ice. "The truth about *me*?" He scans the board members, who still sit in utter silence, too afraid to speak or move. "I'm not sure what you're referring to, Silas, but I can assure you, this board doesn't want to hear your wild accusations. They have no bearing on anything related to Bolton Steel, and you have no say in anything having to do with the company, even if you complied with the trust terms, since you've renounced your inheritance."

He lifts the letter and shakes it smugly.

"I'm afraid you've wasted your time driving into town today, Silas. Why don't you head out so we can continue this meeting with the legitimate board members?"

Silas stiffens, the rage he's barely containing making him so tense he feels like he might shatter beside me. "No. I won't leave until the board has heard what I have to say." He takes a step closer to them. "First and foremost, know I did *not* write that letter, something I am confident I can prove to any competent, *unbiased* court that should review the issue, and I *am* in compliance with the trust requirements."

His warm gaze falls on me, and the smile I never thought I'd get from the man pulls at his lips.

"This is my wife, Lyla, and I'm prepared to fight for my

father's share of this company, what's rightfully mine, as a Bolton."

Marty pushes his chair back and rises abruptly, releasing a sardonic laugh. "Your *wife?*" He takes a few steps around the table and holds out his hand to another board member, who pulls a few papers from a folder and gives them to Marty. "Lyla Lynn Sinclair..."—his gaze cuts to me, the pure joy he got out of what he did to me gleaming there—"my, my, my, aren't you an interesting addition to this story?"

Oh no...

Acid climbs my throat, and I swallow it down before I gag on it.

He keeps reading, flipping through several pages before raising his eyebrows. "Well, look at *this.*" Turning the sheet toward the room, he wanders back to his chair. "You accepted a bank transfer in the amount of $50,000 from my nephew the day *before* you two got married." He sneers. "I wasn't aware there were hookers who were good enough to warrant *that* price."

I can practically see the steam coming from Silas' ears as he struggles to keep from lunging at his uncle and strangling the life out of him right in front of all these people. Only an iron will keeps him from doing just that. He flexes his hands at his sides and reaches out for me.

Sliding my palm into his, I allow him to tug me into his side.

"Lyla is my *wife.* I offered her a wedding gift. That's all it is. And if you ever call my wife a hooker again, I will ensure you will regret it."

Marty only grins at Silas' threat. "Violence again." He spreads out his hands. "Is this the type of person you want involved in running the company?" He looks at each board member. "A mentally unstable, tattooed, violent man who paid a woman of questionable moral character to marry him so he could come in here to try to take what is rightfully mine?"

I've—mostly—remained silent, to allow Silas to handle his business on his own because it isn't my place to intervene, and he certainly doesn't need my help. But I can't stand by any more listening to Marty's bullshit without defending myself and Silas.

Looking at each board member, I try to present our truth in the most sincere way possible. "Silas and I may have met in an unusual way, but I can *assure* you, I am *not* a hooker, nor am I of 'questionable moral character' as this man suggests. If anyone here is, it's *him*."

Marty barks out a laugh, shaking his head, then grabs the papers from the table and flips to another page. "Lyla, where did the fifty grand go?"

Oh hell...

My stomach drops, and my hands start trembling.

Silas wraps his arm around my shoulder and lowers his head, brushing his lips to my ear. "You don't have to tell them anything."

One of Marty's silver brows rises. "Lyla? Where did it go?"

You don't have to tell them anything.

Each pair of eyes in the room is on me now, and I shake my head. "I'm not telling you that. It's none of your business what I do with a gift from my husband."

Marty releases a little chuckle. "Oh, but it is, sweetheart. It *is* my business when your husband is trying to take *my* company while he's married to a gold-digging whore who is using his money to try to get a murderer out of jail."

No. No. No.

All the air rushes from my lungs.

I struggle to take a breath.

Each one comes shorter and harder.

"Lyla, what's he talking about?" Silas' voice echoes, like he's talking to me down some long tunnel. "Lyla?"

It wasn't supposed to go like this...

We were supposed to tell the board about *Marty*.

How did this end up about me?

Darkness creeps into the edges of my vision.

I waver on unsteady feet.

"Lyla?"

This is all wrong.

All of it.

I never should have come here.

My knees give out, and a strong arm wraps around my waist, supporting my weight.

Then the world goes black.

Chapter Sixteen

LYLA

Something cold and wet nudges my cheek, and I press against Whiskey's familiar thick fur and try to push him away. I roll my head to the side to avoid the slobber surely coming from his usual routine when he decides it's time for me to wake up.

I groan. "Whiskey, stop it."

He shifts against me, and I turn in the bed, snuggling back down under the covers and tugging them over my head so he can't keep trying to get me up.

Wait...

My eyes snap open, and I sit upright, my head spinning slightly. I press my hand against my temple, scanning my surroundings and trying to get my vision to clear.

The elegant bedroom in the suite slowly comes into focus.

How the hell did I get back to the hotel?

My eyes land on Silas sitting in the chair in the corner of the bedroom where I waited for him when he had locked himself away in the bathroom yesterday. He's still in his black dress pants and white dress shirt, but he's removed the jacket and tie, the top three buttons now open, exposing several inches of his tattooed chest.

His hair falls free over his shoulders, released from the confines of the tight bun he had it in during the board meeting.

Sharp, icy-cold eyes lock on me.

"How are you feeling?" His voice comes low, filled with concern and something else—an edge of anger.

"I'm..." I take stock of my body, and everything seems okay except for the slight spinning in my head. "All right, I guess. How did we get back to the hotel?"

The last thing I remember was being in the conference room, furious at the bullshit Marty was trying to pull, and getting hammered with questions about the money...

Shit.

No wonder Silas looks so pissed.

He watches me with cool contempt in his gaze. "You fainted. One of the board members is a doctor. He checked you over and said you were fine, likely just dehydrated and stressed. He told me I should let you rest but to take you to the emergency room if you had any other symptoms..."

Acid crawls up my throat, and I fight the gag reflex that makes me want to leap from this bed and go retch in the toilet. "Shit...Silas, I'm so sorry. I..."

He squeezes his eyes closed and shakes his head, holding up a palm to me. "Please don't...I can't..." His Adam's apple bobs with his thick swallow. "I can't right now."

What happened in that conference room shook him badly, so much so that he's teetering on that edge again, about to lose his grip on his tightly held control.

"What happened with Marty? The meeting?"

A deep, aching sense of dread settles over me, waiting for his answer.

Marty wasn't going to let us win that battle, so there's no way Silas walked away unscathed. What might have happened after I passed out makes my gut twist.

His eyes flicker open. "Well, you almost face-planting on the floor kind of ended it. I told the board that they owed it to my father, to me, to hear everything I had to say without Marty's interruptions and diversions into issues that have nothing to do with the company, and I *somehow* got them to agree to hold off on making any decisions until next week."

The vise crushing my chest releases a little of its grip. "So...you bought us some time."

"*Us?*"

I've never considered how much such a tiny, seemingly insignificant word can mean, but the way he says it, with so much uncertainty and accusation, makes me cringe.

"Silas...it isn't what you think."

He pushes up from the chair and slowly approaches me, towering over the edge of the bed, his jaw locked, muscles in his neck straining, tattooed hands fisted at his sides. "Who is he?"

"Who's who?"

The fog still enveloping my head is taking far too long to clear because I have no idea what the fuck he's talking about. He stares at me like I should know exactly what he's asking, but my brain can't seem to process it.

A low growl rumbles in his chest. "Who. The. Fuck. Is. Joey. Danvers?"

Shit.

I squeeze my eyes closed.

Of course.

Of course, he knows his name.

Marty seems to always be one step ahead, to have information he shouldn't, to be able to take things that should be innocuous and twist them into something he can use to drive a stake through someone's heart.

Silas sucks in a sharp breath, like he's preparing himself for something that's about to be excruciatingly painful. "Is he your boyfriend?"

My spine stiffens, and I shake my head, fighting the tears welling in my eyes. "God, no, Silas. I told you; it isn't what you think."

"Then fucking *explain* it to me because right now it looks like you married me to get your murdering boyfriend a fucking lawyer." He flexes his fists at his sides, his nostrils flaring. "I had to stand there in front of the board of my father's company and ask them to trust me, to wait and to listen to what I had to say when my wife is bringing that kind of toxic, media suicide bullshit into the picture—"

"Please let me explain..."

He shoves his hands back through his hair and starts pacing, the tension ratcheting up in the room so much that Whiskey lifts his head from the bed and watches him from beside me, just as worried as I am.

It's finally time to tell him everything.

No matter how badly I may not want to.

No matter how much it will hurt.

"He isn't my boyfriend, Silas." I inhale deeply, then release it slowly, preparing myself for what I'm going to have to reveal to the man who has already been through the wringer and then some. "He's my brother."

Silas' steps falter, and he freezes, looking over his shoulder at me. "Your brother?"

I nod, picturing the sweet, innocent baby Joey once was, which only makes the tears already threatening finally fall. "My mom never really knew my dad. All he ever gave me was some DNA and his last name before he disappeared. She had my brother when I was thirteen, and she died in a car accident when I was nineteen. He was six, about to be seven, and I couldn't let him go into foster care...so I petitioned the court to become his legal guardian."

Silas turns to face me fully, his eyes widening. "At nineteen?"

I offer a half-shrug. "I had graduated high school the year before. I was waitressing and could barely take care of myself. But somehow, I managed to take care of him, too."

Barely.

It was a shitshow.

Even I can admit that.

I had no business trying to raise a child when I was still one myself. Despite legally being an adult, I was drifting, trying to find my place in the world, attempting to figure out what I wanted to do with my life. Because it sure as hell wasn't waitressing.

But Mom's death changed everything.

It shifted my priorities.

What I wanted and dreamed of didn't matter anymore —all that did was that little boy who had lost his mom and only had me.

Silas watches me expectantly, waiting for me to continue. "What happened, Lyla?"

My body starts trembling, and I wrap my arms around my knees. Whiskey shifts up and rests his head across my arm, looking at me like he can sense the anxiety building up by having to talk about this.

"About a year ago, I got him a job part-time at the

restaurant I worked at. I waitressed. I bartended. I did whatever they needed me to do. He bussed tables and helped back in the kitchen with some food prep stuff." I look up at him. "He's a good kid, Silas. *Really*."

"So, how did he end up with murder charges?"

I squeeze my eyes closed and drop my forehead onto my knees, the memory of that night so vivid, it threatens to steal my breath the same way Marty's inquisition did in that conference room. "It was close to closing time. We were both working the late shift. Only the two of us were left, and a handful of customers. One of them was a regular...a guy I was friendly with..."

Reluctantly, I lift my head and find Silas watching me carefully, the tension returned to his body.

"I don't normally drink during work hours. But that night..."—I suck in a deep breath and release it—"he asked me to have one with him at the end of my shift."

If only I had said no.

If only I had been smart enough to see what was happening.

"I did." The feeling that overtook me that night hits me again, making the room spin around me. "After a little while, I got a little dizzy. By then, the other patrons left, so it was just me and *him,* and my brother was in the back. He...*shit*..."

I clench my eyes closed and shake my head, my body trembling.

"He tried to grab me. I managed to scream for Joey, and he came out of the kitchen. I could barely keep my eyes open...the room was spinning. I knew he had slipped something into my drink, but I couldn't tell him what was happening."

The sheer terror I felt that night hits me full-force,

making me almost double over on the bed, pressed up against Whiskey. "Joey hit him over the head with a glass bottle from the bar, and the guy took a swing at him. But Joey punched him, and he fell back and smacked his head against the bar."

Silas winces.

"When I came to, Joey was sitting on the floor, crying, and the other guy was dead. Police were all around us. I didn't remember the fight. I didn't actually *see* it, or if I did, the drugs wiped my memory of it. I couldn't back up anything Joey told them..."

"There were no cameras?"

I shake my head. "The place was a dive, old school. They didn't have anything like that."

Silas approaches the bed slowly. "So, they arrested him and charged him with the guy's death?"

Tears stream down my face, that same feeling of helplessness I had then overtaking me now. A sob escapes my throat, and I nod. "They said it was murder, but he was just protecting me."

I try to take a deep breath, but all I can do is gasp helplessly, unable to draw enough air into my lungs. Silas closes the distance to the bed and sits next to me, pulling me into his arms.

His familiar scent that somehow still clings to him, despite the fact that we aren't on the mountain, fills my breaths and helps relieve some of the panic starting to overcome me.

He rubs his hand along my spine. "When was this?"

"A few weeks ago. It took them a while to assign him a public defender. He's only seventeen, but that makes him an adult for criminal charges. He could go to prison for the rest of his life. I met with his court-appointed attorney once, a few days after he was arrested, and the guy said it was a slam dunk case for the state because all the evidence showed he had attacked the guy. There were no signs of self-defense—"

Silas stiffens. "What about the fact that you were drugged?"

I shake my head. "They never tested my blood. By the time Joey called the police, I was already waking up and they didn't believe him. There was no proof of our story."

A growl of disapproval vibrates Silas' chest. "It sounds like the cops fucked up."

I sniffle and nod. "I know, and that attorney wasn't going to do shit for him. I knew I needed to find a good one."

"Which is why you needed the $50,000."

The resignation and understanding in his voice finally allow me to relax against him. Keeping it from him all this time has weighed on me more than I ever realized, and I nod against his chest. "I needed the retainer fee."

Silas runs his fingers through my hair softly. "Christ, why didn't you tell me any of this, Lyla? I would have given you the damn money, and you wouldn't have had to go through with this sham marriage."

His words make me stiffen, and I lift my head and meet his gaze. I know he didn't mean it like that, but his words still slice straight to my heart.

"I didn't know you, Silas. You didn't know me. You were going to give a total stranger $50,000? You told me you didn't want to take the money in the first place..."

His jaw hardens as he looks at me, and he takes my face in his palm and brushes away my tears. "You should have told me. Maybe not that day, but you should have told me eventually. Those phone calls?"

"To the attorney. I can't even talk to Joey because he can

only make collect calls from the jail where they're holding him, and we didn't have phone service on the mountain."

"Christ..." He presses a kiss to my forehead. "I am so sorry, Lyla. The last thing you need is all this bullshit with my family when you're dealing with all this. I never should have brought you into it, exposed you to Marty, and allowed him to use your personal trauma against you."

"No." I shake my head. "It's my fault for not telling you. But I was worried that you'd see it the same way Marty does, the same way the board might, that it would stop you from going through with the ceremony and giving me the money if you knew what it was for because it could look so bad, you being associated with someone charged with murder..."

"Fuck, Lyla." His eyes drift closed. "Everything is so fucked up." He drops his head back against the headboard and closes his eyes, pulling me down onto his chest and holding me tightly. "What the fuck are we going to do?"

———

SILAS

Jesus, I'm a fucking asshole.

I've been sitting here, pissed off at her, thinking the worst, imagining a hundred different scenarios for who he might be and why she would've hired a goddamn attorney for somebody accused of murder.

For a split second, I even thought maybe she was a scam artist—a *really* fucking good one—and that I had let myself get taken, when she is just a caring big sister who wants to help her brother after he saved her from something horrific.

What the fuck does that make me, besides the biggest asshole who ever lived?

I clutch her to me tightly, burying my face in her hair, inhaling her scent that usually calms me so easily. Not this time—because I *really* fucked up. "Please forgive me, Lyla."

It takes a few seconds for her to respond, and she traces her fingers over the tattoos peeking out of the V of my shirt. "For what?"

"For ever doubting you for a fucking second..."

Because I did.

I never would have asked her what she did with the money because there are things I never want to tell her, either, but as soon as Marty said she had hired an attorney for a murderer, my head immediately went to the worst-case scenario.

How could I ever doubt her?

Lyla wraps her arms around me and squeezes me tightly, pressing a kiss to my bare chest. "Don't apologize. I doubted you, too, in the beginning. I thought you were exactly what you appeared to be. I believed the same thing that everybody in town did about you, what you *wanted* them to think. It took me a while to see who you really were, and I'm sorry for that."

I can't be mad at her confession.

Not when it was exactly what I wanted.

Everything I've done since I left here was to push people away, to keep everyone who might *try* to get within reach from ever getting anywhere close enough to hurt me.

And now Lyla is far too close.

She could hurt me worse than Marty ever did, and for that one moment, I believed her capable of it.

This woman is far too good for me, but I'm too selfish to

let her go now that I have her in my arms, trailing her soft fingers over my scarred skin so reverently.

Gazing up at me, she searches my eyes for an answer I don't have. "What do we do now?"

I release a long, heavy sigh that doesn't even touch the level of uncertainty consuming me and go over the question again, the same one I've been asking myself for the last hour while I sat in that chair and waited for her to wake up. "I don't know. I would say we try to get a hold of Ronald's secretary and his wife to see if he left anything for us anywhere. Try to determine if he ever got a hold of any of the law enforcement contacts he had mentioned."

"You and I both know he never did, right? Or if he did, Marty found a way to stop it."

That's what I'm afraid of.

And if she thinks the same, then it's probably true.

Uncle Marty was too smug, too cavalier today. He knew I wasn't going to have shit to back up anything I said— because he made *sure* it didn't exist.

Lyla shifts slightly, pushing herself up. "What if there's other evidence?"

"What do you mean?"

I brush a strand of hair behind her ear, and she tilts her head into the touch.

At this moment, I'd give anything to be able to kiss her senseless. To wash away the trauma of the day on a wave of ecstasy that would bring both of us to a place where we could just be *us* without the endless complications and painful truths.

But that's impossible.

Still, Lyla looks at me with so much hope. "Well, you said there were payoffs made, right? Other victims. What if you could locate that paper trail or some other sort of written documents?"

I shake my head. "They were too careful to keep that stuff. Ronald said he was supposed to destroy it, and I know Marty did when he realized what Ronald was up to."

"Yeah, but how do you *know*?" The gold in her eyes sparkles. "How do you know Ronald didn't hide a copy somewhere for us? You said he already suspected Marty was onto him when you two spoke on the phone, right?"

I nod slowly, trying to follow her reasoning. "Yeah."

"So maybe he hid it. Maybe he put it somewhere only *you* would find it because he knew he wouldn't be able to get to the FBI and there was no way to get back in touch with you on the mountain once you came back to the cabin..."

"That's a huge maybe, Lyla."

She shifts, pushing herself up farther, the fatigue written all over her face and in her eyes, the same bone-deep exhaustion I feel after today's meeting. "But how do we know unless you *look*?"

I run a hand over my beard, contemplating the millions of possible places he could have left something. "I wouldn't know where to begin, Lyla. I haven't been here in fifteen years. I don't even know where Ronald lives anymore."

There's so much I'm in the dark about. So much has changed since I've been gone. Running didn't solve anything. All it did was put me at a tremendous disadvantage in trying to return and do what I should have from the beginning.

Lyla places her hand over my heart. "I don't think he would've put it somewhere that's important to *him*. He would've put it somewhere you would look, someplace that was important to *you*, before you left."

For most people, dozens of locations would come to mind immediately. But for me, those dark memories connected with my life here cloud my ability to think of a single place I would ever *want* to go back to, let alone one Ronald would have known about.

Still, what she suggests makes sense as something he might have done as a last-ditch effort to salvage our plan. "I guess it's possible. Maybe."

"If he managed to hide the evidence for us, where would he have put it?"

I stare at the ceiling, trying to put myself in Ronald's shoes if I knew Marty was coming for me. "Somewhere I'd have to have access to."

She grasps my beard and tugs on it gently until I dip my head and lock eyes with her again. "The house."

Of anywhere in this city, it's the last place I want to go—where the worst memories and most dangerous demons still reside.

I swallow through my suddenly dry throat. "Marty lives there."

"Actually, that probably makes it the safest place to hide something because Marty would never suspect it, right?"

"Shit." I scrub my hands over my face and groan in frustration. "We should have thought of this potential and planned ahead better before Ronald left Millsburg."

"I know." Lyla tugs on my wrists until I pull my hands away to look at her again. "We have to go to the house. Try to think of any place to look where he might've left it for you. And then we do what Ronald couldn't. We take him the fuck down and make sure he stays there."

The absolute determination and confidence in her words and the passion vibrating through her almost make me believe it's possible.

I take her face in my palms again, dragging her up until I can press my lips to hers. "I know you hate when I say this, but I don't deserve you, woman, not even a little bit. Today fucking proved that."

She rests her forehead against mine, crumpling against me. "You have to keep reminding yourself that that isn't true. You've been good to me, Silas. You've protected me. You've made it possible for me to take care of my brother. You've taken care of me. Since my mom died, no one else has ever done that." A little sigh slips from her lips. "I basically had to become a mom to Joey, and I never got the chance to do any of those things that nineteen-year-olds are supposed to. I was busy making him dinner and running him to school and Boy Scouts and soccer and all the things I thought he needed to try to have a normal life."

"That explains why you're such a fucking good cook."

Her light laughter breaks some of the tension in the room. "That was from years of working at restaurants, being back in the kitchen, helping out when I needed to. My brother mostly lived on frozen chicken nuggets."

I chuckle and press another kiss to her lips. "That sounds super healthy."

She grins. "He's in shockingly good shape, considering his diet as a child."

Almost instantly, her smile falters, and the tears well in her eyes again.

"You're worried about him…"

She nods, trying to fight back a sob. "He's in jail. I haven't talked to him in weeks since I came up the mountain. I don't have any idea what they're feeding him or if he's okay in there with all those criminals. I'm confident he's terrified, and he doesn't belong there."

I know absolutely nothing about the kid, but I know

enough about Lyla to be confident that she would have raised him right. Every single word she told me about what happened is the truth. I didn't have to be there and witness it with my own eyes to believe it. And I'm not going to let her brother suffer for doing the right thing when I didn't do it at his age like I should have.

"We'll get him out, Lyla, I promise. We'll call the attorney tomorrow—"

"I spoke with him when we got here yesterday." She sniffles and swipes at her eyes. "He said he thinks he might be able to file a motion, but we will likely need an expert, and—"

"And what?"

"Nothing." She starts to pull away. "Nothing. Forget it."

I tug her back against me, refusing to allow her to put any distance between us when I already did that today. "No, Lyla, no more secrets between us."

Fear fills her gaze, but I hold her steady, not letting her look away.

"He said he might need an expert to testify at the hearing. I don't even know what kind of motion it is yet because he didn't get into specifics, but experts cost money I don't have."

Christ.

An hour ago, if I had heard her say she needed more money, I would have immediately leaped to the worst conclusion, but I easily brush aside that knee-jerk reaction this time.

Because I didn't misjudge her.

I saw exactly who she was from the beginning.

It terrified me and still does.

But I *saw* her and her true nature that shines so brightly. Now, I don't know how I could have ever doubted it.

"I'll pay for whatever he needs."

The tears stream down her face, and she closes her eyes and shakes her head. "No, Silas, I can't take anything else from you, not now, not like this, not when—"

"Look at me, Lyla." I wait until her eyes lock with mine. "You're my *wife*. I don't care how we ended up here or what your reasons were for coming up that damn mountain. I'll take care of you. I'll take care of your brother. You don't even have to ask."

Her bottom lip trembles as she stares at me with so much trust and affection that I almost have to look away. "You're too good to me, Silas."

She leans in and kisses me deeply, pouring all the emotion we've both felt over the last few hours into the gesture. Her hands clutch the lapels of my shirt, almost frantically tugging me against her.

For the first time in my life, I need someone as badly as they need me, maybe more, and that makes what we're about to do even more terrifying.

Chapter Seventeen

SILAS

For the second night in a row, I lie awake. Staring at the unfamiliar ceiling of the penthouse suite I never wanted, in the city I tried so damn hard to stay away from, wishing it were the rough-hewn logs of the cabin that have stood tall over my bed for so many years.

Sleep eludes me, or maybe I'm actively fighting it because I know what closing my eyes will surely bring.

Being back in Pittsburgh, in *that* building, confronting Uncle Marty, and seeing he's as smug and volatile as ever, has released my demons from the place Lyla managed to corral them for a short while.

They've broken free to run amok inside my head, threatening to overwhelm me and force me to shut down completely to ensure they don't hurt me even more.

Every scar on my body aches and burns, constant reminders that the man we're up against is capable of the worst and more than willing to do it for his own pleasure.

That arrogant sneer that twisted his lips flashes before my eyes.

The feel of his hands on me makes my skin crawl.

And then the pain comes again.

I rub at the scar on my chest left by the hot fireplace poker he pressed to it while he wore that sinister grin of his, getting off on hurting someone smaller and weaker than him. A pirate galleon now covers it, the thick central mast aligned to the marred skin in an attempt to conceal the red, tight, shiny souvenir he gave me from any prying eyes.

A vain attempt to hide what was done to me—just another way to run from it instead of doing something about it.

Lyla rolls closer to me, pressing her hand over mine, stopping me from obsessively brushing my fingers along the raised ridges of one of the worst scars. "Why aren't you sleeping?"

Whiskey's snores fill the room from where he crashed in the chair earlier tonight—finally relaxing once he was assured Lyla and I were both all right. At least, for the moment.

I wish it were that easy for me.

To let go.

To believe that things will be okay.

To relax.

But I can't do either.

"I'm too amped up to sleep..."

Lyla rests her chin on my chest next to our hands and looks up at me with concern darkening her gaze. "Amped up, worried, or nervous?"

Leave it to her to call me out.

"All the above." I huff out a sigh. "I don't even want to think about going back to that house, about stepping foot in there, but I've had to all night. I've been trying to think of every room, each potential hiding spot. Anywhere Ronald could have left something for us before he met his untimely demise. It's definitely not doing anything to help me sleep."

She plays with my beard gently. "Stop thinking about it."

I snort a laugh, and my chest bounces under her.

A grin plays on her lips. "I knew it sounded stupid as soon as I said it."

Rubbing my palms into my eyes, I release a groan, feeling every bit as exhausted now as I usually do after working all day on the homestead—a job I left in Travis' capable hands while we are gone so I won't worry about the animals. "I feel like I haven't slept in days..."

Lyla squeezes my hand. "Because you *haven't*. But you're going to need some rest for what we're doing tomorrow."

"I know." I drop my hands and slowly drag my fingers down her spine, making her shiver against me. "I'm trying."

She presses a kiss to my lips softly. "Let me help you relax."

I am about to ask her what she means when she slips down my body and her hand finds my cock, hardening it almost instantly.

Oh, hell.

After the day we've had, sex was the last thing on my mind tonight when we climbed into bed. Even with her naked body pressed to mine, I just wanted to hold her, to be able to feel that she was safe and all right.

"Fuck." I shake my head. "Lyla, you don't have to—"

"I know." She keeps her eyes locked on me as she shifts between my legs and lightly flicks her tongue across the head of my cock. "I want to."

Sweet mother of God.

I clutch the comforter in my hands as little electric shocks shoot through my body, the promise in her voice enough for me to know what's coming. Lyla offers me a knowing grin before she slowly wraps her mouth around me and sucks me down.

Fuck...

Gritting my teeth, I shift one hand into her hair, the thick, silky locks catching on the rough, work-hardened skin on my palms. She swallows, and the head of my cock brushes the back of her throat, making my hips buck, driving me even deeper.

"Shit..."

I didn't mean to do that—to force myself down her throat and almost choke her—but she moans her approval around me, the vibration making my balls tighten and my entire body tense.

She slowly pulls her head back, letting her lips drag along every inch of me until I'm trembling and my hold on her hair must be painful. It doesn't seem to faze her at all because she doesn't stop. Doesn't seem at all affected by my iron grip.

Lyla just glides my cock back into her mouth, her tongue sliding along the underside and flicking right at the back of the head.

Holy shit.

The room spins, my eyes unable to focus, the feelings consuming me new and overwhelming in the best way. Something I never could have imagined in my wildest dreams, even when they started including this woman.

I am not going to last ten fucking seconds with her doing this, and she seems to know that. She wraps her hand around the base of my cock and strokes on every retreat, working me with her smooth palm while she licks and sucks and drives me absolutely fucking insane.

It doesn't matter how many times she tells me...

It isn't true—I do *not* deserve this woman.

Not even a little bit.

At all.

The pure ecstasy flooding my veins only gets heavier, harder to process any thought through, as she increases her pace and suctions around me even tighter.

"Fuck!" I grit the word out through clenched teeth and lift my head from the pillow to watch her better.

Seeing my cock disappear into her mouth starts a low tingle at the base of my spine. Heat floods my body, and I'm only seconds away from blowing.

I tug on her hair to try to get her off before I come, but she shakes her head and redoubles her efforts, ensuring there's no way or time for me to pull away. My orgasm blasts through me, and I squeeze my eyes closed, bright lights flashing against my lids as wave after wave of pleasure courses through every nerve in my body and I shoot my load down her throat.

The warm contraction of her swallowing against the head of my cock only seems to draw it out of me harder. My hips bow up, shoving me deeper, and she keeps going, sucking me down like she can't get enough.

My body finally jerks one last time before I sag back against the mattress, completely fucking spent.

Lyla pulls back off my cock, giving it light, little licks that make me twitch before she works her way back up and spreads out across me, her bare breasts pressing to my chest.

She kisses me deeply, the taste of my release still on her tongue, and it might be the hottest thing I've ever experienced. Her already slick core rubs along my still-hard cock, and she rolls her hips against me, making a low groan slip from my lips as I tighten my arms around her.

Her fingers twine in my hair. "Feel better?"

"Fucking hell, Lyla. What the fuck was that?"

Little jolts still sizzle through me as she places an almost chaste kiss on the corner of my lips.

"Me trying to take your mind off everything."

"Well, it fucking worked."

Having her in my arms like this, having her touch me like that, makes everything else disappear. All the worry. All the doubts. All the complications we're sure to face.

Though, I know it won't be for long.

We can only ignore what waits for us for a few more hours. And I'm going to savor every single moment I have with her, the same way I do her taste, while I let her know how much I fucking need her.

This woman has taken a broken, scarred man intent on hiding from the world and somehow convinced him there's hope out there for something better, for something *more*.

I have to show her how much she means to me, even if I don't know how to say the words and maybe never will be able to.

———

LYLA

Silas rolls us until he has me pinned under him, my back pressing into the soft, luxurious mattress, and his hard, muscled body keeps me prone. His hair spills forward over his shoulders, brushing the pillow on either side of me, cocooning us like we're the only two people in the fucking world.

That's all I want—to pretend that none of this is happening, that tomorrow he's not going to have to go back and confront his demons in the place that ended up being his torture chamber instead of his home. Where he should have been safe and loved.

I want to show him what that feels like because he's never experienced it in his entire life.

If he'll let me.

Though he's let me in, he still holds back. He still keeps things close to his chest and buried deep inside him when opening up and letting go is the only way for him to move forward.

I reach up and press my hand against his bearded cheek. There was a time, not so long ago, when he would have flinched, but now he leans into the touch. He drops his head and kisses me deeply as he reaches between us to drag his fingers through my arousal.

My hips bow into him, craving it, needing the friction against my already throbbing clit. He brushes across it lightly but doesn't stay long, instead grasping his cock and rubbing it between my slick folds, already rock hard again and ready to go.

It seems my distraction worked—even if only for a little while.

And it isn't just for him.

It's for me, too.

To forget about Joey and the uncertainty that awaits him.

Silas and I both need this, and he appears intent on devouring me, his lips moving over mine, hips grinding. I tear my mouth from his on a gasp and wrap my hand around his on his cock, aligning it, so he can shove into me in one hard thrust that makes me dig my nails into his back.

"Fuck, Silas."

He groans in my ear and buries his face against my neck, kissing me there, his beard abrading my skin in the most delicious way as he draws his hips back and slams into me again.

This isn't the same man I've been tangled with like this before.

This is Silas untamed.

This is Silas, truly ready to fall over the edge, and I'm going to give him a nudge in the right direction.

I squeeze around him and still my hips, keeping him pinned inside me. He lifts his head and searches my face.

"What? Did I hurt you?"

I shake my head. "Fuck no. But I want to turn around."

Heat flares in his eyes, and he shifts back, pulling out of me with a groan. I move onto my knees and grab the headboard, shifting back and giving him the perfect position to enter me from behind.

Only he doesn't...

His rough hands trail down my spine, sending a shiver through me, then Silas cups my ass, almost reverently. He squeezes it and presses a kiss to the middle of my back. "You're fucking beautiful, Lyla."

He's told me before, but this time, it makes something swell in my chest and tears pool in my eyes.

The absolute sincerity in his words.

Knowing he's likely never said it to anyone else in his entire life...

Silas shifts his lips to the base of my neck and kisses all the way down until he buries his face between my thighs and shoves his tongue into my pussy.

I jerk at the contact, but he probes again and again until

my legs tremble, my head shakes from side to side, and my fingers dig into the headboard. "Silas, please."

I need him back inside me.

I need *him*.

He retreats from between my legs and presses the head of his cock inside me. I squeeze around it as he pushes in slowly, this angle making him seem even bigger, me even tighter—the stretch decadent and almost painful.

"Fuck." I drop my forehead against the headboard as he bottoms out inside me and stills.

My legs tremble. He wraps his arm around my waist and tugs me upright, using his other hand to turn my head so he can kiss me—brutal and unforgiving. Like he's trying to take something from me that I'm more than willing to give to him freely.

He consumes me with the kiss and the way he fills my body and soul. Then he releases me and nudges my shoulders forward until I grip the headboard again before he starts a hard, driving rhythm into me.

His fingers dig into my hips. His hair brushes my back each time he thrusts forward. Every stroke is deliberate.

Deep.

Ruthless.

I glance over my shoulder at him, and in the faint moonlight streaming in from the windows, I can watch him completely coming apart.

All the stress of the day, the threats and reality of everything that's happened, has built up in the most unhealthy way. Toxic and deadly, it's been festering inside him, and if he doesn't unleash it, he's going to destroy himself from the inside out.

"Harder."

His gaze meets mine.

The fire burning there flames up as he moves his hips faster, slamming into me, fucking me like the crazed, wild mountain man everybody thinks he is.

It's a primal coming together of two people who need each other, who need this, who want to pretend nothing else exists except this moment.

I tighten around him with each deep plunge, and his low growl of satisfaction from behind me makes my clit throb for attention. Though my grip on the headboard is what's keeping me upright, I reach down with one hand and rub against it as he continues to plow into me relentlessly.

The low heat builds fast.

I'm so fucking close.

Just having him in my mouth, swallowing him down, knowing that I could do that to him and make him come so unhinged, was almost enough to make me come on its own. And now that he's hitting that perfect spot deep inside me, I'm about to come undone completely.

He inclines his body, pressing his chest against my back, and reaches his hand over, nudging mine away so his callused fingertips can take over.

Fuck can they do the job...

My orgasm doesn't slam into me; it consumes me. Burning out from my core through my limbs, my entire body bursting into a conflagration I'm not sure I'll ever be able to put out.

I gasp, my body jerking as he continues to pound into me. He bites down along my collarbone, a sharp sting of pain, making me clench around him as he finally comes deep inside me in short, hot spurts.

He sags against me slightly, gripping the headboard, and wraps his arm around my waist to keep me from fully collapsing under his weight. Then he kisses the spot where I undoubtedly have teeth marks and makes his way up my neck, pushing my hair over one shoulder to give himself access.

I turn my head to peek at him out of the corner of my half-lidded eyes, and he drops a kiss to my cheek, my temple, then buries his face in my hair.

"I fucking love you, Lyla."

His words make me tense and clench my eyes closed.

What just happened was emotional, for sure, and those words getting thrown around at a moment like this are always suspect, but he reaches up and tips my chin toward him.

"Open your eyes."

I do, and I see the truth in his.

His fingers feather over my cheek. "I didn't think I knew what it meant. But this is it; you, me, this. Isn't it?"

Shit, the man actually has to ask what love is.

The tears I've been fighting finally leak out of the corner of my eye, and I nod, swallowing past the emotion threatening to choke me. "It is."

Relief flashes across his face, and I close my eyes again because watching him struggle with something we should so innately understand only makes me love him even more.

He pulls me to him again, then rolls onto his side, taking me with him, his cock still buried deep inside me. Curling around me, he kisses every inch of skin he can reach and holds me tight enough that it feels like he may never let go.

And I might not let him.

Chapter Eighteen

LYLA

The house where Silas was forced to grow up far too fast towers over us like some ancient castle that should be somewhere in remote Europe, not in the middle of Pittsburgh.

A shudder rolls through me as I stand in front of it, and not only because I know what happened inside those walls. The cold, stark exterior can't be helped by the perfectly manicured bushes, flowers, and shrubbery. It still looks like a prison, and that's what it was for him.

I squeeze Silas' hand, and it barely gives, his entire body as rigid as the stone on the building we stare at. "Silas, you need to breathe."

He glances down at me. "I am."

"No, you're not."

The corners of his lips fight a smile, likely remembering me giving him the same advice before we walked into that conference room. Which means I've succeeded at getting his focus off the monstrosity in front of us and broken through the anxiety to actually get a hint of humor from him.

But it disappears as quickly as it was there.

He returns his focus to the house. "I don't know how much time we're going to have."

After waiting all morning for Marty's car to speed away from the house, this might be our only opportunity to get in without him here before we see the board on Monday. If I can get Silas in there without him passing out because he stops breathing.

Just like when we were standing outside Bolton Steel, I tug on his hand, urging him to advance toward the building that holds so many horrific memories of his past. "Let's go."

He swallows thickly but slowly steps forward, putting one foot in front of the other. Today, he dressed in some-thing much more Silas—a pair of well-worn jeans and black Henley.

We approach the house together, and he stares at the double front doors for a moment. Long enough that I begin to think he's going to turn around and walk away, but he squares his shoulders, walks up to it, and turns the handle, pushing it open without so much as a knock or ring of the doorbell.

I lean closer to him, keeping my voice low. "Silas, what are you doing? You can't just walk in!"

He glances over at me. "I own the house, don't I?"

"Well, yeah, but what if someone sees us walking around in here?"

"Let him call the police and try to kick me out."

His confident defiance makes me grin through the tension. I follow him into Bolton Manor and shut the door behind me. The click seems to echo loudly through the front foyer, off all the marble and hand-carved wood, and I wince.

But Silas either didn't notice or doesn't care, too entranced by the interior of the house. He shakes his head slowly as he examines it. "Nothing's changed here. They updated the offices because people are constantly coming and going, but here"—he spins, looking at the massive chandelier above us and the twin staircases wrapping up to the second floor—"this all looks exactly the same as it did almost two hundred years ago when they built this house. Eight generations of Boltons have lived here, but I'm going to end that tradition." His gaze cuts to me. "After today, I'm never coming back. Whatever happens, I won't set foot in here again."

His declaration seems to hang in the air around us for a second before he motions for me to follow him.

"Where are we going?"

He heads up the staircase to the left. "My room. It would be the most obvious place for him to leave something for me..."

God willing.

I don't even want to *think* about what we'll do if I'm wrong and Ronald wasn't able to get a copy of what he had on Marty stashed away somewhere safe for us. We'll be left hanging with the board, whose members were reluctant to utter a single word in front of his uncle.

Stay positive.

It's hard to do when we're wandering around the place where so much damage was done without the benefit of having Whiskey with us as *some* form of protection should anything happen. But Silas insisted on leaving him at the hotel, worried the protective dog might alert someone of our presence far more easily than we would on our own.

I follow Silas up the stairs, keeping an eye out for any of the staff who must be roaming around the house. "Did you spend a lot of time in your room as a boy?"

He pauses mid-step, his hand tightening on the railing. "I did—mostly trying to stay away from my uncle and praying he didn't come looking for me."

My stomach turns at the thought of the small boy cowering in fear in his own bed. No wonder Silas doesn't sleep well. I loop my arm through his and squeeze. "Are you sure you want to do this? Maybe I can go in, or—"

He rests his hand on top of mine on his forearm, and I look down at the scars across his knuckles, only partially hidden by the tattoos there.

"I have to, Lyla."

Ending any further debate, he takes the last few steps up, and we move quickly down the hallway, past several closed doors to the last one at the end on the right. He pulls his arm out of mine and reaches for the knob, his hand shaking as he turns it and pushes the heavy-looking wooden slab open.

Not taking my own advice, I hold my breath and follow him in, unsure what I should do or say as his eyes dart around the room, taking in everything from the ancient-looking fourposter bed to the dresser, still covered in photographs of him as a teenager and various personal knickknacks that he never took with him when he left.

"They haven't touched anything..."

His voice sounds hollow, somehow devoid of emotion when it should be full of it.

I walk over to the dresser and run my finger across it, lifting it up for him to see. "They've been dusting, though. Someone's been in here keeping it up, maintaining it for fifteen years."

He bobs his head. "Ursula, our maid. She never would've allowed dust to collect in here, even if she knew I wasn't coming back."

The affection in the way he talks about her leads me to believe she was one of the only people in this house who was ever kind to him—another piece of the sad reality he lived in for so long.

It makes the solitude he sought on the mountain make so much more sense.

Alone was safe.

This place definitely isn't.

I scan the room for anything obviously out of place, perhaps a clue left by Ronald to alert Silas where he might have left the evidence. "Where would he hide something?"

Silas runs his hands through his hair and wanders over to the nightstand. "I don't know."

He pulls open the top drawer and rifles through the things in it, then shoves it closed and does the same for the drawer under it. Slamming it shut, he lowers himself to the bed, dropping his face into his hands.

"What the fuck was I thinking coming back here? I don't know where he would put anything. This house has twenty bedrooms and dozens of other rooms. It could be anywhere, or it could be nowhere. What if he didn't leave anything at all?"

The panic lacing his voice makes my heart go out to him even more.

I've been there myself—when the police took Joey into custody and said he was being charged. That feeling hung over me until last night, but the moment I told Silas everything and he promised to help him, it felt like a giant weight had been lifted from my shoulders.

And I want to be able to do the same for Silas.

Only I don't know how when we're twisting in the fucking wind.

Settling on the bed next to him, I rest my head against his shoulder. "Let's just look anywhere we can in here, and if we don't find anything, we'll reassess, but we can't give up. We've only been here for five minutes—"

The door clicks open, and we both jerk our heads toward it, tensing, prepared for a fight.

An elderly woman with white hair pinned up in a bun and heavy laugh lines on her face stands in the jamb, staring at us. Her eyes zero in on Silas, and tears start to pool. "Silas, is that really you?"

He rises from the bed and approaches her tentatively. "Ursula?"

She nods vigorously, wringing her hands in front of her. "I never thought I'd see you again."

The corner of his mouth curves into a sad smile. "I never thought I'd be back."

A tear slips from her eye, and she shakes her head. "I'm so sorry I could never do anything for you, that I couldn't intervene, but your uncle would've had me deported, and I—"

Silas closes the distance between them and takes the old woman's shoulders in his hands. "Don't apologize. It was a long time ago."

"But you were only a baby."

"I'm not anymore, Ursula, and I'm going to make sure he pays for what he did to everybody, especially me."

The woman sputters, her eyes widening slightly. "Your father..."

My spine stiffens as Silas narrows his eyes on her.
"What about him?"

"He was acting strange in the few days before he died, locked himself away in his office for hours at a time. I don't know what he was doing, but I thought I would mention it with everything that's happening. That's where I found him."

Silas raises a brow. "*You* found him?"

She nods. "He was slumped over his desk. They *said* it was a heart attack."

The emphasis she places on the word "said" doesn't go unnoticed by Silas or me, and he cuts me a sharp look that tells me exactly what we suspect is likely true. Even the maid believes Marty had something to do with Silas' father's death, the same as he did Ronald's.

"Do you think Uncle Marty could have done something to him?"

Her slim shoulders rise and fall. "They had been arguing for months. I don't know what about, but it got nasty. Things were tense here, so I can only imagine what they were like at the office..."

"What about Ronald? Was he here before he died?"

She narrows her gaze on Silas. "Ronald? No...not that I can recall. I hadn't seen him here in weeks."

Which means, he didn't leave anything here for Silas.

Silas' shoulders slump as he comes to the same realization, but then he glances over his shoulder at me. "We need to go to my father's office."

"Why?"

"If that's where he was spending his time right before he died, maybe there's something there that can tie Marty to his death or something else."

It's a long shot.

But at this point, we don't have anything else to go on.

I rise from the bed and approach the woman standing in

front of Silas, suddenly realizing he hasn't bothered to introduce me yet. "Hi, I'm Lyla."

"Shit." Silas winces and wraps his arm around my shoulder. "Ursula, this is my wife."

Ursula's eyes widen slightly. "Wife?" Her wrinkled lips curl into a genuine smile, perhaps the first one I've seen from anyone since we got into town. "Oh, Silas, I'm so happy for you." She reaches out and takes my hand in hers. "Do what I couldn't. Take care of him…"

Silas presses a kiss to my temple. "She already does."

———

SILAS

The longer I'm inside this house of horrors, the more determined I become to burn the fucking place down when I'm done with it. Each generation that lived here, the people who built our empire from inside these walls, would be absolutely disgusted to know what happened.

And not just to me.

Could Marty really have killed Father and Ronald?

I don't want to believe it, but something deep in my gut tells me neither were "heart attacks." Uncle Marty is smart enough to have it *look* natural so questions aren't asked—like he might have done with Mom—but killing people he sees as a threat wouldn't be out of his wheelhouse.

Ursula said Father was arguing with Marty, and that fact alone raises my suspicions even more—makes what *should* be unthinkable seem almost likely.

Those two were always so close, inseparable, really.

What possibly could have driven a wedge between them? What could have turned them against each other?

Something tells me the answer lies in Father's office, the place that was always strictly off-limits to me as a child. So many kids grow up at their parents' feet, under their desks, sitting on their laps while they work, but not me.

This was hallowed ground, and I was never allowed to step into it. Of course, it didn't mean that I complied; I just tried to make sure I wasn't caught because I knew what the consequences would be if Father or Marty ever found me in there.

But I don't need to sneak around anymore.

I lead Lyla down the stairs and through the hallway to the west wing, where Father chose to set up his office so he could watch the sunset out the massive windows facing the horizon.

Lyla squeezes my hand as we move past several closed doors that I have no desire to open. Having her here with me for this is truly the only thing keeping me grounded. If I had attempted this alone, I never would have made it inside and certainly wouldn't have been able to keep my head on straight.

Even with everything going on with her brother, she's still beside me. Still my *rock*. Still willing to follow me into the lion's den in hopes of finding the answer to our prayers.

We reach the door to Father's office, and I take a moment to try to get my shit together before opening it. Lyla doesn't push me, merely tightens her grip on my hand and waits with me until I grab the knob, twist it, and push.

The familiar smell of stale cigar smoke, wood polish, and bourbon fills the air. I inhale deeply, another flood of memories coming with it.

Father's booming voice coming from behind the closed door...

Pressing my ear against it to try to hear what was being said...

Ursula seeing me and shooing me away before I got caught...

Lyla squeezes my hand again. "You okay?"

I don't know how long we've been standing here in the hallway as I just stare into the room, lost in my head. But I can't avoid going in forever. "I will be."

When this is all over.

When I can go back to the mountain, to my cabin, my land, my freedom.

This isn't the world for me. I left it behind for a reason, and even if we succeed in our mission to save Bolton Steel and crush Uncle Marty, I can't stay.

The people. The traffic. The noises. The smells. All of it is too much.

But I have to push away my reticence, release Lyla's hand, and move forward into the office.

I go straight for the massive wooden desk dominating the room and pull the chair back. The red leather monstrosity he always loved looks garish now, like something out of a cartoon rather than real life, but back then, it seemed like a throne he ruled from.

And apparently died in....

I stare at it for a moment, picturing the old man slumped over the desk, likely with a drink sitting near his hand—the way I almost always saw him. That old feeling that I shouldn't be in here engulfs me, but I slowly lower myself into the chair, pulling open the middle drawer.

Pens, a letter opener, miscellaneous office supplies.

Absolutely nothing of any interest.

Lyla wanders around the room, taking in the books on the floor-to-ceiling shelves along one wall and photographs of Father over the years with presidents and other political figures and celebrities. "Your father sure knew a lot of important people."

I open the next drawer and rifle through it, searching for anything unusual before making my way to the next. "I told you; he and Marty have connections. The kind that ensured they got away with literally anything."

For men like them, without consciences or souls, their power became a toxic drug they couldn't get enough of. And they used it to get what they wanted—by any means necessary.

It did great things to help grow Bolton Steel, but it was as destructive as a hurricane for anyone who dared to get in their path.

Lyla wanders over to the desk. "Did you find something?"

I shake my head, surveying the entire office again, trying to think of where Father might have left anything he might have been working on. "No, but if they were arguing about something, if he was locking himself in here, there has to be a record of what he was doing. Phone calls, a ledger, notes, *anything* that might tell us something useful."

Father was a meticulous record keeper, and I don't believe for a second that he wouldn't have been documenting whatever caused their rift in order to use it against Marty if he needed to.

Against my most base instincts to leave the past in the past, I try to draw up the old memories of the few times I was in here with him.

Angry, harsh words fill my head.

I tighten my fists.

A cloudy memory starts to solidify. "There's a hidden drawer...."

Lyla's eyebrows fly up. "What?"

"There's a hidden compartment."

She immediately starts scanning the front face of the old, hand-carved desk. "Where?"

I shove back the chair and reach under the huge piece of furniture to find the movable pieces of wood that act almost like a puzzle box on the underside. "I snuck in here once when I was a kid and saw him putting something under here. He screamed at me to get out, but a few weeks later, I came back in. I hid under the desk when Ursula came looking for me, and I saw it above me—these pieces that didn't look like they matched the rest of the wood. I think they're the way to open it."

"Let me look." Lyla nudges me aside and slides under the desk—her smaller frame much more agile than mine and able to fit easily. She lies on her back and looks up. "I see three pieces that are stained differently from the rest of them. What do I do?"

"Move them around until it clicks open, I guess."

She releases a humorless laugh. "I was never very good at puzzles, Silas."

"You managed to figure me out, right?"

In the beginning, I absolutely hated the way she seemed to be able to read me so well, how she challenged me and called me out, yet she didn't stop pushing.

And it changed everything.

She grins, then reaches to the underside of the top and begins shifting the pieces of wood around until a click sounds. Her eyes dart to the side, and she pulls out a leather-bound journal, holding it up to me.

My hand trembles as I take it from her.

She slides out and climbs to her feet, wiping off the butt

of her jeans before she settles on the arm of the chair next to me. "What is it?"

I set it on the desk and flip open the leather cover. The first page sucks the air right from my lungs, and Lyla's constant reminders to breathe flood my head.

Lyla leans over to read it. "It's dated a month before he died."

> Dear Silas,
>
> At least, I hope this is Silas, as you are the only one who ever saw me use my secret hiding spot.
>
> I pray that upon my death, you'll return to this house you ran from so many years ago, find this, and understand why I did what I did.

Lyla's brow furrows. "What the hell is he talking about?"

I shake my head as I flip to the next page. "I don't know."

> Your Uncle Marty was always a little off. Even as a child, he was a bit sadistic, torturing small animals, kicking the dog, biting and hitting other children in school. Our parents, God bless them, did everything they could to try to dispel those tendencies. They sent him to special schools, counseling. They warned me to always

watch out for him, to try to keep him in line as much as I could.

Being the psychopath that he is, he was able to convince everyone that he had changed. But I always saw what he attempted to hide just under the polished surface. I saw that he had no conscience. I saw that he actually enjoyed hurting people.

But my parents had tasked me with watching out for my little brother, so I did it, much to the detriment of many innocent people— including you.

Please believe me when I say I didn't know what he was doing to you, at least not in the beginning. Your mother was insanely protective of you, and as long as she was in this house, I believed he never would've been able to touch you without her going straight to the authorities. Though we had people on the force who could have intervened on his behalf, he couldn't risk that potential exposure.

Bile climbs up my throat, and Lyla's hand tightens on my wrist. She glances at me, her eyes wide. "Is he saying what I think he is?"

I nod, unable to form any words right now while reading what appears to be Father's confession that Marty killed my mother.

I don't have proof that he did it. Just a gut instinct. As far as I can tell, that was when the worst of the abuse started, once she was gone. But I didn't know, didn't truly know until that day when you were seven, when I saw the burn mark on you.

The tears start to well in my eyes, but I swipe them away to clear my vision so I can keep reading. As painful as this is to read, it might help resolve so many of the questions I've always had about what went on within these walls.

Lyla flips the page, giving me a moment to try to collect myself.

I should have intervened then. A good father would have. But I was too deep in the bottle, too wrapped up in running the company and doing what was best for Bolton Steel. Too worried about the money and the legacy and the promise I made to my parents. I chose all that over you. And for that, I will likely burn in the fires of Hell and deserve an eternity there.

I would never ask you to forgive me for that. That isn't something that can be forgiven. All I can offer you is what I hope will assist you in making sure Marty pays for what he's done.

Even now, he threatens me, after everything

307

I've done for him. My brother won't stop, and you are the strongest person I know. You can end this.

I love you, son. And I'm sorry.

My hand trembles so badly that I almost tear the page trying to turn it.

A series of dates and names followed by detailed descriptions of incidents fill the paper, starting as far back as their teens.

"Oh, my God." Lyla's hand flies to her mouth. "Is this what I think it is?"

I flip through page after page of Father's elegant scrawl. It goes on and on, filling almost the entire journal. *Decades* of information.

"He documented everything." I glance up at her. "It isn't the type of evidence Ronald would've had—signed contracts, NDAs, bank statements of money transfers—but it's my father's own handwritten accounts of everything he knew about. It's *something*, something we can take to the board."

Father might've been a spineless, self-destructive bastard during his time on this planet, but he left us what might be the only thing that can take that monster who is his brother down.

Chapter Nineteen

LYLA

The longer we've stayed in Pittsburgh, the more agitated Silas has become.

For the last four days, he's been a quivering ball of nerves—far worse than anything I witnessed up on the mountain.

Pacing the penthouse suite.

Running his hands through Whiskey's fur incessantly.

Tugging at his own hair until he practically rips it out.

Obsessively poring over his father's journal, trying to memorize the information within it until I finally had to take it from him because reading and re-reading the horrific things his uncle has done has only made his anxiety worse.

And I'd be lying if I said I haven't been feeling it, too.

Even touching base with Attorney Fields again, introducing him to Silas, letting him know I'd get him the funds he needed for the expert, and finally connecting with Joey on the phone couldn't dispel my anxiety, either.

Too much is at stake.

It all comes down to today and Silas' ability to convince seven people that they need to overthrow the man who has been the number two at the company for over thirty years.

Setting foot in Bolton Steel again still brings the same sense of dread it did the first time, evening knowing we now have ammunition against Marty. That one little book holds the key to ending his reign of terror. It also holds the pain of so many people.

But one name is absent.

Silas' father left what was done to his son out of his confession—though we still don't know whether that was to protect himself from judgment or Silas from having his trauma exposed.

I'd love to believe the latter, given the note he wrote to his son, but the selfish actions of the man over the years he could have been protecting Silas make me question his intent as much as his sincerity.

And looking at Silas today, dressed in a dark-gray suit, you'd never guess what he's suffered. He appears every bit the Bolton he is—save for the long hair tied back and the hints of ink around his neck and hands.

For the first time, it also appears that he *feels* like it. He doesn't even glance at the lobby receptionist who gave us so much trouble last time, just stalks past her like he owns the place—which, I guess, technically, he does at least halfway.

Whiskey trots beside him, ignoring the woman completely.

I scowl at her to make sure she understands that the potential new CEO of Bolton Steel will be firing her if he gets the job he's asking for today. She averts her gaze to something on the desk rather than look at me, and I can't fight the smile of satisfaction, despite what we're about to walk into upstairs.

Another potential bloodbath.

But at least this time, there aren't any more secrets for Marty to try to use against Silas and me. We're ready for anything he might throw at us, any twisted game he tries to play.

We're ready.

We're ready.

We're ready.

I keep telling myself that as we enter the elevator, hands clutched tightly together for the ride up, the journal in Silas' other one. It's the only evidence we have after contacting Ronald's wife and secretary, who were never able to find anything he might've left for us.

Whatever happened to him—whether it truly was a heart attack or something more sinister—it happened before he could prepare anything to alert them about what we needed. And someone ensured nothing was left behind that could incriminate Martin Bolton.

The ding indicating we've reached the tenth floor sounds. I lean closer to Silas, wishing we had one more minute alone so I could give him a pep talk. "You can do this."

I feel like a broken record, yet each time I say the words, I hope he believes them a little more. But Silas is so focused on his mission that he barely acknowledges I've said anything before the doors slide open and he steps out onto the expensive marble.

Whiskey's entire demeanor shifts as we approach the conference room to see the man who so easily derailed us the last time we were here.

Marty has remained suspiciously absent and silent since

the last board meeting. Aside from watching him drive away from the house before we went in the day after, we haven't heard from him at all. Something that sets both of us on edge.

We both, apparently incorrectly, had assumed he would try to pull something before this meeting, that he would show up at the hotel, making threats or otherwise interfere, but maybe he's just that smug of an asshole to think he doesn't need to do anything to stop us because he's confident he's already done it.

And we're about to prove him wrong.

We walk into the same ice-cold reception we received last time. The board members all sit with their spines ramrod straight, refusing to look our way, while Marty stands at the head of the table, head held high, as arrogant as ever.

I was right.

He didn't think he *needed* to threaten us.

He thinks he's already *won.*

The smug grin plastered on his face matches the confident set of his shoulders. "Let's make this quick. Say what you have to say, then get the fuck out of my building."

A few board members shift uncomfortably at his language.

Silas moves to his spot opposite his uncle and looks at each member of the board, when they refuse to meet his gaze. He knows his audience, and he will do whatever he has to in order to convince them they need to remove Marty —even force them to listen.

"Once again, I want to thank you for giving me the opportunity to come back and speak with you again after our less-than-productive meeting last week." He glares at Marty. "Hopefully, I won't be interrupted this time. My purpose in coming here last week that got sidetracked"—he glances my way—"by claims about my wife was to unearth some dirty laundry and buried skeletons now that my father is gone."

Marty lowers himself into his chair, spreading out his hands and appearing bored by the whole ordeal. "I don't know what it is you think you know, Silas, but before you say another word, I suggest you consider the consequences of making baseless accusations."

One of Silas' blond brows rises slowly. "You mean like the ones you threw at my *wife?*"

I want to clap and jump up and down at that jibe, but I try to maintain my composure while I watch for any signs of Silas about to lose his control and attack his uncle again.

If I have to step in, I will.

And Whiskey seems more than prepared to finish the job he started up on the mountain. He watches Marty from beside Silas, his lips curled, teeth bared, ready to protect his owner from the only apparent threat in the room.

I understand the feeling because it's exactly what I've been trying to do for Joey.

For so long, it was only the two of us, relying on each other, trusting each other and no one else. But now that Silas knows the truth, we have him on our side, too. Willing to fight and throw his money at anyone who might be able to help with this horrific situation.

It has to be enough...just like that diary his father left needs to be today.

Silas holds it up. "I have plenty of evidence for what I'm here to say, Uncle Marty, from someone you know very well."

Marty doesn't flinch, but his eyes do cut over to the

leather-bound book in Silas' tattooed hand before returning to his nephew's face.

Silas looks at each member of the board. "Someone all of you know very well. Know and *respect*. Or you did...until he died a few weeks ago. You all knew my father and the type of man he was. And I suspect everyone in this room also knows the type of man Marty is as well; only you're too afraid to do anything about it. Ronald and I were working together before his death, and while I no longer have access to any evidence he had accumulated against Martin Bolton, I do have *this*."

He opens the book and flips to the first page containing the dates, names, and incidents. Every set of eyes in the room narrows on it, but his father's elegant scrawl isn't readable from a distance.

I've practically memorized it by now.

Each instance.

All the names.

Every detail seared into my brain.

An almost endless list of horrors the man at the other end of the table has gotten away with for decades, yet he sits here today in control of one of the most profitable companies in U.S. history.

Unashamed.

Unencumbered by conscience.

Practically gloating over the victory he thinks he has achieved.

Silas runs a finger over the writing. "A detailed list of every horrific deed Martin Bolton ever committed—at least those that my father was aware of. Dates, names, locations, amounts paid to the victims to keep them silent. Hell, even the names of some of the police officers they paid to ensure Marty didn't end up behind bars—"

Marty releases a sardonic laugh, instantly chilling my blood. "All you have are the writings of a man with a bone to pick. He and I have been battling for control of the company for months. He had every reason to write libelous information about me in there to try to sway the board. There's absolutely no reason any of them should believe a single word of it."

Fuck.

He isn't wrong.

Ursula said they'd been arguing. Undoubtedly, Marty was getting tired of waiting for his turn at the helm and wanted his older brother to step down. And since he wouldn't, he found a way to make it happen himself.

Silas glances over at me, the panic in his gaze twisting my gut. He knows his uncle is right. All that's there in that book are accusations made by someone who had a motive to lie.

No matter how much we tried over the last few days to get in contact with any of the people named in there, they were all either dead, unreachable, or unwilling to admit they knew the Boltons—probably because they still feared the man staring us down from across the room. Which means we have no witnesses to back up anything written.

But I know someone who isn't afraid of him anymore.

I watch the panic in Silas' gaze flip to determination.

What is he going to do?

He reaches up and grabs his tie, pulling the knot loose.

Oh God, no.

I rush toward him as he jerks off the tie and lets it fall onto the conference room table beside the book. "Silas, what the hell are you doing?"

He shucks off the suit coat and casually hangs it on the back of the chair, then reaches for the top button of the white dress shirt. His inked fingers undo it, then another, working his way down, exposing more of his tattoos to the men and women seated at the table. "I'm showing them evidence they can't deny and giving them eyewitness testimony."

Shit.

I squeeze my eyes closed and swallow back the bile threatening to make me gag. His hands cup my face, and he tilts it up toward him. I open my eyes and meet his.

The soft sea of blue I could get lost swimming in holds so much affection and confidence. "I can do this."

The words I said to him before we walked out of the elevator ring in my ears, and this time, I know he believes it, too.

I nod, placing my hand over his on my cheek. "I'm right here. I'm not going anywhere."

He gives me a quick kiss and releases me so he can continue to unbutton his shirt.

Marty pushes to his feet, his jaw locked, anger flaring his nostrils. "What the hell are you doing?"

Silas makes it to the center of his chest and pulls the shirt from where it's tucked into his pants so he can reach the rest of the buttons. He turns away from me to face his uncle. "What I should have done years ago. Showing everyone what you did to me."

———

SILAS

I didn't have the strength to do this fifteen years ago, and I wouldn't have had it even a month ago. But the woman standing next to me has given it to me.

Lyla has helped me prove to myself that I can move past what the piece of shit at the other end of the table did. That I can become someone else besides the broken man I had let those memories make me, that I can save other people from the pain I experienced by just speaking up and telling my truth, which is exactly what I fucking intend to do.

I undo the cuff links at my wrists as the wide eyes of the board members roam over the tattoos on my chest and stomach.

These aren't the type of people who appreciate body art, and I know showing them will automatically change their opinion of me—and not for the better.

But there isn't any other way.

Because Marty is right—this ledger Father created doesn't actually prove anything to these people.

They need to see it with their own eyes. Touch it with their own hands. Hear it with their own ears.

I'm the *only* one who can do this.

Lyla trembles beside me, her nerves almost worse than mine, but I can't stop to assure her I'm all right. If I do, I might not be able to go through with this.

I remove my shirt and drape it over the back of the chair, never looking away from Uncle Marty, letting him see he doesn't intimidate me anymore. That he *can't*.

He shakes his head. "No one wants to see your deviant art, Silas. This is completely uncalled for and unacceptable in a place of business—"

"So is abusing your nephew."

The room goes dead still and silent with my words, and several of the board members dart their gazes to Marty, then back to me.

His jaw locks, a muscle there ticcing as he shifts slightly

317

and adjusts his suit coat. "I don't know what you're talking about."

"Yes, you *do*."

And now it's time to show the men and women of the board who the man running Bolton Steel *really* is at his core.

I slowly make my way around the corner of the table to the first board member—Alicia Clayton, one of Father's high society friends and biggest benefactors to our charities. A woman I met countless times growing up. I incline my head toward her. "Alicia."

She clears her throat, looking up at me awkwardly. "Silas."

"Give me your hand."

Her head jerks back, her silvery hair barely budging from the tight bun wound at the base of her skull. "What?"

"Will you please give me your hand?"

She hesitantly raises it, and I take it gently in mine, then press her palm over the scar on my chest that Lyla had hers over only a few nights ago. "This was a hot fireplace poker. I was ten."

I drag her hand over it so she can feel the shape, the warped skin. The things she may not be able to see because of the ink I tried to conceal it under.

When I release her hand, she lets it fall to her lap, her eyes wide and following me as I move to the next person.

Marty watches silently, his face reddening, hands clenched tightly around the back of his chair.

I hold out my hand, and Arnold Peck places his in it tentatively. Father's oldest friend and confidant. I'm quite sure, of all the people here, he knows precisely what I'm going to show him.

His eyes meet mine, and I set his fingers over my left

bicep. "This one was a crowbar. He actually broke my arm and told my father I fell down the stairs."

I shift it over to the spot where a bone had protruded, and he winces and jerks his hand back, closing his eyes for a moment like he doesn't want to process what he heard and felt.

Marty snarls as I move to the next board member. "Enough. Stop these lies!"

I shake my head as I reach Miriam Anderson, the wife of Dr. Anderson, who sits next to her. She gives me her hand, and I lower it against my back, just below my shoulder blade. "Explain this one, Uncle Marty. You can feel the letters *M* and *B*."

She slowly traces her fingers over them where they're concealed by the intricate artwork.

"He literally carved his initials into my back with a fucking razor blade."

Miriam winces as I move to her husband.

"Dr. Anderson, you, of all people, should be able to recognize abuse when you see it."

The old man's eyes rake over me, taking in all the ink, but I know he sees what's underneath it. It's impossible to miss the puckering, shiny, off-color skin when you're looking for it.

I lift my arms and spin so he can see my entire chest and my back, both of my arms, and tilt my head up so he can view the scar around my neck. I drag my finger over it. "This is where he tried to strangle me the night I left and never came back."

Dr. Anderson cuts his gaze to Marty but doesn't say a word, all the color draining from his face.

Marty begins trembling, barely containing his rage. "This is all bullshit." He smacks his palm against the table.

"You can't prove any of it. You have every reason to make it up, every reason to lie, to get your hands on the fucking company and the money."

"I don't give a shit about the money, Marty. I never have. You're the only one who cared about it. You and Father." I scan the stunned faces of the other people around the table. "I'm a Bolton just as much as he is. I'm in compliance with the terms of the trust, which means I have every right to take my fifty percent ownership of the company. But what I want to ask all of you is whether you really want a man like Martin Bolton here in these walls as your CEO. Given the amount of time you've all known him, I don't believe for a fucking second that you didn't suspect something was going on, that you didn't see through the façade and the smiles and the act he put on for everyone else's benefit. You all believe me because you know this man and you know what he's capable of."

On the verge of a complete meltdown, Marty smashes his fists against the table, kicking his chair back behind him. "Shut the fuck up!"

The snarl that comes from the end of the table makes everyone's head snap toward Whiskey. He sits next to the chair I vacated, growling low, slobber dripping from his mouth as he stares down Uncle Marty.

"Even my dog doesn't believe you, Marty, and he's a pretty fucking good judge of character."

Lyla can't hide her half-grin at that, and she steps over next to him and places her hand on the back of his neck, trying to calm him before he tears Marty limb from limb in front of all these people and ruins the expensive white marble tile beneath our feet.

Dr. Anderson finally turns and looks up at me. "What are you asking for, Silas? What do you want us to do?"

"You fucking traitor!" Marty growls low and points at Dr. Anderson. "Don't forget what I know about you, what I could do to your name and your career."

Miriam gapes at her husband. "What the hell is he talking about?"

I snort an incredulous laugh. "He's going back to his old tactics." Returning to my spot at the foot of the table, I stand to one side of Whiskey with Lyla on the other. "He is using intimidation to try to scare you away from doing what you know is right. Remove him as CEO. Put me in place as interim CEO."

Maeve Broderick shakes her head from the other side of the table. "Where have you been, Silas? You've been gone for fifteen years. You know nothing about the company, about what we've been doing, about where we're going. How the hell are you going to run it?"

"With your help. With the help of the staff that I'm quite confident my father and Uncle Marty ensured knows what the fuck they're doing. It doesn't have to be permanent, and ultimately, if the board determines that it's in the best interest of everyone, we'll sell. But I'm the last Bolton, and my family built this company from the ground up. I'm not going to let this man destroy it with his greed and depraved behavior."

"Depraved?" Marty rounds the table but stops short when Whiskey snarls again. "You have a lot of fucking nerve, kid, showing up here and trying to take this from me."

"Do I?" I fist my hands at my sides, digging my nails into my palms to keep myself from doing what I really want to. "You took *everything* from me. My home, my family, the safety and security I should have had. You took my *childhood,* my fucking *life,* and I didn't get it back until I met *her*." I point at Lyla as tears well in her eyes. "We can figure out the future plans for Bolton Steel later. What matters is what we do in this moment, that we do what's right, that we do what should have been done years ago, what my father wanted done." I grab the journal and hold it up. "He wrote this before he died. He laid it all out so that I would have evidence to use against Marty because he *knew* Marty would go to great lengths to ensure that none of it ever saw the light of day otherwise."

Someone clears their throat. "This will destroy the company if it gets out."

I turn to the board member who spoke—a man I've met half a dozen times, at least—Stephan Russell. "We can't be afraid of that, Stephan. We can't be afraid of *him* anymore. I'm not."

And for the first time in my entire life, I actually *mean* it.

Lyla slips her hand into mine and squeezes it.

The whole room watches Marty, his face red as he trembles, staring down the kid he thought he had taken care of all those years ago. He believed he had ensured my silence, broken me so badly that I would never stand up to him. And I was *this* close to letting him win.

"You won't get away with this, Silas—"

I keep my gaze on him. "I call for a vote to remove Martin Bolton as acting CEO of Bolton Steel. Do I have a second?"

Dr. Anderson looks at Marty. "Second."

"All those in favor?"

Every single person around the table raises their hand as Marty gapes at them.

"You don't know what you're all doing. I will destroy all of you."

I bark out a laugh. "You can sure try, but you have no job, no credibility, no home to go back to. I've called and had the locks changed."

His mouth gapes open. "You *what*?"

I grin at him, reduced to the same cowering, distraught child I was when he abused me. "I own the house, Marty. You've overstayed your welcome."

"You can't do this." He takes a step back and then another. "You can't *do* this!"

Every scar on my body tingles with the utter despair in his cry.

The man who got off on creating that kind of anguish in others has been crushed under the boot of the boy who took the worst of it.

And it's time to drive the final nail into the coffin.

"I also provided a copy of this"—I hold up the journal—"to the FBI. I'm sure they'll be contacting you soon..."

His eyes widen, and I see the same fear I once felt reflected back at me before he turns and rushes from the conference room.

Before the door can even close behind him, Lyla wraps her arms around me and buries her face against my bare chest. "You did good, Silas."

I drop a kiss to the top of her head as Whiskey rubs up against my hand, finally relaxing now that Marty's gone.

Dr. Anderson climbs to his feet and makes his way around the table toward me. He extends a hand. "You did well, Silas. Your father would've been proud of you." He motions to the board. "We've all been trying to figure out a way to get rid of Marty for years, but you finally did it. I wish your father would've been here to see it."

"Me, too."

And I actually mean it, despite everything he did to me —or failed to do.

"Everything is going to change for Bolton Steel."

And staring down into Lyla's eyes, I know it's going to change for us, too.

For the better.

Chapter Twenty

LYLA

The familiar, rhythmic sound of Silas slamming his axe over and over again into pieces of wood echoes across the property. I never thought hearing that would be so comforting, that this place would feel so much like home to me. But after being back here for a week, I can't ever imagine being anywhere else again.

Silas was in a rush to return to the mountain after the board meeting, and I finally understand why.

There's just something about this place.

A magic in the air that immediately relieves the tension in my body and unrest in my soul. It allows me to relax even when so much is still unsettled. Though, it might have something to do with the company up here, too.

Except this guy.

He's an asshole.

With my hand on the gate, I stare down Billy in the goat pen and point a finger at him. "Don't even think about it, you little asshole. If you want treats, you can't try to get out this time."

One thing I've learned about Billy since our little walkabout in the forest is he'll do almost anything for a carrot, and I've been using it to my advantage whenever possible to keep him from bolting again.

Whiskey sits next to me, staring up, waiting for me to open the gate. I insisted on borrowing him from Silas long enough for him to help me with the animals, in case Billy decided to make another escape.

I undo the latch on the gate, and Billy immediately runs for it.

Little jerk.

I've learned my lesson, though, and I slip in and close it quickly, turning to face the tiny goat that gave us so much trouble. "Are you going to be like this your whole life, little guy?"

He releases a baa in response, takes the small carrot from my hand, and then runs off toward his brother and parents near the shed where we keep their feed. I make my way over to them, get them fed with only a few playful nips from the twins, then head back for the gate where Whiskey waits for me, tail wagging. After I secure the pen, I turn to pet him and tell him he can go back to Silas, but the sound of the axe no longer hangs in the air.

Once Silas is in a rhythm, he rarely stops, and the utter silence on the property makes Whiskey's ears perk up. I listen, too, for any signs of where Silas might have gone, but he comes around the side of the barn before I have to go looking for him.

My breath hitches like it did the first time I saw him.

Hot damn.

It should be a sin for this man to walk around without a shirt on...

A light sheen of sweat glistens on his chest and arms, and a few drops roll down that perfect *V* of his hips to the waistband of his low-slung jeans. He scrubs a hand over his face, rubbing at his beard as he approaches.

His gaze darts to the pen, then back to me. "Billy give you any trouble?"

I rest my ass against the gate. "What do you think?"

He smirks. "I think he's always going to be trouble, just like you are."

Me, trouble?

I almost object to his statement, but the night he literally had to drag me out of the woods flashes fresh in my mind and stops me. Silas leans in and gives me a quick kiss, then holds something out to me.

I narrow my eyes on it. "What's this?"

"A satellite phone. You need to return a call to Attorney Fields."

"What?" I snatch it from his hand, examining the device. "Where the hell did you get a satellite phone?"

While being back on the homestead has felt incredible, the fact that it also means being out of touch with civilization has weighed heavily on me. With Joey still in jail awaiting trial and Marty still floating in the wind, the peaceful life this place allows is constantly interrupted by mental reminders of the unsettled nature of our lives. Having a phone that *works* up here can help change that, but I never thought Silas would ever get one.

The Silas from *before* sure wouldn't have.

He rests a hip against the fence, crossing his arms over his chest, making his massive biceps bulge. "Before we left Pittsburgh. With everything going on with your brother, I couldn't very well let you stay at the cabin without any way to get in touch with the attorney or for your brother to call you. I had it delivered to the hotel before we left."

"Delivered to the hotel, like your suits?"

He grins. "Sometimes being a billionaire has its benefits."

Like being able to live up here while he's technically the CEO of Bolton Steel, at least for the time being. He still hasn't definitively decided what he wants to do with the company, and he left the people his father and Marty put in place to run it as much as they can without him physically being there. But it isn't the ideal situation for anyone, and he and the board know that.

I wiggle the phone back and forth. "You know they're going to be able to call *you* up here with this?"

His smile falters, thinking about the calls he's likely to get from company headquarters. "Yeah, I know, but we got the win over Marty on the CEO front. I can't blow it by not being reachable when I'm needed at Bolton Steel, right?"

"Right."

He inclines his head toward the device he never would have had on the mountain only a week ago. "Call Attorney Fields. He has a good update for you."

My chest tightens instantly, and I rub at it with my free hand, trying to push away the anxiety that always overtakes me when I have to speak with the man who holds Joey's life in his hands.

"Don't look so scared, Lyla. I said *good*."

It doesn't matter.

When it comes to Joey, it's impossible not to worry and get anxious for any updates. Every day he's in that jail is one too many. He doesn't belong locked away with *real* criminals, and the longer he's there, the greater the chance that something could happen to him within those grimy, dingy, dangerous walls.

I flip open the phone and dial the number I've memorized for Attorney Fields. His assistant immediately connects me with him, and I brace myself for the news.

Please, God, let it be something incredible.

Attorney Fields picks up the line. "Lyla, thanks for giving me a call back so quickly..."

Like I would have waited.

Between Silas staring me down and telling me to make the call and my nerves about Joey, I couldn't have put it off another minute without driving myself mad. "What news do you have?"

"Potentially good. I filed a motion to reduce your brother's bail that will be heard next week. Silas insisted that I list him and you as co-signers."

Co-signers?

Attorney Fields is throwing around terms I don't understand, and I look to Silas, who leans against the fence, looking more comfortable in his own skin than I've ever seen him.

He's apparently already had this conversation with the man on the other end of the line.

"Co-sign? What does that mean?"

"Essentially, that you'll agree to make sure your brother complies with the terms placed on his bail. Ensuring he doesn't miss court and stays out of trouble while the case is pending."

"Okay." I nod vigorously. "I can definitely do that."

Joey has *never* been a troublemaker, and if it hadn't been for what happened, he would have likely never had contact with the police his entire life, save for maybe a speeding ticket or two.

Attorney Fields continues, "It also makes it far more likely for the court to actually grant it. The name Bolton goes a long way around here."

Don't I know it.

Our time in Pittsburgh demonstrated that daily.

People bent over backward for Silas—from the hotel manager, who insisted we stay in the penthouse suite, to the tailor who arrived to bring Silas another suit before the second board meeting, and just about anyone else he spoke with to get what we needed done almost instantly. And he's willing to sign and take responsibility for Joey when he's never even met him, knowing full well that the Bolton name could be the thing that makes a judge actually release him from lockup.

Papers rustle on Attorney Field's end of the line. "I also filed what's called an Other Acts Motion relating to the alleged victim in this case."

I pace along the edge of the pen, Whiskey falling in next to me, cutting his own path through the dirt while staying at my side. "What does that mean?"

"Remember I told you I was doing some digging?"

"Yeah."

It feels like that conversation happened so long ago, but it's only been a few weeks since I was angry enough with Silas to threaten to leave.

How fast things change...

Attorney Fields releases a sigh. "Well, my private investigator discovered some pretty interesting things about the man who died. Like this wasn't the first time he had done something like that to someone."

I freeze mid-step, and my eyes meet Silas'. Given the sympathetic look there, I can tell he's already heard all this from Attorney Fields.

"He found three friends of the guy willing to testify that he's gotten rough with women in front of them before, and my P.I. connected him to one woman who claims he raped her at a party in college several years back."

"Oh, my God."

My head spins, the events of that fateful night still so fresh that I can feel the effects of whatever he slipped into my drink as much now as I did then.

"I have affidavits from all four of them that I'm attaching to the motion. Hopefully, the DA is going to take a look at the evidence I'm trying to present at trial and decide he doesn't want to put a seventeen-year-old on trial for murder when the alleged victim was more than likely trying to sexually assault you when Joey stopped him. We have a strong defense of others case, and this makes everything even stronger."

That flicker of hope that's taunted me so many times over the last several weeks lights again, and I squeeze my eyes closed and inhale deeply, taking in the fresh mountain air as my entire body starts to tremble. "So, he might dismiss the charges?"

"If the DA has any common sense, he's not going to want to take this to trial in front of twelve jurors. All we need is *one* to believe it was done to defend and protect you, *one* person to believe our story, and they lose."

Silas' strong arms wrap around me, holding me tightly. The smell of freshly cut oak soaks into my lungs, and his hard body pressed to mine helps stop the trembling as he supports my weight and gives me his own strength.

"Lyla, are you still there?"

"Yeah"—I open my eyes but keep my cheek pressed to Silas' warm chest—"I'm here."

"This is good news."

"I know. I just...I'm afraid that the other shoe is going to drop, that something else is going to interfere or go wrong."

Because nothing has seemed easy since that night.

God knows living with Silas and breaking down his walls hasn't been.

"There are no guarantees when it comes to cases like this, Lyla. I'd be lying and a real shitty lawyer if I did guarantee you something, but we're doing everything we can. My investigator is continuing to look for other witnesses who might be willing to testify. And like I explained when we spoke last week, I have an expert who is examining the crime scene photos and will meet with Joey to piece together exactly what happened. He will testify about self-defense and defense of others cases and how people react in these situations to ensure the evidence makes sense to the jury—if we get that far. All these things are good for us. Good for Joey."

I fight a sob, swallowing it down as I picture him locked away in that awful place. "Is he doing okay?"

It's been a few days since I've spoken with him, and even though he said he was all right, I could hear the lie in his voice. In my head, he became that little six-year-old boy crying and scared at Mom's funeral again. The way I will always see him—someone I need to protect. Not the other way around.

"I met with him earlier this morning to give him the same update I just gave you. He's okay."

I release a heavy breath, and Silas kisses my temple, rubbing my arm with his work-hardened hand. "Thank you again, for everything."

"We'll need both you and Silas here for the bail hearing next week. The other stuff could take a bit longer to get scheduled for hearing. We have to be patient."

Patience.

I've struggled with it since I arrived on the mountain, growing easily frustrated with the enigmatic man now holding me against him. I pushed and pushed and pushed him, almost to the breaking point.

It worked, in the end, but this situation with Joey is completely out of my hands. No amount of pushing Attorney Fields will get anything done faster because we're at the mercy of the courts, and potentially, a jury. Which means I'll be practicing patience for the foreseeable future.

I end the call, and Silas pulls the phone from my hand and slips it into his back pocket.

He lifts my chin. "I told you it was good news."

Tears well in my eyes, and I press my hands against his chest, running my fingers over the scar near his heart. "Is it too much to hope that we've won two battles?"

The corners of his lips curl. "No. Hope is a good thing."

Words I never thought I'd hear from this man.

"Since when?"

He brushes his thumbs across my cheeks, swiping away the tears that fall. "Since you brought it into my life. I also spoke with the FBI this morning. They're going to issue an arrest warrant for Marty."

"You're kidding?"

Silas shakes his head. "It turns out they've had him on their radar for a long time. Years. They've just never been able to pin anything on him before. They think with my father's journal, they'll be able to track down victims who might be willing to cooperate."

"Jesus...so, he might actually go to prison?"

He nods slowly. "He might."

The slight hesitation in his voice tightens my gut. "But if he doesn't?"

Silas's eyes darken from their usual warm blue to arctic ice. "There are other ways he can be dealt with."

A frigid chill floods my veins, and I press my hand to his chest harder, directly over the scar. "You don't mean that. That would make you just as bad as him."

One of his brows rises. "Would it?"

In all the time I've spent with Silas, I never once considered killing Marty as an option, and I never thought Silas would have, either. He had his chance when he held him at gunpoint only a few yards from here, but he let him go rather than take his life.

To hear he's considering that as a legitimate option pains me more than what Marty did to me that day.

"You're too good for something like that, Silas. I don't like that he's out there somewhere when we know what he's capable of any more than you do. But he's keeping a low profile. He's scared. He's running. Karma will catch up with him eventually, even if the police don't."

Silas' jaw tightens, and he feathers his lips across mine. "God willing."

―――――

SILAS

Even after everything she's seen, Lyla still thinks so much of me and believes that I wouldn't go and strangle the life out of him like I tried to in that conference room. But if I ever found myself alone in a room with Uncle Marty again, I can't guarantee that I wouldn't.

Not after everything he's done to so many people.

Not after I read that journal over and over again.

Not when I was so close to ending all of it before that showdown in the boardroom.

I tighten my grip on Lyla, trying to keep myself from falling down that dark rabbit hole again. "Maybe I should have fired that gun when I had the chance..."

Before I have a chance to continue my thought, Lyla takes my face in her hands.

"No. You don't talk like that. We're moving on from all this, not looking back. Right? That was the plan."

It was the plan.

And since we've been back on the mountain, it's been a lot easier to move forward rather than let the past drag us back into it.

Not simply because we've left behind all the physical reminders of what went down but because this place just has that effect. The peace I found here all those years ago still permeates this land, the immediate sense of belonging here and that the mountain will provide anything I need.

And in a way, it did.

It brought Lyla to me, and having her here with me, now that everything's out in the open, now that we're fully exposed to each other, it feels like a fresh start, especially with this potentially good news about Joey and from the Feds.

Things are falling into place, exactly where they belong —like Lyla being in my arms right now. "Are you done with the animals?"

She raises a brow. "Yes. Why? Are you done with that load of wood?"

I shake my head. "Not even close. I got distracted."

"By the phone calls?"

I press a kiss to her lips. "No, by *you*. I couldn't stop thinking about you and missed having you with me."

Lyla drops her head back and laughs, the sound so natural and free from the turmoil we've been wound up in that it physically warms me. "I was like, what, fifty feet away from you the whole time?"

"It was too far."

I tug her up against me again fully and let her feel my cock hardening against her leg. Leaning in, I kiss her neck where it meets her shoulder. "I was thinking…"

She angles her head to give me better access. "What?"

"That maybe we play hooky from chores for the rest of the day."

I kiss higher, and her nails dig slightly into my chest, right over the scar I used to convince the board to vote my way. All this time, I've tried to hide them, tried to conceal them under something that told a different story, one of adventure and freedom of a childhood that I never had. But now I crave her touch over the marred skin. I need it as a reminder that despite how broken I am, she still loves me.

Her warm breath flutters my hair against my cheek, her lips barely brushing my ear. "That would just leave more work for tomorrow, wouldn't it?"

Nodding, I work my way up the elegant slope of her neck. "It *would*. But you naked on top of me in a hot bath sounds absolutely glorious right now."

I drag my head back and search her face. What I find there steals my ability to speak.

Pure love shines in her eyes.

The way no one else has ever looked at me in my entire life.

She wraps her arms around my neck, twining my hair around her finger and tugging on it gently. "I might be persuaded, but only under one condition."

"Yeah. What's that?"

Because I would do *anything* this woman asks of me.

Literally anything.

If she told me to ride Lasher down to the river stark naked and wade into the middle of it to catch her a damn fish with my bare hands, I wouldn't stop until I came back with a whole fucking bucketful.

"We eat something first." She drops a quick peck on my lips. "I'm absolutely starving."

My cock twitches between us, and I grin at her, picturing her spread out naked on the bed, her pussy glistening and exposed, waiting for me to devour her.

She narrows her eyes. "What's that look for?"

"Oh, I *definitely* plan on eating before we get into the bath. And I have something for you, too."

Her jaw drops, and I take a step back and lower my shoulder, throwing her up over it. She yelps in surprise, dangling over my shoulder, her face near my ass, my arm banded over her thighs to keep her in place.

"Silas Bolton, put me down."

Shaking my head, I stalk back toward the cabin. "No fucking way."

She smacks my ass as hard as she can, but it barely registers. "Put. Me. Down."

The annoyance and hint of anger in her voice only spur me on because she's fucking beautiful when she's all worked up.

"I will put you down when we get to the bed." Her peal of laughter makes me grin as I take the steps up to the porch. "Are you done fighting me?"

Tiny fists hit my back, but I shove open the door, march over to the bed, and toss her onto it. She bounces with another little yelp of surprise but doesn't have time to react before I'm on her, pressing my body over hers and kissing her deeply.

My tongue glides along her lips, begging for entrance, needing to taste her even more when she's being so playful and feisty with me. The entire energy around here shifted as soon as we got home, falling back into a routine of busy days working together on the property and heated nights tangled up in this bed...or on the chair in front of a roaring fire...or in the hay in the barn...

It's the kind of life I never knew existed.

She's the kind of *woman* I didn't think could ever be real.

But she's *mine*.

My *wife*.

Lyla moans and wraps her legs around my lower back, pressing the heels of her shoes into me there. "We are getting the bed filthy."

I pull back slightly. "That's the plan."

She laughs and shakes her head, her dark hair fanned out around her on the pillow like a halo. "No, I mean your boots, my shoes. I was just in the goat pen..."

"We can wash the sheets and comforter. Now, for the love of God, let me get *you* dirty."

She stares up at me for a moment like she doesn't recognize me, scraping her nails against my cheeks through my beard.

"What is it?"

Her lips tilt up into a sultry smile. "You." Her fingers glide across my lips. "When I met you, you were so shut down, and now, you're..."

I raise a brow at her. "I'm what?"

The gold flecks in her eyes sparkle as she figures out

what she wants to say, and her lips twist slightly, as if she's afraid to voice what she's actually feeling.

"Tell me, Lyla. I always want you to be honest with me."

She shrugs slightly. "Well, now you're kind of turning into the brutish, demanding, wild mountain man everybody always thought you were."

Her words give me pause, and when she doesn't continue, I search her gaze for some indication of what she means.

I know what the people of Millsburg have believed about me since I arrived—exactly what I wanted them to. To keep them away. To prevent anyone from reaching out to me the way Lyla has. But now that it's happened, it seems as though the way I've lived for so long could hurt my chances at a future with her because they've left me living between two worlds.

One drenched in wealth and privilege and pain.

One built on freedom and nature and all things primal.

"Is that"—I swallow thickly—"a bad thing?"

She shakes her head. "No." A smile plays on her lips, and she tightens her thighs around me. "I kind of like this version of Silas."

Relief floods my chest, and I grin at her. "Good, because I don't think he's going anywhere...as long as you don't."

She threads her fingers through my hair and drags me back down for another kiss. "You couldn't get rid of me even if you wanted to. You're stuck with me."

"You just want that $5 million."

Her burst of laughter makes her body shake under me. "Oh, *yeah,* you got me there..."

That stupid contract is what brought Lyla to me, and it will always be there, a reminder of why she came to the mountain. I joke about it now, but the reality of our situation hits me so hard I actually jerk back from her.

All the horrible feelings I had when Ronald suggested I *buy* a wife return, and I stare at the woman who owns my heart completely—without a fucking contract.

"I want an annulment."

She freezes, her humor dying as her eyes widen. "What?"

Shit.

That wasn't the right way to say this.

"I think we should have the marriage annulled."

Her soft brow furrows. "What? I don't understand. I thought—"

I press my fingers over her lips to silence her. "Just listen to me. We got married for all the wrong reasons. I want this to be real. I want it to be about how I feel about you. How you make me feel—like I'm alive again. Like I'm starting over the life that was taken from me. I want this to just be about us and not about some stupid piece of paper. So, I want an annulment, and then, I want to marry you for real."

Tears pool in her eyes as she stares up at me. "Are you serious?"

I nod.

Her bottom lip trembles. "What about the trust? It says we have to—"

"I'm not worried about the trust. Not anymore. If the board wants to remove me as CEO, they will, whether I own half the company or not. They have every right to pick the CEO they think will do best for the employees and the business. I think we all knew that was never going to be me in the long run, anyway."

"But what about your ownership interest—"

"I don't give a fuck about that." It comes out a bit

harsher than I intend it, and I feather my fingers over her cheek to try to temper my rough words. "I told you I never wanted my father's money, and that's still true. Besides, he left me more than I could ever spend in fifty billion life-times, completely separate from the trust."

I never told her any of this because it never mattered before.

For weeks, I tried to convince myself she was only here for the money, that there was nothing between us but that stupid contract we both signed.

But I was so wrong.

No matter what Uncle Marty tried to insinuate, Lyla doesn't care about the money. She will never ask me for anything again, except maybe a better gate for the goat pen or some extra jars of pasta sauce to make a delicious dinner.

"Marry me for real, Lyla, and everything that's mine will be yours. No prenup, no bullshit. Just you and me, just us here on the mountain."

"That's really what you want?"

The true uncertainty in her question stabs at my heart. I pushed her away and cut her off for so long that even now, she still doesn't fully believe this is the real deal.

I kiss her again, trying to convey my answer the only way I know how because words always seem to fail me. Her arms wrap around my neck, keeping me in place, returning the emotion and the need I have for her.

Forcing myself to pull back, I take her face in my hands, ensuring she can see deep into my soul when I say this. "And when Joey gets out, because I am fucking confident he will, he can come up here with us, if that's what he wants. I'll build him a fucking cabin of his own, and I'll teach him how to live out here like this...and how to not let Billy escape."

Lyla grins, but she doesn't respond to my offer.

"So, what do you say?"

She stares at me for so long I start to think she might actually say no, before a tear trickles down her temple and she nods. "Yes. I'll marry you for real. I'll be the billionaire lumberjack's bride..."

I crush my lips to hers again, stealing her breath and anything else she might have said.

The first kiss with this woman sealed our fates as much as it did that contract, and the next time we do it, it will be with our hearts and souls truly belonging to each other, with vows we really mean.

Lyla Sinclair saved my life, and I am going to spend every waking moment I have left showing her how much I love her for it.

Dragging my head back, I grind my hips against hers, letting my cock rock between her legs, where I plan on burying my face in about five seconds before I fuck her senseless. "You might not be able to wear white after what I plan on doing to you."

A coy smile spreads across her face, and she lifts herself up until she can feather her lips over mine. "Don't make promises you can't keep, Mr. Bolton."

"Oh, Mrs. Bolton, you are playing with fire..."

That spark I felt when my lips first met hers has ignited a raging inferno I don't ever want to flame out. Lyla is the oxygen it needs to survive, that I need to survive. Without it, without her, all I would be is a pile of ashes ready to blow away in the spring breeze that barrels through the mountain this time of year.

She giggles, rolling her hips against mine, the same heat blazing through her loving gaze. "I'm ready to get burned."

Epilogue

LYLA

The woman in the mirror isn't the same as the one who looked back at me four months ago in the courthouse bathroom. *That* one was terrified, lost, looking for something or someone to cling to. *This* one is stronger, happier, content, for maybe the first time in my life.

Exactly how a bride *should* look on her wedding day.

Ursula steps up behind me and places her wrinkled, frail hands on my shoulders, squeezing them gently. "You look beautiful, child."

I meet her gaze in the reflection.

The old woman who has become like a mother to me—and retaken that role for Silas as well, since he reconnected with her—adjusts the veil on my head, ensuring that it trails down my back in exactly the right position. "You're ready."

"I am this time."

She chuckles and shakes her head, making a little *tsking*

sound. "I still don't know what you two were thinking, mail-order bride..."

I smile at her as I rise to my feet. The heels I'm not used to wearing anymore pinch my feet, but they match my dress perfectly, and I refuse to give up on them until after the ceremony. Then they'll become obsolete on the mountain and I can return to my comfortable work boots and sneakers.

"We're making things right now, Ursula."

Finally.

Bobbing her head in agreement, she slips her arm through mine and leads me to the door of the small changing room at the back of the chapel in the non-denominational church in Millsburg.

Though neither Silas nor I are religious, he *insisted* we do it here this time, with a minister and the people we consider our friends as our witnesses.

The right way.

Ursula opens the door, and Joey whirls to face us from his spot in the hallway.

Dressed in a tux, his dark hair slicked back, he looks far older than his eighteen years, but maybe it was the time he spent in custody or the things he saw there, the things he did that put him there, that have aged him so much, so quickly.

The part of me that remembers him as that scared little boy hates that he's had to grow up so fast. I had to when Mom died, and I wished for something more for him.

His green eyes trail down over my dress, the corner of his mouth curling up. "Has Silas seen this?"

I shake my head, fighting a grin. "No."

He laughs. "He's going to love it."

"I know." I step forward and pull him into an embrace,

344

still not one hundred percent over the need to touch him constantly to assure myself that he's really safe and here and that his ordeal is truly over now that the district attorney has dropped all the charges. "I'm so happy you're here with us."

Pulling back, tears shimmer in his gaze. "Me, too. You and Silas didn't have to do everything you've done for me. I—"

"Yes, we did. And you're always welcome here, with us, for as long as you want to stay...or as long as you can tolerate him."

I grin and Joey returns it, then offers me his arm.

"Are you ready?"

More than ready...

The last few months since we had our *original* marriage annulled and the contract voided, things between us have been incredible. But things felt...off.

Not wearing the rings, knowing we weren't legally bound to each other, left a hole deep in my chest I hadn't thought it would. Silas felt it, too. He cared more about getting the new wedding planned than he did about officially giving up the role of CEO of Bolton Steel.

But once Marty was finally arrested and charged for some of his crimes, it seemed the only thing still unresolved was the two of us saying "I do" and actually meaning it.

And it's finally time.

We make our way to the back double doors of the church, and Ursula slips inside in front of us, giving me the double thumbs up.

I take a long, deep breath and close my eyes as the music starts.

All those months ago, when I sat across the desk from Carly, discussing what it would be like to be a mail-order bride, I never imagined this was a possibility. When she mentioned falling in love, I thought it was a joke, something she said to clients to try to get them to sign on for something so insane. But then I went and fell for the grumpy mountain man who bought me.

And look where it got us.

Here.

Today.

Finally doing it "the right way," according to Silas.

The double doors swing open, letting the music stream out to us.

Light. Happy. Inviting celebration of a day that feels like it's been so long coming.

Our friends stand in the pews toward the front, but my eyes don't even register them. They fall on the man waiting for me at the altar, dressed in an immaculate tux that hugs his perfectly muscled form and stands in stark contrast against his sandy-blond hair flowing over his shoulders.

The first time we met, his eyes held so much anger, distrust, resentment. But now, the pale blue swims with nothing but love, understanding, and need. And from here, as we start moving down the aisle, I can tell he's already been crying.

His gaze drops from mine to my dress, the corner of his mouth slowly tilting as I had hoped it would when I chose it.

We make our way down the aisle, past Jensen and his wife, Travis and his, Ursula, Miriam and Dr. Anderson, and a few other members of the board Silas has grown friendly with over the last few months.

Even Carly and her husband made the trek to Millsburg for the occasion. The tears already stream down her face, and she gives me a little wave, her excitement practically contagious as I make it up onto the altar where Carrie Ann, my only true friend in Millsburg stands waiting as my Maid of Honor.

Joey leans in, giving the same goofy smile he always had as a kid. "You found a good one, sis."

He kisses me on the cheek and moves to stand next to Silas as his *human* best man—on the opposite side of Whiskey, looking dashing with his black bow tie—an arrangement Silas insisted on when we were planning our nuptials, given how close they've become since Joey came to live with us.

Working side by side, building a small cabin for Joey so he has his own space to grow and become the man he wants to be. Caring for the animals, even showing Joey how to ride Lasher, to find his freedom in galloping along the river shoreline or across the mountain meadows filled with the spring wildflowers. Teaching him to swing an axe and passing along the skills he learned that have allowed him to find peace up here.

Joey pauses next to him and whispers something.

Silas gives him a stern look and nods, then steps forward and takes my hand. He brushes his lips against my ear, the light contact and warm breath against my skin raising goosebumps across my entire body. "A red wedding dress?"

I smile even though he can't see it, leaning closer to him and squeezing his hand tightly. "You told me I wasn't going to be able to wear white again...and you delivered."

He pulls back with a grin that makes heat rise in my cheeks. So much promise now lies in his gaze, and the scarred man who once growled everything at me and stomped around the property like I was an unwanted invader now looks at me like I'm the only other person in the world.

Silas' ink will forever cover the evidence of what

happened to him, will always at least partially conceal it from the world, but what he did at Bolton Steel that day set him free from the pain of it.

It gave him the strength to face his demons and chase them away, hopefully for good. But if they return, he knows how to fight them. Exactly like this—with me at his side.

We twine our fingers together and turn to face the minister. After battling for what has felt like forever, we're finally ready to start the rest of our lives together.

Again.

Without contracts. Without secrets. Without the outside world influencing our decision.

Just Silas and me.

Just *us*.

———

SILAS

Nothing could have prepared me for seeing Lyla in this dress, walking down the aisle toward me.

Absolutely fucking nothing.

My knees practically gave out; I was so ready to drop to them at her feet and worship her right here, right now. Instead, I have to control myself, at least until the end of the ceremony, when I can take her home, tear off that dress, and ravage her the way I've been fantasizing about since the day we signed our annulment papers.

She'll be my wife again in a few minutes, taking her rightful place as Mrs. Bolton—again.

The emotion threatening to choke me makes it almost impossible for me to concentrate on what the minister says. I'm too lost in staring at Lyla and how stunning she looks today, how *happy* she is—truly happy—and knowing I'm part of the reason makes everything we went through to get here worthwhile.

Joey nudges me.

Shit.

I'm supposed to be saying something.

Lyla looks over at me, eyes wide, probably wondering what the fuck is going on and why I'm not doing what I'm supposed to.

I clear my throat and nod at the minister. "I'm sorry. Can you repeat that?"

He gives me a little wobbly smile, probably well aware I didn't hear a fucking word he said. "Of course. I asked if you had written your own vows."

"Oh, yes."

I start to reach into my inner jacket pocket to grab what I jotted down over the last few weeks in preparation for today, but I still my hand and pull it out without ever touching the sheet of paper.

Because I don't need to look at my notes to know what I want to say to Lyla.

I've been dying to let her know for so long, but the words always seem to escape me. If there was ever a day, it would be today.

I turn toward her and pull both her hands into mine, squeezing them and looking down at her soft, pale skin next to my darker, rough, tattooed hands. She squeezes them back, giving me the encouragement to finally say what I need to.

"You know I'm not very good at this stuff."

Everyone in the church laughs, and it relieves a little tiny bit of the tension threatening to stop me and send me running like I have before.

"I know you thought it was strange that I wanted to get married in the church, considering neither one of us is religious, but there's a reason for it. A good one." I lock my gaze with hers, needing that connection when I make my confession. "My entire life, I never really believed in God because all the praying, all the begging I did growing up, for help, for somebody to make what was happening stop, went unanswered. To me, I felt like if there was a God, he wouldn't have let it happen to me."

The tears well in her eyes, and she doesn't bother to try to swipe them away. They stream down her cheeks, through the perfect makeup she applied.

"But I changed my mind. *You* changed my mind. That night you got lost in the woods, I prayed for the first time in fifteen years. I prayed that I'd find you and that you'd be all right. It had absolutely nothing to do with the contract we had signed and needing a damn wife. I did it because even then, I was already falling in love with you. I just didn't realize it. I didn't know what it was because I had never seen it. And then, I prayed that God would help us succeed where so many other people had failed, in doing what was right, even if it hurt."

She pulls her hand from mine and reaches out to press her palm over my heart because she knows exactly what I'm talking about, as does everyone else in this room now.

"I now believe in God because he clearly brought you to me. It may have been a long, torturous road full of thirty-two years I'd rather forget, but if none of that had happened, you never would've come up the mountain and shattered the world I thought I was going to live in the rest of my life."

I swallow a sob threatening to slip from my throat.

"I love you, Lyla, and everything that comes with you.

Even when we argue about stupid things, or you call me out on my bullshit." I glance at the minister. "Sorry."

He smirks but doesn't correct or chide me for my language.

"I know it's only because you care, probably more than you should. I love you, and I love this little family we've created." I glance over my shoulder at Joey. "Your brother has become my brother, and I can't imagine the two of you not being on the homestead with me." I turn my head back to her. "So yeah, I want you to be my wife, and I sound like a fucking idiot."

But given the tears still streaming down her face, I must've said something right.

She curls her hand against my chest and looks to the minister, who gives her a nod to go ahead. "God, I feel like what I'm about to say is so stupid compared to that."

I give her a half-grin. "Nothing you say can ever be stupid."

"Well, I hope not." She offers a little laugh. "I didn't write anything down because I thought I knew what I was going to say, but after that, I'm not so sure..."

Watching her struggle to find what she wants to say makes me want to tug her into my arms and hold her, tell her I don't need to hear it because I already know.

But she takes a long, deep inhalation and gives me a sad smile. "I thought my life was over. When Joey got into trouble, I felt like I was twisting in the wind with nowhere to go and no one to ask for help until I walked into Carly's office." Her eyes dart to the blonde sitting in the second row. "It was a last-ditch effort, one that sent me on a car ride into the middle of nowhere to meet a man who absolutely did not want me there."

I can't fight my grin at her completely accurate description of what happened.

She squeezes my hands. "But I saw something in you, felt something, a spark, a knowledge that not everything was as it appeared, and the more I got to know you, the more I realized what a beautiful man you were underneath all the anger and attitude. Everything you just said is true for me, too. When I lost my mom, I felt like my life was over, and then, I lost Joey. So, I didn't believe there was a God, either...until that night you saved me in the woods. I saw you in a whole new light. I saw what you tried to keep hidden from all these people, and I knew I could bring it into the light."

Fucking hell.

If there was ever a way to shatter me, it's with *that* statement, and she has no idea why I'm breaking apart with her words.

I shouldn't interrupt her vows, but I can't keep it in.

She has to know.

"*You're* the light, Lyla."

"Shit." She swallows thickly. "You can't say stuff like that to me or I'm going to start sobbing."

"I'm sorry."

She shakes her head. "No, you're not."

Everybody in the pews chuckles, some of them clearly uncomfortable, but those who know us should have expected our wedding would never be a normal one. Carrie Ann will have plenty of gossip to spread around town after this.

"Silas Bolton, I know who you are here." She presses against my chest again. "You're the man I love more than anything in the world. You're my family, you and Joey, and I'll stay on this mountain with you forever."

The tears finally fall out of my eyes to match hers.

The minister raises his hands. "With those lovely and unique vows, it's now time to exchange the rings."

I reach down to Whiskey's collar and pull the rings out of the small box we attached to the back. This time, when I slip my grandmother's ring onto Lyla's finger, I know it's never coming off again. She does the same with the simple band I wear, placing it over the tattooed one I had added months ago, one that will stay there forever.

With our gazes and hands locked, the minister finishes the ceremony without me hearing another word until he finally says, "You may now kiss the bride."

It's what I've been waiting for since the moment we signed the annulment papers—for her to be my *wife* again. For *real* this time.

I step forward and tug her against me, pressing my lips to hers in a searing kiss, filled with confirmation of all the words we just spoke to each other. She clings to me, her love and passion poured into her mouth moving with mine.

When we finally come up for air, she brushes her lips over me again and again, and then wraps her arms around me, burying her face against my neck. "Thank you for the beautiful wedding. Mr. Bolton."

I squeeze her tightly, inhaling her light citrus scent. "Thank you for agreeing to marry me, Mrs. Bolton—again."

She pulls her head back and takes my face between her palms. "I'd marry you a thousand times if I had to."

I shake my head. "Please, no, I don't think I could survive another wedding."

Her grin lights up her face. "Me, either."

With a quick glance around to make sure no one is close enough to hear me, I kiss my way to her ear. "Now, let me take you home and get you out of this dress..."

She pulls back, humor and heat dancing in her gaze. "I'd hoped you'd like it."

Like it is an understatement.

The woman looks like walking sin in the skin-tight red number, with a nod to a traditional dress in the white veil trailing down her back.

"You knew exactly what you were doing when you put this on, didn't you?"

She nods, giving me another sly grin. "I sure as hell did, Mr. Bolton."

———

I hope you enjoyed *Billionaire Lumberjack's Bride.* The next reclusive lumberjack in *Billionaire Lumberjack's Beauty,* a twist on the classic Beauty and the Beast tale, is available now!

A wounded billionaire known as The Beast. A young woman forced onto the mountain with him...

They call him The Beast of Barker Mountain.

And now, I belong to him.

Sent to settle a debt.

The volatile, reclusive billionaire owns the mountain he lives on...and me.

If I try to run, he'll catch me.

Attempt to hide, he'll find me.

There is no escape.

I should fear him.

His enigmatic moods.

His dark disposition.

The way he handles his axe with such violent precision. Yet the most powerful man in Montana harbors a secret that could change everything between us.
So much of what I thought I knew was a lie.
He calls me Beauty.
But I'm not sure I'll survive The Beast.

Grab this steamy billionaire, age gap, forced proximity, arranged marriage stand-alone twist on Beauty and the Beast about an isolated, damaged older man with a bad reputation, the younger woman sent to settle her family's debt, and the secret that could save or destroy them.

AVAILABLE NOW: books2read.com/ BillionaireLumberjacksBeauty

Meet the other Lumberjacks in Love:

Beau in *Billionaire Lumberjack* - available now at all retailers! books2read.com/BillionaireLumberjack

Wells in *Billionaire Lumberjack's Baby* - available now at all retailers! books2read.com/BillionaireLumberjacksBaby

To stay up to date on news, releases, and sales from Gwyn, sign up for her newsletter here: www.gwynmc namee.com/newsletter

About the Author

Gwyn McNamee is an attorney, writer, wife, and mother (to one human baby and two fur babies). Originally from the Midwest, Gwyn relocated to her husband's home town of Las Vegas in 2015 and is enjoying her respite from the cold and snow. Gwyn has been writing down her crazy stories and ideas for years and finally decided to share them with the world. She loves to write stories with a bit of suspense and action mingled with romance and heat.

When she isn't either writing or voraciously devouring any books she can get her hands on, Gwyn is busy adding to her tattoo collection, golfing, and stirring up trouble with her perfect mix of sweetness and sarcasm (usually while wearing heels).

Gwyn loves to hear from her readers. Here is where you can find her:

FB Reader Group: https://www.facebook.com/groups/1667380963540655/

Facebook: https://www.facebook.com/AuthorGwynMcNamee/

Newsletter: www.gwynmcnamee.com/newsletter

Website: http://www.gwynmcnamee.com/Twitter: https://twitter.com/GwynMcNamee

Instagram: https://www.instagram.com/gwynmcnamee

Bookbub: https://www.bookbub.com/authors/gwynmcnamee

Acknowledgments

Thank you to everyone who helped create Silas and Lyla's world! Renee, Patricia, Stephie, and Caoimhe - you guys are rockstars. I appreciate all that you do for me more than I can put into words.

OTHER WORKS BY GWYN MCNAMEE

The Hawke Family Series

Savage Collision (The Hawke Family - Book One)

He's everything she didn't know she wanted. She's everything he thought he could never have.

The last thing I expect when I walk into The Hawkeye Club is to fall head over heels in lust. It's supposed to be a rescue mission. I have to get my baby sister off the pole, into some clothes, and out of the grasp of the pussy peddler who somehow manipulated her into stripping. But the moment I see Savage Hawke and verbally spar with him, my ability to remain rational flies out the window and my libido takes center stage. I've never wanted a relationship —my time is better spent focusing on taking down the scum running this city—but what I want and what I need are apparently two different things.

Danika Eriksson storms into my office in her high heels and on her high horse. Her holier-than-thou attitude and accusations should offend me, but instead, I can't get her out of my head or my heart. Her incomparable drive, take-no prisoners attitude, and blatant honesty captivate me and hold me prisoner. I should steer clear, but my self-preservation instinct is apparently dead—which is exactly what our relationship will be once she knows everything. It's only a matter of time.

The truth doesn't always set you free. Sometimes, it just royally screws you.

Tortured Skye (The Hawke Family - Book Two)

She's always been off-limits. He's always just out of reach.

Falling in love with Gabe Anderson was as easy as breathing. Fighting my feelings for my brother's best friend was agonizingly hard. I never imagined giving in to my desire for him would cause such a destructive ripple effect. That kiss was my grasp at a lifeline—something, anything to hold me steady in my crumbling life. Now, I have to suffer with the fallout while trying to convince him it's all worth the consequences.

Guilt overwhelms me—over what I've done, the lives I've taken, and more than anything, over my feelings for Skye Hawke. Craving my best friend's little sister is insanely self-destructive. It never should have happened, but since the moment she kissed me, I haven't been able to get her out of my mind. If I take what I want, I risk losing everything. If I don't, I'll lose her and a piece of myself. The raging storm threatening to rain down on the city is nothing compared to the one that will come from my decision.

Love can be torture, but sometimes, love is the only thing that can save you.

Stone Sober (The Hawke Family - Book Three)

She's innocent and sweet. He's dark and depraved.

Stone Hawke is precisely the kind of man women are warned about— handsome, intelligent, arrogant, and intricately entangled with some dangerous people. I should stay away, but he manages to strip my soul bare with just a look and dominates my thoughts. Bad decisions are in my past. My life is (mostly) on track, even if it is no longer the one to medical school. I can't allow myself to cave to the fierce pull and ardent attraction I feel toward the youngest Hawke.

Nora Eriksson is off-limits, and not just because she's my brother's employee and sister-in-law. Despite the fact she's stripping at The Hawkeye Club, she has an innocent and pure heart. Normally, the only thing that appeals to me about innocence is the opportunity to taint it. But not when it comes to Nora. I can't expose her to the filth permeating my life. There are too many things I can't control, things completely out of my hands. She doesn't deserve any of it, but the power she holds over me is stronger than any addiction.

The hardest battles we fight are often with ourselves, but only through defeating our own demons can we find true peace.

AVAILABLE AT ALL RETAILERS:

books2read.com/StoneSober

Building Storm (The Hawke Family - Book Four)

She hasn't been living. He's looking for a way to forget it all.

My life went up in flames. All I'm left with is my daughter and ashes. The simple act of breathing is so excruciating, there are days I wish I could stop altogether. So I have no business being at the party, and I definitely shouldn't be in the arms of the handsome stranger. When his lips meet mine, he breathes life into me for the first time since the day the inferno disintegrated my world. But loving again isn't in the cards, and there are even greater dangers to face than trying to keep Landon McCabe out of my heart.

Running is my only option. I have to get away from Chicago and the betrayal that shattered my world. I need a new life-one without attachments. The vibrancy of New Orleans convinces me it's possible to start over. Yet in all the excitement of a new city, it's Storm Hawke's dark, sad beauty that draws me in. She isn't looking for love, and we both need a hot, sweaty release without feelings getting involved. But even the best laid plans fail, and life can leave you burned.

Love can build, and love can destroy. But in the end, love is what raises you from the ashes.

AVAILABLE AT ALL RETAILERS:

books2read.com/BuildingStorm

Tainted Saint (The Hawke Family - Book Five)

He's searching for absolution. She wants her happily ever after.

Solomon Clarke goes by Saint, though he's anything but. After lusting for him from afar, the masquerade party affords me the anonymity to pursue that attraction without worrying about the fall-out of hooking-up with the bouncer from the Hawkeye Club. From the second he lays his eyes and hands on me, I'm helpless to resist him. Even burying myself in a dangerous investigation can't erase the memory of our combustible connection and one night together. The only problem... he has no idea who I am.

Caroline Brooks thinks I don't see her watching me, the way her eyes rake over me with appreciation. But I've noticed, and the party is the perfect opportunity to unleash the desire I've kept reined in for so damn long. It also sets off a series of events no one sees coming. Events that leave those I love hurting because of my failures. While the guilt eats away at my soul, Caroline continues to weigh on my heart. That woman may be the death of me, but oh, what a way to go.

Life isn't always clean, and sometimes, it takes a saint to do the dirty work.

AVAILABLE AT ALL RETAILERS:

books2read.com/TaintedSaint

Steele Resolve (The Hawke Family - Book Six)

For one man, power is king. For the other, loyalty reigns.

Mob boss Luca "Steele" Abello isn't just dangerous—he's lethal. A master manipulator, liar, and user, no one should trust a word that comes out of his mouth. Yet, I can't get him out of my head. The time we spent together before I knew his true identity is seared into my brain. His touch. His voice. They haunt my every waking hour and occupy my dreams. So does my guilt. I'm literally sleeping with the enemy and betraying the only family I've ever had. When I come clean, it will be the end of me.

Byron Harris is a distraction I can't afford. I never should have let it go beyond that first night, but I couldn't stay away. Even when I learned who he was, when the *only* option was to end things, I kept going back, risking his life and mine to continue our indiscretion. The truth of what I am could get us both killed, but being with the man who's such an integral part of the Hawke family is even more terrifying. The only people I've ever cared about are on opposing sides, and I'm the rift that could end their friendship forever.

Love is a battlefield isn't just a saying. For some, it's a reality.